THE
AVOWED

AN UNBOUNDED NOVEL

BOOKS BY TEYLA BRANTON

Unbounded Series
The Change
The Cure
Protectors
  Ava's Revenge
  Mortal Brother
  Set Ablaze
The Escape
The Reckoning
Lethal Engagement
The Takeover
The Avowed

Colony Six Series
Insight (prequel)
Sketches
Visions
Travels

Imprints Series
First Touch (prequel)
Touch of Rain
On The Hunt
Upstaged
Under Fire
Blinded
Street Smart
Hidden Intent
Checked In

Other
Times Nine

UNDER THE NAME RACHEL BRANTON

Lily's House Series
House Without Lies
Tell Me No Lies
Hearts Never Lie
Your Eyes Don't Lie
Broken Lies
No Secrets or Lies
Cowboys Can't Lie

A Town Called Forgotten
Kiss at Midnight
This Feeling For You
Reason to Breathe

Finding Home Series
Take Me Home
All That I Love
Then I Found You

Other
How Far
I Don't Want To Eat
  Bugs
I Don't Want to Have
  Hot Toes

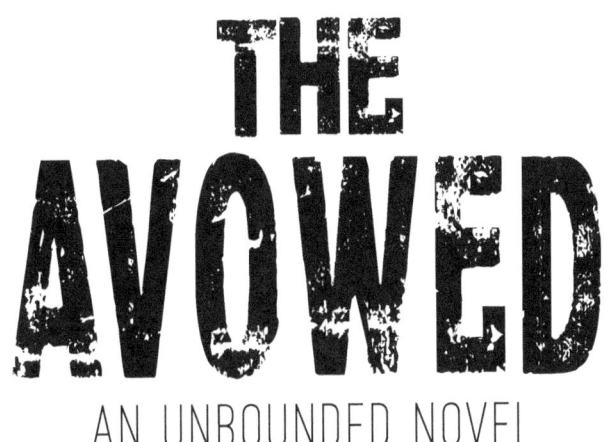

THE AVOWED

AN UNBOUNDED NOVEL

TEYLA BRANTON

WHITE
STAR
PRESS

Acknowledgment

I would like to thank Charmaine Tan for her comments and suggestions during the editing phase of this book. I'll take any opportunity to look better than I am. Thank you!

This is a work of fiction, and the views expressed herein are the sole responsibility of the author. Likewise, certain characters, places, and incidents are the product of the author's imagination, and any resemblance to actual persons, living or dead, or actual events or locales, is entirely coincidental.

The Avowed (Unbounded Series #8)

Published by White Star Press
P.O. Box 353
American Fork, Utah 84003

Copyright © 2021 by Nunes Entertainment, LLC
Model photo copyright © 2015 by White Star Press
Cover design copyright © 2021 by White Star Press

Printed in the United States of America
ISBN: 978-1-948982-26-9
Year of first printing: 2021

Thanks once again to my daughter Cátia
for all her help with this book. She is always willing
to discuss (or debate!) the finer points of grammar, and
she's the calm in the storm when I'm having weird program
issues—which she can always fix by a wave of
her magic wand. You are an amazing friend
and a great mother.

I

am so

lucky

to have

you.

LOVE YOU MORE!

CHAPTER 1

PEOPLE TEEMED ON THE SIDEWALK IN FRONT OF THE MISSION ON Ninth in downtown Los Angeles, spilling onto the street between cars parked along the road. With the neighborhood search for the missing girls, the crowd itself was expected, but the sheer numbers of sign-holding supporters were a surprise. Only the area directly in front of the mission doors was void of people, and there, on the five steps and the threshold leading into the building, lay mounds of flowers, pictures, and stuffed animals, as if people already expected a negative outcome after barely two and a half days.

"What?" I said, catching my new husband, Ritter Langton, scowling as he steered his black Toyota Land Cruiser toward the throng of protestors.

"We'll have to park down the street and walk in. There are easily over a thousand people here."

"At least they look peaceful." This came from Dimitri Sidorov in the back seat.

He had a point. In the four months since the US president's

earth-shattering announcement detailing the existence of Unbounded, we'd seen more riots than peaceful protests. Learning that a society of nearly immortal people lived among you had a way of bringing out the fear in people—and for good reason, especially if they had any inkling of the true history between the two Unbounded factions, Renegades and Emporium. Yet even in blissful ignorance, many mortals had rioted against identified Unbounded, demanded illegal medical tests, and encouraged violent discourse between Hunters, who hated Unbounded, and Believers, who worshipped them in the newly formed Church of the Unboundaried. Sometimes it was hard to keep it all straight.

"For now, they're peaceful," Ritter allowed.

I could feel his anxiousness through the connection we shared, even without accessing my sensing ability. Since our marriage right before the president's announcement, our link barely required an effort—and the connection went both ways to a certain extent, though Ritter was a combat Unbounded and not a sensing one.

"I'm betting it's a vigil, not a protest," I said. "They're worried about the girls like we are." As we drove slowly past, I stared at the pictures littering the steps of the mission, taking out my phone to snap a few pictures so I could zoom in to study them.

Ordinarily, missing teens in this run-down area of LA wouldn't have made it to our radar, but Kimber Wheeler was vaguely related to Dimitri, second-in-command in our San Diego Renegade cell, and her name in the news had triggered our electronic warnings.

"I'm sorry to get you involved, Erin," Dimitri said to me, his careful pronunciation almost completely masking his slight Russian accent. He was a short, broad man with longish dark hair, intense brown eyes, a narrow nose, and a trim mustache. Not good-looking, exactly, but so sure of himself that he exuded attractiveness. "But I'll need the use of your ability when I talk with the pastor and the parents." He was referring to the fact that he had cut short Ritter's and my vacation on our inherited tropical island, but Dimitri was family—and not just because I'd recently learned he was my biological father.

"Of course we're involved," I said. "Kimber is related to me too, after all."

Kimber was Dimitri's eleventh great-niece, to be exact, the third great-grandchild of an Unbounded. Dimitri had been checking periodically on Kimber since her birth, as we did with all descendants who might still undergo the Change. Following our posterity had been vital before we had taken over the Emporium, whose murdering ways had made it necessary for most Renegades in the past to sever all ties with our mortal families and obscure any connection to them, even to the point of faking our deaths. It was too soon to know how that practice might alter in the future without Emporium interference, but for now we were still very much at risk from a world newly apprised of our existence.

At seventeen, Kimber was nowhere close to a Change, which usually happened between the ages of thirty-one and thirty-three, and though the chance was small at six generations removed, it was still a possibility. That meant she was doubly important to Dimitri. To us. We needed to find out what happened to her and why.

Ritter pulled over to take the space of a departing car, squeezing the Land Cruiser expertly into an impossibly tight gap.

"Wait a minute," I said, studying the pictures I'd taken, immediately recognizing Kimber with her bronze skin and long black hair. "A lot of pictures on that step aren't of Kimber or the girl she's supposed to have gone missing with. There are a couple of boys too." I shoved my phone over the seat in Dimitri's direction.

He glanced at it and nodded. "Could explain why so many people are here. Families and friends of other missing children must have come to offer support. Makes sense. The girl's family isn't large or wealthy enough to evoke this kind of response on their own."

Before hopping out of the Land Cruiser, I put my phone away and smoothed the skirt of my blue dress over the thigh holster that held two guns and a knife. The top of the casual dress was tighter on me now than I liked, but the fuller skirt allowed a full range of movement in a battle, which was why I'd chosen it—not that I expected trouble. It was just in case. For the same reason, my long blond hair was pinned in a tight knot at the nape of my neck.

Ritter met me on the sidewalk, his dark eyes already scanning for potential threats. He was a good head taller than I was, his muscles rippling noticeably under his gray button-up shirt. Every part of him was strong, from the determined set of his square jaw and wide shoulders to the hands hanging loosely near his hidden weapons. His black hair parted on the left, the strands falling to the right and grazing a mole on his cheek. A shadow of growth already marked his face, thanks to our rapid metabolism, though he'd shaven barely hours earlier.

"Ready?" he asked, his hand gently brushing my bare arm in an intimate gesture.

I took a moment to scan the area. No life forces hiding between or in parked cars, though there were plenty of glowing life forces inside the surrounding buildings and up ahead on the sidewalk near the Mission on Ninth. But none were dimmer, which meant no one nearby who was trained to mask thoughts from those with my sensing ability. Only the rare few could hide all their life force glow from me, and even those couldn't hold out for long.

"Relax, Your Deathliness," I said with a grin. "No one knows we're here." No one threatening, I meant.

The slightest arch of one eyebrow was his only response as he started down the sidewalk ahead of me, close enough that people would know we were together but far enough away that he could easily move to block anyone who might confront us. On another day, I might remind him that I didn't need his help against mortals—after all, he'd trained me himself, as he did all our cell members. But things had changed this past month, and I was fine with letting Ritter strut his protectiveness. For now.

My ego aside, Ritter had a right to worry because we *were* different from those in the crowd ahead. We weren't dressed in our customary black clothing, and we had no weapons in the open—and certainly not the swords we'd found necessary when facing Emporium hit teams—but any keen observer would know there was something different about us. Being Unbounded not only meant that we physically aged a mere two years for each hundred we lived, but we had the best genes our human lineage offered, and our healing ability meant we carried no scars or imperfections. We also radiated the confidence and vitality that came with the Change. Mortals translated this into beauty, but for those who had dealings with us, our nature would be exposed.

Currently, our most challenging enemies were Hunters, whose solitary goal for more than half a century had been to eliminate all those with the active "devil gene." We were negotiating with leaders in the Hunter Circle to change this, but decades of hurt and indoctrination were a hard battle to win. Since the announcement, thousands of discontents had joined their ranks, either hotheads with little education or "educated" intellects with an overactive sense of fairness. Since they could never be like us, they would enjoy the opportunity of trapping and cutting us into three precise parts, even if it meant jail time. While Hunter leaders claimed never to target children, who by their very age could not have Changed, we knew that if any of their violent new recruits were involved in Kimber's disappearance, her chance of survival was slim.

They shouldn't know about her or her connection to us, I thought, stamping down on the worrying thoughts. We lived in a completely different world now than we had even a few months ago, and I was dredging up trouble where there was none. There had to be another explanation for her disappearance.

We'd reached the crowd now, who milled about, talking and holding their signs that proclaimed a variety of information and demands. Dimitri had been correct in his assumption that this gathering went beyond Kimber's disappearance. Despite the heat already blistering the streets on this late-May Saturday morning, several small groups of protestors had dressed in head-to-toe black, some wearing long, high-collared coats and boots and various weapons, including the occasional sword strapped to a back.

These were Believers, their presence not a surprise since the pastor at the Mission on Ninth held a Sunday service for those who had adopted their ways. Kimber herself was a member. I had to admit that the costumes of these particular Believers were rather accurate depictions of Unbounded, except our clothing was specifically designed to hide numerous weapons, not display them. Even our tightest metamaterial bodysuits, necessary in certain operations, could hold a dozen or more weapons and first aid supplies with barely a bulge. But these faux Unbounded made no attempt to mask their thoughts, their life forces glowing as brilliantly as the average mortal's.

I paused when a young woman in jeans and a purple blouse stepped into my path. Tears slid down her cheeks as she waved a poster with the photograph of a smiling young male high over her head. *No one cares about my brother,* the single, piercing thought stood out from her despairingly, a resolute grimace on her face.

Curious, I delved deeper, stepping into my mental representation of her conscious mind. A sandlike stream of thoughts flowed from top to bottom of my awareness like a waterfall, appearing overhead and vanishing into the stage of her mind at my feet. Disjointed scenes rushed at me, glimpses I couldn't hold and study but only peer at as they rushed by with lightning speed. Finding the right place to jump into the stream to observe was the challenge, but the thought about her brother had given me a place to start.

There, I had it. The thoughts and memories came in an instant dump of knowledge.

Her parents had washed their hands of their rebellious son years before he'd gone missing from their home, and they hadn't bothered to look for the sixteen-year-old. Life had been much easier. But this woman, his older sister, had looked for him repeatedly in the two years since. I saw the boy in her thoughts—a too-bright teen who couldn't fit in with his peers at school. She'd traced him as far as this mission, but aside from a few days of eating here, no one had any idea where he might have gone. The single most feeling in the forefront of her mind was one of failure—her failure. She moved away without appearing to notice me.

As I continued forward, a young man's solemn face calmly met my gaze, though his thoughts cried out wildly: *Where are you now? I should have let you stay in my garage when you asked. I wish you knew how much I regret saying no.*

That could be related to Kimber, and I had to know more, so I studied his thought stream. But his thoughts revolved around a girl he'd known from school, who had run away from her home a year earlier and had never been seen again. He'd talked to the police, but when her drunken father hadn't shown interest, they'd written her down as a runaway and stopped actively looking.

More thoughts came to me, each event unique but all following a common theme of loss and guilt. I stopped walking, swept up in the emotion. I was perhaps the strongest sensing Unbounded to have been born in the past millennium, my line-of-fire training having propelled me to that status, but the emotions here by these unshielded mortals were overwhelming. I hadn't been around so many ordinary humans since before my Change—before I was able to sense.

Ritter's arm closed around me, urging me on, and with effort, I shoved the emotions back while still keeping watch for anything that might jump out as important. Someone in this crowd might have been the last one to see Kimber. Maybe they even knew where she was right this moment. Ritter shot me a questioning gaze, but I didn't have answers. Not yet.

Before we reached the steps, a tall, full-figured woman in a peach-colored suit picked her way through the pictures, toys, and flowers that littered the stairs and began speaking through a megaphone.

"Thank you for being here, everyone. Together we can make a difference!" Cheering met her shout, and people surged forward, momentarily blocking our progress. "Eight hundred thousand children go missing every year in the United States, and too many of them are from California," she continued. "We will—we must—bring our loved ones home!"

But she was lying. Her thoughts screamed out that she didn't believe even this many people could change a thing. Her granddaughter had been gone for four years now, and she'd given up hope. Yet organizing this rally and those like it made her feel she was at least doing something. Besides, there was always the longshot that these Believers at the mission would be able to call upon the new angels they worshipped for help.

"The news reporters have arrived," the woman continued as the crowd quieted. "We will hear from Kimber Wheeler's parents shortly, but until then please feel free to come up here one at a time to tell your own stories while we pass out flyers for you to share in our march today. Make a line at the base of the stairs. Let's tell the world what we know. We need to find all our kids!" More cheers, and then a line began to form.

Ritter tensed at the mention of the media. We had expected a few people coming to pay their respects and maybe a bored freelance reporter angling for an exclusive interview with Kimber's grieving family, but with over a thousand people swarming the sidewalks, there was bound to be more unwanted media attention. Unlike me, Ritter and Dimitri's faces were well-known, both to Hunters and any stray Emporium soldiers who hadn't yet gotten the memo that we were no longer at war. We'd agreed disguises weren't necessary, but things could quickly go wrong if they were recognized.

We pushed past the protestors and hurried up the five stairs to the mission's steel-reinforced glass door. Heads turned and gazes fixed in our direction, but no one made a move to stop us as we let ourselves into a vaulted entryway, gratefully leaving the crowd behind. Inside the mission, the sparse furniture and aluminum accents of the entry hall screamed cheap, but that was to be expected at a mission designed only to save souls and feed the poor.

A man rose from a couch against the back wall where he sat with a couple, all three radiating brightly to my senses. "Welcome," he said, hurrying toward us and holding out a hand to shake Dimitri's.

I recognized Pastor Mike from his picture. He had piercing green eyes, a chiseled face, and deep brown hair that spiked up in front and somehow looked stylish rather than too short. I hadn't been sure whether to expect a formal minister or an Unbounded wannabe, but he was neither of these. He wore nice black jeans and a short-sleeved, gray shirt, and except for the white tab on his collar and the one-inch sword pendant hanging from a silver chain around his neck, the Believer symbol, he could have passed for any of the protestors in the street. He was, by any yardstick, a handsome man.

"Good to see you, Mike," Dimitri said quietly. "I wish it were under better circumstances."

"Yes. Me too." Pastor Mike glanced briefly over his shoulder at the couple behind him. "But I appreciate your coming, Sam. Are these colleagues of yours at Steel Cross?" He gave us a wide smile.

"Yes, they are." Dimitri, or "Sam," didn't introduce us, and Pastor Mike didn't ask our names.

I focused on the couple. Already their grief and sadness reached out, the emotions like cloying fingers threatening to strangle me. I understood their loss. Just over a month earlier, the former Emporium Triad had killed my mortal grand-mother and one of our closest Renegade Unbounded, Cort Bagley. Permanently killed, and we were still grieving his loss. I also knew neither of my losses was the same as what these parents were going through. My grandmother had been in her eighties, and Cort had already lived five hundred years. But my niece and nephew, whose family lived with us in our San Diego Fortress, would never Change, which meant that sooner or later, I'd lose them too. And I would likely bury many of my own children before I physically aged another year.

Ritter's hand brushed my bare arm below the sleeve of my dress, drawing me out of the despair emanating from the couple. Concern came through our link—and a rush of protectiveness.

Giving him a faint smile I knew wouldn't fool him, I moved toward the parents, stepping over a huge, dark stain in the thin carpet where someone had perhaps spilled a pot of food or maybe a pitcher of coffee. Pastor Mike came with me, beating me to the couch where the couple watched us with achingly hopeful expressions. Even with the reddened eyes and smeared makeup, the woman was beautiful. She had short, raven hair that curled slightly under at the ends above her neck and ears, flawless dark brown skin, and a curvaceous figure. Her husband was more non-descript, with light brown hair, pale eyes, a decidedly large nose, and a painfully thin figure. The man had one arm comfortingly around his wife's shoulders, his pale, angular face almost skeletal.

"These are the people I told you about," Pastor Mike said to them. "They're from the Steel Cross Syndicate." He stumbled on the alliteration. To us, he added, "These are Kimber's parents, Isaac and Nyomi Wheeler."

The Wheelers stood as one, Mrs. Wheeler wiping a tear. "Are they the ones who awarded Kimber the scholarship?" she asked the pastor.

"Yes." Pastor Mike said with a brisk nod. "Anonymously, I might add, so let's keep it between us. And it's not the first help they've offered over the years. They have been instrumental in keeping our programs open in these difficult times. My father and his predecessor also worked with them."

I glanced at Ritter, whose mouth gave a tiny quirk, which told me the scholarship and Dimitri's apparent relationship with the mission through this so-called syndicate was a surprise to him as well, but I bet Dimitri's involvement coincided with the Wheelers' participation at the mission—or Mrs. Wheeler's family, as she was Dimitri's descendant.

Mrs. Wheeler's gaze brushed over Dimitri and Ritter before fixing on me. "Thank you for choosing our daughter." More tears dripped from her eyes as she leaned heavily into her husband. "I only hope she'll be able to use your generous gift."

That Kimber would be around to go to college, she meant. I was in her mind now, sifting through the sands of her thoughts. The ache for her daughter was nearly paralyzing; she found it hard to even breathe.

"I know you'd planned to speak to the Wheelers after talking with me," Pastor Mike said to us, dragging two chairs away from the wall to face the couches, "but they have to speak to the group outside in a few minutes before they pass out more flyers, so I thought it would be okay if you talked to them first."

"That's fine." I sank onto one of the chairs, mostly because I was worried both Wheelers might collapse. Dimitri took the other chair while Ritter and the pastor remained standing. "Mr. and Mrs. Wheeler," I said, "our organization has many branches, and because of our long relationship with the Mission on Ninth, we have decided to look into your daughter's disappearance."

Mrs. Wheeler started sobbing softly, so it was Mr. Wheeler who spoke. "Thank you so much," he said. "We appreciate your time and anything you might be able to do to help."

"I would like you to tell us everything that happened, anything you think might be useful, and even things you don't think matter. Keep in mind that we do have access to the police reports, but hearing details from you might lead us in another direction." The police reports had been hacked into, not given to us, which meant we didn't have the impressions of the responding officers, but the Wheelers didn't need to know any of that.

"I don't know what happened," Mrs. Wheeler said through her sobs. "Kimber just didn't come home for dinner on Wednesday night. She was here working with the kids, and she texted to say she was stopping at the park with a friend. I didn't even notice that she hadn't come in until Isaac said we'd be late to bowling if we didn't eat." Her voice grew higher at the end of the sentence as she struggled to speak. "So I was getting ready in my bathroom when . . . when whatever it was happened. Oh, my poor baby!" She curled into her husband and cried.

"You have to understand," Mr. Wheeler said, his arms wrapping around his wife. His skin looked even paler against her dark bronze. "Kimber is a good girl. She's a straight-A student and would never miss school like this. She's not the kind to go anywhere with strangers. She's a little shy, except for when she's here with the young kids in the afternoons. She's also kind and considerate. She would never do this to her mother." Or to him—I saw that in his thoughts. Kimber was a respectful child.

"Did you notice anything different in the days before her disappearance?" Ritter asked. "Tell us what the weeks leading up to Wednesday were like."

This was my cue to watch their minds carefully to catch anything unsaid, but as the Wheelers each described the days and weeks before, nothing stood out in the chaotic jumble of their minds. The only thing they did besides go to their jobs—Mr. Wheeler as a middle grade teacher and Mrs. Wheeler as a city secretary, was to watch TV and go bowling on Wednesday nights. Kimber would usually accompany them. They were ordinary people with seemingly no secrets or vices. On the surface, they were a little too good to be true, but they were so caught up in their loss that the single thing consumed the other difficulties they might have.

I pushed back partially from their thoughts, dulling their emotions enough to give me a little perspective. "What park did she say she was going to?"

"The one near our house, I think," Mrs. Wheeler said in a breathy, painful whisper. "They like to go there and hang out sometimes."

"And is the friend the other missing girl?"

"I don't know." She gave a despairing snort. A vivid picture came to me of her carefully adjusting the wig she was wearing now over her naturally kinky hair on the night of Kimber's disappearance, a memory that would no doubt haunt her for the rest of her life. "What kind of a mother is so preoccupied that she doesn't ask?"

"The kind of mother who trusts her intelligent daughter." I leaned forward to touch her on the arm. "You can go outside for your speech now. They're probably ready for you. I'll get your contact information from Pastor Mike if we need to talk further." They could tell me nothing more than I'd seen from their thoughts as they'd spoken, and I wanted them and their crushing emotions gone before I questioned the pastor.

"Oh, right." Confusion registered on Mrs. Wheeler's face, as if she'd expected more questions, but I was sure she couldn't help us more than she had, and the police documents already contained anyone who knew Kimber. By the time we returned to the Fortress, our technopath Stella should have backgrounds on all of them.

Pastor Mike strode across the room to open the door as Mr. Wheeler led his wife across the entryway. Seconds later, as the pastor closed the door and walked toward us, we heard clapping outside and the megaphone woman announcing them.

"Kimber was last seen leaving the mission with Brenna Dabney," Pastor Mike said, sitting on the empty couch. "They had just helped with the kids in the afternoon who come here for lunch and play while their parents work—it's a program we offer to save parents money in daycare and to encourage them not to leave young kids at home alone. Usually, they only need a few hours overlap, and both girls were volunteers. Well, Kimber more than Brenna. We never counted on Brenna as her appearances were sporadic, but she came a few times. The girls seemed to work well together."

"And now they're both missing." Dimitri leaned forward in his chair, his voice grim.

"Yes and no," Pastor Mike said. "In truth, we don't know that Brenna is missing. She's only been around a few months. But sporadically. During that time there have been stretches of a week or more when I haven't seen her. I believe she's a homeless teen, probably a runaway. She could have simply gone back home."

"You don't report runaways?" Ritter asked from behind my chair.

Pastor Mike studied him for several heartbeats before shaking his head. "Not unless the kids agree. Because they put them in the foster system, where many end up running away again. Sadly, I know of too many situations where these teens are abused in the very place that is supposed to be helping them. And I'm not just talking about being given too many chores. I'm talking big-time emotional, physical, and sexual abuse. Sometimes I can place them with members of my congregation, and I was hoping to do that with Brenna. But in the meantime, I knew she was sleeping up on our roof when she was around. There are worse things for these kids."

Ritter nodded, satisfied, but Dimitri frowned. "This other girl, Brenna, she's two years younger than Kimber?" he asked.

"Yes. And I thought Kimber was having a positive influence on her, but . . ."

"It's possible it went the other way," I finished.

Pastor Mike nodded, his handsome face twisting as his eyes glistened with moisture. He clenched and unclenched his jaw. Just like Kimber's parents, his thoughts told me he felt guilt at what he hadn't done, but he had done more than simply allow Brenna to occasionally sleep on the roof. He'd provided blankets, clothing, and food—even a mirror.

"Maybe Kimber went with Brenna to wherever she's from," I said. If so, Brenna was the key to finding Kimber.

He shook his head. "As far as I know, Brenna told Kimber nothing about her family. The only thing she got from her was that Brenna believed herself to be a descendent of Unbounded. She's a most devoted Believer."

"Which explains why she chose your mission," I said.

"Likely." Pastor Mike gave a shrug, one corner of his mouth twitching in an ironic smile. "Although it could also have a lot to do with the free lunches."

"So she dressed like a Believer?" Ritter asked, disapproval in his tone.

"Very much so. All the time." Pastor Mike smiled widely. "Not a bad thing. Mimicking the angels is a tenet of the faith, though not required outside of worship service."

Angels? I wasn't familiar enough with the Church of the

Unboundaried to know if this was a common belief or if the idea came only from his sect. They all seemed to believe we had come to save them.

"Was there anyone else here close to Brenna?" I asked. "Anyone who might know where she's from?"

"No, she kept to herself," Pastor Mike said, "though she did a few odd jobs for our handyman, Jim James, in exchange for a little money. And before you ask, that's not unusual for us here."

We'd have to find and talk to the man. "You saw nothing out of the ordinary in the past weeks?" I pressed, though his thoughts were showing nothing useful. "No one odd hanging around?"

Many of the original Hunters were mortal offspring of the Emporium Unbounded, thrown away or abandoned when they didn't Change, so unlike most mortals, they'd known about us long before the announcement. They kept a database on known Unbounded and could have possibly traced Kimber through her heritage. Still, Dimitri would probably have had some idea if this branch of his family had been on their radar.

Pastor Mike shook his head. "No, nothing like that. We're a quiet bunch. In fact, only a few dozen parishioners come to the morning Believer sessions, and they're mostly new here. My longtime members prefer a more traditional service."

"I bet," Ritter said, half under his breath.

"Where can we find this Jim James?" Dimitri asked.

"Oh, he's around somewhere." The pastor stood, and his mouth opened to speak again, but his words were overrun with shouts and screams coming from outside.

Then the shouts were overrun by the buzzing of several small engines.

Ritter looked down at Dimitri. "Are those—?"

"Chainsaws. Yes." Dimitri jumped from his chair, heading toward the mission door. Ritter beat him there, his movements so fast they blurred. Pastor Mike and I ran after them.

Outside, the feeling had changed. More than a dozen men had surrounded the Believers, two brandishing chainsaws and at least two other wielding axes. One man carried an assault rifle. Everywhere, people screamed as they fell over each other, trying to retreat.

The life forces of the newcomers were dimmer to my senses, but their mental protection was poorly done, which hinted they were also mortal. I knew each of them would have the logo of a man with rifle on their plaid shirts. A mixture of dread and anticipation puddled in my gut.

"Hunters," Ritter gritted, saying the word like a curse. With one hand on the railing, he vaulted down the five stairs.

Giving Dimitri a quick glance, I leapt after Ritter.

Chapter 2

EVEN AS RITTER HURLED TOWARD THE HUNTERS AND THEIR PREY, dodging around hapless bystanders, a slit in his mental shield opened, inviting me in. I understood the level of trust this required. The crack in his barrier was dangerous to Ritter because those with the strongest sensing ability could incapacitate him with a targeted flash of light, though I'd be watching for intrusion and could protect him to an extent. But with this connection, I could channel his ability, which gave me faster reflexes and excellent coordination. It meant the ability to judge someone's skill at a glance, anticipate their moves, and know the best way to make them stop moving forever. I hadn't yet met another Unbounded who could channel abilities, but then I didn't go around advertising I could do so. Only those closest to me in our Renegade cell even knew.

Dimitri didn't need such a crutch. After a thousand years of fighting the Emporium, he was more than capable of holding his own, even if his ability was healing and not combat.

"Assault rifle!" someone screamed. The excitement inside

me ramped up. It wasn't something I could help. The gene remade us into confident people who craved action.

Ahead of me—only slightly now that I could move as fast as he did—Ritter pushed through the circle of Hunters and grabbed the hilt of a sword from the back of a cowering Believer, whipping it out with a resounding *briiiing*! He jabbed it at the nearest chainsaw, where the blade wedged between the vicious teeth and stuck. The engine howled an ear-shattering scream before cutting off abruptly. Ritter punched the Hunter hard. Down the man went without a sound, his fall oddly graceful. He hadn't yet hit the ground when Ritter kicked out at the Hunter holding the assault rifle, curling him over, and pulling the man into his fist with the strap of his own gun.

By then, I had reached the man with the second chainsaw, who threatened a woman Believer. She pulled a gun from a holster, her hand shaking wildly as she pointed it at him.

"I'm going to cut you in three!" the Hunter shouted over the loud noise of his machine. "I don't care if you're a fake!"

Three cuts to sever the focus points of mind, heart, and reproductive organs was one of the two ways to kill Unbounded. Unfortunately for this woman, one cut would permanently send her to the grave. Her finger tightened on the trigger, and Ritter's ability told me she would probably fire in the next second. Worse, her shaking meant she was more likely to hit someone in the crowd than the Hunter.

I punched a round-faced Hunter next to the chainsaw-wielding idiot, sending him to the ground. Jumping over him, I pushed the woman's hand down and slipped a throwing star from a slit pocket in the bodice of my dress. I threw it at the chainsaw guy, the points ripping into his hand and clinking into the machine, where, as calculated, it killed the motor and saved his miserable life. He screamed and collapsed in an agony that was so bright, I had to block the emotion. My method wasn't as elegant as Ritter's but far more satisfying. The Hunter wouldn't be quick to pick up another chainsaw any time soon.

Meanwhile, Ritter had flattened three more Hunters, and Dimitri at least two. I was vaguely aware of their battles but careful not to focus on them. I wasn't invulnerable, especially now.

"Put that gun away," I yelled at the woman.

The man I had previously hit was up again, and I slammed my own gun into his head with enough force to knock him out. Another Hunter leveled a pistol in my direction, but I kicked it out of his hand. The weapon clattered as it skimmed across the sidewalk and onto the street under a parked car.

A warning shout came to me from Ritter's mind. I moved instantly but not quite far enough. The blade of an ax sliced into my upper right arm where my sleeve ended. Even with the adrenaline racing through my veins, white-hot pain registered in waves throughout my body. Whirling, I slammed my left fist into my attacker's face. Blood spurt from his broken nose.

He tried to swing the ax again, but I easily stepped too close for him to reach, my gun against his throat. "Drop it."

He did—and ran.

I let the ax lay where he'd left it and leveled my gun on the man who'd tried to shoot me. He was young, maybe not even eighteen, the only Hunter left standing.

"You're one of them," he muttered, his voice breathless. "All of you. Fiends from hell."

"Then why aren't you dead?" I flashed him a glimpse of my teeth that was more grimace than smile.

He had no answer.

"But don't run," I added. "I'm a very good shot." He couldn't know that I wouldn't shoot, not here in this crowd. Was it already too late for him to see that we weren't the enemy? That there was no enemy now after we'd taken down the Emporium?

Ritter hurried to my side, giving me a solid perusal. His ability told him I would be fine, but he'd probably tease me about my reaction time later.

"Unbounded aren't trying to hurt you," I told the boy.

"Oh, yeah? We have proof that one of *your kind* is behind the missing children." His lip curled with angry disgust as he began cursing at me.

"Come now," came the voice of Pastor Mike, stepping over the circle of fallen Hunters to begin comforting his parishioners. "It's not like that, son. Unbounded aren't here to hurt us but to protect us through the difficult times foretold in scripture. They are angels, gifted with immortality and abilities we know nothing about."

"Well, we'll have to disagree about the angel part," Ritter said, his tone slightly mocking. "I suspect these 'angels' are just as good or bad as the rest of us, depending on who they are."

He was right, of course. Renegade Unbounded might have defended mortals for hundreds of years, but we weren't angels. We also weren't exactly immortal, though two thousand years of life and immunity to normal causes of death might seem a lot like immortality to shorter-lived mortals.

Pastor Mike shifted his stance to stare at Ritter. In his mind, I glimpsed a clear memory of a man he'd seen with his father as a child, a man dressed in black, his face shadowed. The man's body shape and movement reminded me of Dimitri, and though Pastor Mike didn't make the connection, he secretly believed his father had received an Unbounded at the mission. No wonder he'd become a Believer. But if Dimitri had worked with both Pastor Mike and his father over the past several decades, neither noticed how Dimitri hadn't aged in all that time.

"Do you think the rumor that there are fallen Unbounded is also true?" Pastor Mike asked. "That maybe these men"—he motioned to the Hunters, a few of whom were moaning and moving slightly—"have good reason to hunt them? The fallen angels, I mean?"

Ritter's cringe was obvious to me through our connection, and I stepped in before he told the pastor what he really thought. "You'll have to excuse us," I said. "I need to clean up." My wound throbbed in response, as if pleased to be acknowledged.

Pastor Mike was slow to pull his gaze back to me, but his eyes widened at the sliced flesh angling out awkwardly and the blood dripping down my arm, though the flow of blood had already slowed.

"Time to go," Ritter said, clamping a handful of gauze over my wound. Traffic was completely stopped as the crowd, now paused in their fleeing, jammed the roads, talking madly. The news crews were filming, all cameras turned in our direction.

"Should we call an ambulance?" Pastor Mike asked.

As if on cue, the wail of sirens cut through the voices of the crowd. The police was my bet, which was a faster response than I'd expected given this poor area of LA.

"I'm a doctor," Dimitri said. "I'll tend to her." He continued talking, but his words became muted as Ritter and I moved away.

Dimitri caught up to us seconds later. "Inside," he said, placing himself on my other side, his arm going around me protectively. "There's a back exit, but we won't be able to get our vehicle out of here now." The crowd cleared before us as we swept up the steps and into the mission.

I experienced a rush of warmth in my arm as his ability began working to encourage my healing process. He'd let me ride along in the past as he traced veins and arteries and blood cells, but today his mind was tightly shut.

"I'll call Stella." Ritter pulled out his phone. "See if she can make that footage of us disappear or at least alter it. But it may be difficult, depending on how many people were filming versus how many were running away."

"You and I are already in the Hunter and Emporium databases, so we don't matter," Dimitri said. "And Erin was on the side farthest away from the camera."

Ritter nodded shortly and spoke into the phone. "Hey, Stella. We need a little help."

Dimitri drew me to the couch where the Wheelers had been sitting moments before. He pulled a small first aid kit from some hidden pocket.

"No stitches," I said firmly.

He chuckled. "It's pretty deep, but we don't have time for that now anyway, so I agree. Glue and tape will do for now, and by the time we get to the safe house, it'll be enough." He drew out a syringe with a thick needle.

"No curequick," I said. The mixture of sugar and proteins reduced to their most usable forms would increase my already rapid healing by up to five times, but its effects were addictive, which I couldn't risk at the moment.

Dimitri frowned. "You haven't needed it for a month. It's okay."

"I'm fine." I could endure the pain for the few hours my body would take to repair the damage. "And don't tell Ritter I refused it."

Understanding dawned, and Dimitri chuckled under his breath. "You haven't told him yet, have you?" he said, his voice low enough that I could barely understand the words.

I stared at him in shock because I hadn't told anyone yet. But of course Dimitri would know. With his ability to heal, he could trace every part of a person's body. The question wasn't if he knew my secret but *how long* had he known.

"No," I said.

"Better do it soon." His jaw twitched in exactly the same way mine did when I was forced to confront something I wanted to reject. In fact, the wide oval shape of his eyes was mine too. And right now, they looked a little too innocent.

I gave a sharp nod. Today was the day I'd planned to talk with Ritter on the island, but here we were on Unbounded business. Again. Since my Change nine months earlier, that had become a regular occurrence. Protecting humanity from our own kind wasn't something any of us took lightly, but I'd thought it would be different since our last battle.

"Do you think that boy Hunter could be right?" I asked as Dimitri tortured me with disinfectant. "Is there still a faction out there determined to take over the mortals?"

He shook his head, his fingers working quickly to tape my wound together. "I don't know, but it's not something we should dismiss out of hand. Your brother has only been in charge of the Emporium Triad for five weeks. There hasn't been time to reorganize everything. And with Kimber's disappearance, I think we need to research other missing people in the area to see if there is a connection to the Unbounded. It's possible Kimber was targeted because of her link to us. If we find more links like that, it'll be something to look into."

"Right, and Hunters have records that even we don't." Records that had been stolen when they left or were kicked out of the Emporium fifty or sixty years ago. Those had been the lucky ones. More recently, those who didn't Change had been forced to remain in the servitude of the Emporium, and anyone trying to leave was eliminated so the secret could be maintained. I hoped Dimitri was wrong.

Dimitri blotted blood from the hem of my short sleeve before folding it up inside, hiding the stain. Together we stood to face Ritter, who walked in our direction.

"She's sending someone to collect the Land Cruiser," Ritter said. "Come on. We'll have to make our own way to the safe house."

Dimitri held up a set of keys. "Pastor Mike was kind enough to lend us his vehicle. We need to go through their gym to get out the back."

I laughed. "Let's go then."

"Wait." Dimitri turned up my other sleeve. He was a man of good taste and attention to detail, but for some reason the action struck a tender chord in me. I'd once asked him if he regretted not being part of my childhood, instead of allowing the man I'd thought was my birth father raise me, but he'd reminded me of all the centuries we would have together, years that my mortal father couldn't possibly match. Dimitri had helped give me life, but he'd also allowed me a wonderful, normal childhood with a mortal who still loved me today. I wouldn't change that. I hadn't missed Dimitri growing up, but I was glad to have him in my life now.

We hurried down a hallway past an aluminum accented staircase. Like the entry, the hallway was free of litter and notable dirt, but the color of the carpet and the scuffs on the wall gave off a worn sensation as if too many feet had trod down this path for too many years.

At the end of the hallway, an older, heavyset man in jeans and a T-shirt stepped out in front of us. "I'm sorry, but we're closed until the kids' activities this afternoon," he said in a friendly voice, "but grab-and-go lunches will be passed out by the gym doors in about two hours. If you have a problem . . ." Whatever else he'd been planning to say was lost as he took better note of us, his eyes settling on Ritter as the most obvious threat. His hand went to his back pocket, and I quickly reached out to his mind to see if he carried a weapon.

No, a cell phone. I kept my hands away from my own weapons, knowing Ritter and Dimitri would pick up on my cue. "You work here?" I asked, ignoring the impatience emanating from Ritter. He wanted us out of here before any policemen arrived, but we couldn't pass up the opportunity to question this man.

He nodded. "I'm the janitor, handyman, watchman. You name it. Jim James is the name." He extended a hand, which I shook. Dimitri and Ritter followed suit, which seemed to make Jim relax.

"Right. Pastor Mike told us about you." I was determined to focus on his chaotic rush of thoughts as quickly as possible. "We're from the Steel Cross Syndicate and are looking into Kimber's disappearance. We wanted to ask you about Kimber and her friend." The name of the other missing girl had escaped me for the moment.

"Brenna," supplied Dimitri.

Jim glanced around before replying. "It's a terrible situation." Pity rose from him in a wave, and in his mind, I caught a glimpse of Kimber as she played basketball with a group of younger children. Jim had been changing a light in the gym, and his ladder had been hit by the ball. He'd laughed and stopped to watch them for a few minutes.

"I'm guessing you knew Kimber?" I asked, satisfied that his thoughts were benign—at least toward Kimber.

"Some." Jim gave a slight shrug. "I mean, she didn't tell me any deep, dark secrets or anything like that, but she was here most every day this summer to help with the kids. She and her parents are members of the parish, so I also see them on Sundays."

"Did you see her on the day she went missing?" Ritter asked in a surprisingly casual voice that belied the tenseness still radiating from him.

"No, but I heard she was here to help with the lunch. I didn't see her myself because I was in the mechanical room trying to fix the water heater. We've been having issues. This building is as old as sin." He gave a dry laugh. "Probably built by one of those new people everyone's talking about."

I laughed. "Unbounded? You ever see any of them around here? Or anyone looking for them?"

"Nah, none of them folks around here." Jim shook his head, raising a hand to scratch at his grizzled head. "Except for the wannabes. To tell you the truth, I doubt much of what everyone says is even true. I mean, I know Pastor Mike is convinced they're angels from God, sent to protect us, but reporters like to make up stories. I mean, obviously, there's something to it, or the president wouldn't have announced them, but I'm betting it's an evolution kind of thing. You know, nature's way of making sure the human race survives amid all the famine and global warming. But all the rumors and hype about mysterious powers and immortality"—he shook his grizzled head—"it's just a way to sell advertising."

His take was one I hadn't heard before, but then most mortals I spent time with these days knew Unbounded personally. By my way of thinking, this handyman was more right in his attitude than the pastor.

"I take it you're not a Believer?" I gave him an appreciative smile.

He laughed. "Not in any immortal humans, but I worship like the next man. I believe in doing good, and that's why I'm here. I like helping these kids. Never had any of my own."

"What about Brenna?" Ritter said, glancing down the hall as if expecting someone to appear there any minute.

"Oh, I know her even less than Kimber. She did some work for me here—and she was surprisingly good at it for a runaway kid. But she's all muddled up, believing she's something she's not. I don't blame her. I suspect she came from an abusive home."

"You know where she's from originally?" I could see the girl in his mind. If an Unbounded ever decided to incorporate the gothic look, Brenna would fit right in, but the image was jarring to me. Her face, however, had good lines underneath the makeup.

Ritter's gaze brushed mine, and I shook my head to his unasked question. If Jim James knew anything about either girls' disappearance, he wasn't thinking about it.

"She wouldn't say," Jim said. "But she was from the South—Georgia, if I'm not mistaken—or has spent time there. My deceased wife was from there, and the child had a tiny bit of the same accent. Even fifty years here in LA couldn't change that for my wife."

"And there's nothing more you know?"

"I told it all to the police—but I can tell you again."

"We'll read the reports," I said. "If we think of anything more, we'll contact you. Can you show us the gym doors? Our ride is waiting."

Jim thumbed to his right. "Through them doors. But no one is there. You did say you're here with the knowledge of the pastor, right?" He pursed his lips as we nodded, and he stepped backward, his eyes riveted on us as if loathe to let us out of his sight, a mixture of fear and admiration coming from his thoughts. It was a reaction we were accustomed to receiving, but I wished I'd come in disguise now. We couldn't allow him to put the police on our trail.

"Of course we have permission." Dimitri held out his hand. "Thank you for your time."

Jim shook, then his eyes opened wide. "What was that? Something pinched—" His eyes rolled up in his head and only Ritter's fast action stopped his head from hitting the wall on his way down.

Ritter picked him up, his muscles flexing under the man's weight. Without speaking, we hurried to the gym, where Ritter settled Jim James into a chair on the edge of the basketball court. "You got it?" he asked me.

"Almost."

The man's unconscious mind had become a placid lake of water that I slid into. Underneath the water, I examined bubbles of thought passing by. These memories were much less detailed and often more misleading than those in the sand stream, but I welcomed the peace of studying them without the chaos. Finding the thoughts containing our encounter was easy, and I reached out and pulled it toward me. The memory popped and vanished.

Jim James would never remember us or be able to tell the police where we went.

"Let's go," I said.

Still, I kept my link with the man, examining other thoughts, searching for those of Brenna to hear her accent for myself.

Ritter reached the door first, opening it to look out, and what he saw must have satisfied him because he motioned us forward. The alley was narrow, only wide enough for the space of a garbage truck.

"Hopefully, this will take us out after the traffic jam in front of the mission," Ritter said. "And before they have time to lock down the area."

We'd reached the pastor's ancient, nondescript van when three men barely out of their teens appeared in front of it, blocking the alley. I recognized the sandy hair and chubby face of the young Hunter who pulled the gun on me earlier. This time he was wielding an ax instead of a gun, but his two friends each carried a pistol. Behind us, a truck was pulling up, and six more men with axes and a chainsaw blocked our retreat.

The young Hunter smirked at me. "Thought I might find you here. You'll be coming with us," he motioned to those with the truck.

"Like hell we will," Ritter growled. As one, the three of us pulled our guns. Ritter, two pistols in hand, faced those behind us while Dimitri and I faced forward.

"We *will* fire," Ritter said. "Even if you shoot, you won't kill us before we get most of you. And you'll stay dead. Are you wearing body armor like we are? How many are you willing to risk?"

A frustrated growl came from the round-faced man, but he lowered his ax. "Put them away," he said to his friends as he moved to the side.

Dimitri and I jumped inside the van, our guns still targeting the Hunters. Ritter pounced onto the top, crouching, one gun toward those behind and one pointed at their apparent leader as Dimitri drove away.

After we turned into the alley leading toward the street, Ritter pulled himself in through the window. "Remind me next time to bring a tranq. I really, really wanted to shoot them."

I knew the feeling, but I also knew we'd have regretted

shooting them. At least with the Emporium, we had the chance of taking many of those we killed to Mexico to recover, where they would either be reeducated or prosecuted for their crimes. If we pulled the trigger on the Hunters, however irritating they were, they would be snuffed out permanently.

They are human, and so are we, I reminded myself. I could never forget that we were trying to protect them along with the other mortals.

"Now what?" I asked.

It was Dimitri who responded. "Now we find those girls—and whoever is behind this. If they're targeting our people, we need to know how."

Chapter 3

WHEN WE ARRIVED AT THE SAFE HOUSE IN AN UPSCALE CONDO near the ocean, we found not only Stella Davis, our technopath, waiting at the door, but also Ava O'Hare, my fourth-great grandmother and the leader of our San Diego Renegade cell.

"Good, you're back." Her gray eyes lingered only a moment on my arm and the bandage there. "We've got another problem on our hands."

She fell into step beside me. Her hair was a yellow-blonde, rich with color, almost golden, and her smooth, clear skin was wrinkle-free. She had high cheekbones and a nose that spread a tiny bit more than necessary, reminding me of my mother. Physically, she was only a few years older than I was, but the wisdom in her gravestone eyes and the regal way she carried herself hinted at the three hundred plus years she'd lived. She was also a sensing Unbounded, and every time we were together, I felt the ferocity with which she cared for all of us in her surface emotions.

If not for her interference in my mother's insemination, I wouldn't be Unbounded, and I wouldn't have survived the fire that had once killed me. There had been a time when I wasn't sure surviving was a positive thing, but the me I had become was grateful.

Her steps slowed as she let the others go ahead into the safe house family room. "You're hurting," she said. "What happened?"

I could feel her like a butterfly on the outside of my mental barrier, and because I knew the safe house had been wired with a net that wouldn't allow outside sensing to reach us, I released my shield to allow her entry. No one could get through my shield—I'd killed the only person who'd been able to. Now, I concentrated on focusing on the events to make it easier for her. Ava couldn't break through shields the way I could, and she couldn't channel others' abilities, but I respected her experience and knew she might see something I missed.

All she said was, "You haven't told him yet."

I sighed. Of course she'd pick up on my worry about that. "I should have done it before."

I hadn't because that week on the island had been our last shot at being alone. Then, instead of bringing the others for an extended vacation, Mari, our shifter, had shown up to bring us here.

Which reminded me. "Are the kids disappointed?"

My niece and nephew had endured a lot in the nine months since the Emporium murdered their mother, and my brother Chris had married Stella. The island was supposed to be, in part, a gift for both children who had celebrated birthdays this past week—Kathy turning thirteen and Spencer eleven.

Ava laughed. "No, the kids are on the island. Chris flew

them there as planned. They're upset that you guys and Stella aren't there with them, but they'll survive."

"Good. I'm glad." It was still strange that I owned an entire island. Cort Bagley had left it to Ritter and me in his will, and after his death, I hadn't imagined being able to go there without experiencing overwhelming grief, but Cort's island had been exactly the right place for us to contemplate a future without him.

We entered the family room, where Ritter and Dimitri were talking with Stella Davis and Mari Jorgensen, who was Stella's fifth-great niece. To my surprise, my younger brother, Jace Radkey, was with them, and he enveloped me in a hug. I winced as pain pierced my arm.

"Ha," Jace said with a grin. "Looks to me like you didn't move fast enough."

"Something like that." My eyes drank in his lean figure. From his white-blond hair and blue eyes to the tips of his worn tennis shoes, he looked well. Recently turned twenty-nine, he'd Changed on the early side when Emporium soldiers had nearly killed him. He'd spent several months enjoying his new life of Renegade battles until circumstances required him to take over his birth father's place in the Emporium Triad. He'd always been the fun, playful brother, the one I could count on to make me laugh, but also the one I needed to look out for and protect because he didn't always make the best choices. Never in a million years did I think he'd be running a multi-million-dollar enterprise as a member of the Emporium Triad.

"They still let you go out dressed like that?" I teased, eyeing his worn jeans and black T-shirt. His birth father, Stefan Carrington, now sedated and imprisoned in Mexico, had flaunted his wealth and expensive tastes. I didn't suppose my brother's Costco deals fit in at Emporium Headquarters very well.

He grinned. "No, Jeane has insisted on a bunch of five-thousand-dollar suits. But I hid these bad boys at the back of my closet. In my safe. Which is as big as a regular closet, I might add."

We laughed, and for a moment, it felt like old times—before we knew about Unbounded and Renegades and the war for the lives of the mortals.

"How is Jeane?" I asked a little reluctantly. She was also a new member of the Triad, taking over for her brother—the one she'd permanently killed during the takeover. He'd had it coming, but the brutal act still unnerved me.

"As crazy as ever. She's useless at helping me run the businesses, but she does know about people, so that's been some help. Keene and I are doing the rest." Jace snorted. "Who am I kidding? Keene's the one who is really making it work. So far. Since he was raised by the Emporium, he already knows much of what goes on." Jace's sigh hinted that he'd come across more challenges since we'd all left him and Keene in New York a week earlier.

"I can imagine. So is that why you are here? For a break?" I was starting to feel the toll of events at the mission. Was it too much to hope that this was a social call?

"Well, I—" Jace began.

Ava interrupted with a clap. "Let's sit down and get right to business."

Jace and I headed to a beige leather couch, with me sinking into its comfortable depths gratefully. The others settled around us as Stella, her blinking neural receiver on her head, brought the huge screen on the wall to life without even looking in that direction. This "family room" in our LA safe house might not be quite the up-to-date technology we had in our conference room back at the Fortress, but someone had gone to the trouble of making sure the systems it did have were integrated with her equipment. With her straight dark hair, flawless features, and heart-shaped olive face, Stella was a most compellingly beautiful woman, even among Unbounded circles and even at five months pregnant. The nanites she controlled in her body as a technopath were continually remaking her face. Slight adjustments came to her as naturally as breathing, such as playing up the Asian part of her heritage or enlarging her eyes.

Stella settled next to Mari, who resembled her in her dark hair and eyes, though Mari had only a hint of Asian in her features. Dimitri and Ava took the third couch in the semicircle, and only Ritter remained standing on the far side of the room by the small bar, his arms folded over his chest, his eyes riveted on me.

I met his gaze and smiled, but he didn't return the gesture. His eyes were unreadable, almost black under the interior lighting.

I have to tell him, I told myself. Pushing aside a rush of regret that we weren't still on the island, I concentrated on the image Stella brought up on the screen. It appeared to be an ordinary eighteen-wheeler carrying a huge metal shipping container.

Ava nodded at Jace, and he uncrossed his legs and leaned forward. "As you know, Keene and I have been combing through all the Emporium records as we try to get a handle on everything they're into. Mostly, it's pretty straightforward. We buy things we need for our various businesses, either to resell or to use in manufacturing. Or items for our own use. They—we—have a hand in pretty much every industry. Of course, Keene and I have also been working on righting abuses that have continued for generations."

"Because they pay poor wages or cheat or threaten their suppliers or distributors," Ava chimed in.

"Right," Jace said. "Then a few days ago, I ran across a large shipment of goods I couldn't identify."

The lighting in the room dimmed slightly as an image of two semitrucks appeared on the screen. Everyone was concentrating on it, except Stella, who was staring into the air, looking at something only she could see. Her neural receiver allowed her brain to connect directly to the network, and she could process information faster than dozens of people, so whatever else she was doing, she didn't need more than a stray thought to keep pace with our discussion.

"One shipment originated from a warehouse we own in Oregon," Jace continued. "It contains mostly electronics. The second truck came from Texas, and I believe it contained at least some foodstuffs, but it seemed to take an odd route along the Mexican border to join up with the other truck here in LA, where they were put on a cargo ship. The interesting thing is that there seems to be no final destination for these particular items, and I found no payment. When I tried to talk to the truck drivers, they didn't know anything, and the cargo ship had already taken off. I have no idea where it's headed."

"Could be Chile," Stella said. "I see online that the boat plans to pick up cargo in Chile before returning to the US, but as Jace says, there is no record of the Emporium shipping anything with them. It's a medium-sized boat, as far as cargo ships go, but there are at least thirty businesses using the company to ship stuff to and from Chile and back."

Jace nodded. "Interesting. Well, the lack of information made me curious, so I did a couple of searches and found fifteen more trucks that came to LA at the same time to drop off shipping containers. No record of what was inside, but the contents are now also on that cargo ship. When I finally tracked down the Emporium manager responsible for signing the loading orders for the first two trucks, he was all fun and games until I pressed, and then he only wanted to speak to Stefan."

"Who isn't actually in charge anymore," I said, folding my right hand into my left across my stomach, which eased the throbbing in my right arm. The pain was already fading but not fast enough. I'd grown soft these past five weeks of inactivity. "The plot thickens."

Jace looked at me gravely. "More than you know. Because I discovered this has all happened before. About a month ago, more foodstuff and electronics were shipped. No final invoices. And it happened the month before that. And again. Stretching back at least twenty years. So whatever is going on, it'll likely happen again next month."

Stella's headset blinked furiously. "He's right. It's all here in the Emporium database, though it's in the section that was formerly restricted to the Triad. I'll need more time, but on the outset, I don't think there is anything else to show, aside from the general description of foodstuff and electronics, at least in black and white, as we used to say. It's a huge coverup."

I grimaced, thinking of Stefan and his plan to take over the US presidency and Congress. We'd nearly been too late to stop him, and if this was something he put into place, it couldn't be good. "Stefan never did anything unless it would benefit the Emporium and him specifically," I said.

"Right," Jace agreed. "The more I learn about him, the more I detest him." But there was something else in my brother's voice, a fascination as well. I understood that. At first, I'd believed the doctored sperm used for my conception had come from Stefan, and meeting him under those circumstances had been life-altering.

"The real thing we should be thinking about," Ritter said

into the silence, "is what happens when we stop the shipments next month."

"No." Ava shook her head. "We can't do that until we find out what they contain and who they're for. That means we need details before the next shipment. I would like suggestions on how to find those details."

Jace leaned forward again, eagerness in his face. "The obvious thing is to board that boat and see for ourselves."

"The boat will take time to arrive at its destination in Chile," Dimitri said. "Assuming that is their actual destination, and there isn't a drop-off before that."

Ava sighed. "Which there very well could be."

"If we could pinpoint the ship's location, I could shift us all there," Mari said. "Well, I'd probably need a bit of boosting from Keene."

We all nodded. Keene McIntyre's ability was synergy, which allowed him to increase the action of anything. While it had seemed a relatively volatile and confusing ability in the beginning, it had turned out to make him one of the most powerful—and dangerous—Unbounded alive.

"A moving target?" Ritter asked. "I would rather not end up in the ocean. A plane drop nearby would be better."

Mari laughed, seemingly unconcerned. "Moving isn't a problem, not if we can find it in the first place. I can calculate the exact position and fold it around us." Her reply was challenging, which showed how far Mari had come since joining us. She'd changed from a desperate woman sold out by her fake Hunter husband into a strong fighter and the only known Unbounded shifter alive. She was a vital part of our cell.

Ritter nodded, though I could tell the idea still gave him pause. I didn't blame him. Until recently, shifting had been a nearly forgotten ability, but I had channeled Mari many times, and to her, moving between two locations came as naturally as breathing, especially now that she and Keene had figured out how to pinpoint her accuracy at pretty much any distance.

"It would still be easier if we were at least in the general vicinity," I said. "I think a plane is a good idea." With Chris on the island, though, Dimitri would have to shake off the dust on his flying skills.

"I had the computer estimate the total shipment value based on what we do know," Stella said. "Of course, there's a large degree of extrapolation since we don't know what was on all the trucks, but I'm placing it between one and five million dollars."

Jace gasped. "Who are they giving that to?"

"Or paying it to," I said.

For a moment no one spoke, but then Ritter pushed off the bar where he was leaning. "It could very well be a payment, which is why Ava's right that we need to know what's going on before we stop it."

"Maybe the first place to start is the manager Jace talked with." Ava's gaze went to him as she spoke. "You and Erin should go. Can you find him on a Saturday afternoon?"

Jace's grin stretched wide. "Oh, yes."

"I'm coming too," Ritter growled, "and this time, we're dressing the part."

Ava turned to look at him, and for a moment, I thought she'd reject his offer, but instead she nodded. "Okay, but keep a low profile. After what happened at the mission, every cop in LA is going to be looking for you."

"Actually," Stella said, "I've been monitoring the local chatter, and the police don't much care about them. It's the man who was hurt by Erin's throwing star who's making a fuss and wants to press charges."

I rolled my eyes. "Uh, he had a chainsaw pointed at me."

Stella laughed. "That's what the police saw in the videos and why they don't care to pursue it. By the way, I was able to blur your face in the official videos, and you were on the side, away from the press, so I don't think you'll be identified."

Jace snorted. "Well, officially, she's dead. So good luck if they do identify her."

I nodded and smirked with him, but a part of me was disappointed. Maybe I'd even been planning on coming back from the dead now that Unbounded weren't a secret.

Ritter paced a few steps to stand in front of the couches. "We'll take precautions." Again, his eyes lingered on me, and I knew he suspected something. But our business would have to wait.

"Before we go, I would like to show Stella the accent of the missing friend in Kimber's case," I said. "If she's from Georgia, or lived there, we might be able to locate her family and see if Kimber is there with her."

"Good idea," Dimitri leaned forward to grab another laptop from the coffee table. "I'll cross-reference any other missing people in the area and also across the United States to see if there's a correlation."

"I've already input most of that data," Stella said. "If you'll send any additional particulars, to my regular mailbox, I'll put them in my search."

"Wait," Mari said. "Before we get off the subject of the boat entirely, are there any islands in the area? I mean, on the way to Chile, or some other likely target? I think we need the ship's manifest."

Jace snorted. "Good luck. Patrick Mann was trying to help me hack into it from New York. They're sealed up tight."

"Probably don't want to say that too loud." I punched Jace on the shoulder. "If news got out that the president's Unbounded son is hacking into private companies, there would be trouble." Patrick, a technopath like Stella, had become the official public face of the Unbounded.

Mari laughed. "If Patrick couldn't get in, they've definitely got something to hide." With the softest pop, she disappeared from the couch and reappeared near the bar. "Anyone want a drink?"

"Water," I said, raising a finger, more for something cool than for thirst. I'd been absorbing from the air to recoup my energy, but I was still feeling weak.

When no one else answered, Mari grabbed a bottle of water from the mini-fridge and appeared behind my couch with the drink. I smiled my thanks.

"I'd like to hunt down the manifest at the shipping company," Mari said, "but I'll need a flash drive or one of Cort's inventions to copy the . . ." She trailed off as if suddenly remembering that Cort wasn't around anymore to invent tech for us to use. He had been our scientist, gifted to see patterns on an atomic level, which had meant that he was good at any kind of inventing, even to the point of helping Dimitri with medicine. "Sorry," she added.

"It's okay." Ava's voice was atypically gentle. "We all do it."

Tears pricked my eyes. Cort would be laughing at us all right now, if he were here.

"I can get you something to use," Stella said. "It'll help get you past their encryptions, but I may need to walk you through a few things onsite. Better take an earbud."

"I'll go with Mari to get the manifest then," Ava said. "Ritter, Jace, and Erin will question the Emporium manager. Stella and Dimitri will continue researching the missing girls."

Ritter folded his arms across his chest, staring down at Ava. "I'd feel better if Jace went with you and Mari. If the cargo people have been paid off, they could be dangerous."

Ava usually gave in to Ritter's requests, trusting him as op leader, but this time she shook her head. "Jace will need to set up the appointment with the Emporium shipping manager. However, you could come with us. With Erin channeling Jace, they'll have two combat Unbounded, and it's unlikely they'll need force anyway since he does work for us. Well, for the Emporium anyway."

Ritter was torn, but he shouldn't be. His senses had to be telling him that was the best option. Why weren't they? "Okay," he said shortly. His eyes strayed to me at the word, digging and searching. I frowned at him in a clear message: back off.

"Okay, we'll leave in thirty minutes." Ava stood, a hint of satisfaction in her expression. "Keep your phones handy, and I want all of us to take earbuds as a backup. We'll stay on different channels unless we need support from the other group. Stella will monitor for us."

Meeting over, Ritter and I headed back to our room that overlooked the ocean. I leaned over and began unstrapping my gun and knife sheaths from my thighs. I'd be using the built-in ones on my bodysuit for the next op.

He watched me, his eyes hungry. Heat curled in my gut, and I turned my back toward him teasingly. "Unzip me, would you?"

He leaned over to kiss my neck, sending goose bumps over my skin. Then slowly, he dragged down the zipper—and froze. "Hey, you're not wearing body armor."

"Uh, yeah." I'd forgotten that was something I didn't want to bring up. "This dress is already too tight, and in my defense, I didn't think we'd run into Hunters at a church mission."

These days the body armor, even the lighter, short-sleeved version, made me feel as if I were smothering, so I avoided it.

"You need to wear it when you go with Jace."

"Of course." I'd use the bodysuit with the built-in armor, which was less stifling than layers.

His hand ran over my bare back. Desire radiated from him, filling me as well. "You're not wearing much else, either."

"Nope."

Careful of my arm wound, he helped me remove my dress before tossing it to the floor. Then he kissed my neck and back all the way down to the fastening of my bra. I groaned under his ministrations. The bra and panties followed the dress, leaving me wearing only a gold necklace with two rings as pendants. His own clothes dropped next, clunking as the weapons inside the folds hit the ground. Then he was kissing me again, his tongue hot on mine, pushing me toward the bed.

He hesitated before we fell onto it. "Something is different," he growled, frustration lacing his voice. "I need to know what. You're holding back in training, and it wasn't just because we were on vacation. My senses tell me you're at risk, but you fought as well as ever today. There's something . . . new." He radiated both hope and concern through our connection, and my senses sharpened.

I put my arms around him, my breasts against his chest. "There is something," I said, lifting myself on tiptoe to glide my tongue along his lower lip. "I was going to tell you on the island today. I've known for a few weeks, but I didn't want to share you. Not yet. We never really had a honeymoon until then."

His eyes widened, and he pulled back slightly, his gaze dropping to my still-flat stomach. "You're going to have my baby." It was more a comment than a question.

"Yes. We're having a baby." Tears welled in my eyes, sliding down my cheeks. *Hormones,* I thought, because as a Renegade, I'd learned to compartmentalize emotions. Still, nothing had prepared me for this, for becoming a mother. "During all the commotion with the takeover, I forgot to channel Stella's ability, and the nanites didn't do their job." Nanites because otherwise pregnancy was nearly impossible to prevent.

With a hoarse cry, Ritter dropped to his knees in front of me, his face pressed against my belly. "Hey, little guy. Or girl. It's your daddy." He looked up at me, his eyes filling with tears I had rarely seen him shed. "Can you talk to him yet?"

I shook my head. "No, but I can sense an awareness. I can see thoughts forming. Dimitri should be able to tell us what it is. I just didn't want to tell him before you. But today he told me he already—"

"Knew." Ritter gave a strangled laugh. "Of course. He's a healer. And I'm betting Ava knows too."

I nodded as he kissed my belly, murmuring words I couldn't make out. Emotion coming from him cracked through his mental shield and spilled into the room, threatening to overwhelm us both. I felt it all—everything he'd been and done. Most of it I already knew, but coming at once, inspired by this tiny life we'd created, was a new level of intimacy.

Ritter had Changed two hundred and forty-one years ago, his entire mortal family subsequently murdered by Emporium agents, including his mother, younger sister, and the woman he was engaged to marry. Until recently—until me—Ritter hadn't been able to imagine a future without the hate that had consumed him.

Our baby moved inside me. At only five weeks since conception, seven since my last cycle, he or she was aware, and I could feel the mental response and the beating of a human heart in my mind.

Ritter began to sob. This strong, powerful man, who had waged war against oppression and evil for over two centuries, wet my belly with his tears. So many times this past month, I'd dreamed of how I'd tell him the news, but none of my imaginings had gone here. I thought he'd whoop for joy and begin planning toddler training sessions, but I never expected this display of vulnerability.

He looked up at me, the corner of his left eye slightly drooping. Not a defect that his Unbounded genes would have hurried to fix, but a feature programmed into his DNA. One more thing I loved about him.

"I've been fighting so long," he said. "Killing, pushing love away. What if I . . .? I don't know how to do this."

"You did it with Blaze," I said. His adopted son had been thirteen when his Unbounded parents, Ritter's friends in England, had been killed by the Emporium.

He shook his head. "Even with Blaze, there was a separation. And he was a snotty teenager. This is different. What if I screw up?"

"We'll figure it out like everything else we've done so far." I leaned over to kiss him.

He kissed me back as he stood, his passion flaring, overtaking, and blending with mine until I didn't know where the emotions originated. I'd once told Ritter I wanted it all, to have someone worship and love me with all that he was. Ritter had taken on that role, and the depth of his commitment and emotion still surprised me. And to be honest, it frightened me too. Because up until recently, our lives have been filled with violence and death, which made loving someone that much more dangerous.

But now all thoughts of danger and the uncertain future vanished. Because lovemaking was something my husband and

I did particularly well. There was only Ritter's touch, and my touch, igniting fire over every inch of our bodies, the linking of our minds doubling each sensation until we lost ourselves completely . . . and found each other.

I could even—almost—push aside the mistake I'd made that meant our child might not have the same chance at immortality that I'd been given. But that was a worry for another day.

Chapter 4

RITTER AND I WERE LATE IN MEETING THE OTHERS FOR OUR RESPEC-
tive ops, but we were dressed and armed to the hilt when
we arrived in the entryway where the others waited. Ritter
was disguised as a businessman with glasses and pasty makeup
that couldn't quite hide his virility. He also couldn't hide his
reluctance at our separation, but I wasn't about to let him start
treating me like a liability.

"You need to be careful," he said in a tone low enough for
only me to hear.

"I have been. We were going to see a pastor this morning,
remember? Besides, the ax hit was a fluke. I would have shot
any of them if they threatened our baby."

"I would have too," he said. "I knew something was up."

Which meant he'd been watching me. So it was a good
thing we were going our separate ways for the next op. I didn't
want him distracted any more than he'd want me to be.

Strange how different it all was now. Many times we'd put

our lives on the line, knowing we might never see each other again, but now we had hope. A seemingly tiny change made an entire world of difference.

Mari and Ava looked little like themselves under wigs, glasses, and makeup, and the long expanse of Mari's bare legs in her mini-skirt probably meant no one would be focusing on her face anyway. Jace looked like me—black bodysuit and a long coat riddled with hidden pockets for weapons. It would be hotter than Hades in the sweltering LA midday heat, but we wouldn't be out of our air-conditioned SUV for long.

"Earbud check," Ava said.

I put my hand to my ear and turned on the mic with a click. "Erin, testing."

"Loud and clear," Stella said in my ear.

Jace was next, and we left before the others were finished, Ritter staring holes in my back. There was no sign of the emotion he'd shown upstairs in the room, but his surface emotions were still jubilant.

"Want to tell me why you two were late?" Jace asked as we climbed into the SUV. He took the wheel, which was best since he knew where we were heading.

"None of your business."

"Oh, yeah? Then I take it you don't want this?" He reached into the back and dragged a large, pink pastry box forward over the middle console. "I got your favorite donut."

"I don't have a favorite."

"That's why I got one of each." Dropping the box in my lap, he started the engine. "Open it, would you?"

When I did, he snagged an iced chocolate donut and bit into it. "Mmm."

I felt hungry with the smell wafting up to my face, though absorbing nutrients came like second nature to me now. Still, absorption wasn't nearly as satisfying as a sugar rush, even though that was muted with our speedy metabolism.

I reached into the box, but Jace leaned over and slapped my hand. "Not until you tell me what's up with you. I wasn't just being nosy when I asked why you were late. I can feel a difference. Plus, Catrina has been hinting at something for a month now."

Catrina, the new sensing Unbounded for the Emporium Triad, had been the first to note the light inside me that signaled pregnancy. And Jace might not be as skilled as Ritter, but he was still combat gifted and his gift was giving him warning signals.

"Fine," I said. "I'm going to have a baby, and I was telling Ritter." I waited a few seconds and added, "I wanted to tell him on the island."

Jace laughed, choking a little on his donut. "That's fabulous news! Congratulations. How did Ritter take it?"

I grinned. "His Deathliness . . ." But telling Jace about Ritter's reaction was a breach of privacy I knew my husband wouldn't appreciate. "He's happy."

"I'll bet. He's been waiting a long time."

I took a glazed donut with mystery filling from the box, biting into it and chewing with a sigh. "I forgot how much I love these things."

"I know." Jace shoved the rest of his donut into his mouth and reached for another. "Once, I forgot to eat for a week because I was so busy." His words were garbled, but I understood.

Three minutes later, I was regretting the two donuts I'd ingested. "Jace, pull over, quick!"

He glanced behind him as if expecting to see someone following us. "What, why?" But he did as I requested.

I pushed the door open and heaved bits of mashed donuts on the side of the road.

"Really?" Jace said, handing me a bottle of water when I finished. "Unbounded have to do that too?"

Guess he hadn't been around enough to see Stella being sick.

"First time," I said. "I've been feeling perfectly fine before today. Maybe I'd better stick to absorbing instead of eating." At least until I officially saw Dimitri as my doctor. He had medications that hadn't made their way into mortal distribution channels yet, and maybe he could help. I tossed the box of donuts unceremoniously onto the back seat, their aroma now making me nauseated.

Jace drove in silence for a moment and then said, "Maybe you should channel my ability for a while. A physical ability might help with the nausea."

I didn't see why not, so I slipped into the mental crack he opened. Instantly, I was more aware of the life forces we were passing, the cars around us, and what I might have to do to avoid them. My gift plus his. It made me feel almost invincible.

And still nauseated.

I reclined my seat a few inches. "Tell me more about the meeting you had with this manager."

"His name is Stanwood Bastian. We video-chatted on one of our secure channels. He clammed right up when I mentioned the shipment and asked to talk to Stefan. Bastian is combat, and a big guy, so I don't think I can beat it out of him." He flashed me a grin. "Together we could take him."

I rolled my eyes. "You could just fire him."

"Maybe. But since this is some kind of secret operation, you might have to channel Stella and use nanites to change your face to Stefan's to do that."

I shook my head. "No." Even if I could tell the nanites to change only the surface of my face and body, and though I'd posed as someone else during the takeover before I'd known about my pregnancy, I wouldn't risk miscarriage now because I was suddenly more male than female. "If he's combat, I'll be able to get through his shield with time. You just keep him talking."

Jace frowned. "He's over a thousand years old. He's probably tougher to crack than most."

"I can do it."

For centuries, the Emporium had strived to create combat Unbounded, overlooking the need for sensing and other rare abilities. It was largely their own fault that we were able to use these gifts against them during our final battles. This was the first weakness we were trying to eliminate.

"You finally put a stop to their breeding program?"

Jace laughed. "You mean ours. We've got to stop thinking of it as us versus them. No more Renegades and Emporium. We're all just Unbounded now."

"Whatever," I said.

"But the answer is yes. We are phasing out all mandatory breeding programs, and we stopped forcing early Changes since more kids die from the procedure than survive. I put Catrina over the couples that are currently expecting. We're registering abilities internally, but the program is now voluntary. Hopefully, the new reproductive freedoms will help the lost abilities to emerge naturally." He frowned as a car cut in front of him. "That still won't change the fact that even with manipulation, only fifty percent of our offspring will actually Change."

His words hit me like a slap in the face. Though our scientists had been able to identify the gene that caused the Change, they couldn't replicate the gene, splice it into any mortal, or force a person with the non-active gene to become Unbounded, unless it would have happened in time anyway. We had no idea why it didn't activate in most of our descendants or why in all but one family in Russia—Catrina's family—the gene waited to activate until around the beginning of the third decade.

We had, however, figured out a way to manipulate Unbounded sperm to increase our offspring's chance of developing the active gene, though fifty percent was as high as that went, compared to thirty—if both parents were Unbounded in the first place. Egg manipulation had proven impossible as the eggs died upon leaving the mother's body, or we might have increased the chance even more.

Therein was my guilt. Because I'd been lax with my nanites and channeling Stella's ability every day, my pregnancy had occurred without manipulated sperm. That meant my child still had a thirty percent chance of Change, but it should have been more.

"What?" Jace asked, glancing over at me.

I shook my head. "Now that we're not trying to kill each other, we need to get all our scientists, both Emporium and Renegade, working on how to activate the Unbounded gene when it doesn't kick in on its own. If we did, maybe Chris and the kids could have a chance." Maybe my baby could have a stronger chance.

"I'll push for that." Jace placed a hand over mine, his eyes still on the road. "But you know Chris is seventh generation from an Unbounded, and the kids are eight. It makes it harder."

Impossible was what he really meant. We had to accept that our long lives would eventually separate us from most of those we loved. They would grow old, living their lives as fast as a cloth in a furnace, before we aged another year. Mourning them was a fact, and even though I was only recently Changed, I understood that on an increasingly personal level.

"Just remember that we have each other," Jace added quietly.

I turned my hand so I could squeeze his. "I know. We're lucky." When I'd first learned he was like me, I had thought I'd never want anything again. But things change. Now I wanted more. A lot more.

Time for a new subject. "So, how are you and Catrina getting along?" I'd seen the looks between the two in the month after the takeover at Emporium headquarters in New York, or at least on his part.

Jace sighed and didn't take his gaze from the road. "Catrina is amazing. She's everything I never thought I'd get a chance at—smart, beautiful without being fake, and very knowledgeable. It's just . . ."

"Just what?"

"Our age difference is a little daunting."

I blinked at him. "I know it's a big difference, but she's hardly a child. She's lived among Unbounded all her life, and she did Change, so that gives you two plenty of time together." It was an easier choice than falling in love with someone who might never Change. "You shouldn't hold her youth against her if everything else is going well. A ten-year gap might be a lot now when she's nineteen, but in another ten years—or even in another five—you won't even notice."

He slowed the SUV at a light and stared in my direction. "What are you talking about? It's not her age that's the problem. It's mine. She might look nineteen or twenty, but that's only because she hasn't aged in the past *fifty* years." His stress on the fifty was pronounced with distaste. "Catrina's actual age is sixty-nine, which makes her forty years older than I am."

"No," I said. "When we met, she told me she'd Change six months ago." That would make it seven now.

He snorted. "That was when she was still on their side—

before she made the choice to help us. She was supposed to gain your trust."

I should have known. Her sweet, innocent face had made me suspicious at the time, but after everything happened, I'd assumed what she'd told me then was true. Even for a sensing Unbounded, her mental shield was one of the best I'd ever seen. No wonder she'd been able to sense my baby before I did. She'd had a lot of practice.

"And she's rather good at lying," Jace added. He huffed a breath when the people behind us started honking for him to go now that the light had changed. He punched on the gas. "And I don't mean she's ordinarily a liar. She's just very good at her job. Like I said, she's perfect. It's me that's not. She sees me as a kid, even though I'm supposedly running the Emporium now. Well, with help from Keene and the rest, of course. I don't blame her, though. She's old enough to be my mother and then some."

I tried to wrap my mind around that. "Well, what I said still stands. Your inexperience might make a difference to her now, but in fifty years, it's not going to matter."

"Well, it does right now." He sighed. "How about you and Ritter? I mean, he's like hundreds of years older than you are. How do you make it work?"

I had no idea what Ritter found so attractive in me, but I wouldn't confess that to my little brother. "This isn't about me. It's about you. All you can do is be yourself. Be confident, do your job. Don't hesitate to ask for input. You have a tendency to be a know-it-all."

"Yeah, well. That's easy for you to say. Every time I'm with her, I feel about sixteen."

I laughed. "That's not all bad. I remember you had quite a few older girls after you at sixteen."

"It's not funny!" But he laughed with me. "Anyway, sometimes it creeps me out thinking I'm that attracted to a woman who's as old as Mom. Doesn't that bother you, knowing Ritter is really old? Like some dirty old man."

"If there's one thing Ritter isn't, it's old. And neither is Catrina. You're still thinking like a mortal."

He sighed. "I know. And I keep telling myself there's plenty of time, but headquarters is dripping with experienced soldiers who take every chance to throw themselves in her path."

I opened my mouth to say more comforting words, but Jace pulled onto a ramp leading down to an underground parking lot of an expensive high rise. The building looked amazingly new, all steel and glass, and I couldn't sense anything beyond it. Not a single life form, thought-blocking or no.

"It has an electronic grid," I said as we approached the manned booth.

Jace nodded. "Most of the buildings did already, and we added to those that didn't. Stefan may have been a diabolical master, but one thing I can say about him is that he kept people in line. Without his brutal control, we're bound to have problems from some of our people in the future, so the grids are now more for our protection from disgruntled former employees rather than to control them."

"It also means we're cut off."

He tapped his ear. "Not really. These will get through. We worked with Stella and Patrick on passwords and protocols. They're routine now at all our facilities."

The guy at the guard booth—a mortal, given his faulty mental shield—registered surprise as he pointed a camera in Jace's direction. "Good to see you, sir. I'm sorry, but we'll need a fingerprint." He held out a device, and Jace put his finger on it.

"You too, Miss Carrington." The guard repeated the protocol with me, his eyes lingering on me as if I were some movie star.

I hated being called Carrington, and I hated even more that people within the Emporium still thought I was Stefan's daughter when it was only Jace who carried his genes. I continued to bear that shame only because my obvious support made Jace's position that much stronger in the organization, which was still too volatile to leave to chance.

The metal bar swung inward, and we drove into the garage. All the life forces registering in the surrounding buildings went blank, and those inside the building flared to life instead. We drove up to the second floor of the garage, where we parked in the executive section. I could tell by my brother's grin that he was enjoying the perks of being a Triad leader.

We rode up in an elevator, which wasn't manned by guards like in New York, but then this was only one of their businesses, not Triad Headquarters. Even on a Saturday, scattered life forces glowed from the floors we passed, more bright than dim, which told me they employed more mortals than in New York. But the previous Triad had always preferred to surround themselves with Unbounded.

"Do they have anyone gifted with sensing here?" If so, I'd have to be prepared to protect us mentally.

"Not that I am aware of," Jace said, "and I poured over the employee roster quite thoroughly before coming. I knew you'd ask." He cast me a grin. "They might have an unreported one. I would if I was under Stefan's rule."

I thought about that for a moment. I had met various Emporium agents who had hidden family members—or thought they had until the Triad needed something from them. Family members, especially mortal ones, had long been a weapon for the Triad.

"Let's stay connected so we can communicate," I said. "I'll keep an eye out for mental intruders."

"That's my thought," he agreed.

On the eighth floor, we exited into a hallway lined with glass walls on both sides. A guard sat behind a desk in front of the only door, his bulging muscles riveling Ritter's. No doubt he was combat. His inner thoughts were masked well, but his surface emotions swirled with excitement.

He glanced up from the screen of a thin tablet supported by a fancy plastic holder. "Good afternoon, Mr. and Ms. Carrington. I let Mr. Bastian know you are here. He will meet you in the conference room." He stood and added, "Come this way." He opened the glass door and ushered us to a long hallway lined by rooms with glass walls. So far, I couldn't sense any others on this floor, but that didn't mean we were alone.

The guard led us to a room at the end of the hallway, where a table large enough for twenty was set with a banquet spread the likes of which I hadn't seen since . . . well, ever.

"Please help yourselves," the guard said. "Mr. Bastian will be here shortly. And may I add that it's a real pleasure to meet you both." He inclined his head as the door began to shut.

Jace stared at the table. "I don't remember this being a lunch invitation, but now I'm sorry I ate all those donuts."

"Guess this is coming out of the business account, though I can hardly blame him. We are making him work on a Saturday." I snagged a grape from a cluster, popping it into my mouth.

"Are you sure you want to do that?" Jace mimed gagging, making me laugh.

"I promise to go slow."

I sobered as a heavyset man in an expensive business suit appeared on the other side of the glass. Despite his bright, friendly smile, he mentally registered as dark. Jace was already facing the door, every line of his body ready for battle.

"Ah, it's the heir apparent and the spare daughter," the man said as he opened the door. The wide smile made it clear that his words were meant in fun, but I wondered if something lurked beneath. I felt not even a slight hint of his surface emotions.

"I'm Stanwood Bastian," he continued. "I, of course, know who you both are." Again with the wide smile. A barrel-chested man with long, glossy brown hair cut too long for his expensive business suit, he appeared to be in his fifties, which made him around a thousand, give or take two hundred.

He came forward in a wave of cologne, offering his hand to me. "We're honored to have you visit. Usually Stefan makes me go to New York for our business. Torturous flight, even in first class." Instead of shaking it, he kissed the top of my hand.

"Oh," I said, not hiding my surprise.

He laughed. "You'll have to excuse me. I miss the old days when we got to kiss all the beautiful ladies, or at least their hands. Alas, it's rare to find anyone who appreciates bygone eras, even among our kind."

"I know a few," I said, thinking of Dimitri and even Cort, who had once taken me to a formal French restaurant where the delicious food had made me swoon.

"Of course, of course." Bastian shook Jace's hand. "Please, sit down. Let's eat while we talk."

"I'm afraid we've already eaten," Jace said.

Bastian waved the words aside. "I'm sure you'll find room." He took an oversized plate and began filling it with grilled meat, followed by a huge helping of roasted potatoes. By the time he sat at the head of the table, his full plate was in danger of toppling. He'd have to eat that much five or six times a day to stay ahead of his rapid metabolism and maintain his stockiness, but he was apparently willing to make the sacrifice. Most of us gave up and let our bodies absorb exactly what we needed.

Jace put a token serving on his plate while I simply sat kitty-corner from Bastian and began exploring his mental shield. Definitely strong. I'd need my machete talisman. I had the real machete back at the Fortress, and holding it made me feel stronger, but the mental rendition would do almost as well. Slowly, I tested the surface.

"We're here to talk about the shipment," Jace said, taking the chair opposite me.

"I know why you're here. And I'll tell you the same thing I told you when we last talked. I can't release any information except to Stefan."

I slammed the machete into a section that seemed thinner than the rest. The machete didn't even make a dent. If he wasn't sensing, he shouldn't be able to keep me out or even realize I was breaking in, but if Jace had made a mistake about him being combat, we'd know it soon.

"Well, you need to know that my father put me over this operation entirely," Jace said. "He thought hearing the details from the man in charge would be the best."

Bastian chewed thoughtfully as he listened. When he swallowed, he shook his head. "That's not the way we set things up. Are you telling me you are now the head of the Triad and not only the heir? Has something happened to Stefan?"

His resistance registered on my senses, just a flickering. Bastian was digging in. *Keep him talking,* I told Jace, releasing the thought into his mind. He'd guess the abrupt prompt came from me.

"With the new merger between us and the Renegades," Jace said, "there have been some structural changes. Why don't you walk us through it? What are the shipments for?"

Bastian's emotions had vanished again behind his shield. I couldn't even sense clear surface thoughts. I needed more distraction.

"Would that bother you, working with us instead of Stefan?" I couldn't call Stefan "father." Never. I made my voice hard. "We can always replace you."

Bastian took another bite, his jowls bouncing with the chewing, but I sensed nervousness now. "That wouldn't be wise. It's a delicate situation."

"What are you saying?" Jace pressed.

"Just that it's a very delicate situation. It needs experience and discretion."

I envisioned slamming the machete once again into Bastian's shield, and this time there was a crack of light. Instantly, I was on the stage of his mind, his thought stream falling over me. I grabbed onto the most recent thoughts and realized that he saw us both as babies, wet behind the ears. Incapable. Besides, his instructions from Stefan had been clear. But what were they? If this man knew we had Stefan in an induced coma awaiting trial, would he sound the alarm or spill his guts? I was betting on the former.

In the next minute, I saw I was right. His subtle pressing of an intercom inside one of his rings had been a signal to his combat-gifted employees waiting somewhere down the hall, soldiers strong enough to hide their life forces from me, though now that I knew they were there, I could sense them dimly. Ten at least, coming fast in our direction, though I couldn't yet see them through the glass. Bastian didn't plan to give us anything, and there was no way we would win against so many.

Fury burst through me. *He's got men coming,* I told Jace. *Whatever is going on here, it's more important than we think.*

Get behind me if they attack, Jace thought. *You need to protect the baby.*

He'd have no way of knowing I'd heard unless I put another thought into his mind telling him I was still in his mind. *They won't dare hurt us.*

I didn't know that for sure. If Bastian really believed Stefan was compromised, maybe he had enough power in the Emporium to stage a coup. Or to entice enough Unbounded away to start another faction.

Men appeared outside the glass in the hallway. By their black attire and the swords on their backs, they were obviously experienced Emporium hit teams.

I need to get control of Bastian's mind—and fast.

Chapter 5

I FORMED A THOUGHT, RELEASING IT CAREFULLY INTO BASTIAN'S thought stream so he would believe it was his own. *Hold them back for now!* Usually it worked, especially if the target hadn't often been controlled by a sensing Unbounded.

At the same time, I said aloud, "You need proof, you mean? That we were sent by Stefan? Is that right?" I already knew that was what he wanted, but I had to discover what this "proof" required of us.

He raised a hand at the men in the hallway, and the lead soldier paused with his hand on the door. At least that had gone my way.

I smiled at him, ignoring the men completely. "You've been in this position for how long?" I didn't know if he'd tell us, but the thought appeared in his mind. "Fifty years, I think Stefan said," I added.

"That's right." The day appeared in Bastian's mind, the details racing toward me, filling my mind with scenes. There, I had it—everything I needed.

You have to write down a code, I told Jace. *Get something to write on, and I'll tell it to you. You do it. He needs to trust you since you'll be running things.* Bastian wasn't even supposed to tell us there was a code, which explained his reluctance and reaction.

"Oh, but I'm forgetting the code." Jace reached into one of his hidden pockets and withdrew a pen. "Let me get that for you." He spread out his napkin.

I rattled off a thirty-digit number that would have made Jace look like some kind memory genius in the mortal world, but Bastian's mind prompted me over and over. He'd memorized it very carefully.

As the last number appeared on the napkin, Bastian relaxed and waved his men away. "Good," he said. "I was beginning to worry this wasn't what it seemed. That maybe you didn't have Stefan's permission."

"Are you kidding?" Jace's laugh sounded genuine. "You've known him longer than I have. There is no way anyone could go around him. Besides, they'd have to go around us now, too. We are fully united." Jace's comment was casual and a complete lie. Even so, I could sense that he was both revolted and fascinated with everything Stefan had accomplished in his life.

A knot formed in my gut. My brother wouldn't be safe until Stefan was dead. I tried to shove the thought away but felt it deep in my core.

"Where do you want me to begin?" Lifting his fork, Bastian shoved it into a mound of meat, cutting it delicately with his knife.

"At the beginning would be nice," I said. "We know about the shipments, but Stefan has been too busy to deal with this himself. We have all been busy since the merger."

"Right. Well, just over fifty years ago, we were approached

by . . ." Bastian froze with his fork halfway to his mouth. "I want to say organization, but they are really a people."

Jace and I exchanged a look. "You mean another faction," I prompted. "Someone not Renegade, Emporium, or Hunter. Or mortal."

"That's exactly what I'm saying. Although they have mortals among them as well."

"But they are from Earth?" Jace said, a bit too eagerly. There were rumors that Unbounded hadn't originated on Earth at all, a theory of which I was skeptical, so Jace's comment wasn't all that out of place.

Bastian's smile was tight. "Oh, they're from Earth." Seemingly he remembered his fork and took a bite, chewing only twice before swallowing. "And they are our people— Unbounded, I mean. They are very much like us."

"We would have heard about them." Jace gave him a skeptical look, shaking his head. "Where have they been all these years?"

Bastian didn't crack a smile when he said, "In the ocean. Or rather, below it. In Antarctica, currently, though they indicated that in the beginning they were mobile."

Jace and I were too stunned to respond, but mentally I was soaking in Bastian's thoughts. He'd been surprised too when first learning of these people, but in the end, he came to the same conclusion I did: only in the ocean, still largely unexplored, could they have escaped notice for so long.

"What about sonar?" I asked. "The water might have hidden them a hundred years ago. Maybe even fifty years ago. But not now."

"A hundred? Try thirty-six hundred years." Bastian waved his fork. "Or thereabouts. They're advanced like we are. Maybe even more so. They use a grid to prevent spying eyes from sensing Unbounded."

"And from shifters," I said.

Bastian's smile was tight. "That's right. I heard we have one of those now. That's certainly an ability that would come in handy during a battle. Anyway, from what we know, these people, who numbered only a few thousand at the time, lived somewhere in a city called Sinalta near Greece around sixteen hundred BC. Give or take a century. They were a little vague on dates. They were apparently prosperous and technologically advanced, but then something happened, and their entire city sank under the ocean. They didn't give details, except to imply that it was a war of some kind. We don't know if mortals were the cause or if they themselves were, but that's when they left. Seeing as Unbounded only live two thousand years, we have no eyewitnesses to prove it either way, but these Sinaltans claim all Unbounded came from Sinalta at one point, and that we are descended from the same ancestors. They, however, call themselves Avowed instead of Unboundaried."

"If they were advanced enough thirty-six hundred years ago to create a city that could survive under the sea," Jace said, "they would be formidable enemies."

Bastian stabbed his fork at Jace. "Exactly. That's what we thought, so we were determined to deal with them until we knew more. We still haven't had enough time to uncover much about them."

I bit my tongue so I wouldn't blurt out the obvious that fifty years was more than enough time to learn something about a potential enemy, even in immortal terms. It wasn't like Stefan to let an enemy grow stronger, which meant there had been some kind of agreement benefitting him.

"So what did they want?" I rose and went to pour myself a glass of water, hoping it would ease the nausea that still twinged in my gut.

"Food, electronics mostly. But also medical supplies." Bastian was back to eating again, chewing rather noisily. I wanted to shove the fork down his throat.

"In exchange for what?" Jace growled, hitting on the same question I wanted answered.

"Raw materials. Gold, rhodium, silver, platinum. They've been mining—in Antarctica, no less. From down below in the ocean, cutting into the continent or other underwater formations—anywhere they can near their cities."

"Cities?" Jace asked, emphasizing the plural.

"That's right. There are at least two that I'm aware of, but they have kept details to a minimum. They also agreed to back us up when it came time to combat the US armed forces, if that became necessary."

Silence fell over us. We'd been aware of the former Triad's goal to enslave the mortal population by taking over the government, but maybe the new Triad hadn't been clear about the recent changes. "You are aware that our goals have shifted in that respect," I said, moving back to my seat.

"I am. But what I need to know is how that affects our agreement with the Avowed." Bastian scooped up potatoes with his fork. "Last month, the Avowed pressed for more information about when they'll be able to surface. And this time they also requested information. Actually, demanded would be a more accurate term. But because of this business with the Renegades, we are nowhere close to having things ready."

In his mind, I saw a glimpse of what would come next, and I gasped. "What more have you promised them?"

Bastian bristled at the thinly-veiled anger in my words. Jace shifted slightly, and I caught the gleam of a blade between his fingers where they lay next to his plate.

"Not me," Bastian said, chewing and swallowing. "The Triad. From the beginning, the Avowed asked for either South America or the southern half of Africa for their people. Stefan thinks they would probably settle for Australia, though." When neither Jace nor I responded, he shrugged. "We'd have to move out the existing Unbounded, unless they wanted to stay."

"And what about the current residents?" I asked.

Bastian shrugged. "The mortals could be placed elsewhere, or they can stay and serve the Avowed. Either way, you can't blame the Avowed for wanting surface land. Your father, along with the rest of the Triad, was hoping to ally with them because they see our place in the world as we do. And quite frankly, I don't believe the Avowed are going to be pleased with the change in our direction." Displeasure dripped from his words, and his thoughts told me exactly how he also detested the new direction of the Triad. "I believe if we can't give the Avowed what they want, they might come and take it anyway." Bastian's words hung in the room like a promise of destruction.

"Exactly how many are there?" Jace demanded.

"My guess is millions. But I have no real idea. When I took over the shipments from the Triad, who oversaw them in the very beginning, I tried repeatedly to plant devices to determine their numbers, but all those attempts failed."

I took a sip of my water. "So what makes their request different this time? And how did they communicate with you?"

"Same way as always. Their latest shipment to us arrived on Monday, and last night, an employee delivered a missive from the warehouse along with their order for next month." Bastian nodded at Jace. "This was after our virtual chat yesterday morning. In the message, they demanded an exact date and time for their removal and transfer. But as I said, we don't even have ships in the area."

"You mean they wouldn't bring their cities up?" I asked.

"Apparently not." Bastian shrugged. "Or at least not both of them. Sometime back, they sent us a list of how many aircraft carriers and planes they'd need and how many months to accomplish the move, which is why I believe they have several million residents. They didn't ask for submarines, so maybe they do plan to bring one city up or use their own crafts to get to the surface. Maybe they plan to keep things as they are and leave people there to run the mining operations. I'm not sure. Our deal with them was for the trading we've been doing, plus the ships, planes, and a destination. And autonomy for their new country. They would like to send their first groups beginning next month—or the month after at the very latest. With the hope of finishing before the end of the year. The shipments are to continue both ways until then."

"Why didn't you report this?" Jace's voice was calmer than his roiling emotions.

"I did. I sent the message on our private server last night. I was most concerned when Stefan didn't respond, which is why I had my men here today."

It wasn't an apology, though I appreciated the explanation.

"I realize Stefan is busy, and agreement with those deceitful Renegades can't be easy." Bastian set down his fork, his plate nearly clean, though I could have sworn it was still full a few minutes ago. "But I assume you are Stefan's response since he sent you with the code, and frankly, I'm happy to leave it in your lap. I take it you want to see their recent message and the details of their previous requests?"

"Yes," Jace said. "I also want to know exactly what was

included in each shipment, where it was picked up, and when our latest drop is scheduled—and where."

"I'll get the shipment details for you," Bastian said. "The shipping company, however, is the one with the final destination for this and past shipments. As per Avowed request."

"That's convenient," I muttered. *What idiot agreed to that?* I said to Jace silently.

Jace gave me a warning look, and he was right. We still needed to tread carefully while those men waited down the hall, though I'd argue that they should be taking orders from Jace, not Bastian.

"It's clear they don't trust us," I amended, feeling like an idiot stating the obvious.

"And the feeling is mutual," Bastian said. "But they were promised land when this accord began, back when the Triad was not strong enough to control the governments, and we have profited financially from the Avowed shipment, which bought us more power. They will be better allies than enemies." Bastian pushed back from the table and stood. "Should I prepare the next month's shipment as usual, or will there be another course of action?" His gaze held first mine and then Jace's.

Jace glanced at me, but I had no answer. "Continue with the shipment," Jace said. "I'll take this news back to the Triad."

Bastian nodded, turning toward the door. "You should know," he said, "that part of the shipment is unconventional."

Jace snorted, sounding almost like his playful self instead of a Triad leader. "This whole arrangement is unconventional."

"It is." Bastian smiled. "But that's for you to sort out now. All the details will be included in the documentation I'll give you. I'll just be a moment. Please help yourself to more refreshments, if you'd like." With a dip of his head, he reached for the door.

I was still wondering what could be more unconventional than sending secret million-plus-dollar shipments to an unknown, questionable ally in the middle of the ocean. Surely Stefan had to know more than this man who, despite his advanced years and experience, was still little more than a Triad lackey.

I mentally stayed with Bastian as he went to his office to be sure he was giving us everything and not planning to send his hit team in after all. He seemed to have accepted us, though.

"Everything okay?" Jace asked.

I knew he was asking about Bastian, and I nodded, drinking the rest of my water. I was feeling better.

"We have to find out more about these Avowed," Jace said.

"We'll discuss it with Stefan," I lied through gritted teeth. Neither of us dared say much more than that, not knowing if the room was being recorded. We would be recording in Bastian's place, though maybe Stefan's warning not to even mention the code had prevented Bastian from activating listening devices.

Jace sighed, and before I could see what was bothering him, he began trying to put his shield back in place, and I let him lock me out, wanting to allow him privacy. But again, worry rose inside me. If we actually did end up needing to talk to Stefan, I would make sure to protect my little brother from that monster.

Minutes ticked by as I poured myself more water, and Jace found room for sliced fruit. When my earbud crackled to life, I jerked with a start.

"Erin? Jace?" The voice was Ritter's. He was far enough away that I couldn't sense him, but the tone of his voice was enough to kick on all my warnings. To talk to us directly, he'd have switched over to the channel we were using instead of the one assigned to his own team.

Clicking my audio on, I said, "What's up?"

"Need a little help here." He waited for a heartbeat before adding, "If you have the time."

Jace and I exchanged a glance, my worry reflected in his eyes. "We're nearly finished here," Jace said. "What do you need?"

"For Erin to remove a memory." He gave a mirthless laugh. "Unless you want me to remove all his memories permanently."

A shiver crawled across my shoulders. Renegades didn't kill casually, not even their enemies, and for years that very mercy had caused them to lose repeatedly to the Emporium. But Ritter had been one of those who had killed. And killed. And killed again. He'd gone into the worst battles and saved the day numerous times, never caring what the struggles had done to him.

"What about Ava?" I asked. "Can't she do it?"

"She's occupied at the moment."

Jace tapped his earbud. "We'll be there in twenty."

"We may not have twenty. I can send Mari."

"That works," I said. "We'll be out of this building and out of its grid in a few minutes. We'll let you know."

Three impatient minutes of waiting later, Bastian gave us a thumb drive, and we headed down in the elevator. At the SUV, I climbed into the back seat, and Jace squealed out of the parking lot, pulling over immediately to the side of the road.

"Okay, Ritter," I said. "Send Mari. I've got coordinates if she can't find me."

"She's already found—"

The rest of his sentence was gone as Mari appeared on the sidewalk outside the car, the hair of her blond wig swinging free, her dark eyes gleaming with anticipation. She climbed into the back seat next to me. "Ready?"

I hesitated only an instant—because of the baby. But Stella had shifted with Mari during her pregnancy, and all was well. I nodded.

A scene opened up before us, obscuring Jace, and then folded around us. We were in an office of some kind, quickly standing from our sitting positions so we wouldn't fall to the floor. Ritter was waiting there, no longer wearing his glasses, standing by a man slumped over a desk.

"He came in when I was getting the data," Mari said from behind us. "I had to pull my knife on him."

"Do we need a hospital?" Knowing Mari's affinity for knives, my eyes wandered quickly over the man's body. No blood that I could see except a bit on his face that likely came from his nose.

Mari put her hands on her hips, her pale face stern. "Of course not. I punched him." She smirked at Ritter. "All by myself."

I could feel something churning in Ritter's surface emotions at the comment, but I was already focusing on the man. The lake of his unconscious mind was almost an invitation, and it was easy enough to remove the memory of seeing Mari in the room.

"Did you get any information from him first?" I asked.

Mari shook her head. "Turns out that he's a surly, closed-mouth kind of a guy. Big surprise."

"What about Ava?" She might not be able to break through mental shields, but she should have been able to get something from a mortal.

"She couldn't get much either. He just kept thinking about having us thrown out. She was supposed to keep trying while I shifted up here, but he got suspicious and came looking. Now she's downstairs keeping watch." Mari pointed to a window that overlooked a warehouse, where metal girders lined the walls, and ceilings and huge shipping containers crammed together with barely a walkway between them. Beyond these, the garage doors were open, and more containers filled the yard.

"Or rather, she's distracting anyone who might come up here," Ritter said.

"Good. Guess you two better get back to wherever you were supposed to be before he walked in," I said. "But shift me out first." I tapped my earbud. "Stella, you'll need to turn off the safe house grid for us."

"Uh, not yet." Ritter face contorted into a grimace. "There's more."

"More?"

Mari heaved a sigh, and I turned to see one arm crossed over her abdomen, the other elbow resting on top as she nibbled at the inside flesh on her left middle finger. "Okay, right," she said, pulling her hand away when I looked at it pointedly. It was a habit left over from her nervous mortal years. "This guy," she tapped the unconscious man on the back of the head, "had time to call out, and a few of his goons showed up. Ritter had to take care of them."

That explained the feelings I sensed from him earlier. "Take me to them."

Mari went over to a bathroom where I found not one but five men piled up inside. "We were worried more would come in," she said. "So we hid them."

I arched my brows. "And they're suddenly all going to wake up and think everything is normal?" I frowned at Ritter. This was a big-time screw-up. No wonder Ava was downstairs trying to make sure we didn't have to add more employees to this pile.

"I don't care what they suspect," Mari said, holding up a flash drive. "We got what we need."

"We don't want them to call the police," Ritter said. "They have cameras in the warehouse down there, and we haven't been able to locate the feed or where it's saved."

"It's not just the police I'm worried about," I said. "Jace and I have disturbing news about a new player in this game. Bottom line, we can't let this guy report anything to them."

Ritter's gaze asked for more, but I shook my head. "Later."

"There's an old furnace out in the hall," Ritter said. "If you can take care of these guys, I'll arrange a gas leak. Then we'll join Ava, and since I was one of those who ran up here, I'll stagger back downstairs and report the leak so they really don't die."

I nearly laughed out loud, but a commotion in the warehouse below caught our attention. Ritter's hand ran over my arm. "I suggest you hurry."

By the time Ritter started the gas leak and returned to us, I'd extracted the men's painful memories of meeting his fist. "All finished," I said. "Just need to drag them to the hall."

"I'll do it. Go!" Ritter had picked up a man and was hurrying toward the door when Mari folded the space of our safe house family room around me. For a moment, her mind shield was open, and I could see the numbers she used falling into perfect sequence. The next instant, she was shifting out again to wherever she'd been before shifting into that office, and I stood alone in front of the coffee table.

"You're back," Dimitri said, looking up from his laptop.

"Did you find anything?" Stella rested one hand on her swelling stomach. I knew the urge. I already had it, and I was barely at the beginning of my pregnancy.

"Yeah, and you're not going to like it." I held out two thumb drives on my hand, one from Bastian and one that Mari had pressed into my hand during the shift.

"Make that double for us," Dimitri said, setting the laptop on the coffee table and coming toward me. "We've found Brenna, and it's not what we thought. She's not a runaway teen Believer at all. She's Unbounded."

Chapter 6

WHILE I GAPED, STELLA TOOK THE THUMB DRIVES, HER EYES EAGER. "One of those drives is from Mari," I recovered enough to say. "They didn't seem to have gotten much from the shipping company employees, so I'm hoping the drop site is there. As for the Emporium manager we saw . . ." I paused and sighed. "I don't even know where to begin."

Dimitri put a hand on my shoulder and led me to the couch. "Why don't you have a seat?"

I sank down heavily. "Okay. But how can a teenager be Unbounded? Catrina's family in Russia are the only ones who have been known to spontaneously Change early—and not all of them, either. The others we know about were all forced, which came at a great cost." The cost being years of life—forced Unbounded only lived about four hundred years. I tried not to think about Jace's half-brother, a forced Unbounded who had died during the takeover, but I couldn't help myself. If Jonny had lived, I believed we would have become friends.

"Ah, but Brenna Dabney isn't a runaway teenager," Dimitri said.

"What?"

"We did track her to Georgia, and we found footage of her, but not from any missing person's database. Stella, can you show her?"

Stella had apparently been keeping abreast of our conversation even as she examined both thumb drives—her neural headset blinking madly—because immediately, a pale, young girl with thick, dark lines around her eyes stared out at us from the big wall screen. Short and slender in an oversized trench coat, at first glance she looked very young, especially with all the makeup and black hair showing several inches of blond roots. But a closer examination revealed knowing blue eyes under the black makeup, and the set of her chin was assured. Moreover, she lacked the numerous piercings that normally decorated every available surface of similar youth. With our rate of healing, piercings were annoyingly difficult to keep up with, having to be turned often and never removed so our skin didn't grow over or even eat away at the metal. Ears could be managed, but repeated piercing of other body parts wasn't something any Unbounded I knew had the time or desire to continue.

"She doesn't look thirty," I said, studying the pale face. Not a wrinkle, though that wasn't unusual. "But I agree that she's probably not fifteen. Who is she, and why do you think she's Unbounded?"

"We found her on footage the police released involving the separate disappearances of two pre-teens." Dimitri paused as two different pictures of Brenna with a young girl appeared on the screen. "These disappearances were ten years apart, however, and either Brenna has an identical older sister, or it's the same girl going by a different last name. Witnesses in both cases say they saw her with the missing girls and even wondered if someone took Brenna at the same time."

"Just like now."

"Right." Dimitri shook his head. "And that's not all. Over the past twenty years, she also came up on police radar in New York, Texas, and Utah, and in each place, a child went missing around the same time. Though she wasn't seen with the children and was never connected with any of the cases, the reports are all the same: an unfortunate, at-risk runaway who escapes police or family services custody in one way or another. There's only one mention of Brenna in each state. Well, except in Georgia, where we have the two cases. Since she's retained a faint accent, she might have a place there."

"She's been hiding in plain sight," I said. Pretending to be a child herself was a perfect cover to get close to kids. But for what purpose? "Is there a connection between the missing children?"

Stella looked up from her laptop and said, "We don't know yet. Right now, I'm just finishing up on the children, going back twenty years. As I compare more occurrences, there will be a greater chance of finding the right connection—if there is one. It might be random."

Disgust, horror, and anger rose from Stella's surface emotions, and I knew she believed Brenna was trafficking these children. I had to agree. Whoever she was, I was going to make sure Kimber's was the last family she ever hurt.

I sensed Ritter pulling up outside, our connection flaring to life. Ava and Mari were probably with him, but all I could sense was a hint of blocking, which was probably Mari. Maybe it was knowing they were safe, but I settled deeper into the couch, suddenly relaxed. "You might want to turn the safe house grid back on," I said. If I could sense Ritter, it wasn't on yet.

Stella nodded. "Done."

"Feeling better?" Dimitri asked.

"Yeah, I—" The way he was staring at me clicked. "Hey, wait a minute. Were you fixing me just now?"

No wonder I was feeling better. Dimitri had touched my shoulder and then sat close to me on the couch, apparently soothing away my tiredness and nausea. I no longer even felt twinges from my ax wound.

He shrugged, giving me a little smile. "I can't help myself anymore than you can help sensing."

Stella grinned and arched her back slightly. "I don't know how I'd get through pregnancy without help. Chris thinks it's his back rubs that are saving me, but between you and me, it's really Dimitri. If he can ease the pain in your wound, I say enjoy it while you can."

Which reminded me that I still hadn't told her about my baby. But the others were coming in now, even Jace, who must have arrived around the same time.

For the next few minutes, I listened to Jace, who stood in front of the coffee table, telling everyone about Bastian's information regarding the Avowed. Differing levels of shock and disbelief marked their faces. Only Ava and Dimitri remained calm, though their surface emotions were dark and unhappy.

A vein bulged in Ritter's throat. "We can't exactly call South America or half of Africa and ask them to kindly move over for these Avowed or Sinaltans or whatever they're called." From his place next to me on the couch, I could feel the heat of anger wafting off him.

"Exactly." Jace rolled his eyes. "And can you imagine what

Australia would say? They began as a penal colony. They've fought hard to get where they are. They're not going to willingly give up their country to some mermaids."

"They are not mermaids," Stella corrected. "What they might be is Atlanteans." That sent another shock running through all of us. "Atlantis is supposed to be fiction," she added, "but fiction often has a way of springing from real life, or the legends created from real events."

We took a moment to digest this. "Wait," I said into the silence. "If these Avowed have been wanting to surface from the beginning, does it make sense that they'd hold off for fifty years since first contact? I mean, if they are supposed to be advanced, why are they waiting, and why do they need help from the Emporium?"

"If most are Unbounded," Ritter said, "fifty or a hundred years isn't that much of a wait if it avoids casualties."

"Yeah, but how many of them are mortal? Mortals must far outweigh the Unbounded if they are anything like us." I would do anything for my human relatives—anything except wait fifty years to make them happy. That would be too late.

Ritter's gaze met mine, and I knew he got my gist. "Possibly they might not be as advanced as we imagine."

Jace snorted from the front of the room where he was pacing. Tension and energy rolled off him. "They built an entire city and took it underwater—or two of them, though one might have been built underwater—and they're mining in Antarctica. That's advanced as you can get, short of space flight."

"I agree," Ritter said. "Baring some great cataclysmic event among them, it does sound likely that they've continued to progress. But events do happen, and the fact that they have waited so long is suspect."

"Or maybe they know how to pass on the gene to *all* their

children," Stella said, glancing down at her distended belly. "That would make waiting more logical."

"Which means we must make finding out about them our priority." Ritter leaned forward on the couch, looking past me at Dimitri. Sorrow radiated from his surface emotions—and a blackness that made me know he was thinking about the deaths of his own family. "You know this has to take precedence over the girl's disappearance, right? We have to know what's going on. We might be on the brink of a massive world war."

A pit formed in my stomach as Jace and Stella nodded in agreement. Mari's eyes widened, her mouth ajar with a protest she didn't voice but that screamed out at me from her thoughts. Of all of us, she was the newest Changed and her shield the weakest.

"No." Ava held up a hand from the end of the couch closest to the door, her gaze locking on Dimitri, who awaited her judgment. A world of emotion swirled between them, but if she was talking in his mind, I was blocked out. After several long seconds, she said, "We will work on both cases together. We'll bring Patrick in on this, and also the technopaths in the Emporium if we need to. Whatever else they're doing can wait. The Avowed are a serious threat, yes, but we will not abandon any of our posterity. We never have, and we're not about to start."

I was glad to see nods of agreement. Kimber might not be one of us—yet or ever—but she was still one of the mortals we had sworn to protect. She was also family to Dimitri.

Stella nodded. "Of course. You're right. We can work through the night on both cases."

"Good," Ava said. "We'll need to trace all the shipments, incoming and outgoing, and comb Emporium files for mention of these Avowed or their city, Sinalta. Assign as much out as you need to, but I want you in charge of finding Kimber. Time is of the essence in her case."

That was Dimitri's cue to tell everyone what he and Stella had already uncovered about Brenna Dabney and her likely targeting of Kimber. Ava listened, her arms crossed and her face grave. When he finished, she sighed. "I don't like any of this. We need to know who this Brenna is."

Mari pushed off the wall where she'd been resting. "Give me something to do. I'm ready to help."

"Me too," Jace said.

"First, we do a little training," Ritter said to Jace as he rose from the couch. "You're about ready to burst."

I was glad he'd also noticed Jace's anxiety. He'd probably been too cooped up at Emporium Headquarters to put in much training, and without the hit teams to fight, well, he would have extra energy that needed release. We all did to some extent, but those with the combat ability were especially susceptible.

"Oh, yeah? You think you can take on all this?" Jace pointed to his body and did a little jig.

"With one hand tied behind my back," Ritter said dryly.

Jace snapped his fingers. "You heard him, everyone! Handicap accepted. I'll do the tying."

We all laughed, but they hadn't yet made it to the door when Stella said. "Wait a minute." Shipping logs began appearing on the big screen, flipping so fast I couldn't see details. "This can't be right," she muttered.

"What are you seeing?" Jace asked. "TVs, tablets, phones, cookies, sugar, ultrasound equipment—that sounds about right." With his combat reflexes, he was apparently better at catching words from the manifests than I was.

"Just a minute, almost there. There are eighteen containers, not just the seventeen you tracked. And here's the manifest for the last one." Stella's flipping stopped abruptly, and I leaned forward to read what was on the page. Columns filled the screen with the headings QTY, SEX, AGE, ETH, and GEN. Below, single numbers filled the first column, the second was either M or F, the third was a double number, the fourth a single letter, and the last had only single numbers again. I struggled to understand what I was seeing.

"It looks like quantity, sex, age," Mari said. "But what are ETH and GEN?"

Obviously not computers. "Some kind of wildlife?" I knew as soon as the words left my mouth that it probably wasn't right, but what else could it be?

"I don't know what GEN means," Stella said slowly, "but I'm pretty sure ETH means ethnicity, given that the letters below it are W, A, H, B, and I—white presumably means White, Asian, Hispanic, Black, and Indian. That would mean this cargo is human. And as you can see"—a circle appeared around the total at the bottom of the log—"there are twenty males and twenty-nine females in this shipment. All between the ages of twelve and twenty-two."

We stared at each other, unbelieving. Bastian had said some of the cargo was unconventional, but could it really be human? That seemed farfetched, but as Jace had said, everything about this was suspicious. Yet compared with how many kids went missing in the United States every year, forty-nine was a drop in the proverbial bucket.

"And just like that, our two cases suddenly might not be that unrelated," Dimitri said quietly. "When did this last shipment leave the harbor? Before or after Kimber went missing?"

"Looks like it left Wednesday evening, the same day she disappeared," Stella said. "The scheduled time was six, but

notes say that a couple of hours either way is standard procedure with this company. So it's close to the time she went
missing, which makes a connection possible even if it's not
probable, given the timeframe."

"Kimber could still be here in LA." Mari said. "Or in Georgia
or anywhere else with Brenna. I say we talk to the people on
the list we got from the police, and anyone connected with
the Mission on Ninth, especially the Believers. Erin and I can
do it." She grinned. "We can go as ourselves to the Believers.
It might be nice to be worshipped for a change instead of
dodging bullets or knives."

Near the door, Ritter shook his head. "Not Erin."

"Why not Erin?" Mari said. "You can spare her, can't you?"

Jace smiled mockingly at Ritter. "Yeah, why not Erin?"

"I'm waiting to hear too," I said.

"Because of the . . . you know why." His face flushed with
indignance.

I pulled my feet onto the coffee table next to Dimitri's
laptop and folded my arm across my abdomen. "I guess this
is when we make the official announcement, though some of
you have already guessed. Looks like Ritter and I are going to
have a baby." *And His Deathliness is a little worried,* I added,
though only to myself.

"Oh, that's wonderful!" Mari jumped up from the couch
to come hug me, followed by Stella, her neural headset still
blinking. Dimitri looked smug while Ava grinned. Babies for
Unbounded weren't unusual, as the gene was determined to
survive, but there hadn't been babies in our cell for generations. There had been too much pain involved in walking away
for their protection. With the peace between Renegades and
Emporium, and with Unbounded now known to the world,
all that might change. I hoped so. Family to Unbounded,

especially to those born centuries ago, was everything, and children were infinitely precious.

"It's not coming for ages yet," I said, "and I certainly can help track Kimber."

Mari faced Ritter. "She can channel me and shift out at a moment's notice. With both our gifts, the danger is probably lower than getting in a car accident."

Ritter frowned, likely trying to come up with some logical reason to protest. That was another issue with older Unbounded. Those with a few centuries under their belts sometimes forgot that women didn't follow traditional roles from bygone eras.

"That sounds reasonable." Amusement showed in Dimitri's voice. His swift exchanged glance with Ava suggested they might have already discussed my situation. Or perhaps the glance was a hint of some other private conversation. Which made me wonder if they were any closer to realizing how much they meant to each other.

Ritter's eyes locked onto mine, resignation in his eyes. "Jace and I can help with the names from the list."

"And frighten them to death?" Mari asked, her hands on her hips. "No freaking way. You guys go work off steam. We'll call you if we need backup."

"She's right," Ava said to Ritter. "This is more up their alley. And the police and the Hunters could still be on the watch for you after those videos this morning. Anyway, as soon as Stella pinpoints the shipment drop location, we'll need you to devise a plan of attack. We won't have a large window of opportunity, and waiting another month for a new shipment isn't an option, especially if Kimber is on board that ship."

"I know the direction and general location of the boat right now." Stella was still standing after congratulating me, but that hadn't stopped her from using her headset to keep sifting through information. "According to the itinerary we took from the cargo company, they should be heading south along the Mexican coast. It looks like their first container drop is scheduled for two to four days from now, and matching their manifests with the Emporium records, that is the drop we're interested in. But the exact location and time will be radioed several hours in advance, which means only ship personnel will know the details. We only have a general northwest direction, which I assume the boat will head toward soon."

"We'll have to track the ship by satellite," Ritter said.

Ava nodded, uncrossing her legs and rising from the couch. "That means calling in favors. I'll start the dialogue."

Ritter's gaze caught mine again, and heat rushed between us. "I'll see you later." With another glance at me, Ritter waved at Jace, and they left together.

Mari sat down beside me. "Whew! For a moment there, I thought he was going to tell you to wear your armor like a good little frontier wife."

I laughed. "He already did that. But since when did frontier wives use body armor?"

Ava frown at my levity. "And he's right. You need better protection."

"I can get you sturdier armor," Stella said. "I've had it made at every stage. You're taller than I am, but they're adjustable enough in the shoulders that it should be okay. You'll have to go back to the Fortress to get it, though."

"I'd like that."

"And you'll need a disguise," Stella added. "I blurred your features in all the videos I could access online, but I missed a few, and some of the people you're visiting might have been there in person, and you could be recognized."

"Good call," Ava said. "You can dress like an Unbounded

for the Believers, but we don't want anyone connecting you with the altercation at the mission."

"Fine. I'll go as a brunette, I think. We'll get ready back at the Fortress."

"Could you shut the grid down again?" Mari said to Stella as she stood and pulled me to my feet. "Ready?" Her mind was open, inviting me to channel her ability. This time she'd shift using the *in between*, which was easier for her to use for long distances but harder to take others with her, so I'd shift myself.

I held onto her hand. "Let's go."

Numbers filled my mind.

Chapter 7

L OTS OF NUMBERS. I SHARED MARI'S JOY IN HOW THEY ALL FELL perfectly into place. So easily. Here and there—I could feel both locations the numbers described. Then the safe house vanished, and we were outside the gates to the mansion that was our San Diego Fortress, with perhaps a heartbeat of time between for us, when we were neither here nor there, and I couldn't see anything but numbers.

Mari waved to Charles, one of our mortal security guards, as I punched in the gate code, and we laid our hands against the readers to be allowed in. Charles was a big, strong man with pale skin, brown hair, and a serious expression, who liked watching Star Trek and loved strange pizza toppings like white sauce and kelp. Like the other mortal employees, he was former military black ops.

His eyes took in Mari's blond wig and my black attire. "Not going to have fun without me, are you?" he said, coming from the booth where he sat in a padded chair before an array of monitors.

"Sorry, Charles. It's just some questioning."

"No luck finding the girl then?"

"Not yet."

"Well, don't hurry to let me know when I can be of use," he deadpanned, turning back to the booth. "I'm *really* enjoying cleaning my fingernails for the six figures you pay me. It's been nothing but excitement since we beat those weirdos in New York."

Mari and I laughed. "We'll let you know. Thanks, Charles."

We shifted once again, this time into the house now that we were past the protective grid.

Fifteen minutes after that, we were back in LA, getting ready to drive to the first Believer's address. Mari balked at using the car instead of her ability.

"Abilities among the Unbounded are only a rumor at the moment," I reminded her. "We don't want to add fuel to that fire by appearing out of nowhere."

"I can put us out of sight," she insisted.

"Using color numbers?" I knew Mari saw people as numbers that related to colors, which made sense in a strange sort of way since people weren't like physical locations that stayed put, but I'd thought she could only find certain people.

"Well, I can still only locate people by their color numbers if I know them well, but I can change locations at the last moment, so you can look for life forces before or as we appear. No matter how long we stay in the *in between*, no time passes out here. We can take our time."

The thought of trying to park in LA got me over my trepidation fast. "Okay, let's do it. But we should try to stay out of sight. Remember that Brenna is Unbounded, and she might be able to block enough that I wouldn't even see her watching us until we were on top of her."

"Right. But she's not likely hanging out at any of these addresses. I mean, unless they're harboring her, which is unlikely since Kimber is part of their congregation."

"Who knows," I muttered. "The Believers already seem a bit crazy to me. Someone might figure out a way to use them."

Mari frowned. "Guess it's just as well that we're going to visit the Believers first."

We appeared inside the lobby of the first apartment building with no one the wiser. "I could get used to this," I said to Mari.

She only laughed.

The elevator was broken, so we jogged up the three flights in the sweltering stairwell and banged on the door since the doorbell appeared broken.

"Two people inside," I said, on high alert. Both life forms glowed brightly. One was closer to us, but the other was in what might be a back bedroom.

As we waited for an answer, Mari's eyes wandered down to where the tiny light of my baby nestled in my stomach. I studied her face to be sure she was okay about the baby. Before knowing Mari had Changed, she'd pleaded with her husband to have a child, and he, a Hunter who would later give her up to be sacrificed, hadn't wanted anything to do with possible demon spawn.

"Your color number is still red," she said, catching my stare. "But there's something more now. It's a brighter shade. Must be the baby. I thought it was just me when I saw it before, but there's a more notable difference since I saw you last."

"About that," I said. "I know it must be hard with Stella and me. . . both . . . expecting."

"Not at all." She waved the words away with a careless hand. "Once, I thought I'd die if I didn't have a child, but now my time isn't running out, and I have years to make a decision. It's changed the way I look at everything. And I don't want a baby with someone like my ex. Never in a million years."

"Things are going well between you and Keene?"

Her smile widened. "I think so. We've been horribly busy, and I don't see him much. But when I do . . ." She lifted her eyebrows a couple of times. "Well, let's just say there's a lot of heat between us."

"Uh, you know conventional birth control doesn't work for us, right?" Someone might not have told her. "I mean, short of getting a technopath to redirect nanites every time."

She snorted a laugh. "Yeah, I know—believe me. But it's actually a lot less pressure. We're more like kids making out in the backseat at this point. We're a taking it a day at a time because it's not like we have only sixty years ahead of us."

The understatement of the year.

The door opened and a mousy blond woman stood in front of us. She'd come from the back because I could sense the other person was still in the same place closer to us. The woman's eyes widened as she took us in. Mari was wearing an actual sword on her back, and while I'd opted to leave mine at home, I had a gun at my waist in plain view.

"Hi, who are you?" she asked. "I don't recognize you from church."

"We've been asked by Pastor Mike to look into Kimber's disappearance," I said. "May we ask you a few questions?"

Again, her gaze ran over our black bodysuits and the long coats that were more for carrying weapons than for comfort on this scorching day.

"Uh, sure," she said. "I guess if Pastor Mike sent you."

I wanted to demand that she take more care about who she let into her home, but I followed her silently into a small, slightly cooler living room where a teenage boy was playing video games.

"Joshua, we have visitors," she said.

He glanced up at us carelessly, then did a doubletake when he realized what he was seeing.

"Hey, that's a real sword you got there," he said to Mari.

With relish, Mari pulled out the sword for him with a *briiing!* that reverberated off the walls, her love for the piece evident in her gleeful expression. She held it out for his examination on the palms of her hand.

"Wow." Joshua reached out, stopping short of touching the blade. "I don't know anyone who owns one this nice."

"Most people can't afford it," she said. "This sword was made a hundred years ago by the best artisan in Russia." Who was Unbounded and still alive, but she didn't elaborate.

The boy's eyes flew open, the laziness gone. "By the Unboundaried," he said in a hushed whisper. "You are one of them, aren't you?" His gaze widened to include me. "You both are. You're the real thing!"

"That's right," Mari said, replacing the sword on her back. "And we're helping Pastor Mike find Kimber Wheeler. Now tell us, have you ever met Brenna Dabney?"

"You mean the homeless girl who went missing with Kimber?" the woman asked, her eyes so wide they bulged.

I nodded. "Yes."

"She was at church," Joshua said, "but that's the only time I ever saw her."

He was lying. I could sense it from his surface thoughts, though I couldn't see the details in his mind yet. I'd have to direct his thoughts to find the right ones.

"You didn't ever see her during the week?" I asked.

"No," he said, which was true.

"But you saw Kimber with her at church?"

He nodded. "Yeah, for the last few weeks, I guess."

"You ever talk to Brenna about anything?"

"Not really. I mean, she came to church, and that's all." He hesitated. "Kimber liked her a lot, though. She was always trying to help her, I guess. The way they talked, they were together a lot."

I still hadn't uncovered his lie, but I turned to the mother. "What about you? Did you see Brenna during the week? Or Kimber?"

"We don't go to the mission any day but Sunday," she said. "I work, and Joshua here just plays video games." She gave him a hard look.

He shrugged. "It's summer vacation. I'm gonna have piles of homework soon enough."

"Did either of you notice anything strange about Kimber in the few weeks before she went missing?"

They both shook their heads.

"But you saw them both that Sunday before?"

With a nod, Joshua said, "Yeah. They asked me to go for coffee at that new Unbounded café at the end of Ninth, the one that also sells ice cream."

I'd been to one in San Diego. They had flavors like Endless Strawberry, Boundless Blueberry, and Immortal Mudpie, and I guessed the coffee names were every bit as silly. "You didn't go?"

"No." He glanced at his mother. "She won't let me." Yet he had gone once, and from the scene in his mind, it hadn't been that exciting, except for being with Kimber, who he secretly had a crush on.

"It's too dangerous," his mother said. "I've seen on the news that those hoodlums like to rough up the clientele just because they're Believers. We go to the church meetings, but I don't want my son exposed without the pastor and others around. Things are too crazy these days. Those Hunters even attacked

Believers at the mission this morning during a rally for Kimber. I tell you, it's crazy."

"Kimber's parents let her go to the café with Brenna?" I asked her.

"I guess. Or they don't know. They mostly attend the regular church, not with the Believers. Kimber always goes to both meetings, though. At least she has for the past month or so. But we know Kimber pretty well from before we divided to include a Believer session." She smiled. "That's what I love about Pastor Mike. He's always ready to embrace new things."

"Good thing he did, or a lot of us would have left," Joshua said.

I stifled a grin. No doubt losing parishioners was one reason the pastor had been so open-minded, but Pastor Mike seemed to be the real deal.

"People in the café even thought Brenna was Unbounded," he said, exposing his lie since he supposedly hadn't gone with the girls or seen them since Sunday. "They all knew her by name and even gave her free coffee because she could do some cool tricks with her knives. But she was way too young to be real, of course."

"She was only fifteen, I think," his mother added, not catching on to his prefabrication.

Joshua's eyes gleamed. "Is it true that you only Change at thirty? And what else can you do besides grow a new arm or leg?"

"We live a very long time," I said.

Mari snorted a soft laugh, and I narrowed my eyes at her in warning before turning back to the boy, who was once again staring at the hilt of Mari's sword poking above her shoulders.

"I got a sword too," he said. "I wear it when I dress up. You know, when I go to church." He didn't seem all that anxious to show it to us, so I didn't ask.

Nothing of what they'd said seemed to be of any help, but we asked a few more questions before finally excusing ourselves. This time they both walked us to the door, the mother apologizing profusely for forgetting to offer us refreshments or asking us to sit during our discussion.

"It's fine," I said. "We don't need to eat."

"They absorb nutrients like all the time, remember?" said Joshua. "But one thing I want to know. Do you go to church? Are you Believers?"

I exchanged a glance with Mari, and for once she wasn't grinning. I didn't want to destroy anyone's faith, but worshipping Unbounded was no more useful than worshipping a mortal.

"Look," I said. "I'll say this: my mortal parents go to church every week, and my oldest brother too, but they are not that kind of Believers."

They only stared at us as we walked into the stairwell.

Twelve more visits went the same way with other Believers until it almost felt like we were reliving the same scenes.

"This is going to take days," Mari said as we stepped from an elevator into a lobby. "There are still twenty on the list. Maybe we should let Ritter interview them." She cast me a mischievous glance.

"He'd be banging his head against the wall right now." I felt like doing the same. One thing for sure, these interviews were getting us nowhere.

"I wish we could talk to the police officer who's investigating Kimber's disappearance to see if anyone raised suspicions," she said. "I mean, all the adoration was fun at first, but it's getting old."

"I doubt he's even talked to this many people. Anyway, he'd have started with Kimber's family and those close to them, not focus on a homeless girl. And if Brenna was planning this all along, she wouldn't leave casual clues. She even did odd jobs for the handyman at the mission for cover, who said she did a good job for a runaway kid, which make sense now, given that she wasn't either of those things."

Mari drew in a deep breath, and I could sense she was absorbing nutrient molecules from a nearby hamburger joint. I tasted grass, too, on my tongue, and also a hint of dirt. I'd have to ask Dimitri if I was low on iron. At least I wasn't in danger of throwing up anything that wasn't in my stomach.

We were debating which address to go to next when we both got a text from Ava: *Brenna spotted ten minutes ago at an ATM in Atlanta, Georgia. Coordinates sent to your GPS. Locate and observe only. Then report.*

Mari was already downloading the location. "They're three hours ahead of us, so it's nine there. What does she need money for this late at night?"

"It's Saturday. I can think of a million things. I wonder if Stella can hack into her bank, and not just the footage of whatever camera snapped her picture." I was imagining the trail we might find, though if Brenna was like the rest of us, she had multiple bank accounts and emergency cash in several safe houses.

"I'm sure she'll let us know if she can. You ready?" Excitement punctuated Mari's thoughts as she put a hand on my arm.

"Yes." I was trying not to regret the past wasted hours, but maybe something we'd learned would come in handy. If anything, I felt I knew Kimber quite well. She was a good kid, and I was going to find her.

Numbers filled my mind, coming from Mari. Together we shifted, but this time we stopped moving, still inside the shift as she briefly searched to find a place we could emerge out of view of the numerous lifeforms I could sense at our destination, a breath away. Or maybe an eternity. It was hard to tell in this place where nothing existed.

It was neither hot nor cold in the *in between,* and I could detect no sound or color. There were only the numbers in our minds, logical and precise and safe. Then Mari's hand tightened on my arm, and we finished the shift, coming out into a deserted alleyway. The narrow street was quickly being swallowed by night, warded off by a single lamppost at the end of the street where it met the main thoroughfare.

"How far from the ATM?" I asked.

"Three minutes on foot."

We'd gone less than a minute before we saw people on the streets, heading toward movie theaters, dance clubs, or bars. Or maybe even home after a nice dinner. The crowds seemed to grow with each step. The ATM was apparently located in a hopping downtown Atlanta.

By the time we reached the ATM, Brenna was, of course, long gone, and a quick investigation into restaurants nearby garnered nothing except stares.

"We need to change our clothes," I said as we emerged from a bar. "Something tells me they are not as friendly to Unbounded here as they are in LA."

"You're calling the place that tried to chainsaw you today friendly?"

I laughed. "Those people notwithstanding. Anyway, I haven't spotted one Believer here. And as expensive as these wigs are, they're hot." I wiped the sweat from my forehead with my fingertips. It might be evening, but the air felt sweltering and heavy.

"I say we keep looking. She had to be going somewhere, and if we go back to change, we might miss her."

"All right."

We started walking again, only to find three men blocking our path.

"Well, lookee here. What have we got?" said a brown-haired man with a six-inch beard, who wore a red flannel shirt and jeans.

"Looks like more of them Believers," said one of his companions, a short, squat man with long hair and a clean-shaven face.

"We know what to do with them, don't we?" said the first.

"Come on," said the third. "We're going to be late." He was younger than the other two and probably had the equivalent of both their IQs. He ran a hand over the scruff on his chin.

"Just a minute. I gotta make sure these misguided ladies know what side they should be on. The *human* side." The bearded man reached for my arm. I grabbed his hand and stepped into him, flipping him over and pushing him face-down to the cement, where I held his arm back, one boot on his neck.

The other men grunted and stepped forward, but the glint of Mari's knife stopped them.

"I can break his arm, and I will if you don't start walking now." I tugged the man's arm, and he screeched in pain.

"Go," he screamed at his friends.

With a look of hatred, the second man hurried away. The other paused and whispered, "Sorry about that. He's drunk. Please don't hurt him."

I nodded and sent him a little mental encouragement to be on his way. In retrospect, maybe I should have tried that in the beginning, but an entire day of examining thoughts and emotions and shifting on top of that, had me feeling a little worn.

A crowd was gathering. "Do we need to call the police?" someone asked.

"He attacked us," Mari protested. "Can't a woman walk on the street without being attacked?"

"It's true," a woman said. "I saw the whole thing."

"Well, maybe if you weren't dressed like crazies," a deep voice muttered.

"Hey, they can believe what they want," the woman retorted. "Last time I checked, it was still a free country, or are you one of those socialists?" An argument ensued, with people jumping in from all sides.

I let the man go, and Mari and I slid away, turning our backs on the few phones pointed in our direction. I was glad to be wearing the wig.

Mari was lagging behind, so I slowed my steps to meet hers. "Well, if she was nearby, we scared her away with that little show," I said. "We seriously need to change our clothes."

"Okay, but before we shift back, let's talk to Ava and make sure there isn't new information."

Ava picked up immediately. "Still no sign of her," I said, adding to the brief text update I'd sent earlier.

"She's probably still nearby. Maybe even working at taking another child. I wish we'd been able to uncover more of her habits." The tone of her voice told me there was more.

"What else have you learned?"

"Stella found Brenna's image connected with one other missing child two years ago, and we've discovered a link between all four children the eyewitnesses have connected her to. They are all descendants of Emporium Unbounded."

A sinking sensation filled my gut, and I stopped walking. "That's not good."

"Right, because we did a search in the Emporium database, and there have been over two thousand of their descendants who have gone missing over the past decade alone."

The number seemed astronomical. Both the Emporium and Renegades kept track of descendants, with the Emporium trying to indoctrinate or eliminate them while Renegades tried to protect them from Emporium hit teams or murderous Hunters. Yet that hadn't stopped Hunters from finding and almost killing Mari and others. Could they be involved with Brenna in this deliberate targeting of Emporium descendants?

"Wouldn't they have noticed that many children disappearing?"

Ava gave an angry snort. "Apparently not—or at least not the descendants of their rank and file. We wouldn't be making this connection now without access to Emporium records. The missing are mostly descendants of those fallen in battle, murdered by Hunters, or eliminated by the Triad themselves."

"So these are descendants no one was personally responsible for." But still children with a chance to eventually Change.

"That's right. We all know how easily they've discarded those who don't Change. We wouldn't have the problem we do with Hunters now if they'd treated mortal offspring with respect instead of making them work like slaves or throwing them out. Even placing them for adoption would have been kinder." Pain laced her voice, and I knew it was for all the mothers who had made similar choices instead of risking their child's death at the hand of Emporium hit teams.

After a few seconds of silence, she said, "We're matching names in their database now to see how many of our descendants they knew about and were possibly leaked to whoever is responsible. If some of our Renegade descendants went missing when they were children, and they weren't murdered, it's possible they're still alive somewhere."

"But how far back does it go?" I had to ask.

For a moment, the question hung there between us, but

finally Ava answered. "We've just finished ten years now, plus any missing children connected with Brenna, but we'll check as far back as they have records."

"Or at least fifty years."

Another silence. "You're thinking this is connected to the Avowed?"

"Well, Brenna Dabney was in LA when the boat left." I didn't know if it was worse to imagine those children being trafficked or sent to live in some underwater city. Or maybe both were true, and the trafficking was taking place in Sinalta. The idea made me sick.

"We'll keep scanning to see if we get another clue to Brenna's whereabouts," Ava said. "In the meantime, go to the safe house there and get some rest."

"We can return to LA." It wasn't as if we'd have to catch a plane.

"No. You must both be exhausted, and if we have to move fast, you'll be fresher if you simply stay at the Atlanta safe house."

"Ritter's not going to like that," I said, finding the idea rather amusing.

She chuckled. "Give him a break. This is his first child. They're always that way, and it's a good thing. But just because I sent you to Atlanta doesn't in any way mean this is permission for you to approach this woman alone. We have no idea how dangerous she is or who she's working with. That's why Dimitri will be flying Ritter and Jace out there. It's going to take us time to get back to San Diego and the plane, but it'll be faster than a commercial flight. They should be there in the morning to back you up."

"Seems a waste when Mari can shift everyone." Though now that Ava had pointed it out, Mari was lagging.

"She can shift *our* people," Ava corrected. "But we are going to catch up with this woman, and until we know more about her and who she works for, I don't want her or anyone knowing what your abilities are. So we'll need the plane anyway."

"It's too bad Chris is on the island." The island where I was supposed to be relaxing in the sun right now. "Then Dimitri could stay and help you."

"Actually, Chris is on his way home. He won't get here for this flight, but if we send a full team to board that boat, we'll need him to fly us. I told him we could borrow a pilot from the Emporium, but he was adamant. He and Marco are already heading back. They left George on the island with the kids."

At least someone would get to enjoy the sun and sea.

"That reminds me," I said. "You might want to send Charles with us when we board the boat. He's going crazy watching the Fortress."

Ava laughed. "I'll mention it to Ritter, but the final plan of attack and who goes will be up to him."

Her words sparked a warning in my mind. "What does that mean? Look, I'm going. You need me." Ritter had promised never to stop me from going into battle, even if all his instincts demanded that he protect me, but that was before the baby.

"Erin." Ava's voice was tinged with censure. "Your child means a lot to all of us. To Ritter especially."

The idea of my team going into battle without me made me want to shout and scream with frustration, but that tiny, burning life force inside me also evoked emotions I had never experienced before.

"To me too," I said finally.

"Talk to him in the morning. A lot will depend on whether or not these cases are connected. I'm still not convinced of that.

Check the server for the address of the safe house. Get some rest, and I'll let you know if there are any developments." The line went dead.

"What?" Mari said at my sigh.

"The others are flying out here with the hope that we get another sighting and can take Brenna back. So we are ordered to the local safe house."

Mari rolled her eyes. "Ava thinks I'm too tired."

"Aren't you?" I wouldn't admit that I felt like dropping into a coma.

She laughed, stifling a yawn. "Maybe. What's the location? Unless it's super close, shifting will still be easier than walking or finding a taxi. There's not an electric grid, is there?"

"If it's empty so it shouldn't be activated."

I gazed around the street once more, my eyes searching each nearby face. I felt . . . something. But what? I couldn't quite catch the idea hovering just out of sight.

I pulled back into an alleyway that appeared deserted. "Let's go."

My words came too late as Mari was already folding the location of the safe house around us. The next instant, I was staring at an apartment entryway in surprise. Not exactly what I'd been expecting.

"What's wrong?" Mari asked, her knife already out as she scanned for danger. "Is someone here?"

"No," I assured her with a chuckle. "I guess I was hoping for one of those plantations. Like the one Ava owned when she was a southern belle." I gave the words a hint of an accent that fell miserably short of the one Ava could pull off.

Mari laughed, sheathing her knife. "Her? Well, I guess I can see it. But those dresses must have been a very big pain for her."

I had to agree.

"Let's send out for pizza." Mari shed her jacket. "If I can find a place open after eleven."

I opened my mouth to say no, but it suddenly sounded perfect. Even if all I ended up doing was absorbing some of its molecules, I suddenly craved pizza with spicy pepperoni and gooey cheese. "Good idea."

While we waited for our order, I investigated the upscale, three-bedroom apartment. There were fresh linens in the hallway closet, cupboards full of canned foods and medical supplies, and a safe with money and fake IDs. Each of the bedroom's walk-in closets also contained numerous sets of clean clothing.

I'd barely shed my coat and removed my wig in my chosen bedroom when Ritter called me on our server's private video chat. "Hey," I said, sinking into an easy chair.

"Hey." His eyes ran over my face as if searching for signs of distress.

"You on your way to San Diego?"

"About to leave. Did Ava fill you in?"

"About the Unbounded connection?" I nodded.

"There have been Renegade descendent kids going missing. Besides Kimber."

I sat up a little straighter. "They've verified it?"

"Not yet. But I remember it happening several times when we'd check up on them to see if they'd Changed, and we were years too late. I thought it was the Emporium. If Kimber's disappearance hadn't triggered alarms, it would have been the same story."

Anger flared inside me. "We need to find Brenna. We'll make her tell us."

He nodded. "If only we knew a little more about her. Habits make people predictable."

"We talked to half of Pastor Mike's Believer congregation, but no one knew much. She's good at pretending."

"Everyone messes up. We'll find where she made a mistake." Silence fell between us. Then, "I wish I were there," he said.

"I wish you were too." I wish he would make love to me so my mind would stop rehashing the fact that innocent kids were at risk, or that we had no idea what Stefan and this new faction had been planning. And also the very real possibility that my baby might grow old and die before I physically aged another two years.

Ritter decided right then to tell me exactly what he'd do if he were there, things involving a lot of bare flesh and creativity. His words brushed my skin like a caress, leaving me both aroused and amused.

I was about to tell him what I would do when Mari burst into the room without knocking. "Pizza's here," she sang.

Ritter arched a brow. "Pizza? Do you even like pizza? How come I don't know that?"

"Chalk it up to weird cravings," I said.

He laughed. "We're leaving now anyway. I'll see you in the morning."

After gobbling two slices of pizza and taking a brief shower, I collapsed into bed, my body tired but my mind still racing. Something was bothering me. But what? Had I missed something in the street?

I went back over the night since our shift to Atlanta, expecting exhaustion to take me, but sleep didn't come. I rubbed my arm where the ax had sliced my flesh, now little more than a narrow, itching cut that would be gone by morning.

What was I missing?

When it came to me, I couldn't believe I hadn't remembered before. We hadn't learned the information in Atlanta but back in LA at the very first apartment when we'd talked to the boy and his mother. He'd said that Brenna liked to go to the Unbounded Café for coffee. With all the Starbucks and drive-thrus available, that was a choice—and personal information about Brenna.

Could the café be a place she also visited here?

In my former life, I would never drink coffee at night if I wanted to sleep, but it made no difference now. Maybe Brenna, with her fast metabolism, would return to her habit.

Grabbing my phone, I looked up the location of the Unbounded Café nearest the ATM where Brenna Dabney had been sighted. There was one a mere two blocks away from the ATM. Not an area we had reached in our search.

It was open until one in the morning, which was only twenty-five minutes from now.

Pulling on too-big jeans and a shirt from the closet, I filled the hidden pockets with weapons and grabbed a pair of pristine white Nikes on my way out the door. The apartment was dark, and when I peeked into Mari's room, all that greeted me were soft snores. I was probably wrong anyway, so it was better to let her sleep. I took car keys from the cupboard and let myself out of the apartment quietly, the electronic lock latching with my code. Downstairs in numbered parking, I found a black Jeep.

Ten minutes later, I was walking into the Unbounded Café in downtown Atlanta. The place was remarkably busy, but the fact that it was situated between a bar and a movie theater, with a restaurant across the street, probably added to the crowd. There were just as many people eating ice cream as ordering coffee.

I ordered Unbounded Preferred Pistachio ice cream, thanked the teen employee with the pale blond hair, and sat in the corner where I had a good view of the entire room.

The traffic cleared within minutes, and the employees began watching the clock and sending me pointed looks.

Then I recognized a woman coming from the back room with a mortal male employee in his late twenties. She wore black dress pants and a silky red blouse that matched her bright red lipstick. Her eyes were expertly made up, and her former straight black hair was now a dark blond, curling naturally in loose rings. She didn't look at all like a teenager, but I recognized her at once.

I'd found Brenna Dabney.

Chapter 8

AS AVA'S WORDS RANG IN MY HEAD, I FOUGHT THE URGE TO PULL my gun, force Brenna into my car, and take her back to the safe house where I could grill her without an audience. I was to watch and wait and listen—no action without backup.

One-handed, I texted Mari using an emergency number that would keep beeping until she answered. *Found her at the Unbounded Café here in town.*

Absently, I licked dripping ice cream while I sent out a mental probe. Brenna's shield was shut tight, as I expected. Surprisingly, the mortal employee also had a shield, though it was a flimsy thing, leaking his excitement at being so near her. That told me he knew about sensing Unbounded and had been taught to protect his mind. It also told me he had little exposure to Unbounded, or his shield would have been stronger. The man looked like a Believer, with his long hair slicked back, his black trench coat, and the sword on his back—likely cheap replica.

I smashed his shield with a single mental blow. Even though I could tell at a glance that he was mortal, his thoughts of

Brenna confirmed it. What was more, his ardent admiration and worship told me he knew her true nature—and it made it difficult to get anything but blind adoration from him. Questioning him would direct his thoughts in the way they needed to go, but with her there, doing so was out of the question. However, that didn't mean I couldn't listen in.

"Coffee to go?" he asked.

"Yes, of course. The usual."

"I'll be right back. Have a seat."

Brenna looked around and chose a seat near the door. I had a clear view of her, but I pretended to look at my phone when she glanced in my direction.

The two female employees, dressed in black but without long coats or weapons, glared at the male employee as he returned to the counter. "Sheesh, Newton," said the teen who'd served me. "Finally, you come to help. Why is it that every time she shows up here, you suddenly stop knowing how to work? We still have a ton of stuff to do before we can leave."

"I *am* working. And it's something important."

"Getting her coffee is important? Is that what you were doing in the back room during that last rush? Besides, we're closing in five minutes."

"Don't forget that I'm the night manager. And I was getting an update. She's been out of town for a few days for important work."

"She's always out of town for a few days," said the other female employee, a Hispanic woman who looked older than the pale teen but younger than Newton. "What is it you do for her anyway?"

"It's on a need to know," he said importantly as he began filling a coffee cup. "If you were a real Believer, she might tell you."

I saw a flash of thoughts in his head—wide eyes in a darkened room.

The Hispanic woman rolled her eyes. "I am a *believer*—in paying my bills—or you can *believe* I wouldn't be working here." In a lower tone, she added, "Some of the people who come in here are weird, not to mention the management."

Newton glanced behind him at Brenna. "Don't you get it? She's one of them, the Unbounded." And his mind was back to the complete and total worship, blotting out the more interesting thoughts he'd begun to have after his co-worker's question.

"Who gives a crap?" The Hispanic woman sneered. "They have to use the bathroom just like we do. We all dump, and that makes us all equal."

"Never mind." He began adding cream to the coffee, expertly drawing a tree-like design before hurrying back to the table where Brenna was sitting.

My phone gave a faint chirp. The text was a reminder from Ava: *Observe only.* Which told me Mari had not only received my message but had contacted Ava, as per protocol.

I was considering releasing into Newton's thought stream a glimpse of the wide eyes I'd seen in his mind. Maybe he'd follow through on the thought. But I decided it was better to break into Brenna's head and see what she knew about Kimber. Her shield was a whirling, silvery gray, though, and it looked as strong as steel.

That didn't mean I couldn't get through. Grabbing my imaginary machete, I slammed it into her shield. It bounced off without making a chip or dent or anything I could detect. I was about to try again when Mari sauntered into the café, which told me she'd shifted here after receiving my text.

She waved and headed toward me, barely glancing in

Brenna's direction. "Sorry, I'm late," she called out. "Some guy rammed into a car a couple streets over. Stopped up traffic good."

Someone really needed to remind her to stay away from facts that could be easily checked. I faked a smile. "No problem." With a nod, she turned toward the counter to order.

I refocused on Newton's mind to follow his conversation with Brenna. "I'll be here tomorrow with the package," she was saying.

"What time?" Excitement filled his mind, but it dimmed when he noticed Brenna's nostrils flaring with irritation.

"I'm not sure. During your shift. You come in at five, right? It will probably be earlier than tonight, and I won't need to use your back room. Please tell me now if that's a problem."

A burst of panic filled him at the tone of her voice. He knew what happened to those who had problems, and as much as he worshipped her, he didn't want to disappear. Not now when he was finally moving up.

"It's Sunday, so we close early tomorrow. I'll be in at three. But there's no problem. I got it." He swiveled to glance at his co-workers. "I'll have someone waiting for the drop. Just like tonight and yesterday."

"See that you do." Again, the odd note in her voice that both thrilled and terrified him. "You've been a devoted Believer," she said. "I know you will continue to serve us for a long time. And you'll receive the usual funds, of course." She gave him a flat smile that made his heart pound faster. Was she looking at him differently tonight? A rush of desire accompanied his thought.

I had to bite my tongue to stop from snorting. Couldn't he see that she thought of him as no more than a tool for whatever agenda she was carrying out?

"Th-thank you." He mentally cursed himself at the stutter.

She was so perfect, and she'd chosen him. That meant a lot. He'd call the others tonight and make sure tomorrow went off perfectly.

Brenna sat back and took a sip of her coffee, each movement translating into beauty as seen by Newton. He could look at her all day. "How is the girl from yesterday?" she asked.

The music playing in his thoughts cut off abruptly. This was a question he'd dreaded. "She's not settling down the way most do." His voice took on a reverent note. "Is she an embryo? Or a-a—" *Slave* was the word in his mind, but instead he said, "Worker?"

What? I thought, trying to sift through the sands of his thoughts for more details, but he'd moved on. Searching thought streams was a little like being on a busy freeway and trying to find a certain car without being smashed to bits by the other vehicles.

"Potential embryo." Brenna swallowed more coffee. "We won't know for sure yet until later."

"I'm honored," he said. "I'll treat her with every care—I promise. Please tell your friends that. But will you consider coming to see her? She's making things difficult for the others."

Clearly, he believed a few words from her would solve everything.

Brenna pursed her lips. "I've got too much work right now to risk a visit. I'll bring you a little something to give her until transport day. But there should be no problem with the one tomorrow. That one needs no special care."

Newton hoped the child wouldn't be too young. Those always cried the most—at least until they understood that being chosen was an honor. Brenna always made them see that in the end.

I blinked at that and lifted my eyes to see Brenna climbing

to her feet. *Oh, no you don't,* I thought. I brought my mental machete down on her shield again. And then more times. The result was not even a tiny crack.

I jumped to my feet, meeting Mari as she came toward me with coffee. "Let's go," she sang as if leaving had been our plan all along.

Brenna strode out to the street, not glancing in our direction or bidding farewell to Newton, who stared after her like an addict watching his dealer leave with his drugs.

I hit Brenna's shield again and again, blowing out a soft sigh of frustration.

"What?" Mari spoke in a low whisper as we followed Brenna outside.

"I can't get inside her head." Only the very oldest and strongest Unbounded could keep me out, or those who shared my gift. Brenna definitely wasn't old—unless she was a new breed of Unbounded altogether.

Ahead of us, Brenna was striding down the street with a catlike grace that made people leaving the theater stare.

"Could she be sensing like you?" Mari asked. People were now staring at us for the same reason they watched Brenna.

"No." If Brenna had been like me, she would have known that I was blocking the minute she walked into the café eating area, but she hadn't looked twice at me or tried to get into my head. "I'm almost sure she's a hypnopath or something similar. She completely controlled that employee with her words." We knew only one other hypnopath, Tenika Vasco, who was a psychologist by day and the leader of the New York Renegades by night.

"Awful." Mari shivered. "Tenika tried it on me once, and I totally caved even though I knew she was using her ability on me. I guess that would make it easier for Brenna to talk

Kimber into going with her. Kimber's parents were quite sure she'd never hurt them that way."

"Right. The only good news is that Kimber might be here in Atlanta." I quickly gave Mari a rundown of the conversation I'd overheard.

"Slave?" she asked, riveted on that part of the conversation. "Are you sure you saw that in his thoughts?"

"Absolutely."

Mari groaned. "If the press finds out about this, there goes all Patrick's PR attempts."

"They won't find out." The words came out as a growl because Brenna had stopped near an expensive sports car at the end of the block.

"We can take her," Mari said. "Even if she turns out to be combat, there's two of us. And we can both shift."

"No."

Mari snorted. "You're just scared of Ava."

"I am." But I was even more concerned that Ritter would use my breaking protocol as a way to keep me from participating further. "But Brenna is coming back tomorrow with another child. If we take her now, we might find Kimber, if she's wherever that employee stashed her, but we'll possibly lose the other child. And I'm betting Brenna has plenty of plan Bs and Cs. She might have something set up to get rid of evidence permanently if she doesn't show up wherever she's going. It's what I would do." If I were a rogue Unbounded, that is. You couldn't question dead people.

Mari nodded. "All right. So we wait until we can find out for sure where she's keeping Kimber."

"If she has Kimber. And there might be others."

Brenna's car sped away, but we kept walking in case she was looking in her mirror.

"What do you think embryo means?" Mari asked.

"I think it means an Unbounded descendant." It was the only thing that made sense—if any of this did. "It goes right along with them taking children who might Change. Which means someone gave her a list, and Kimber must have been on it."

"And what if they don't Change? Kimber's chances are slim at best."

"That, I don't know. Let's go back to the café to see if I can find out any more from that employee. We'll have to be careful not to spook him, but he might have more available in his head."

But when we returned to the café, the door was locked and the outside fluorescent light off.

"What now?" Mari asked.

"We report to Ava and the others. But one way or the other, I'm going to be waiting here for Brenna tomorrow. This is going to end."

"We need to let the drop happen," Ritter said twenty minutes later from a split screen, coming to us from the plane Dimitri was flying to Atlanta. "So we can go to wherever they plan to take this 'package' and still grab Brenna without a lot of fuss. It'll take two teams."

"Agreed," Ava said from the other screen. "What we need is a way to lure her somewhere. That term embryo is really disturbing. I think Erin's right that it means a potential Unbounded."

"It could have several meanings." Ritter's face appeared dark and angry, reminding me of the way he'd looked when we'd first met. "Maybe it means one who will carry a child. With all the people out there obsessed about gaining immortality, one of our descendants would go for a high price on the black market."

Mari and I exchanged a look. Neither of us had gone there, but I couldn't deny the sense he made. His long experience with the former Emporium Triad had taught him that darkness was their methodology.

Ava gave a long sigh. "Or it could mean both of those things."

"It's only been three days since Kimber went missing," Mari said, "and already Brenna is taking more. It seems fast."

"Two thousand children go missing in the United States daily," Ritter said. "From what we know, Brenna is taking kids no one wants, as well as these embryos. She was probably recruiting every day she was in LA. Some kids might take only a few minutes while kids like Kimber with families who love them take longer."

"Right," Ava agreed. "There's also no doubt in my mind that Brenna went after Kimber because of her connection to us. That means Brenna has a list, and at this moment she could already be laying the groundwork for one or two or a dozen more kids exactly like Kimber."

"So what we need is a kid." Jace was seated next to Ritter in the plane. "Too bad the kids aren't coming back with Chris. Kathy would be a perfect lure."

We all stared. "Are you crazy?" I shot. "One slip, and our very mortal niece would be gone."

Jace rolled his eyes. "I'm teasing. When did you get so touchy? Must be the pregnancy." Which made me angrier.

"Shut up." Ritter nudged him hard. "Even I know that's a stupid thing to say."

"I could do it," I said. "Dress like a homeless teen, pop some gum, ask for money. Get her to recruit me."

Now everyone stared at me. "Sorry," Mari said. "There's no way you could pass as a teen."

"And excuse me for saying so," Jace added, "but you're scary when you have that look in your eyes. She's going to smell something fishy."

"Well, who else would be able to withstand her hypnosuggestion?" I asked. "If that's what's she's doing? I think I could to some extent, and I can increase my mental shield strength to help. Who else could do that?" I wasn't quite sure I could block suggestions from a strong hypnopath, but I had confidence in my team to step in if it became necessary.

Jace snapped his fingers. "That's why we use Catrina."

Catrina, the woman who had more years of experience than I did and whose shield was impressive. Jace's crush on her aside, it was an excellent suggestion.

"That," I said, "might work. Would she be willing, you think?" I knew that being the new sensing Unbounded for the Emporium was a full-time job.

"Of course." Jace took out his phone a little too eagerly. "She's as upset about this as we are. I'll talk to her now. She can take one of the Emporium jets and meet us in Atlanta." He moved off-screen, his phone pressed to his ear.

"Okay then," Ava said from the other side of the screen. "I'll want final op details before noon. We'll be monitoring, but we're too far away to help if something happens to your earbuds, so we'll need a backup system in place there."

"Always," Ritter said, not a trace of rancor in his voice.

"We must bring her in alive if possible," Ava continued, "though temporarily dead is okay if it's necessary. We still don't know why she's doing this, and we need to know if it ties into our other case and also trace all the other children she's been involved with. Waiting for her to heal takes time we don't have."

"What about our other case?" I asked. "Any progress on tracking the boat?"

Ava shook her head. "It's going to take another few hours to get the satellites into position, and after that, we have a lot of ocean to search. But I'm confident we'll have it on radar by morning. Then we'll try hacking into their onboard communication. Until tomorrow." With a nod, she terminated the connection.

Once again, I didn't sleep, though all the efforts against Brenna's shield had taken their toll. Something was still bothering me, so maybe making the connection between Brenna and the café hadn't been the only thing on my mind. Maybe I needed to go deeper.

When Delia Vesey, former Triad member and sensing Unbounded, had failed in her attempt to move her consciousness from her aged body to my younger and stronger one, she'd left behind many of her memories and experiences. Thankfully, nothing of her actual conscience or much of her opinions or conclusions about the memories survived her death, but the fact that they existed troubled me enough. Sometimes I knew things I shouldn't, mostly dates and facts and events. It was hard to make it all clear in my head, but now that I'd exhausted all other avenues, it was into these memories that I looked.

And found Brenna.

She was reaching out for a list, given to her by none other than Stefan Carrington, the Triad leader who was Jace's biological father.

"We give you these names as a token of our good faith. It should help your situation while we work on a mutually beneficial future of Unbounded reign."

"Thank you." Brenna gave him a smile, her face sickly pale compared to his robust coloring. "I am honored at this trust."

When she was gone, Stefan's gaze shifted to Delia. "Now we watch the funds roll in."

Delia's returning laugh was high pitched and mirthless. "Then ka-boom!"

The stray memory cut off there, though I searched the other wisps of silver and black floating on the stage of my mind. But it was like piecing together a puzzle of over a million pieces and finding only a few, none of which connected.

Regardless, it was enough.

I knew where Brenna had gotten her list, which meant the Hunter at the mission had been right. Unbounded were behind many of the disappearances. I also knew that whatever was going on with Brenna, Stefan had a plan that might still be in play.

We needed more than ever to talk to Stefan Carrington. And when we did, I had to find a way to make sure he never had the opportunity to hurt Jace.

Chapter 9

THE NEXT DAY AT FIVE I WALKED BACK INTO THE UNBOUNDED CAF',
bought a coffee, and sat in the same seat I'd used the night
before. I wore last night's jeans over my borrowed body armor,
which felt less confining around my hips but more like an iron
jacket over my chest. Catrina Silvaski was at the next table,
having been there already for several hours, during which time
we'd been in constant mental contact. We'd both probed the
night manager's thoughts, but besides bouts of nervousness
and thoughts of Brenna, he'd been focused on work.

I had to admit that Catrina looked the part. She was tiny
and sweet-looking, with large green eyes and dark strawberry-
blond hair, the kind I'd always thought of as orange. A splash
of freckles warmed her face, and an artful fake bruise on her
jaw made people stare. The ripped jeans, bedroll, and worn
backpack stuffed to brimming hinted she was homeless. Her
tank top revealed another impressive bruise on her back, near
her shoulder, where observers might conclude she wasn't aware
of the story that it told. She was about the same height as my

twelve-year-old niece, and she likely weighed less. Without makeup, she looked about sixteen.

"Look, miss," Newton said, coming up to her, his slicked-back hair making his face seem overly large. "You can't be hanging out here all day. We're not a hotel." He was dressed much as he had been last night, except this time he openly carried a knife sheath on his calf, which looked bulky already because of the boots he wore under his black slacks. Very tacky.

"Why? It's not like you're that busy." She looked up at him, her eyes wide and innocent. Her words had a slight exotic lilt that I knew was a Russian accent, which like Dimitri's hadn't quite been eradicated in all her years of education. "And I'm still drinking my coffee." It was her second, to be exact, but she'd spent most of the hours here pretending to do a cross-word puzzle.

He lifted her cup, shaking it. "Empty. And business is picking up, as you can see." He waved an arm at the short line in front of the counter, though most people were leaving with their ice cream or coffee, not staking out tables.

Catrina's shoulders slumped. "Okay, okay." She began gathering her things, swiping the back of her hand across her eyes as if trying to rub away signs of tears. When she stood, she barely reached his chin. "I, um, is there a park nearby?" she asked.

That was my cue to release a carefully constructed idea into his thought stream, like a slip of paper into a river: *Looks young. Might be a runaway.* I also had another thought ready in case he overlooked the first, but he jumped at the idea.

"Hey, are you a runaway?" he asked.

Terror flooded her eyes. "Of course not. I'm eighteen."

"You don't look eighteen."

"I don't answer to anyone!"

"Is there someone I could call for you?"

"Please, don't tell anybody." A tear slipped from Catrina's eye. She shouldered the backpack, wincing as if feeling the bruise on her back. "Forget it. I'm leaving."

I released a new idea into Newton's mind, a picture of Brenna with a smile on her face as she stared eagerly at Catrina. For all his desire to serve Brenna, he was sure slow at picking up on this golden opportunity.

"Wait, are you hungry?" he asked, stalling for time.

She turned back to him. "I-I don't have any more money."

"It's okay. Come with me and—"

"No," she said, and when he tried reaching out to her, she backed away. "Don't touch me!" Her voice was loud enough to cause people to stare in their direction.

"I was just going to say that I know this woman—she helps people like you. Look, you can even sit here while I call her."

"You mean call the police more likely," Catrina hissed at him, clutching her backpack as if it were the only thing she owned in the entire world.

"Hey," I said, striding toward them. "I couldn't help overhearing. There's a park on the next block, and there's always a great food truck there. Well, if you like hot dogs. Here, it's on me." I extended a twenty-dollar bill in her direction.

Catrina stared at the bill, looked back at Newton, and then again at me. "Thank you." She snatched the bill from my hand and ran out the door.

Newton glared after her for a few seconds, barely remembering to smooth his face as he turned toward me. "That was nice of you," he said stiffly. "I'm sorry if she disturbed you." Inside, he cursed at the interfering busybody.

I stifled a smile at the contradiction. My interference had been a plan B because he'd decided to put Catrina in the backroom until Brenna arrived instead of calling her as we'd hoped. We needed Brenna to come here first to drop off her package and then go find Catrina, who would delay as long as possible before leading her to where Jace and Mari were waiting to take her into custody.

Meanwhile, Ritter, Mari, and I would follow whoever Newton brought to relieve Brenna of her so-called package, hopefully releasing Kimber and anyone else who might be with her. Timed correctly, we could free the kids around the same time that Jace and Mari took Brenna into custody.

If Kimber is there, I reminded myself.

"She didn't bother me," I said to Newton. "It's obvious the poor kid has no one. She can't be more than fifteen or sixteen, can she? I bet she plans to sleep at the park. A policeman might pick her up."

He thought about that for a moment, and then without a nudge from me, he had the brilliant thought all by himself: *If a cop grabs her, Brenna will lose her chance to give that girl purpose in life.*

I gritted my teeth at the pretense. He talked the talk, even mentally, but could he really believe it? More likely, he was trying to convince himself.

At least it worked, Catrina said, still connected to me mentally. *He needs to call her, though. If she doesn't show up there with her package until later, it's going to be a long day.*

He's calling, I said, sending her a mental image of him escaping into the backroom. I sat back down at my table, listening from Newton's mind as he eagerly reported his encounter with Catrina.

"She's a beautiful child," he said. "Looks like someone has been beating her. I tried to keep her here, but she ran off to the park, the one with the hotdog vendor."

"You expect me to know which one?" Brenna was obviously amused. "Unbounded don't eat hotdogs."

"No, of course not. I'll send you the address. It's close. On the other block. You can't miss her red hair or the bruises. They have benches under the trees, so she'll probably be on one of those. I'm just hoping a cop doesn't pick her up first."

"Why would he do that? Not until after eleven anyway. And I'll be there long before that."

"Uh, I . . . you once mentioned that there's a finder's fee." His gulp sounded loud in his own ears as he thought about other opportunities he'd missed in the past, kids he'd never told her about. "In addition to the transportation and housing, I mean."

Brenna chuckled. "Oh, yes. Welcome to the big boy club, Newton. With any luck, I'll take you with me on a future shipment." Her laugh made him shudder, but I couldn't tell if it was from anticipation or fear.

"Thank you, Brenna."

But she'd already hung up.

I pretended to drink coffee, using the cup to hide my mouth. "Looks like it's a go," I told the others through my earbud mic. "But still no timeframe from Brenna."

"Stay there as long as you can." Ritter's voice came through my earbud. "We're in place." Which meant Ritter was staking out their employee entrance, and Dimitri was parked in front. "If we don't spot her first, signal us as soon as she shows up there with her package." He hesitated a heartbeat and added, "Jace and Mari, you have eyes on Catrina?"

"Yep," Jace answered. "She's almost at the intersection. Not too far from the park now where we are. I can't wait to get to that food truck, though. It's been ages since I had a hotdog. We really need to start carrying them in the headquarters café. These look just like the ones from Costco."

A snort came from Catrina, who'd also been listening to Newton and Brenna's exchange about hotdogs.

"Eat one for me," I told my brother.

"Two, you mean," he said. "Since you're eating for two."

I laughed. "Right."

Now all we had to do was wait.

THE FIRST SIGN THAT SOMETHING HAD GONE WRONG WAS CATRINA'S voice in my mind. I'd kept my connection to her without effort, which was easy with another sensing Unbounded, who I had to admit appeared every bit as strong as I was on the surface.

Erin, she's here.

Not even twenty minutes had passed, which told me Brennabeen nearby when Newton called. And she hadn't come here first with her package, as we'd hoped.

Maybe she's checking you out before she comes here, I said. *To see if it's a real lead or if there's any reason she should cancel her drop—because she can't expect to convince you to go with her so quickly. Is she alone?*

I don't see anyone else. If she talks to me, what should I do?

Play along for now.

I relayed the information to Ritter. "Tell her not to go anywhere yet," Ritter said. "Jace? Did you see what car Brenna came from? Maybe she left her package there. Or she's sending someone else with it."

"We didn't see her arrive," Jace answered. "Must have come across from the other street."

"If it's the same car as last night, I can find it," Mari said.

"Go, then," Jace told her.

I stifled the urge to ask Mari permission to use her ability.

We were still close enough for me to channel her, but my job was to watch the café, and Newton was still somewhere in the back, texting cryptic messages on his phone that I copied and relayed to the others. The two employees at the counter, a man and a woman, were giving me sideway stares, probably wondering why I was still there, so I decided it was time to trade my coffee cup for ice cream.

For my cover, that's all. I was not craving it. Well, not too much.

Two people were ahead of me, but they were served quickly. With a triple scoop of Boundless Blueberry, I returned to my table, leaving behind a tip. Not so much as to be remembered, but enough that the employees didn't watch me settle at a new table behind a larger group that might provide a little cover.

Catrina? I asked.

My request was met with nothing but a strong barrier where she used to be. "Guys, can you see Catrina? Something's wrong."

"I got her." Jace's voice sounded tense. "They're just talking on the bench."

"She's blocking me."

"Can't you get through?"

"I'll try." Ordinarily, breaking into an ally's shield was out of the question, but this wasn't supposed to happen. "From this distance, if she's blocking I really shouldn't be able to find her at all," I added. That was happening either because we'd already been connected or . . .

Or because she wanted me to find her.

I took out my talisman machete and slammed it into Catrina's head. Once, twice. Three times. I was breathing hard with the effort. It took five times until I got through. But I shouldn't have been able to get through at all. Not at this distance, and not with Catrina, who had been a student of Delia Vesey.

What's going on? I asked Catrina.

You're not supposed to be here. This is a secret conversation.

With Brenna, you mean. I suppose she ordered you not to tell anyone about your conversation. I could see it in her thought stream: Brenna's order and Catrina's interpretation of closing her mind.

She's strong, Catrina said. *I told her my real name.*

You're stronger. Push out your shield against her, I said. *Push hard.*

No response. Words coming from Brenna interfered. I focused on them, seeing firsthand through Catrina's thoughts.

"So, Cat," Brenna was saying, "you're from New York."

"Yes," Catrina answered. It wasn't the entire truth, of course, but too close for comfort.

"What brings you here?" Brenna's tone now held command. "Tell me about your family."

I wanted to open my mouth and tell her about my parents, Jace, Chris and his kids, and Ritter, of course, and the others in our cell. I sensed Catrina struggling and came back to myself.

Don't tell her anything real, I said. *She is using her ability on you. Say you are a runaway. Your parents died in a car accident. Your uncle is abusive, so you ran away.*

But that's not the truth, Catrina told me.

You don't owe her the truth. We are trying to save people. If you give in to her, we can't do that. You must not tell her about us or that you're Unbounded. You'll put us all in danger.

Jace and Mari . . .

Yes. We don't know who else she has, working with her.

"Tell me," Brenna said with more power.

"There's only my uncle." Catrina's words came hesitantly. "He took care of me after my parents died. But he drinks—a lot. So I decided . . . I have a cousin in Pensacola. That's where I'm going. Please don't call the police."

"I won't call the police. Don't worry about that." Brenna smiled. "In fact, I'll help you. I'm headed near Pensacola if you'd like a ride."

"No, I'd better not."

"I'm a friend." Brenna reached out and touched her hand. I felt the shock through Catrina's mind. Brenna's gift was stronger with touch, just as ours was. "You can come with me."

"I don't know." Catrina clutched the strap of her backpack.

Brenna took that as her cue to back off, and she began talking about the park and the people. I felt Catrina relax, which had to be Brenna's intention.

I updated the others through my earbud. "I'm not sure what to tell her."

"Tell her to go with Brenna," Mari said. "If something happens, I can find her, even if her tracer is deactivated. I'll shift her out."

"I'll flag down a taxi," Jace added. "We'll follow her."

"Catrina could still use that excuse about her puppy and lead her to the original location we planned to take her," I suggested. "We should be able to find Kimber though the employee here."

"But we lose the other child Brenna is supposed to be bringing to the cafe." Dimitri weighed in for the first time. "And if she has more accomplices, it'll just start up all over again."

"Tell her to go," Ritter said, reluctant but firm. "We'll track them for the time being, but we need to know the instant she's in any danger."

My ice cream was melting over my hand. "I'll stay with her.

She can't kick me out if I keep a foot in. Unless she really wants to." I was beginning to regret that I hadn't told her about channeling. I'd have to soon since we were on the same side. If anyone else could do it, she should be able to.

During my quick conversation, Brenna had upped her game, giving Catrina a fifty-dollar bill. "Stay safe," she said, standing to go. "Unless you're sure you don't want to come with me." The last three words were an order.

Go ahead, I told Catrina. *We'll be following.*

I'm feeling dizzy. I think she did something to me. It must have been something on the money. Catrina shoved the bill into a pocket of her backpack.

"Are you okay?" Brenna asked, bending over to touch her shoulder and stare into her eyes. "Come with me. I'll help you. You do not have to fear. I am your friend."

"Okay." Catrina's voice was faint.

I'm right here with you, I said. *And Mari will shift to you and get you out the moment you need us.*

I don't have a choice. Catrina's thought was slightly panicked. *I have to go with her.*

I know it seems that way, but once you remember it's only her ability, you can ignore her. And you can block her if you try. Push out your shield like I said before and strengthen it. You know how. But don't kick me out.

Relief came through Catrina's thought. *Right. I'll try.*

I felt her shield strengthen around us, except for the crack where I'd gotten in. I layered that area with my own shield.

Brenna led Catrina not across the park but to a white sedan partway down the block, all the while telling Catrina how she would be helped and how happy she would be. "You will meet angels," Brenna promised. "You will be safe. You have nothing to fear."

I relayed the information about the car to the others, including the license plate number. Jace was also tracking her internal chip on his monitor, but I liked to cover all the bases.

Inside the car, I glimpsed a strong-looking male driver dressed in all black and a thin, pimple-faced boy of about fourteen in the back seat. The first was definitely Unbounded, but the ragged clothing of the child suggested he was a runaway.

"Who's this?" the boy asked, clutching a fast-food bag in his hands and glaring at Catrina with mistrust.

"A friend," Brenna said.

"She's not going to take my job, is she?"

"Of course not. It's a huge place we need to have painted. You'll both have work for days. And plenty of food. You are safe with me."

"We're safe." Catrina was struggling to keep her eyes open. I hoped the words were part of her act.

"That's right. You'll be working for the Unbounded," Brenna said soothingly. She shut the door behind her and slid into the front passenger seat.

Catrina? She'd shut her eyes, and I was worried.

So tired.

"Brenna's given Catrina something," I told the others. "A sedative, maybe something on the money she gave her. She's still conscious but feeling dizzy. And there is a boy in the car. I think he's Brenna's package."

"Have Catrina wipe off her hands," Dimitri said. "With water, if she's got some. If there's residue, it'll prevent more from getting into her bloodstream."

You have water? I asked Catrina. She didn't have to respond because I saw the answer in her mind. *Pour some on your hands and wipe them off on whatever else you've got in there. Don't let Brenna see.* Catrina unzipped her backpack to obey.

"Uh-oh," Jace said. "The signal to her tracer just cut off. And I don't have eyes on the car yet."

"I can't see her color anymore either," Mari said.

They weren't the only ones. I'd lost contact with Catrina too.

Chapter 10

"I'LL HAVE STELLA SEARCH THE STREET CAMS FOR THE LICENSE PLATE," Ritter said. "But we have no reason to think they won't come to the café, so everyone get back here. She should still be dropping off her package. And maybe now with Catrina, it will be two packages."

His words caused the knot inside me to relax. The child in Brenna's car had seemed convinced he was with her for work, which was better than Catrina's drugging. The good news was that her sped-up metabolism would help her recover much faster, and that would mean another surprise Brenna wouldn't expect.

For five minutes we waited, with me eating ice cream and tasting nothing, Ritter and Dimitri watching the entrances to the café, and Jace and Mari in transit. Then Dimitri said, "Heads up, I see the car arriving in front. Catrina is inside."

Relief spread through me. One part of our op had failed, but we'd known that was a possibility from the start. At least Catrina and the boy would soon be safe.

A minute later, Brenna Dabney walked through the door with Catrina and the boy. Catrina still looked dazed, but Brenna's driver had his arm around her. I reached out and we connected again.

I'm okay, she said. *But this guy is combat. He moves too fast not to be.*

"Okay," Ritter said in my earbud. "Here's plan C. Once Brenna and her guard leave, I want Jace and Mari to follow them. The rest of us will follow whoever comes to transport Catrina and the kid. Only once we find the children will Jace and Mari grab the other two—if they have an opening. If not, they'll wait for us to back them up."

"Will do," Jace said, sounding alive and eager. "We already put a tracker on their car. Not sure if it will work with whatever tech they're using, but the tech might not cover the tailpipe."

I turned slightly to observe Newton coming around the counter, grinning at Brenna. "I see you found her," he said.

"Yes. That makes two to take to the job site." Brenna's voice was low enough not to carry past their circle, and me, of course, as I was linked with Catrina. "They'll be fine additions to the painting crew, don't you think?"

"Absolutely." Newton had his phone out, and he sent a one-handed text. "The van will be here shortly. Um . . . " he paused and motioned to Catrina. "Can she walk okay?"

"She's just feeling a little tired." Brenna handed him an envelope. "Here's what you asked for. One a day. No more."

"Got it." Newton stuffed the envelope into his pocket, and I realized they must be pills for the "embryo" they'd discussed yesterday.

"And get the boy some ice cream," Brenna said. "After all, he's headed for greatness." She bestowed a gleaming smile on the boy and turned to the counter. "Coffee?" she asked her companion.

"Sure." He pushed Catrina toward Newton, who nearly dropped his phone as he encircled Catrina with an arm.

"Come this way," Newton said to the boy. He took them to a tiny back room with a love seat, a small table, and two chairs squeezed into the space. "Wait here in the breakroom. I'll get you some ice cream." He lowered the boneless Catrina onto the loveseat and turned to go—only to run into his male employee.

"Man, we need your help out there with the espresso machine. It's on the blink again, and that witch out there wants her coffee now."

"Don't call her that," Newton growled.

"Why not? She's annoying the way she orders everyone around. And why are these dudes here, anyway?"

"Future employees."

The employee checked Catrina out. "Hey," he said to Catrina. "You have a boyfriend?"

"Get back out there. Flirt on your own time." Newton pushed the employee out in front of him before shutting the door behind them.

Catrina stretched and came to life. "Hey," she said to the boy. "I'm Cat. What's your name?"

He didn't smile, and the glare didn't leave his eyes. No, not a glare. His eyes were simply crossed—or something. "Roger," he said, sitting on one of the hard chairs near the table.

"So, how did you meet Brenna?"

He shrugged. "I was standing outside the hardware store last week picking up jobs with some guys I know. She gave me her card, and I finally got around to calling her. We arranged to meet today." He paused before rushing on. "Look, I don't know what drug you're using, but don't ruin this for me. I got a sick mom and a little brother who need me to work for as long as I can."

Catrina nodded. "Okay." To me, she added, *So not a runaway.*

No, but that's what his family would have thought. I was as glad as Catrina that the boy wasn't any younger. But what did Brenna want from them? Because Roger was as ugly as any child I'd ever seen, with his ravaged face, sunken chest, and malformed eyes. He wouldn't exactly get top dollar if Brenna was selling. Catrina, of course, was a different story.

"Does your mother know where you are?" Catrina asked next.

"Why should she? As long as I come back in a few days with the money, that's all she needs to know." Roger folded his arms and turned from her.

Out in the dining room, Newton had reset the espresso machine, and Brenna had her extra-large coffee. "She's heading out," I said to warn Jace.

"Motorcycles all ready," he answered. I could imagine him and Mari at both ends of the street. "Jace and Mari out." That was their signal to let us know they'd be communicating on a different channel until it was time to meet up again, but Stella was monitoring both channels and would alert us in case of an emergency.

"We have incoming," Dimitri said. "Blue van heading down the alley. It says Church of the Unboundaried. These have to be our guys."

I was already tossing the rest of my cone into the garbage and heading toward the entry. "No surprise there." But I was surprised. How had Brenna enticed the help of a religious group—or at least some of their members?

I walked across the street to where Dimitri was parked and slid into the front seat.

"Two people just went inside the alley door," Ritter said in my earbud. "Van is running, and we have at least one other still inside. I'll have to use the launcher to place the tracker." A few seconds of pause and then, "There. It's working. They're coming out now. Catrina still looks a little groggy."

"She's mostly okay," I said.

"Stay with them." Ritter sounded slightly distracted. "I'll catch up."

He appeared a short time later behind us on a motorcycle as we followed the blue van. Ritter and Dimitri took turns tailing the van with a finesse that was probably overkill.

They have no idea you're behind us, Catrina said.

The driver of the van kept up a rapid pace through the city, as if uncaring that they might be pulled over by a police officer. On the outskirts of Atlanta, they slowed through a small residential area before suddenly entering a wealthy neighborhood with old houses from a bygone era. The houses gradually separated until the owners would have to take a car—or horse and buggy in the old days—to visit their neighbor. I might get to see a plantation after all.

The van finally turned down a tree-lined lane toward a regal mansion that had seen better days. Dimitri continued down the road and pulled over in front of a large tree, where the car wouldn't be easily noticed if the van happened to leave or someone else arrived. Ritter did the same with his bike.

Any sentries? I asked Catrina as we left our vehicles.

Not yet. I'll let you know. But this is a Church of the Unboundaried. There's a sign on the front door.

Kind of expensive for a new church that began a few months ago, I said.

My thoughts exactly. It could have been another church before that, or maybe Brenna bought it for them. The employee at the café has only been involved a few months.

I took her at her word since I hadn't seen that thought in his mind myself.

Ritter arched a brow at me. "How many?"

"Besides the five people in the van, I'm picking up only three people inside the building. But there could be more Unbounded I'm not seeing."

He shook his head. "This doesn't feel like an Unbounded operation."

"Feel?" I asked, grinning.

He grinned back. "Wait here. I'll do reconnaissance." He disappeared into the surrounding greenery.

While he was gone, I removed my jeans and overshirt, which left me wearing only Stella's body armor—my bodysuit on steroids, as I was fondly beginning to think of it. Without the jeans, I'd have better movement and more access to its hidden weapon pockets.

Ritter was back within ten minutes. "No sign of lookouts. The best way in will be from the back."

"Stella," I said, tapping my earbud. "Any word from Jace and Mari?" I'd tried to reach them mentally, but they were too far away.

"They're staking out an apartment in town," she responded. "I've forwarded the location to your phones. It seems a bit busier there than we anticipated, so they're holding position."

Ritter and I exchanged a glance. Was he thinking like me that we'd chosen the wrong op? We'd expected more resistance here.

We followed Ritter through lush greenery and a garden so overgrown that we had to push our way through the bushes and trees. The rear of the house was clearer, as if someone had tried to give at least a nod to yard work. The grass was trim, and the flowerbed around a large statue of a woman with a huge water jug was free of weeds. However, stagnant water lay in the basin below the stone woman's jug, the fountain long fallen into disuse.

"It's a beautiful house," I said as we paused behind a thick copse of trees. "I mean, it needs a lot of work, but wow."

Ritter blinked at me and then at the house. "Yeah, I guess." He stared at me while longer, and I could tell from our mate connection that he wondered if the question stemmed from my pregnancy and some kind of primordial nesting instinct. Maybe it did.

"Let's go," I said. "No one is near the windows or doors back here." No one who wasn't blocking me, I meant, but he knew that.

"Cover me." He sprinted toward the house, then motioned for us to follow. The back door was locked, but a little glass-cutting had us inside in under a minute. No alarm triggered, or at least not one we could hear, but a soft beep signaled that the door had been opened.

We sprinted to an adjoining room, but no one came to investigate. "All upstairs," I mouthed to Ritter, pointing upward with a finger. "Back side of the house. On left."

He nodded and hurried ahead, motioning again to us. We passed several cavernous rooms full of antique furniture, most of which was layered with dust. A ballroom was fitted with pews and a pulpit, and one wall there featured a picture of Christ with a thorn crown surrounded by what could only be Unbounded soldiers. Or angels, I guess Pastor Mike would call them. It felt wrong.

The grand staircase was large enough for five people abreast.

Ritter went up first, then paused at the top to cover us as we sprinted after him.

Erin, hurry. They're hurting her. Catrina's voice in my mind propelled me past Ritter and into the hallway upstairs. I motioned to the last room, where I once again saw through Catrina's eyes. She was struggling against one of the captors who held her back as two others forced a young girl nearby to put something in her mouth. The child contorted, twisting away, her face and features mostly obscured by long, dark hair.

Any guns? I asked.

Holstered only, Catrina answered.

I'd barely transmitted the info to Ritter when he kicked down the door and burst in, Dimitri on his heels. By the time I got into the room, Ritter had taken down the two mortals struggling with the young girl, Catrina had decked her assailant, and Dimitri had taken out the man who had apparently been tying Roger's hands. None of our weapons had been needed. For me, now channeling Ritter's combat ability, it was a decided letdown.

Another child—no, a young woman really—sat on a couch in front of a television, her eyes wide. "It's okay," I told her. "You're all free. We'll help you get back to your families."

"No, no, no!" the woman-child shouted, jumping up from the couch. "You don't understand." She motioned to Catrina, Roger, and the sobbing teen on the gray carpet, who now had her arms over her mass of black hair. "They don't yet understand. We are chosen vessels to the Unboundaried. Please go away. I don't want to leave."

"You want to see Unbounded?" Catrina asked as we both slipped into her mind.

She nodded. "Yes, please. I've only seen two before. Brenna and her friend. She said I could serve them."

Catrina gave me a look that fell short of rolling her eyes. *I'm Unbounded,* she said in the woman's mind. *You will come with me.* Catrina would have to extract the memory of those words later, but for now, it was a good solution to keep her calm.

The girl fell from the couch to her knees, bowing her head to the floor. "I will, my angel."

I smirked at Catrina. *Good luck with that,* I told her.

Meanwhile, Dimitri had squatted next to the crying teen. "It's okay," he said gently. "You don't have to be afraid." She stopped crying and peeked at us past her wall of hair. She was young. Maybe twelve. Too young to be Kimber.

Hiccupping loudly, she hugged Dimitri, holding on to him as if he were the only person she could trust. "I want my Mom."

"Shhh," he said, stroking her hair in comfort and showing no disappointment at her identity. "We'll take you to her. I promise."

Roger glared at all of us with his hands on his scrawny hips. "Does this mean there's no job?"

Catrina laughed. "Don't worry. You'll still get paid." She nodded at me, and I fished a hundred-dollar bill from an inner pocket of my armor and handed it to him. It wasn't enough, not in the light of what one of my kind had tried to do to him, but we'd make it right. Somehow.

It took time to sort it all out. We couldn't exactly call the police and report the kidnappings because we needed the employees for questioning. They apparently both ran the church and worked on the side for Brenna. I didn't have to guess which gave them more money.

"Just tell me one thing," I said as we put them into their own blue van that we were going to use to transport them. "How long have you been doing this?"

"We ain't telling you nothing," said the one who'd driven

the van. But I was already in his mind. They'd only been doing this since the announcement about the Unbounded, when his buddy at the Unbounded Café had first met Brenna and she'd offered them the house and a way to bolster his failing ministry. The guy was a snake, a charlatan of the highest order, not a real man of faith. Together these men had held over sixty children at the house for varying amounts of time. Mostly the kids were runaways who were happy to have a place to stay for a time, but others were those who had been made to believe their life's goal was to dedicate themselves to the Unbounded, who would save their souls and make them immortal.

"When did you ship out the last batch of children?" I demanded. He folded his arms and glared at me, but the answer was there.

I rolled the van door shut before telling the others what I'd found. "They took one group of kids to a semitruck last week. And another six to a private airfield on Wednesday morning." The day Kimber had gone missing. "They didn't know where it was going, but Brenna and at least three others were at the airport. They might know more, but I don't have time."

Dimitri turned to Ritter. "We'll have to take them to the hanger. Ava will want to question them."

Ritter gave him a flat grin. "Time enough for that after we help Jace and Mari. We might need the van."

"Right. Sedatives should keep them quiet."

"What about the kids?" Catrina asked, glancing at the three former captives, who were sitting or standing on the porch stairs. "I'm not taking them in that van with those creeps." Her voice lowered. "And we are *not* sedating them."

Ritter nodded. "Take them in the car to the safe house to sleep tonight. Start finding out where they're from." Relief waved from him, and I could tell he was happy not to have the children to worry about. From a fighting stance, losing Catrina was to our disadvantage, but she wasn't combat, so it was a risk we'd take.

"The older one will need deprogramming," Catrina said in answer. "I'll have to take her back to New York, or she'll just come running back here. I'll make sure to find out if anyone is looking for her."

"We'll need contact information for all of them," I added. "We have to make this right."

Catrina nodded solemnly, shifting her gaze to Dimitri. "You think the little one will go with me? She seems sort of attached to you."

"I'll talk to her." Dimitri strode over to the young girl sitting on the bottom step, her face still blotchy with tears. He sat down next to her.

"You good then?" Ritter asked Catrina.

"Yeah, yeah. Go," she said. "We need to get Brenna now before the guy at the café figures out something's wrong and tips her off. That could be bad for Mari and Jace. They both don't have a lot of experience."

So Jace was right about her thinking of him as a youngster. "Jace is strong and smart," I said. "He learns fast. I'd have him watching my back any day."

She grinned. "He has been doing a good job at headquarters."

"Right. Plus, he's hot to look at." I winked at her. There, that might help get her thinking in his direction. Possibly. Or she might decide I had a weird thing about my brother. "I mean, if I weren't his sister, he would be," I added, wishing I'd stayed silent.

Minutes later, I was on the back of the bike with Ritter, bending into the curves as we headed into town, which was aglow with evening lights. I loved the hard feel of his back against my chest and the beating of our hearts as they pounded together. Satisfaction sank into my bones. We might not be on the island, but working together like this was almost as good.

We switched over to the com channel Jace and Mari were using, and Ritter contacted them at the light. "On our way to your location."

"Stella filled us in," Jace said. "I'm glad you're coming. This might not be as easy as we thought. Thirteen people are here now, besides Brenna. She seems to be having a dinner party. If I had to guess, I'd say at least six are caterers and servers, but that still leaves us with a good number of Unbounded—especially if they are all combat."

"You recognize any of them?" I asked.

"The ones we've been able to photograph are not in our database, and when I say that I mean Renegade or Emporium databases. Stella has double-checked each one." He didn't have to tell us how weird that was. "What's your ETA?"

"Fifteen minutes."

We found Jace and Mari parked next to a row of expensive-looking, gated townhouses with luxury cars in the driveways. Jace pointed to a house two down from where he and Mari had left their bikes.

"The door is locked," Mari said as Dimitri pulled up behind us in the van. "I checked. But I can get us inside." She seemed more than ready, bouncing on her toes with pent-up energy. No wonder Jace had let her shift over to test the door.

"Or we could just walk in." I jerked my head over to where we could see someone smoking outside, the door to the town-home standing slightly ajar. From the white apron and bright glow of the person's life force, it had to be one of the caterers.

Mari laughed. "Or that. But I'll need to take care of him before you all go jumping over the fence."

Dimitri, who had finished parking and joined us, handed her a couple syringes. "A quarter for mortals. Full for the rest."

"Right." She turned to look at Ritter. "Well?"

"Guns with silencers only," Ritter said. "Mari will visit our friend out in front before we go in. Once inside, Erin will identify the Unbounded. She'll also channel me."

"And me," Mari said. "Just in case."

I could do both, even at the same time, though not perfectly. But I should only need one ability at a time.

"Either sedate or use the tranqs on the mortals," Ritter added. "But shoot to kill the others if they don't surrender. We'll keep only one alive for questioning. The rest will revive soon enough. I want no chances."

His eyes held mine as he said this last part, hesitating. We were at a numerical disadvantage, and he knew our chance of success without taking hits was low. But he also knew I could shift out and that I would shield my body as well as my mind. Because my barrier was mental, it wasn't reliable for repeated physical assault, but I had been able to temporarily deflect a bullet or a blow from a sword. He knew all this, but still he hesitated.

"Go," I told Mari. I started walking, knowing the others would follow. I reached the gate as Mari appeared behind the man with the apron, plunging the needle into his neck and easing him to the ground without a sound.

I hopped over the gate, joined by the others, Dimitri in the rear. Inside the entry, I held up two fingers and made an M in our abbreviated sign language, pointing to the back of the house in what must be the kitchen. I couldn't see them, but their life form brightness could only mean mortal. Ritter signaled to Jace and Mari to take care of them while we moved up to the doors of what appeared to be a sitting room with elaborate furnishings. I counted eight Unbounded and three more mortals.

Each of the Unbounded seemed to have mental shields as strong as Brenna's, which made no sense. Delia Vesey had spent nearly two millennia telling Emporium agents that simple blocking was enough, all the while plundering their minds. These people obviously didn't believe such a thing if they were so guarded here among apparent allies where wine and food flowed freely.

Jace and Mari were back. *Second entry,* Jace signaled with his hands.

Ritter pointed at Mari with the signal M for the three mortals in the room, obvious because of their white aprons. That left two Unbounded each for the rest of us, and Ritter pointed out sections of the room, assigning them to us rather than the targets themselves, who were moving. Next, he pointed at Jace and Dimitri, holding up ten fingers, indicating seconds. They nodded and slipped away to the second entry.

I brought my shield up around me, leaving only the tiniest cracks that linked me to Ritter and Mari. Seconds ticked by. The combat ability to count wasn't nearly as refined as Mari's ability to always know the time, but it was accurate all the same. As one, we rushed into the room from both sides with our guns drawn.

They fought back. Of course they fought back. They were Unbounded after all. Since my assigned section was on the left, Brenna and a man I'd never seen before were my targets. Ritter went for the two men on the right, one of which was her driver, who we suspected was combat.

I pointed my gun at Brenna. "Tell everyone to stand down, and no one gets hurt."

She gave a harsh laugh. "Go to hell."

The man next to her lunged, and my first bullet slammed

into his chest. He staggered backward but didn't fall. Brenna fired at me with her own gun, but I moved quickly enough that the bullet missed even my shield. A punch sent her gun spinning to the carpet. I kicked her in the stomach, pleased to see her crumple, then turned in time to dodge a blow from the man who'd recovered. My fist slammed into his throat as I quickly bounced away. He was experienced but not combat. He moved too slowly.

Brenna was right. There was no stopping this now.

Vaguely, I was aware that Ritter had eliminated one target and was now grappling with the driver, whose lightning-fast responses matched his. Jace and Dimitri had also each downed an opponent but now fought with their remaining targets, who were well-matched.

Brenna brought out a new gun. I moved rapidly, channeling Mari and shifting only a few feet to grab her hand to point her weapon at her companion. I pulled the trigger. Brenna's bullet rammed into his chest, and this time he fell.

But Dimitri was in trouble. For each blow he gave his hulking opponent, two landed on his own body. Blood ran from his forehead into his eyes. I could see how it would end. Still holding onto Brenna, I twisted sharply, throwing her to the ground. I turned toward Dimitri. But in that instant things changed. Dimitri's next punch made his opponent grab at his chest. I knew what Dimitri was doing then—wearing out the man by attacking his body from within. Every jab would cut off a vein or weaken the man's heart.

The man seemed to know it too. With a loud grunt, he pulled a deadly-looking sword from his back and began to swing. Mari was there before me, standing close behind him, her knife slipping upward between his ribs.

He jerked, then screamed. Curtailing the arc of his sword,

he rotated, slicing into her torso. Linked as we were, I felt the slash—a horrific pain that was almost immediately counteracted by a rush of adrenaline that caused a strange kind of euphoria, a sensation of high. It wouldn't be enough to keep her alive. Not for now.

She collapsed as Jace blew the man's head into pieces, his brains splattering over Mari, the floors, and the walls.

Something pinged off my shield, and I turned to face Brenna, who still lay on the floor, her face a mask of rage. Her knife lay at my feet where it had fallen. I dove toward her.

"Hold!" she screamed with such authority that everyone in the room who was still standing paused.

Except me. Protected in my swirling black mental shield, I slammed into her, my hands on her throat so she couldn't utter another word.

Finish this! I yelled in Ritter and Jace's heads, breaking through my brother's familiar shield with hardly a thought. But they were already shaking off their momentary stasis. With a few hard punches, they downed their opponents with final blows.

I needed to be with Mari. I needed to hold her hand in case . . . in case . . . I wanted her to know she wasn't alone. Instead, I stayed where I was and squeezed Brenna's throat until she began choking.

"Where is Kimber?" I demanded. "Where did you take her?"

A flash of amusement came into her eyes. She tried to speak but choked, so I loosened my hands slightly. "Don't use the voice," I said. "Or I *will* kill you."

"Is Kimber what this is all about?" The mocking in her voice was clear. "It's too late. She's a potential embryo. Highly valuable. She's already gone."

Dimitri rose from where he'd been kneeling by Mari and came toward us with a syringe. "Erin," he said calmly, breaking through my rage, "I think we've alerted the neighbors with all this crashing around. And some of their bullets weren't silenced. Someone's banging on the front door. You go talk to them and make sure they stay away. We'll get these guys ready to take back."

Terror filled Brenna's eyes. "No! Please. I'll tell you everything. Just don't send me back. I can't survive there, not after being out in the sun. I'd rather die than return to Sinalta."

I lifted my gaze to see Dimitri's jaw clench. Sinalta. Before, we'd only suspected that our two cases could be linked. This was confirmation.

It also meant we both knew where Kimber was.

"You *will* tell us everything," I snarled at Brenna, flipping her over and zip-tying her hands. "You don't get a choice."

Dimitri's needle sank into her neck.

Chapter 11

"**H**OW LONG?" I ASKED THE NEXT MORNING AS DIMITRI, STELLA, Ava, and I stared down at Mari in our San Diego Fortress infirmary. She lay in a coffin-like container of curequick with double IVs snaking into both wrists. She looked completely and utterly dead. Only my gift told me a life force still burned within her. The blow had killed her, though not permanently so. But if our opponents had been stronger, things could have ended differently. Her death shook me because not only had we been linked, but in the instant of her fall, I'd relived the moment when Cort's father, Tihalt, had used the prototype of his newest laser invention to sever all three of his son's focus points.

Needless to say, I had not slept well on our night flight back to San Diego.

"Three days minimum. So Thursday morning. Though she may gain consciousness by Wednesday night." Dimitri's hands rested on Mari's body, enhancing her healing with his own gift. "She'll have to regrow much of her heart. Several arteries were completely severed. Someone put a couple bullets into her stomach as well. Healing will go faster once she has a beating heart again."

"We won't be able to wait for her," Ava said from the other side of the bed. "The ship left a port in Mexico this morning after refueling. While its ultimate destination is Chile, we have no idea at what point they'll pass the cargo off to the Avowed. The logs said two to four days, and we're at nearly two days now. It could happen any time. I suspect it'll happen away from any known dock, though, maybe even at sea. Seeing as that's where they're from."

"And since at least part of their cargo is live," I muttered.

Next to Ava, Stella pulled her hand from stroking Mari's hair and glanced down at a tablet she'd placed on the bed. "I concur. The ship seems to have taken on more fuel than necessary to reach their next scheduled stop, which isn't as soon as I would expect given their current speed. That could mean they're heading further away from the shore. Mexico and South America are not as strict as we are about exact travel logs or what they consider their waters, so the exchange could happen at any time."

"What do our prisoners say?" I asked. Ava had been with Brenna for several hours after our arrival while Ritter and Jace had taken turns with the others in their separate cells.

"Not much." Ava's lips pursed. "Brenna does claim to be from Sinalta, which she says is currently located in the Antarctic region."

"That's too far for the cargo boat to get there anytime soon, right?" If it had taken days for the boat to get to Mexico, where they had refueled, they certainly wouldn't make it all that way in another day or two.

"Way too far," Ava confirmed. "According to Brenna, the

Avowed will be meeting the cargo boat. They don't trust anyone with the exact location of their cities. Not even her."

"How convenient," I said. "Guess that answers my next question."

"As Erin learned from Delia's memories, Brenna has been working off a list provided to her by the former Triad leaders. The list also contained known Renegade descendants, and one of Kimber's ancestors—not in Dimitri's line—was on it."

I glanced at Dimitri's solemn face. "So that's how Brenna found her." All this time, Dimitri had protected his descendants only to have another branch of the family make a mistake.

"Right." Ava gave Dimitri a sympathetic smile. "Brenna and three of the others—all with similar abilities—were assigned to bring both mortals and what they call embryos to Los Angeles, where they are loaded into a shipping crate with supplies before being taken to the dock. The other four are combat gifted, also from Sinalta, but are apparently here in a subservient role to Brenna and her ilk."

"What do they want the kids for?" Stella asked.

"She claims not to know."

I shook my head. "I don't buy that. Last night she made it very clear that Kimber was important. She has to know more."

"I agree. So I thought we'd go together to see if you can get inside her mind. But I don't want her to know about your gift yet. She thinks you're combat, and I don't mind keeping her in the dark, especially if it helps us breach her shield."

"Oh, I'll breach it," I said, patting my hip where I wore the real machete I'd picked up in Mexico on my second adventure with our Renegade cell. After consciously absorbing all morning and accepting an anti-nausea solution Dimitri provided, I felt more than ready for a mental battle.

"You'll probably have to get into the others' minds as well when Jace and Ritter are through with them. We've got them next door in holding. With the rooms sealed, they won't be able to absorb anything, which should weaken them."

"I tried when they were unconscious," I told her. "On the plane. But they didn't relax their shields at all, even while partially drugged." I hadn't tried too hard because I'd been exhausted and worried about Mari.

Ava started to respond when a rustling at the door called our attention. "Oh, here you all are," Jace said from the doorway. "How's she doing?"

"As expected," Dimitri answered.

"Well, did someone tell Keene yet?" Jace made a face as he strode over to my side. "Because he is not going to be happy. I think we ought to let Mari tell him. After she's awake, that is."

"Chicken," I said.

"You bet I'm chicken. He's scary—and crazy about her."

"Well, if he's coming with us, we'll have to tell him."

Jace shook his head. "There's no way. With me gone, someone has to keep Jeane in check. And Keene's the guy they really trust. Without Mari to bring him back and forth, he'll have to stay."

He had a point. Though my brother was jointly running the Emporium and all its associated conglomerates, that didn't mean there weren't stray Emporium agents still loyal to the former leaders hanging around. But Keene had people loyal to him that would cement his leadership.

"In fact," Jace continued, "now that we're on the subject, we really need to announce that Tihalt is dead so we can officially put Keene in his father's place. The inheritance paperwork we created looks solid, but we'll need to figure a good time for Stefan—or rather, Patrick looking like him—to announce it.

With no fighting going on, it'll be hard to sell Tihalt's death even with an appearance from my dear old dad."

I frowned because there was nothing dear about Stefan. "Except there *is* fighting, and maybe it's time we let a little of that information leak. The knowledge that another faction has attacked their—our—posterity won't be appreciated by most."

Jace slapped me on the back. "Good idea. And I say let's have Tihalt publicly come along for the op so he can have an accident. His body is still preserved, so we can show it, and that will be proof enough." He made a face and groaned. "Guess I'll have to run that past Keene, which means I'll have to tell him about Mari."

"She's going to be fine," Dimitri said.

Jace looked down at Mari. "Yeah, but she'll be furious when she wakes and finds we left without her."

"At least she'll recover." Not having Mari around would set us back. We'd grown accustomed to her ability and the advantage it gave us, but we'd manage as we always did.

"What about the prisoners you were questioning?" Ava asked Jace, nodding a farewell at Dimitri and motioning for the rest of us to follow her from the room. "Any more details since we last talked?"

"They told us pretty much nothing except that they were following orders. But we did discover something both odd and interesting." Jace raked a hand through his hair. "Ritter and I set a few of their broken bones and stitched them up, but they don't seem to know anything about curequick."

"How can that be?" Stella asked. "If they're supposedly so advanced."

"No idea." Jace shrugged, lifting his hands helplessly. "Anyway, I think something is stopping them from talking."

"I'm not surprised." Ava's gaze met mine. "I was just about

to tell Erin that I suspect they've been using Brenna's hypnopathic abilities to make them keep their shields up and not give out certain information."

I snapped my fingers. "Yes, that could give them added protection."

"But I don't think Brenna could have done that to herself," Ava continued. "So maybe they're doing it to each other."

"Either way, we have to get inside her mind." I paused at the entrance to the holding cells.

"I'll leave you to it then." Stella glanced down at her tablet. "Chris is almost here from the airport. I'd like to fill him in."

Her surface thoughts radiated joy, which I'd felt from her before in regards to him, but it still took me by surprise. Stella had been deeply in love with her former husband, and Chris was supposedly a stand-in, a way for her to replace the unborn child she'd lost. At the time, he'd been grieving his wife, grasping onto anything good he could find, and I worried both would be hurt. But months later they were married, expecting their first child, and . . . happy. Somehow. Chris's children also adored Stella.

Love and loss, then love again. It was incomprehensible. I couldn't imagine loving any man except Ritter. But I'd been almost engaged before, and Ritter had spent hundreds of years exacting revenge for the death of the woman he was supposed to have married.

I pushed the thoughts aside. Nothing was going to separate us.

"I'd better go talk to Keene," Jace said, moving after Stella. "I'll be back. Don't have too much fun without me."

Ava placed her hand on the lock pad that let us inside the holding area. A long hallway had tiny cells on one side, all of the rooms together not even half the size of my third-story suite.

The cells were constructed of metal and had sealed doors. The ventilation filtered nearly all particles that could be absorbed. If we turned off the ventilation, it would be the second way to kill Unbounded, though after suffocation, it would still take months or years for the tissue connecting the three focus points to degrade to a point where there was no coming back. We weren't going that far, of course, but these Avowed couldn't know that. With only ten cells, we were over capacity today, and the four mortal church members had to share two of the cells.

Ritter emerged from a cell, a frustrated expression on his face. "Either they're dumb as rocks, or they really don't know anything." His next words were a growl. "Short of actually starting to cut them into pieces, I don't think we'll get more. We don't have time for this."

Ava nodded. "We think hypnosuggestion is why they won't—or can't—answer. And also why Erin can't get past their shields."

Ritter's gaze brushed mine, and the violence in him ratcheted down a notch. He nodded. "So, we need to get Brenna to order them to speak."

"That could work, especially if she put the order there in the first place. And I think she probably did—or they did it to each other. Because they've been here for at least twenty years."

"Closer to fifty," Ritter said. "I've been able to verify that."

Ava gave a swift intake of breath. "Then there are many more victims to find."

"Yes," he answered grimly. "Let's go talk to Brenna."

In holding cell three, Brenna took a deep breath when the door opened, as if already feeling the lack of sustenance. Her unlined face was even paler today, and her rumpled clothing and matted hair made her look as homeless as the children she kidnapped.

"Back for more?" she asked mockingly from her seat on the narrow bed. But her appearance made the words fall flat.

"Actually, yes." Ava set her hand on a metal folding chair attached to the wall, bringing it down to sit on. I did likewise, but Ritter remained standing, his hands loose at his sides, ready for anything.

"I told you I'm a sensing Unbounded," Ava said. "Under your bravado, I can sense you're afraid."

Brenna's smile faded. "I don't want to go back, that's all."

"You understand that we can't allow you to keep taking our children—or any children."

"It was the agreement between our people. That's all I know."

"No," I said. "It's not."

Her head whipped toward me.

"You said Kimber was important." I fingered my machete. Mentally, I already had it drawn and was tapping lightly on her mind shield. "Why?"

"Because she's an embryo."

"Why are embryos important?" Ava asked.

"Because they might become Avowed. So potential embryo is more the correct term."

"Why do they need more Avowed?"

Brenna opened her mouth and then shut it. "I-I—we don't need anyone."

"You know more than you're saying," Ava said. "Think."

Abruptly, my mental tapping sounded different. I slammed my mental machete into her shield, again and again. My breath caught in my throat, and my real-life hand ached from gripping the hilt of the physical machete. The man who had given it to me believed it held special properties. I didn't believe that—exactly—but it did help me focus.

"I told you all I know," Brenna said, a bit breathily.

"You don't find that strange?" Ava asked. "Why wouldn't you know this? You've been targeting children for years."

Again, Brenna opened her mouth and shut it. I slammed the machete again. A chink of light shone through the blackness, and it was all I needed. I slipped into her thoughts.

Immediately, Ava was there with me. *Look for whatever is stopping her from speaking,* she told me. *Because I believe she really is frightened of going back, and that gives us leverage. If you find something, grab onto it and hold.*

She might feel it.

Unlikely. She isn't sensing.

"I'm in your mind now," Ava said. "Past your shields. You think I'll have to give up. Well, I won't. I believe someone ordered you not to speak about these things, but you *will* speak of it."

"You can't be in my mind," Brenna said. "The ability to break past a mental barrier has been lost by the few sensing Avowed that remain."

"Maybe in Sinalta, but not here. Surely, the Emporium told you this. Delia Vesey was a master at controlling others."

"I . . . no." Brenna squeezed her brows tightly.

"Who did this to you?"

I saw the answer in the stream of her thoughts. One of her companions, also a hypnopath, had only last night strengthened the order, but behind that was yet another figure—a man Brenna feared. Ava saw it too. I reached for the thoughts, but they streamed past, unaffected by my touch.

Look for a block, Ava suggested. *Like the constructs Delia used on you.*

I could see that Ava didn't know if constructs could actually be created by a powerful hypnosuggestion, but it sounded reasonable to me. I felt my way around the rest of Brenna's mind—but saw nothing unusual.

"So the Avowed need more embryos," I said. "Either they're perverts, or they eat children, or they . . ."

"Or they need more bloodlines," Ritter finished.

I'd forgotten that our mate connection would transfer some of my thoughts and emotions to him, especially when I was currently so open.

Brenna sucked in a breath—and then I saw it. Thoughts rushing at me, encased in a glittering crystal substance. Raising my machete, I slammed it into the stream of thoughts as they rushed downward toward where I stood, as if I were at bat and hoping for a home run. The sands scattered momentarily, flying everywhere and stinging me with their force as they shattered.

More crystal-encased thoughts followed the others, and both Ava and I worked furiously to destroy them all. The original hypnopath who had done this to Brenna had to be powerful—because I saw that the additional strengthening carried out since then was merely a bandage to the original order.

This isn't only created by a hypnopath, Ava said. *This is more like what Delia did to you. I think it was two people—one creating the order and one sealing the job.*

I had to agree. Finally, we seemed to reach a critical point, and with a burst of light, the crystals melted away like ice in a furnace.

Brenna gave a shocked cry that was both frightened and relieved. "Okay, I can tell you." She glanced at Ritter. "He's right. After so many years apart from the world, we needed new bloodlines."

I stared at her in horror. "You're breeding children?"

Brenna drew back, looking appalled. "Sinaltans may only

reproduce if they Change. So no, they are not children." But I could see in her mind that it wasn't quite true. Some of those who hadn't yet Changed were allowed to reproduce earlier—but only with an Avowed.

"So you need more Unbounded blood simply because you've been isolated so long," Ava pressed.

"Yes," Brenna said. This time I saw several odd gaps in her memories, permanent gaps she didn't seem to be aware of, as if someone had removed more than a simple thought bubble.

I see it too, Ava said.

"And the other children?" I asked tightly.

Brenna shrugged. "It's only a few mortals, and that's nothing compared to how many go missing in your country every year." Her voice was again mocking. "America is dripping with unwanted children. It is a culture of me, me, me—if you haven't noticed."

"Forty-nine children," Ritter growled, moving so fast to stand next to Brenna that she blinked. "That's how many you sent this month alone. And we know you've been working with the Emporium for fifty years."

"How did you . . . Never mind. I could have supplied a lot more if they didn't also want the embryos," she said. "Those generally take much more time to set up. As for the mortal children, we choose those who are heading nowhere and give them a better life. We only take as many as we need to replace the workers we lose each year."

Ritter's fury increased, but a look from Ava quelled further outburst. "And what do these captives do?" she asked.

Brenna pushed herself up from the bed. "What does it matter? You are Unbounded, and your ultimate goal must always be the same as ours." For the first time, there was an odd lilt to her voice that wasn't from Georgia—or maybe it was the odd word choice. "In Sinalta mortals are the general workforce, exactly as they will be here in the new world we'll create."

"The Emporium is under new leadership," Ava said.

"*Our* leadership." Ritter's jaw clenched and unclenched. "We need to know specifics of how the drops are made to the Avowed."

Brenna laughed. "Sorry. My crew just makes sure our shipping crate is delivered to the cargo company on time. That's where our jobs end. The Emporium works out shipping and the drops with Sinalta. If you really are in charge of the Emporium now, you'll have to ask your own people."

I inclined my head toward Ritter, indicating that Brenna was telling the truth, at least as she knew it. "How do you know our language so well?" I asked. Because she could pass for a native better than even Dimitri, who had been here far longer.

Brenna's soft snort was derisive. "We've been receiving your country's communications from the time you finally learned to send them. Of course we learned your languages—at least all the important ones."

"Whatever accent you learned in Sinalta," Ava said without admiration, "it has been corrupted by the local speech in Atlanta. In fact, that's part of how we traced you."

Brenna's face flushed, and she opened her mouth to speak but closed it again without comment. Further questioning revealed nothing more except the location of her safe houses and where we could find her notes on the targets she'd taken over the past half century. It was a start, even if many of the non-Unbounded descendants were likely runaways using false names.

As we turned to leave, Brenna said, "Look, I've done everything you've asked, and I'll even order the others to tell you everything, which might help you break through their mental barriers faster. Can't you just let me go? I'll disappear. You'll never see me again. I can't go back to Sinalta, especially now that I've failed at my mission. They don't look kindly on failures."

Ava pivoted on her heel to stare at Brenna. "For now you will stay here."

"Please!" Brenna begged. "You have no idea what it's like to live without the sun. They have light and air, but it's all . . . fake. I can't go back. They'll never let me leave again."

"Yet it is exactly to those conditions you have sentenced thousands of children." Ava's voice held ice, frigid and hard. "You have been part of a conspiracy to commit crimes against our people, both mortal and potential Unbounded. Make no mistake. We consider this an act of war, and you and the people who conspired with you are traitors to the human race. So, no. You will not go free. You will go with us to confront your Sinaltan leaders."

Ava took a step toward the door before saying over her shoulder, "But that does not mean we plan to leave you with them. The manner in which you carry out the duty we assign you will help determine your ultimate fate. Remember that."

Brenna stared at us in horror as the door to her cell shut.

"Are we going to question the others?" I asked.

"It'll waste too much time," Ritter said. "As long as you're sure she wasn't holding back?"

"I am," I said. "Though there still might be questions we don't know we should ask."

Ava nodded in agreement. "She wasn't holding back, but something isn't adding up because, by all accounts, they have only been in contact with us for fifty years. Why, after thousands of years under the ocean, do they all of a sudden need more bloodlines?"

Ritter nodded solemnly. "Something happened to change things."

"We saw nothing of that in her thoughts. But we didn't ask either." Now I worried I'd simply missed something.

Ava shook her head. "If there was something important, we would have seen it. It's possible some of her memories have been removed. If those in charge of Sinalta are anything like the former Triad, they don't leave much to chance."

"Someone has to know more," Ritter said. "Someone inside the Emporium. Why else agree to this trade?"

"Stefan," I said with a sharp stab of disappointment. We'd been circling to this all along, no matter how much I wanted to avoid it. "He may know something."

"Right. We'll have to talk to him," Ritter said quietly.

Ava glanced at me and then met Ritter's gaze. "We're flying to Mexico anyway to board the cargo ship. We'll make a stop at the prison. We can also drop off our Avowed guests there."

A tight knot filled my gut. "Okay, but I want to be the one to talk to Stefan, not Jace."

Ava's gravestone eyes chided me. "You can't protect him from Stefan. It has to be his choice. Trust your brother." She drew out her cell phone. "You two go ahead and prepare the team for takeoff. I'll make sure Brenna talks to her companions before we transfer them to the plane. We can question them on the way." Someone on the other end of the phone answered because she turned from us and said, "Charles, I need you and Marco up in holding to ready some prisoners for transport. And I hope your go-bag is up-to-date because we're all flying to Mexico within the hour."

Ritter and I left Ava in holding and hurried down the hall. But in the elevator up to our quarters on the next floor, he said,

"You should stay here and question the church leaders. They might have more information."

I rounded on him. "She doesn't need my help. You just don't want me to go."

His jaw ticked. "No, I don't. These people are dangerous."

"You need a sensing Unbounded."

"We have Ava."

The bell dinged and the door slid open. I tightened my fists at my side and willed myself to be calm. "Ava can't break through strong mental shields, and she can't channel others' abilities. She can't extend her mental shield to protect you. Now, whether I can do all that because of what Delia did to me or because I was born with it, it doesn't matter. I'm the only one, and you need me."

"I need you safe." His voice was tortured, his eyes dark pits that threatened to drown me. Seconds ticked by. The door started to slide shut again, but his hand shot out to stop it.

"I know," I said finally. "I need me safe too." My hand went to my belly, where the ember of life burned in my uterus. There was so much trust in that relationship, and only now had I begun to understand what Stella went through when she lost her first baby.

But I also knew that a technologically advanced group of Unbounded was a danger to the entire world, including my child. The Emporium had ruthlessly fought their way into government positions and nearly destroyed all the Renegades over the past century, crushing any mortals in their way. Mortals were always expendable. That was Emporium history—a history that had been repeated far too many times. In no possible way could we sit back and let a new faction grow strong enough to hurt the world again.

"If we lose to these Avowed," I continued, "we go back to fighting. That means we lose everything we've gained. Renegades are finally able to connect with families they had to abandon for their own safety. We may no longer need to fake our deaths or worry about being cut into three, but fighting again changes all that. I don't want to raise our child in that kind of world. We have to make it safe—for everyone."

He considered for long moments, his hand on the door, his eyes locked on mine. At long last, he nodded. "You once asked me why I want you, why I see you as my equal when you are comparably so young and inexperienced. This is why, Erin. You don't accept the chance of defeat. You aren't dead inside—resigned—like so many of us . . . like I was." He released the door and stepped close, one arm going around me and one hand resting on the tiny mound of my belly. "I also find you incredibly sexy."

"Ah." That part I knew.

"Show me my son." His mental shield dropped—an invitation.

"Or daughter." The elevator door closed.

He laughed. "Or daughter."

I reached for them both and made the link to the consciousness inside my womb. My baby. Our baby. Moving, growing. Not just an awareness but a tiny being already beginning to learn inside this sanctuary.

Hey, there, I said in a thought-whisper. I could feel the baby's heart beating faster than mine and Ritter's.

"Hey," Ritter echoed aloud. For a brief but dizzying moment, his face and heart and mind were full of emotion. There was no end or beginning to either him or me. It was just us and the spark of life we'd created.

Then he stepped away and jabbed the elevator button. "Get

your stuff," he said. "I'll meet you downstairs. My bag is already there. I'll need to brief Chris."

I stepped from the elevator, my gaze locked on his. As the door shut between us, I hoped I was making the right choice.

Chapter 12

WHEN I MADE IT DOWNSTAIRS, I FOUND MY BROTHER CHRIS IN THE entryway with Stella. Seven years my senior, he had gray eyes like me and our mother and darker blonde hair than either Jace or me. His face was red with sunburn, and I guessed his single day on the island without his new wife had meant no sunscreen. Or maybe Stella wouldn't have bothered since her skin would heal as fast as it burned. I hoped someone was reminding the children to lather up.

I stepped past our dog, Max, and gave Chris a hug. "Sorry for cutting short your vacation."

"Hey, Blondie," he said, using the old nickname even Jace had stopped using after I kicked his butt a few times in our sparring matches. "Not your fault. I'm rather glad to get out of the sun."

"I can see that." I gingerly touched his cheek.

"Dimitri already stopped the pain. Just have to peel now."

"The kids?" I asked.

"They're fine." He bent down to pet Max's long golden

hair as the Collie-Chow pushed his pointed nose into his leg. "Stella packed them sunscreen."

"It was for everyone." Stella shook her head at Chris.

He picked up his bag with a grin. "Everyone ready?"

"Yep." I needed to tell him about the baby, but that could wait.

Tensions were high as we finally received permission to leave Benito Juárez International Airport, the first and only stop on our way to a private airport south of Villahermosa near where our prison compound was located in the Mexican Rainforest. By the time we arrived, it would be after five in the evening.

We'd taken our corporate jet, the larger of our two planes and the same one we used in Atlanta. Though it wasn't a luxury liner, the plane was spacious compared to the smaller one Chris had taken to the island and compared to cramped commercial flights. One side of the plane held two sets of four seats around a table. Across the aisle, there were two single-facing seats, also with a table. Ten comfortable, high-backed seats altogether. A refrigerator and microwave took up the remaining space behind the single seats, with storage space for additional food supplies. Two small bathrooms separated the seating section from the final segment of the plane, which held three triple bunks on one side and a storage area on the other. The bunks were tightly packed with metal grates locked into place over each opening.

Seven of the nine bunks were currently occupied by Brenna's former companions, currently unconscious. Ava and I had questioned them earlier in the fight, but they only confirmed what little Brenna had told us, and each expressed a desire to join us rather than return to the city under the sea.

Not exactly a good recommendation for the Avowed. They'd all be kept in Mexico at the prison until they could be tried for their crimes.

Early in the flight, a rough plan evolved, which had all of us except Stella, who would be running communications from our prison facility, boarding the cargo ship. Ritter had arranged a helicopter to get us close, and the minute the ship stopped, the helicopter would drop us and a combat rubber raiding craft, the same used by Navy Seals, which would get us close enough to board—maybe without them noticing. The timing would have to be precise, but as the ship was currently heading out to open sea, Ritter was concerned we wouldn't have enough warning before their meeting with the Avowed. We might have to drop from the helicopter directly onto the boat, which would leave us more exposed. He and Ava were in the second four set of seats with Charles and Marco, discussing options, while Jace, Dimitri, and I sat in the first set. Brenna was alone in one of the seats across the aisle, cuffed to the armrest, and Stella was in the cockpit with Chris.

"Any news about the kids we found in Atlanta?" I asked Jace, who was seated next to me.

"I've been meaning to ask Catrina." He tilted a tablet from its inlaid position in the tabletop and tapped on it. "I know she let the boy go back to his mother. Since he is from Atlanta, that was easy."

"Something is wrong with his eyes," I said, looking over the screen at Dimitri across from us. "Did you notice? You think he can be healed?"

He nodded. "From what I saw, he's mostly suffering from malnutrition, and we can for sure correct that, but yeah, I can fix the crossed eyes. He'll need surgery, though. We'll have to find a way to get his mom to accept it."

"Or I could kidnap him again." I smiled to show I was kidding. "Shouldn't be a problem getting her to agree. He seems to have the run of the streets."

Catrina's face appeared on the screen. "Hey," she said. "Keene's filled me in on the plan about pretending to take Tihalt with you. It's a great idea. People keep wanting to run their scientific ideas past him, and I'm getting a little tired of making excuses as to why he won't see them."

Jace preened a little, which I could see amused Catrina, but it had been his idea after all, even if my comment sparked it. "So what about the kids?" I asked. "Sorry to leave you holding the bag."

She wrinkled her nose, which made her look even younger than usual. "I'm still figuring out what to do with the oldest one. She has no family to speak of and has been on the streets for years. For now, she's going to be my assistant."

Jace's laugh exploded from his lips. "Ha! Oh, you're going to love that. You can let her run interference for you."

"Actually, she's quite annoying, but she's learning. If I can teach her not to pray to me, I think she might actually find a place here. At least she'll have a chance at a future."

"Better you than me," Jace said.

"And the little one?" I asked.

"She was reunited this morning with her very worried family. She'd been taken from a park in Augusta. She's of Unbounded descent, third generation. Her ancestor was one of those the Emporium labeled a traitor, which is why I assume she was on the list."

"A potential embryo." The words tasted bitter in my mouth.

"Right." Catrina looked away from the screen, her attention diverted. "Can I help you?" she asked someone out of sight.

Jeane Baker, also known as Norma Jeane in another life

before the Emporium faked her death, came into view and settled, catlike, on the tan leather couch next to Catrina. Every part of her screamed sex appeal, from the blond hair she dyed every day and the painted face mole to the figure-hugging svelte pants and pointed bra.

"I hear you're dealing with hypnopaths," she said breathily. "They can be very dangerous." Her grin widened. "Except to me." As a null, she was correct.

"I can block you," I reminded her, which meant I could still use my ability, even to get into her crazy mind, but I couldn't understand her thoughts, and I hadn't been able to fix the damage her brother had done to her.

"Yes, but you're the only one." Jeane glanced pointedly at Catrina, giving her a satisfied smile.

Catrina heaved a sigh. "Forget it. You're not going with them on this op."

Jeane's lips pouted. "Why?"

"First we might talk about Tihalt's missing laser," Jace said. "You know, the one you used to kill your brother."

"You mean the snake of a man who killed the love of my life, changed my memories, and tried to murder all of us?" Jeane's smile became like a shark's. "You were the one who had it last, remember?"

But the laser had gone missing during the final clean-up, and we all suspected Jeane. She, however, adamantly refused to admit to anything. And if we were honest, maybe we were hoping that with it missing and Tihalt's death, the technology behind his portable weapon would remain a secret.

"All these new Unbounded and their delicious technology," Jeane continued, now assured of our attention. "As one of the Triad, I should be involved in the negotiations."

On the surface, that was true, but we intended her to be a temporary member. Only the raiding of her mind had kept her from serving time in the Mexican prison for her former involvement with the Emporium.

Jace offered her a conciliatory smile. "Thank you for the offer. But we're already too far away for you to join us."

"Well, where's Mari?" Jean's voice turned petulant. "She can take me there."

Catrina gave us a sympathetic smile but didn't respond.

"On another assignment," Jace said. "Look, we gotta go. We'll stay in touch." He cut the transmission.

I rose and checked on Brenna. "You want something to eat or drink? We still have another hour."

"No," she sneered, yanking at her cuffed wrist. "Unless you're going to remove these, just leave me alone."

"Your choice." I started toward the kitchen area for a snack of white bread that contained next to no nutrition. I'd learned on the last flight that it settled my stomach, especially in an enclosed space where there wasn't a lot to absorb. Her next comment stopped me.

"You're taking me back for a life sentence, you know. How can you live with yourself?"

I grinned at her. "A life sentence for you would be far too lenient."

She huffed and turned her face away.

Time passed rapidly as we discussed options, during which Ritter kept giving me glances that worried me. Finally, the loudspeaker came to life with Chris's voice.

"Buckle up, folks. We're approaching the runaway now. Might be a little bumpy. I'm teaching Stella how to land."

I looked past Jace and out the window to see a narrow

runway in the middle of what appeared to be a jungle. Since the son of the owner had betrayed us the last time we were here, I was leery about our reception.

Seeing my expression, Jace laughed. "Don't worry. That's been handled. After Chris whomped all of the bandits the last time we were here, they've left the owner and his traitorous brat alone."

"Good to know," I said.

STEFAN WAS CONSCIOUS AND WAITING FOR US WHEN WE ARRIVED AT the holding facility. He was awaiting trial for his crimes against humanity, but after temporarily killing a guard and trying to escape, he had been kept mostly sedated the past five weeks since we removed him from New York. Thankfully, Ava and Ritter had agreed that I was the best one to talk to Stefan, seeing as he had a mortal hatred toward them, but they'd be watching from the next room. Jace, however, insisted on going inside the room with me.

"Ah, a visit from my dear children," Stefan said when we came inside the room. He sat back in his chair as far as the handcuffs and chain allowed, looped as it was through a large iron ring in the granite table. "How good of you to come visit."

Aside from the shackles, he still looked every bit the wealthy and powerful Triad leader. His shoulders were squared, his clothing impeccable, and his white-blond hair that reminded me so much of Jace perfectly in place. The wrinkles around his eyes were more prominent than they'd once been. He was fiftyish in Unbounded years, which put him around Dimitri's thousand human years.

"Although, I have barely begun to recall any memories of

you, Erin," he said, his blue eyes pinning me in place. "The doctors here are not the best in the world at uncovering raided memories."

I shrugged. "It's not like I'm going to send you a Father's Day card any time soon." I glanced at Jace. "Either of us. And for the record, we have a father."

"You have a mortal placeholder," Stefan retorted. "After his bones are rotted in the earth, I'll still be here."

"Yes, you will still be in this prison, paying for your crimes." I permitted myself a smile while some part inside me screamed to tell him that Dimitri was my biological father, not him. But I wouldn't do that until the Emporium leadership was more stable and Jace no longer needed my support. Besides, at least this way, even though Jace knew I didn't carry this monster's genes, we could stand here together—united—as if it were true.

"You know why we're here." Jace slipped into one of the chairs on our side of the granite table. "Or at least you should have been briefed. We're on a clock."

Stefan's cocked his head, giving the appearance of staring down a rifle scope at him. "Right, down to business. A man after my own heart." Which wasn't really true because Stefan was all about the long game. "You want to know what happened to bring the Avowed up from the sea." He shook his head. "I'm afraid you've come here for nothing. My guess is overgrowth. The city I visited was packed."

"You've been there?" I reached out to his mind, finding his powerful, swirling mental shield activated. Surprisingly enough, it wasn't even as strong as Brenna's, but it would still take me a while to get through. Good thing I was wearing the physical machete. I pulled the imaginary one and got to work.

"Yes, I've been there," Stefan said. "I took a delegation and went to meet with them. I wanted to make sure they could hold up their side of the bargain. If I were going to pledge millions of dollars of aid, I wanted to make sure we'd double or triple that in return."

"Of course you would." Jace looked disgusted, as if only now realizing that his father was a complete waste of space. I understood the feeling. Even knowing Stefan was a soulless bastard, I'd hoped for more when I'd thought he was my father. The flip side was that I'd learned Stefan loved and rewarded his posterity with the same quickness and zeal with which he disciplined them. He might give his child more chances than the average Emporium agent, but he wouldn't stay his anger or be above filicide if he decided it was in his best interest.

"Oh, come on." Stefan leaned forward abruptly, his eyes eager. "You are running my empire now. You know we must keep the profit growing or lose everything."

"You went to meet them," Jace said without answering the implied question. "Tell us about it."

Stefan sat back again, the chain jerking him to a stop when he tried to go too far. "The first thing I noticed was all the gold and other precious metals. Their buildings and streets are lined with it—at least in the inner circle where the prominent Avowed live."

"They have separate areas?" I asked.

Stefan nodded. "It was one of the things I liked best about the place. I mean, they have workers coming in, lesser Avowed and mortals, of course, but those people live in the outer or middle rings."

I arched a brow. "I hear they do a lot of mining."

"Right. Or their mortals do."

"Their slaves," I corrected, slamming my mental machete once again into his shield.

Stefan's laugh boomed a little too brightly. "Mortals are obviously a lower species—the Avowed have come to the same conclusions as the Triad did about that." He looked at Jace, tilting his head. "The former Triad."

Jace didn't respond, but I could feel anger coming from him in waves. Maybe it was a good thing he was here, so he wouldn't fantasize that his biological father would ever be anything but a danger to him.

"Did you see the mortal areas?" I asked.

"Not up close. I did see one of the mines, and I was given a brief tour through their two outer rings. They are admittedly overcrowded. Even parts of the inner circle have skyscrapers that would rival ours in New York. Sinalta is home to millions of people. Unfortunately, time didn't allow a visit to their other city, which they said was quite a bit larger." He smiled, shifting his weight as if crossing his legs on the other side of the granite table. I heard the clink of more chains. "What is it that's different about you, Erin? Let's talk about that."

Of course, his combat gift would hint at my pregnancy, just as it had to Ritter and Jace. I hit his shield once more with my machete and finally broke through. I gave him a wide, confident smile. "So let me get this straight. You agreed to give the Avowed finished products and food, mortals, and potential Unbounded—which they seem to be in need of, despite your claim that their cities are supposedly crowded. And in exchange they give you raw materials, including precious metals."

"You forgot about giving the Sinaltans a country," Jace put in.

"Right. Australia? Or the southern half of Africa?" I held Stefan's gaze while studying his thought stream for the answers. He had to know more.

He lifted one shoulder in a lazy shrug. "In the beginning,

they agreed to wait until we finished our plans, and it has been very profitable."

I narrowed my gaze. "Only now they've become anxious about surfacing. What changed?"

Stefan shrugged. "Who knows. Maybe they got sick of being under the sea, living like rats in the dark. That's fine for their slaves, but not for Unbounded."

"So you are not aware of any reason why they are sending missives to speed things up?"

"They've been doing that for the past year, and if you hadn't interfered, we would be well on our way to providing what they need."

"Which brings us back to why they need it now when last year they could wait," I said.

"And what about their technology?" Jace added. "If it's as advanced as our people believe, they're a danger to the entire world."

"Oh, they're definitely a danger." Stefan smiled, and I could see the amusement in his thoughts. "Why do you think I agreed? It wasn't only the money that stopped me from sending a missile to destroy their cities."

"You know their location?" Jace demanded.

Stefan shook his head. "I have no idea. That was another factor. Sinalta is incredibly advanced. They have electronics, lighting, a fake sky, and every luxury a man could ever want. All miles under the water. And they have ships, small and large craft, that are so far beyond what we know that it's like a rocket ship compared to a frontier buggy."

"You wanted that technology." My heart pounded at the idea of Stefan controlling all that.

"Of course," he said. "And you would be a fool if you don't want it too. I was delaying as long as possible to put things in place so that we had control over the technology once they surfaced. Or no one did."

That might explain the *ka-boom!* I'd seen in the remnants of Delia's memories. "You were going to destroy them if you didn't succeed."

"Yes," he said simply. His thoughts told me he believed that once the Sinaltans surfaced, it would be easy enough to find and destroy them before they created any strongholds and while they still trusted the Emporium.

"How? Do you have people there?" Jace wanted to know.

"A few. But they are all mortal, or they were when we included them with the shipments. Because they have at least one person gifted in sensing who would know if they were Changed." He frowned. "But so far, there has been no notification from any of our people."

Jace glanced at me, and I dipped my head a fraction to tell him Stefan was telling the truth. Ava must have also caught the signal because in the next instant, she was in Stefan's mind with me.

"I guess we'll have to chat with those contacts soon," Jace said. "But first, we're going to relieve the cargo ship of the current batch of slaves you're sending them."

Stefan chortled at that, nearly choking with amusement. "Let me guess. You'll get a helicopter and a raiding craft and wait for the ship to stop. It won't work. They'll be too fast, and you'll all be killed." His eyes shifted from Jace to me. "You're so willing to give up my grandchild's life. He or she may be Unbounded, you know."

"What we do is none of your—" Jace stopped when he noticed my stare.

"You have a better way?" I asked.

"Of course I do." Stefan glanced past me at the one-way

mirror behind us before raising his voice. "I have one of their smaller craft. They were kind enough to gift me one after nearly a half century of asking. It can travel ten times faster than any of our ocean subs, or more."

"Where is it?"

Again, he looked past me at the mirror. "I know you're there, Ava, Dimitri. I'll give you the ship. It's even close by—or can be before too long. Lot faster than a plane or a helicopter. With it, you can approach the ship, keep pace with them, and even board while they're moving, if you feel so inclined, though I'd recommend that my daughter wait until the ship stops. Either way, you're there in plenty of time to ambush the Avowed when they surface."

"You know how to drive it?" I asked.

"Yes, but it's difficult. Only I can do it." A lie, I saw. Apparently, the controls were intuitive, and he had an electronic instruction manual in English. There was also an auto-drive.

The intercom crackled. "And what would you like in exchange?" came Ava's voice, cold and precise.

"You exonerate me, and I'll give you the ship. I'll even go with you."

"No deal," I said.

"Absolutely no deal!" Jace jumped up from his chair. "I've spent the last five weeks cleaning up your mess. If you think I will ever be a part of freeing you, you're crazier than I thought!"

Stefan sighed. "That's my deal."

"Where is the ship?" I demanded, eagerly wading into the sands of his thoughts. Could he feel me there, disrupting things? I wasn't being overly aggressive, but he was experienced.

"Sorry," he said, not looking sorry at all.

I saw something in his thoughts and reached for it. "You said it's close. Mexico then."

"Close for it to come to us. Not for us to get there," he clarified.

I got it! Ava said, showing me the thought in his mind. *I know that place. It's Acapulco. The Emporium has an installation there.*

I stood up abruptly.

"What? Leaving so soon?" Stefan's voice was mocking. "We haven't even discussed baby names."

I smiled sweetly. "If you're not going to help us, we'd better get back to our fumbling, old-fashioned ways."

He snorted, lowering his voice in a threatening manner. "If you'd been raised by me, you would have a spine."

I planted my hands on the granite table and leaned over it, staring down at him. "If I'd been raised by you, you would already be dead."

He jerked at his chains, trying to startle me, but I'd seen it coming. I laughed. "Goodbye, Stefan. I truly hope we never meet again."

Then, just because I could, I released a thought into the stream of his mind, so I could watch him react. *She knows it's in Acapulco. I'll never get free.* Despair chipped away at his confidence, which was exactly what I'd intended. It might not be moral or right, and could even be a little petty, but it was less than he deserved.

Erin, Ava chided. *You are not his judge and jury.*

I know. I wasn't even his offspring. Jace was, and he'd somehow refrained from breaking the man's nose. I had a lot to learn before I could be as selfless and far-seeing as Ava was. Maybe after a few hundred years.

Jace and I joined the others in the next room to discuss our next step.

"Flying to Acapulco will take you close to four hours," Stella said. "And then there's the whole driving to the compound and knocking on the door and making sure we can get in."

"Oh, they'll let us in," Jace said confidently. "They were included in our latest upgrades, and as Stefan's chosen heir, my face will get us in. They'll have no choice."

Ritter shook his head. "I hate to be the negative voice here, but there's too much risk using unfamiliar tech. We should continue with our original plan while the cargo ship is still en route to wherever it's going."

Irwin Stafford, who helped run the prison facility, thumbed over his shoulder at the room beyond the glass where Stefan still awaited a full contingent of guards to return him to his cell. "That old crocodile is not to be trusted, so I have to agree with Ritter." His Australian accent was prominent, and his deeply tanned, ruddy skin made it almost impossible to tell his age under his mass of thick blond hair—but I knew he was around three or four centuries. "We may make up the two hours with their boat, or waste more time getting it."

I fought disappointment, though I also agreed. All we had done by coming here was lose precious time.

An urgent pounding at the door had Irwin diving toward it. Yanking it open, he revealed a prison guard standing with Charles, who we'd left at the plane with Marco to watch Brenna. The big man's brown hair was matted with blood, and his pale face flushed with red. Spatters of blood dotted his khaki shirt.

"Are you okay?" Ava said.

"Yes, but she's gone." His voice was tense, his face expressionless. "I was talking with the airstrip owner when she jumped me. She somehow managed to get loose."

"Impossible," Ava said. "Even if she'd been able to get past the gag to use her ability, I have the only key to free her."

He held up a blood-soaked duffel bag. "She had help." He reached in and pulled out a woman's hand, holding it by the tip of a finger. "But obviously not enough time to break the cuffs."

Ava eyed the hand—Brenna's hand—still dripping blood. "Well, that's one way to do it. Those cuffs are impossible to get off without a key."

"She must have an internal tracer," Ritter said. "And an ally who followed it."

"We scanned her," Stella protested. "Thoroughly."

Dimitri stood from the chair where he'd been sitting. "We've heard time and again that they have advanced tech."

"They also zapped Marco with something." Charles dropped the hand back into the bag. "Made all his muscles go weak for a couple minutes. That was after she hit me on the head. But he recovered quickly, and he's tracking them now. They headed deeper into the rainforest instead of back to civilization. He'll check in on the sat phone when he has news. The only good thing is that we'd already transferred the others to the prison since she was the only one going with us."

"This changes everything," Ritter said. "Brenna knew we were heading to intercept the cargo ship. If Marco doesn't catch up to her, she may have time to report us to her leaders. We need to move fast to get on the ship and hope the captain makes the drop to the Avowed before she contacts Sinalta."

Irwin scratched at his bushy hair. "Maybe . . . if the Emporium has someone in Acapulco who can drive the Avowed ship, and if it's as fast as Stefan says, then it should be able to meet us in Puerto Arista—and I can get us there in just over two hours. I'll have to tell the chopper to meet us at another runway instead of the current one, but it's really not that different from our original plan, except you'll only be taking the chopper to the bay instead of out to sea. If things fail, you won't be hours but only minutes later than the original schedule. And if it works, well, you'll be ahead."

"Maybe even far ahead," Jace added. "Depending on the fueling situation of the Avowed ship. Because the chopper may or may not get us close to the drop point before we need to rendezvous with a refueling ship."

Refueling issues had been one of the challenges we were hoping not to face, but the longer the cargo boat continued heading out to open sea, the more likely that became. That or dropping onto the moving ship itself.

"Agreed," Ava said. "Jace, get on the phone and find us that Sinaltan craft and get it to Puerto Arista. Bribe, threaten, or do whatever you have to. Irwin, we'll leave you to provide backup for Marco. Stella will help you monitor the case. And Chris will need the coordinates of the new runway. Hurry, the clock is ticking."

"Will do." Irwin's grin made it clear he anticipated the challenge of tracking Brenna. I wasn't surprised. Before he faked his death and was sent to hide out here, he'd been famous for wrestling alligators in Australia.

Minutes later, as Irwin drove us to the plane in his Jeep, hurtling over washboards and exposed roots on the dirt road with undisguised joy, I couldn't help wondering if he had contacted his wife and children after the announcement to tell them he was alive. If so, would they ever forgive his lie?

Chapter 13

"**B**RENNA MIGHT NOT CONTACT THE SINALTANS," JACE SAID AS WE traded our plane for a helicopter less than an hour and a half later. "She might just disappear, especially now that she knows Stefan isn't in control of the Emporium, and she no longer has a free pass."

"I'm more worried about whoever freed Brenna," I said. "Because there wasn't another plane, which means that whoever freed her either has more technology we don't know about, or they were already here. And how many more are among us?"

I was also worried about Marco, with his olive skin, square chin, and dark eyes that were always moving. He'd fit right in here, with his Hispanic ancestry, but I didn't know if he even spoke the language. And his going after Brenna and her companion alone made me furious. Months before, we'd lost one of our mortal security guards, and I didn't want to lose another one for any reason.

Across from me on the forward-facing chopper seat,

Ritter's knees clamped both of mine between his, the action soothing me. Despite the fact that it sometimes irritated me to have him sensing my emotions for a change, our mate link was also comforting.

At the tiny seaside community of Puerto Arista, a few of the native children gathered to watch as our helicopter landed on the rocky beach, east of the sandbar. They gaped even more enthusiastically as a small ocean craft as large as our corporate jet and with a similar aerodynamic shape emerged from the water, floating fewer than twenty feet out.

A man climbed from a hatch on the deck and was soon speeding toward us in an inflatable raft with an onboard motor. He jumped out as he hit the sand and thrust a tablet toward Jace, speaking in heavily accented English.

"I will need your handprint." By the feel of him, he was Unbounded, but he was less tense than most of those I'd met in the states. He was also definitely a native with his darkly tanned skin, black hair, and accent. Since I couldn't speak Spanish at all, he was one up on me.

"Of course." With barely a grimace, Jace planted his hand on the small device, which registered a happy little beep.

"Okay, then." The man handed him the tablet. "This has a rundown of basic maneuvers. She's all yours. Unless you need anything else?"

"You said the craft has its own fuel source?" Ritter said. "Can you explain?"

"We call it the submersible," the man said. "Because it's similar to our subs, only a lot smaller than those in the navy. It has a backup nuclear fuel source, but the primary system is hydrogen derived from seawater. Never seen anything like it." He chuckled. "If the government knew we'd solved all the problems they're having with their similar process, they would confiscate it for sure. You can go anywhere in the world on this ship, even all the way to Antarctica."

Jace laughed a little too loudly. "No need for that."

"Right. Anyway, this raft deflates here." The man pointed to a box on the inflatable's stern. "A simple pull and then hook up to a deflation tube inside the hatch of the submersible. That's where it stores too. You can't miss it." His eyes ran over us. "You sure you don't need another hand?"

His mind shield was a flimsy thing, and I could see he was worried about what he thought of as his baby, and he was also very much in the dark about the Sinaltans. He believed Stefan and the Emporium had invented the submersible.

Ava looked at Ritter, indicating that as ops leader, the call was his. Ritter appeared tempted to accept the man's offer, and I knew why. We were short-handed without Marco, but there were worse potential problems having someone along that we couldn't fully trust. In the end, Ritter shook his head. "We're good."

"Thanks, though." Jace shook the man's hand and smiled to soften the abruptness of Ritter's refusal. Jace pointed at the helicopter, surrounded by gawking children. "Our pilot will be flying you back."

"Okay." The Unbounded gazed at each of us before adding, "Sorry to ask, but is Triad Carrington okay? Because this boat was supposed to be a secret."

"My father has no secrets from me," Jace assured him. "We'll have it back before you know it."

He didn't quite believe us, but with a nod, he started toward the helicopter and didn't look back.

We began throwing our gear into the inflatable raft, including the weapons we'd gotten past customs in the concealed hatches of our plane. When we reached the submersible, Ritter boarded first to give us the all-clear, then helped the others load the gear and deflate the rubber boat while I studied the tablet. With only a couple of attempts, I figured out how to broadcast it to Stella, whose face appeared on the screen.

Jace dropped down from the hatch into the control room and began looking around. "Man, what a letdown. Here I thought it would look different from our subs."

"You've been on a sub?" Chris went to the control panel and began poking around. "I didn't know Army got to ride on subs."

Jace shrugged. "It was a recruiting tour, is all. Before I Changed, I was thinking about switching to Navy."

Chris pulled up a screen on the wall of the submersible, and an image of the ocean around us appeared. "This does feel similar to a plane, but it's going to take a minute to experiment."

"I'm going through the database now," Stella said from the tablet. "Can you plug in the drive I gave you? It would be faster if I could just see the raw data."

We looked around. "Uh, there doesn't seem to be anything compatible."

"Well, you're going to have to hook me up the old fashion way then," Stella said. "But let me warn you right now that if you go down beyond a certain depth, we could lose contact."

"What about the cargo ship?" Ritter asked. "Any change?"

"It's still moving," she said. "But their angle has shifted south again. I suspect they've received new instructions."

"Because of Brenna?" I asked.

"No way of saying, but Marco and the others are still tailing her. We know nothing about how the Avowed communicate. Depending on their relays, they may need to wait until their ship rises to a certain depth—that's my hope. Things could get hot once their ship begins to surface."

"Which it won't do before they get close to the cargo boat," Ritter said. "So for now, let's not waste time second-guessing Brenna's plans. We need to get this submersible going in the right direction."

"Chris can put in the coordinates I've sent," Stella said. "That's easy enough, but someone needs to get me connected. That way I can check out the rest of its capabilities. And I want to download all the information and specs." Her eagerness was clear.

Chris began tapping at the controls labeled by odd symbols. "Okay, I think that's it. It really isn't all that hard," he said as numbers appeared on a lower screen embedded into the control panel itself.

The next second a loud beeping filled the control room, and both screens flashed. "Warning," a pleasant female voice said in English with an accent I couldn't identify. "Hatch must be closed before movement."

The lower screen now showed an image of a ship and an arrow pointing downward. "Even if it's not as intuitive as Stefan's thoughts indicated," I said, "that's pretty clear."

A clink above us sounded, and the noise stopped. "Done," Ritter called before half jumping, half sliding down the short flight of hatch stairs. The ship began moving.

The control room was crowded now, with all six of us standing, so I left Ritter, who was opening a panel to connect the tablet, and went to explore the rest of the ship. There wasn't much more to see except small crew quarters with five bunks, an even smaller cafeteria, a minuscule bathroom, a machine room, and an engine room, the latter two larger than the rest combined. All the floor space in the crew quarters was taken by our bags, and I started stacking them in the empty lockers and stuffing them onto one of the narrow bunks.

"Easy," Jace said, taking a heavy duffel of assault rifles from my hands.

"I'm pregnant, not an invalid," I retorted.

"Pregnant?" a voice said from behind. "Really?"

I turned in the confined space to see Chris standing behind me. "Sorry," I said. "There hasn't been time for a proper announcement."

He hugged me, smelling of cologne that he must have put on for Stella's benefit. "That's fantastic. Our kids will grow up together."

I grinned. "I'm pretty happy about that, I admit."

"I didn't think I would ever have any more children," Chris added. "Until I fell for Stella. She wants a lot of them, and I guess we have time."

She had time, and he . . . well, I wasn't going to think about that.

Chris gave me a final squeeze that stole my breath away. "At least now I know what that psychopath Stefan was going on about at the prison. And don't hate me, but shouldn't you have stayed back with Stella?"

"Stella's a technopath," I said. "We have different skills. I can make a difference here." I didn't add that I would come back after a death, which he couldn't. But he had the same training as the rest of us and knew the dangers. "Let's rescue these kids and take care of the Sinaltans. After that, I'll go back to the island and get sunburned too."

Chris laughed. "As if. Anyway, I came to let you know that we're going under now. Want to come watch?"

The control cabin had only five seats, which matched the number of bunks and either meant the submersible was intended for five people or ten people on rotating shifts. I guessed it was the former since Stella hadn't found weaponry of any kind.

"I'm taking the ship down now," Chris said. "If we lose you, we'll rise until we connect again." He glanced at the tablet that Ritter had hardwired to the controls.

"Roger that," Stella said distantly. "As long as you don't go deeper than I told you, we should be okay. And it'll be deep enough to hide a ship of this size unless someone is particularly looking for it."

Which we knew could be the case with Brenna running loose.

The ship began moving faster, now tilting downward. The larger wall monitor flipped between views of each side, showing us the water, which changed color as we dived. It was fascinating, and even though I knew I couldn't permanently drown, I felt unsettled.

"My guess is that this is a private craft," Stella said from the tablet. "Maybe used to travel between their cities. The tech, though? I know why Stefan wanted it. If we can reverse engineer it, it will bring a fortune from the military alone."

"I bet he intended to keep it for himself," I said. "He hasn't had it long, but if he built an army of these things and weaponized them . . ." I let the sentence trail off, leaving them to their own imaginations. Stefan had almost put a Triad member in the White House, and a sizeable number of congressmen were also involved.

"I think a thorough investigation of the facility in Acapulco is next on my list," Jace said.

Ava nodded. "Indeed." She sank into a chair. "Just when I think our job is done." Waves of apprehension rolled from her.

What is it? I asked, pushing the thoughts in her direction.

She felt my attention and reached back. *These people are potentially more dangerous than the Emporium ever was. Yet why do they need Stefan? They have to be using him just as they are being used.*

We both knew it was dangerous to play with fire.

AS WE'D BEEN WARNED, THE SUBMERSIBLE WAS FAST, AND WE CAUGHT up with the cargo boat near midnight, easing into a position far under them where Stella calculated it would be impossible for them to detect us. She'd ingested volumes of digital data within that time, and she appeared confident enough for all of us. Chris made each change in course with ease that spoke of his long practice in the air.

Meanwhile, Brenna and her accomplice were still on the loose, which was bad for us, but we had forty-nine reasons on board the cargo ship for why we couldn't back down.

For the next five hours, we took turns resting in the bunks or sitting in the chairs. We didn't break into our rations as the submersible had a system that brought in ocean matter so we could absorb nutrients. The smell of the sea was strong, though, and the changes in direction made me nauseated. Seeing my difficulty, Dimitri made a habit of standing close to me, his hand on my shoulder. We weren't fooling Ritter, though, and I knew a time would soon come when he'd order me to stay behind.

I didn't know what I'd do then. Torn was only the beginning of how I felt.

I was dozing in a lower bunk around one o'clock early Tuesday morning when Ritter pushed in beside me, wrapping his arms around me in the too-tight space and pulling me against his chest. I could feel the pounding of his heart against my back as he nuzzled my neck. All worries fled. This was what we were fighting for. For love, for family, for freedom—for everyone in the world.

A soft warning bell chimed, and the ship spoke in a female voice, first in a language I didn't recognize and then in English and various other languages. "Target craft is slowing and will soon stop. No collision course detected. Do you wish to continue?"

"Looks like they reached their coordinates," Ritter said, rolling from our cramped bed. He pulled me from the bunk and put me on my feet in a way that was both possessive and sweet. I rolled my eyes at him, but he saw my smile. His head came down in a long, lingering kiss, tasting of both desire and anticipation about the coming op. I felt exactly the same. Finally, we were doing something.

Jace was suiting up as we entered the control room, checking his weapons and pulling a dark hood over his blond hair. He was using our latest version of a bodysuit made of metamaterials that would bend light around them so he would seem almost invisible. The darkness would do the rest. I'd brought a cape made of the same metamaterials, since I still wanted the added protection of Stella's specially made body armor, which didn't have that capability.

"Give me five more minutes, and we'll be locked to the starboard side of their hull," Chris said. "With how small and deep we are, there's no way they'll see us coming. I doubt they'll notice once we surface. But it's a long way up the hull of their ship. Climbing will be difficult, even with them stationary."

"Jace and I will go first," Ritter said. "We'll throw down the ladder." His gaze shifted to Chris. "You're the last up. If you spot the Sinaltans, let us know. Everyone check coms."

Outside on the narrow deck of the submersible, the wind was blowing and the boats rocked, but our smaller boat was magnetically clamped to the side of the freighter, and they rocked in sync as if part of each other. The sharp smell of seawater filled my lungs.

Balancing on the far edge of the submersible where he could barely see past the curve of the cargo boat to the railing, Ritter shot a grappling hook with a launcher, securing it on the first try. He and Jace began climbing rapidly, their progress steady and sure despite the rocking while the rest of us covered them with our rifles. Above the railing, barely illuminated by the moonlight, not a soul was in sight, only a massive stack of shipping crates like a huge Jenga puzzle made of different colors.

The ladder rolled down ten minutes later, soundlessly hitting the hull on the way down, or at least it seemed so to me.

"You next," Ava said.

It looked terribly far, at least forty feet, so I began channeling Jace's ability. Combat Unbounded were good at physical things, and I needed that extra boost because climbing even on the ladder was a challenge for me. After long hours on rooftops, I'd conquered my fear of heights—mostly—but swaying and banging against the side of a ship was a lot different than standing on the edge of a roof. I'd chosen Jace to channel because I knew he'd be less likely to worry about me, and Ritter was already watching me too closely.

The baby was well protected in Stella's special body armor, which I bet could take a bullet without breaking my ribs. She'd worn it to Emporium headquarters in New York after the takeover, just in case. It had been invented to keep its shape, even under fire—the latest Emporium technology. The downside was that the armor was heavier and bulkier, which made it harder for me to climb the swaying rope ladder.

Though now that I was channeling Jace, I scoffed at such a minor inconvenience. I knew exactly where to place my hands and where not to place my feet, and I made it up to the top only a little bit out of breath.

Ava was next, then Dimitri followed by Charles. I was already fanning out with Jace before Chris started his climb. Our assignment was the ship's control room and its occupants while the others cleaned up the crew. From the data we'd stolen from the shipping company, we knew there were eighteen employees on the boat, including the captain, or the master, as he was called. Eighteen against seven of us seemed rather unfair—on their part. Unless we weren't fast enough to take over the ship before the Sinaltans showed up.

On our way to the control room, Jace and I were to sedate anyone we came in contact with before reaching our goal. The company didn't have permits for weapons in Mexican or international waters, but someone on board could still have them and be a danger to us.

Life form ahead, I warned Jace as we neared our target.

"Hey, is someone there?" came a voice with an accent I didn't recognize.

I stood my ground while Jace stayed in the deep shadows of the container behind me, his metamaterial hood drawn over his face.

"I'll get him," Jace muttered and disappeared into the darkness.

I pushed back the folds of my cloak so the sailor's eyes wouldn't make him think I was some kind of a bodiless ghost. I waved to the sailor in the dim lights as he approached. He was a thin, swarthy, wiry man with straight black hair that fell into his dark eyes.

"I'm a stowaway. I need to parley with the captain." I lifted my hands to show I was unarmed. My tranq gun was within easy reach in my long sleeve, but I wouldn't need it, not this close.

He stared at me while I gave a little shrug. "You think this is some kind of movie?" he demanded. "The captain will throw you overboard."

"I hope not. I don't know how to swim."

"Maybe I save him the problem." He leered at me. "Unless you got something for me."

I didn't know if he referred to sexual favors or money, but I could see from his thoughts that he had no intention of chucking me overboard. He was, however, definitely admiring my curves despite the bulky protective armor—or at least trying to in the dim light.

"What's that you're wearing anyway?" He reached toward me, and I stepped out of reach so fast he blinked. A breeze chose that moment to blow the cloak back around me, and he stared at only darkness where the dim light should be reflecting off my side but left a pit of blackness instead.

He raised his forefingers to form a cross as a barrier between us. "What are you? *Mohini*?" He clamped his hands over his ears. The word wasn't familiar, but I understood because his stream of thoughts revealed the image of a magical, naked woman who lured sailors to a watery death with a mere song.

Jace appeared behind the sailor, one hand raised in question. Should he send the man into la-la land?

I preferred the idea of an introduction. "Take me to your captain, or I'll sink the boat and all the cargo," I said, giving the man a smile that showed all my teeth. My scary smile, as Jace would say.

"Okay, okay." The sailor stepped back, nearly into Jace, so focused on me that he didn't think to turn around. "But he has a gun. He has shot pirates before."

"But not Mohini? Good to know."

The man turned, looking ill, and motioned to me. He didn't see Jace, who had silently scaled up several shipping containers and now hovered overhead like a spider on a web. I knew he'd used one of Cort's inventions for the climb, and a flash of sadness followed the realization. Even in death, Cort was still an integral part of our team.

Leaving Jace to trail us and tell the others about the captain and his gun, I followed the uneasy sailor through narrow passageways until we came to the control room, which was right where the schematics said it would be.

He opened the door without knocking. "Permission to enter, Master Smith," he said before crossing the threshold. "I captured a stowaway."

Captured? I guessed the seaman was angling for a promotion.

"Bring him in," the master growled.

"Uh, her." The seaman cast another nervous glance in my direction and motioned me inside. He shrank back as I stepped past him, making sure my cape was again trailing behind me. Only a faint scuffle behind the closing door told me Jace was taking care of business.

The captain reached for the gun at his waist, but when he saw I was a woman, he paused. The light was bright in the control room compared to out on the deck, but my eyes, with Jace's ability, were already adjusting.

"Who are you?" he demanded.

I made a show of studying both him and the sailor who was seated at a control panel further into the room, likely the first mate. Both were tall, burly men in their fifties, the master with a full head of short-cropped hair while the mate had a receding hairline and long blond hair in a ponytail.

"Your sailor called me a Mohini," I said finally.

Master Smith made a show of examining me from the tips of my black boots to the tight knot in my hair—and snorted. "You are no mythical siren. What do you want here, and how did you get on my ship?"

"No need to be so brusque," I said. "You might hurt a girl's feelings." When he had nothing to say to that, I added, "I came in a specialized submarine, and I'm interested in cargo container five-eight-seven-three-nine-one."

That made him draw his gun and growl, "I kill pirates."

I saw in his mind that he had indeed done so four years ago, and on this same run, but it had been in self-defense, and he'd never reported it. Though he told himself the scumbag deserved it, visions of the man bleeding out on his deck still haunted his dreams.

"We may be in international waters now, but we are protected by maritime law," he continued.

"Right, which prohibits human trafficking and weapons. Unless under a special permit. Do you have a special permit? For the gun, I mean, because we both know there is no permit available for human trafficking." I drew on my metamaterial cloak for emphasis, giving the full view of its properties. The tech wasn't perfect, but the way it bent light around me would give my body the appearance of near invisibility. Because of the imperfections, they would be able to see my outline, and I hadn't put the hood on, so my face was visible, but the reek of technology should give them pause.

His face reddened. "Are you CIA?"

"You won't find me in any official database." Which was true, seeing as I was dead.

He took a step back. "We aren't traffickers, not in humans or weapons. Or in drugs, if that's your next accusation."

I arched a brow. "So you know what's in container

five-eight-seven-three-nine-one? Then you won't mind showing it to me."

I could feel his panic and his heart rate speeding up, and I could also see the thoughts that told me there was at least one container they hadn't inspected because the Emporium had paid extra, just as the Sinaltans would soon pay him for making an at sea delivery. Which meant he didn't know there were people inside or wonder at their care after being locked inside a crate for days on end.

I fought anger as Ava's thoughts came to me through the careful mental opening I'd left for her and so I could channel Jace. *Erin, we've secured the ship, but the submersible just sent a ping to the tablet. Something else is out there. Deep but surfacing fast. We don't have much time.*

The container would have to wait.

"Your customers are coming," I said.

The first mate stared at his controls. "There's nothing on radar."

"They're deep yet," I told the master. "But it would be in your best interest to surrender your gun to me right now. Because I'm not here alone, and we aren't letting them take the forty-nine children you have locked up in that container."

The first mate gasped, and the two of them shared a look. It was the opening I needed. In six steps, I was at the master's side, my nine mil at his back. "Drop it," I said. "Or I *will* shoot."

Master Smith snorted and nodded at his first mate, who stood and pointed his own gun in my general direction. But his hand was shaking. Since my nearly invisible body was completely behind the master's, it seemed a silly move.

Uh, need a little help in here, I told Ava.

There was no immediate response, so it looked like I'd have

to do this the hard way. I raised my left hand, pointed it at the first mate, and fired my tranq pistol.

My shot missed as the boat rolled slightly, sending nausea through my stomach. Ritter was not going to be happy. He'd force me to practice on a balancing board for hours every day to make up for it. To be fair, though, we might need the man if the master didn't cooperate.

The door burst open at that moment, spilling Ritter and Jace—armed with assault rifles and looking bodiless—into the room. They fanned out and were in position before the others had crossed the threshold.

"Okay. We surrender." The master held his gun out to Ritter, not to me, the muzzle pointing downward. Maybe he felt better surrendering to a man. "You can have the cargo. You can have the whole damn ship. Just don't hurt anyone." He nodded at the first mate to give Jace his weapon.

"You've already hurt someone," I retorted. Did the children even have necessities in their container? And how hot did those containers get?

Chris went to the communications panel, comparing it to the tablet in his hand. To the master, he said, "What time are they supposed to contact you?"

He shrugged. "Any time. I'm to wait here until they show up. That's how it works. Sometimes it's an hour. Sometimes it's a whole day."

"How did you know to come here?" Dimitri asked.

"A note was delivered when we refueled in Mexico."

"A physical note?"

"Yes."

Dimitri and Ava exchanged a glance. "We know they have operatives on land," she said.

Ritter pulled out some zip cuffs and secured the master. "They'll contact you before they board?"

"Yeah. And we'll have to show them where the containers are. They bring the equipment to do the actual moving themselves, but we'll need to unlock the containers and replace them with the ones they're bringing so we remain in balance. It's a lot trickier doing it at sea than at the dock. Impossible, I would have said, but they manage."

"How hot does it get inside those containers?" I asked, the idea still running through my mind.

Master Smith didn't answer, but his wide shoulders drooped. "There's one container we run electricity to, but it's not in our refrigeration section. It's their lightest one, so it's on top."

"Let me guess. It must be container five-eight-seven-three-nine-one."

"I don't know." Smith glanced at the mate, who was now cuffed and sitting several feet from the controls.

"I can che—" the first mate began when a transmission sounded in the room.

"Payload, Payload, Payload," said a voice. "This is Avowed Four. Are you ready for transfer? Over."

Chris glanced back at him. "What's the protocol?"

"Just answer. We're already on the channel they indicated. Say we're ready at their convenience. They'll tell you what they want you to do."

Chris pressed the mic button. "Good evening, Avowed Four. This is Payload. Ready at your convenience. What is your ETA? Over."

"ETA twenty minutes," came the voice again. A male voice with a slight British accent. "Is it all clear there? Any issues we should know about? Over."

"Only that we're going to send you back where you came from," Chris muttered half under his breath.

Ava looked sternly at him. "Not a word more," she said, glancing at the master and mate. "We don't want to have to scrub them." She meant scrub their memories, but the master and mate would probably take it otherwise, which might help them play nice.

Chris pressed the mic button again. "Everything is right as rain over here. We're standing by, awaiting your arrival. Over." Chris glanced at me and winked. We'd be waiting, all right.

"Tell them to rendezvous on the starboard side," the master said.

"No, don't!" I countered. "That will alert them. The containers are on the port side near the stern." The lie was obvious to me from the master's thoughts, even if Stella hadn't already pinpointed the location of the Emporium containers for us.

The master glared at me, but the mate, sending a nervous glance at Ava, said, "Even after they surface, it will take more time for them to move safely close. They'll call again when they're ready to move the containers. But it's just permission to board."

"Sit." Ritter pushed Master Smith roughly toward a chair. "Chris, you'll have to stay here until that transmission comes in. We'll make sure these two don't get in your way. In fact, we'll gag this one since he doesn't know how to speak the truth."

"My men will need to help release the containers," Master Smith protested. "They have to get them ready."

"Sorry," Ritter said. "None of them will be up for another two hours. They're all taking a nap. Well, those who were above deck. And you'd better hope no one else comes up, or they might get caught in the crossfire."

"Crossfire?" The master was aghast.

"Don't worry. We'll be on hand to help the Sinaltans." Ritter twirled a finger in the air, urging us on. "Let's go." Over his shoulder, he added to Chris, "Let us know when they contact us again." He tapped his earbud.

"Will do. Kick some Avowed butt for me."

Chapter 14

RITTER WALKED BY MY SIDE, HIS ARMS LOOSE AND HIS EYES SCANning the deck. The light was dim, and I wondered how the Avowed planned to transfer the cargo in such poor light, but maybe it wasn't that complicated. Ritter removed the top half of his metamaterial suit, which would now be unnecessary in the next phase of the plan. For now, I kept my cape snug around me.

"I really want to go check out that container." I felt anxious about the time that had passed since Kimber's disappearance. For the last few minutes, I'd been trying to sense where the life forms were, but either the container was blocked from mental scrutiny, which I wouldn't put past the Emporium or Sinaltans, or they were too far away. But I didn't think the cargo ship was that massive.

"You could go check it out while we deal with the Sinaltans," Ritter suggested—a little too casually.

"You think I don't know that you're trying to get me out of the way?"

Ritter glanced at me, the tiniest tick of a smile at one corner of his mouth. I knew what he was thinking, not from reading his thoughts but from the amusement coming through our link. He thought this was pregnancy-induced grouchiness. I ignored him because maybe he was right.

"There will be enough time to check on the captives after we secure the Avowed and their ship," he said. "They've done this exchange hundreds of times before, and we know they don't want them to arrive dead. Besides, if you're in the container, you might accidentally end up in the Sinaltan hold. Speaking of which, I have no idea how they plan to transfer the heaviest containers onto their ship first, which is what usually happens, but they must have some method of rotating them."

At times, he was such a pragmatist, except maybe where I was concerned. "We know they send someone with the pay-off for the crew, but we have no way of knowing how many will actually board."

He nodded. "If they don't know we're here, the initial fight should be over quickly. And we may be able to entice more into our trap, but either way, we'll need to be ready to board their craft. It could be bad."

Having dealt with Emporium hit teams, we both knew how bad it might get. Mari was currently paying the price for our last encounter with these Avowed monsters.

Ritter, Dimitri, and Charles changed into work overalls topped with florescent lime-green safety jackets we'd brought along for the purpose, but only big Charles with the dark makeup he'd rubbed into his pale skin managed to look the part. Ritter radiated the air of a hardened black ops soldier rather than a sailor in his getup. In fact, with their flawless skin and Unbounded appeal, neither he nor Dimitri could really pass as a sun-worn seaman, but with caps pulled low over their eyes, it would fool the Avowed long enough. Unless they had a sensing Unbounded among them. Brenna had indicated that the gift of sensing was rare in Sinalta, and those who remained weren't powerful. We were banking on this being the truth, but we really didn't know for sure.

Ava, Jace, and I melted into the surrounding darkness, pulling up our metamaterial hoods and readying our weapons—real ones this time, not tranqs. I moved into position, close to the railing. I'd be letting everyone know if those boarding were Unbounded—or Avowed, rather. It was hard to keep the names separate when they meant the same thing. My gut was tight with anticipation at the coming battle.

Thirty minutes ticked by. Finally, Chris said in my ear. "Something surfacing off the port. It's bigger than the submersible by a lot but still small compared to this ship. Gotta be them."

The swell was further out than I expected, but even so, the cargo ship rocked with the incoming waves created as the ship emerged from the water, glistening darkly under the light of the moon. Finally, it stopped rising, looking much like our submersible but far, far larger. As we watched, people began scurrying around its deck. Huge holes opened, and a circular tube slid out, reaching into the air, telescoping higher and higher.

"Awesome," Jace said in my earbuds. "Guess that's their version of a crane. Wonder where they plan to—" He cut off as a third of the deck opened up, each side folding like a child's paper fan. "Never mind. Looks like they *have* done this a time or two."

His words were meant as a joke, but anger burned inside me. All the displaced children they'd taken, all the "embryos" they'd stolen from their families. What were those children doing now? Were the street children better off, or were their lives even shorter and harder? After meeting Brenna, I was betting on the latter.

The ship that had been slowly and steadily approaching us during all the activity now stopped. The cargo ship was much taller, so I could see deep inside the opened hold of the Avowed ship, which appeared to be half full of containers. *The exchange shipment,* I thought.

A slight crackle in my earbuds sounded before Chris came back on the line. "They're hailing us," he said. "They're requesting two to board. And that means you need to lower the ladder they have there on the port side."

"Only two? That should be easy enough." Ritter sounded almost disappointed.

"They apparently have a list of container numbers and weights and a way to shuffle them," Chris continued. "But get this, they want container five-eight-seven-three-nine-one first. And the first mate here has verified for us that it's the top container."

"Well, they're going to have to go through us to get it." Ritter's response was distracted, and I could see why. The Sinaltan ship began lowering a rubber boat that resembled the one we used to get to the submersible, but Ritter hadn't yet started on the heavy-duty steel and cable ladder. Together, he and Dimitri opened a panel in the railing and sent it clanging loudly downward.

We all held our breaths as rubber boat approached with three figures inside. Finally, two began climbing the ladder. Both were men, and their surface emotions exuded tight concern. Was that for the transfer or because Brenna had managed to warn them, and if she had, why were they here?

"Blocking," I said. "And strongly. Definitely Unbounded."

"Can you get in?" Ritter asked.

"Eventually." I pulled out my mental machete and began hammering. That was when I noticed the dull glow of other life forms in the boat, hidden under a tarp. As the first two reached the top and began talking with Ritter, three others started climbing up a rope that the third person had attached to the railing with a grappling hook. Even as I watched, he shot another grappling hook, and three more people under the tarp began to ascend.

"We've been made," I said. "Got at least a half dozen more coming up in two different spots. All Unbounded."

"I see 'em," Jace said. "I'll cover the right group. You got the other, Erin?"

Ava stepped out of the shadow of a container. "We do," she answered for me.

"Dimitri, to Jace!" Ritter barked as he slammed his fist at an opponent's face. The man dodged, and the two began fighting in earnest.

Ava jumped to the side and fired down at the figures coming up near us. With a grunt, one fell into the water.

It's too easy, I thought.

"Watch your backs," Ritter said. "If it were me, I would send another boat to the other side of the ship. Make sure to get them before they speak. We have no idea how many might be hypnopaths."

"I'll head starboard," Charles volunteered.

Ritter's reply was strained. "Angle past the control room. If they try to take it, Chris will need back up."

"I'll get into a better position," Chris said.

I left Ava to deal with the remaining two on the ladder, a disadvantage fight they couldn't win. Channeling Jace's speed, I sprinted down the deck along the last line of containers, making sure my hood and cape were secure. Sure enough, I spied two figures coming fast in my direction.

"Two more, starboard near the stern," I reported.

Jace crowed triumphantly. "Got one. That belly flop's going to hurt. Dimitri's got the rest here. I'm going starboard."

I knelt and fired, taking one person in the chest. He flew backward, slamming into some equipment. He was still moving but barely. Lucky happenstance because they were obviously wearing body armor.

I was aiming for the second when a pistol touched my neck. "Put it down," came a man's voice. The command was overwhelming. Hypnosuggestion. His mental shield was so tight that he barely registered on my senses, which explained the lack of warning.

I pushed back against the command, tightening my shields. *Ugh, how many hypnopaths do they have?* I wondered. The others were prepared and resistant, but if we weren't fast enough, even one strong hypnopath could be our destruction.

I tried breaking through his shield, but it would take time, so I slumped and started to lower my weapon as if obeying.

"Thought you were too invisible for me to see," the man said with a heavy accent, "but we also have inventions. Now give it to me." This last was said with the power of his gift.

So I did.

Turning quickly, I fired twice at his chest at close range, ducking as shots came from the man across the ship. The Sinaltan's bullets went wide, clinging harmlessly against the side of the container. I returned fire, but the man had disappeared.

The hypnopath fell, trying desperately to raise his weapon. I snatched it from his hands. He was helpless now. In his place, Ritter or Jace would have managed to fight past the pain and calculate exactly where they'd have to hit me in order to get away. This man had no such ability.

"Stop," he ordered. The command was weak this time.

For an answer, I rolled him over and cuffed his hands tightly. He moaned. That was the broken ribs talking, but at least his armor had protected him from a temporary death.

The other man had disappeared, and I faded into the shadows, looking for him. "Two down," I reported. "One got away."

"Erin!" Jace said in gargled response, his voice strained.

Strengthening our link, I saw he was facing a woman who was grinning at him as she pointed her gun at his chest. "That's right," she said. "Drop it. No use in fighting me."

Oh, yeah? I said so Jace would hear me. Pushing out, I strengthened Jace's shield.

It's not working, Jace said after a moment, panicked. *I got rid of her weapon, but now I can't even use mine against her.*

Fear drove me to action, and I slammed my machete against the woman's mental barrier. It didn't seem as strong as the shield of the man I'd just dropped and nowhere near the strength of Brenna's. Plus the woman was distracted, which gave me an advantage. Another slam. There, I was through!

I channeled her ability and told Jace silently. *Do not drop the gun. Punch her out!* Jace laughed as he obeyed.

The slightest wisp of sound had me tumbling to the side seconds before a bullet hit the container behind me. I sent off a shot of my own and then sprinted to another hiding spot behind more equipment.

Abruptly, Jace's combat ability warned me of danger, but I turned too late. The Avowed was to my right. Too close. Would Stella's gear protect the baby? Regret washed through me, bigger than the cargo boat and far more weighty.

He fired.

The bullet went wide at the last moment, and, unthinkably, the man collapsed. Something—no, someone—was behind him. Relief rushed over me.

"Dimitri?" I called. The figure was too far away to see clearly in the dark, but the person was definitely Unbounded and blocking. It wasn't Jace or Ava because I was connected to them, and it wasn't Ritter because I'd know him blindfolded.

In the next instant, the figure was gone, and I was alone with three unconscious Sinaltans. I secured the last and first ones with cuffs before making my way back to the port side of the ship, scanning the shadows for more attackers.

Sounds of hand-to-hand combat came to me before I reached the place where I'd last seen Ritter. He was there, alone, fighting four Avowed who must have boarded from another direction. He'd managed to disarm them but was holding back, so I knew he intended to capture and not kill them, even temporarily. My guess was that he'd identified someone in charge, someone he wanted to question.

I pulled my sticks out from the pouch on my back and waded into the melee, knocking one man down with a blow to the back of his head as I hurtled past him. I brought my sticks up again, this time facing a husky woman with short-cropped blond hair. She ducked under my first blow, sweeping up a pipe from a pile of junk. The movement was fast.

Combat Unbounded, I thought.

I slammed my stick into her pipe, the clash reverberating up my arm. She kicked out at my knee, and I whipped my other stick down at her ankle, hearing a satisfying crunch before following with a twisting blow at her pipe that made it go flying. She dived into a roll—and came up against Ritter, who had dispatched his own opponents.

He pointed a ballistic knife at her. "Your companions have already surrendered. Do you wish to remain conscious or be dead? Your choice."

Nodding sharply, she raised her hands and let him cuff her, grimacing as he attached them to her ankles as well—something he hadn't done with the others who didn't have her speed.

Ritter's eyes flicked over me as if reassuring himself that I was okay. Something in him eased.

As we lined up our captives on the deck, Jace appeared, carrying the woman hypnopath. "Got two more back there. But it'll be a while before they wake. Oh, you have a few that are conscious. I figured Dimitri might wake this one." He lowered her next to the others.

Ritter pointed at a strong-looking blond man with blood running down the back of his head—the guy I'd hit. "No using your ability," Ritter warned him, pointing the ballistic knife at his heart. "I've had enough of that."

"Who are you?" the man demanded, not quite a hypnosuggestion but almost. His eyes were so brightly blue they were startling.

Ritter's jaw worked. "A better question is why you came on board this ship with the intent of doing us harm. Are you pirates?" Ritter's glance at me was serious, but I sensed the amusement underneath.

"Of course not," the man said. "We had a report that Renegades were trying to subvert our cargo." He spoke in English with that odd lilt that had become familiar after talking to the other Avowed.

"No, not Renegades." Jace squared his shoulders and threw back his hood. "I'm Jace Carrington, son of Stefan Carrington, leader of the Emporium Triad."

The man stared, shaking his head. "That's not what we were told."

"You were lied to then."

"We wouldn't betray the Emporium," the man insisted. "They are our allies."

"Well, see, that's part of why we're here," Jace said. "I've just come from a meeting with my father. There has been a change of direction in the Triad. From here on out, I'm over all future negotiations. And things will change."

The man considered the words, glancing down at his cuffed hands and then back to Ritter's face. "Look, I think we got off on the wrong waterway. My name is Leyton Vasile, and I'm in charge of delivering the goods we agreed upon and transporting those you've sent to Sinalta. That's all I'm over."

"Yet you decided to send armed soldiers after us." Jace folded his arms and stared at Leyton until the man looked away. It was a move so like Stefan Carrington and so unlike my little brother that my stomach lurched.

"We thought you were Renegades," Leyton protested. "It is what we were told by our operative."

"And what is the name of this operative?" Ritter clenched and unclenched his fists as if in emphasis. Sensations of pain came from his surface thoughts, originating in his fist and side. He'd paid a price to capture and keep these Sinaltans conscious.

"Brenna Dabney," Leyton said. "That is the name she currently uses. She reported to our leaders that Emporium enemies would be on board this cargo ship, and they ordered me to retake the ship so we could obtain our cargo."

"Did they now?" Ritter glanced at me with an obvious plea to do some digging. I'd been trying. The man's shield was as strong as Brenna's, and my energy was flagging. So instead of wasting more of it, I concentrated on absorbing to boost my strength. The slight taste of salt and fish came to my tongue.

Dimitri approached, carrying an unconscious man in his hefty grip. Laying him down gently behind the others, he began binding a wound in the man's arm.

Silence fell over us, and then Ava stepped from the shadows where she been observing for the past few minutes. "We'll need to talk directly with your leaders. As Jace already told you, there will be changes. As of this moment, human cargo will no longer be a part of our shipments."

"Oh." Surprised registered on Leyton's pale face. "I'm sure that will be of interest to our leaders, and they'll want to discuss it. But . . . does that mean you have a continent for us? That we can finally surface?" He glanced at his three conscious companions, who stared back with guarded hopefulness.

"We'll definitely continue working on that." Ava inclined her head. "But as I said, we'll need to chat with your leaders."

"I'll need to return to my craft to raise them on the com." Leyton hesitated before adding, "But do you think my men could continue with the transfer of the cargo? All but the um, embryos and workers, of course."

Ava considered a moment, looking first at Dimitri and then at Jace, who nodded. "Jace is in charge of that, and it looks like he's in agreement."

"I'll release you," Ritter added, "but we'll be keeping your weapons for the meantime."

"I understand." Leyton turned in alarm as Dimitri approached from behind, carrying a medical kit.

"I'm a doctor," Dimitri said, "and also a healer. Looks like your head is probably hurting a lot." He laid his hand on Leyton's head as he began mopping up the blood.

"It is," Leyton agreed. "But does that mean . . . you're an Avowed healer? You have the gift?"

"We call ourselves Unbounded, but yes," Dimitri said, releasing him to dig in his kit. "I'm sure I'm like the Avowed healers you are accustomed to."

Leyton shook his head, then winced. "We don't have any healers. Doctors, yes, and a few empaths—sensing, I think you call them. But no healers. That ability died out. So I'll be happy to see what you can do."

"First, I'm going to give you an injection of something that will speed up your own natural healing. This one will be mixed with a good old-fashioned pain killer. We won't need my ability for that." Dimitri chuckled. "I'm certain your physiology is the same as ours, though living underwater likely has had some significant effect on your body."

Leyton inclined his head. "I am grateful for your assistance."

"You do live under the water all the time, right?" Jace asked. "Or maybe as the master of a ship, you surface more than others."

"We used to come up often." Leyton let Dimitri tilt his head forward so he could administer the injection. "But all that changed when your people discovered radar. We have shielding for our cities, but we're too exposed when we come in ships. The mortals up here are a little . . . how do you say it? Uh, trigger happy." He smiled to show no ill will, but it was too strained for belief. Clearly, Leyton was upset at the changes in the world above that had cut off his freedoms—and perhaps that anger extended to all mortals in general.

"This will start working right away," Dimitri said. "You'll be feeling a lot better soon." His eyes rose to meet Ritter's. "I'd like to look at the others if you can gather everyone here."

"Then I'll need a complete count of those in your team," Ritter said pointedly to Leyton.

"There's twenty of us who came on board." Leyton's eyes swept the deck as if searching for them. "Plus, the mate who brought us over."

"Six went into the water." Ava walked to the railing and looked over. "Looks like your sailor has found most of them."

"I think you reset some of them," Leyton said without emotion.

"Reset?" I asked. "You mean temporarily killed."

"They're not dead," he said. "We do not travel with mortals."

"Unless they're in a container," I shot. I didn't like the man, and I wasn't for a moment repentant for having hit him.

"I'll have to go down to treat them," Dimitri said, giving me a steady gaze. "But let's round up the others first."

"Charles and I have two over here," Chris said over the earbuds.

Jace chuckled. "Awesome. I'll come help move them."

It didn't take long to find the fallen, and as Dimitri worked on them, I turned on my mic that I'd switched off after the battle. "Chris," I said. "Give me directions to container five-eight-seven-three-nine-one. You said top, but which top? There are a lot of stacks."

"Only one problem," Chris said. "There's no way to bring them down and get them out, though apparently, there are enough berths below deck to house them until the ship gets back to land. Even trying to open the container is difficult if you don't have good access."

"We're not leaving them in there."

"Right. So the Sinaltans will have to take the container to their ship and let them out. We can have boats standing by to bring them back."

I glared at Leyton and the others, though I was too far in

the shadows for them to see me. "And we're going to trust that they'll give them back? You realize they just tried to kill us."

"Right. My feelings exactly. I've been pressing for another option, and I might have found one. Not perfect, but more under our control. The Sinaltans can move the container and a couple of others around, leaving a sort of stairway. It's too far for kids to jump, but the mate tells me they have ladders, and I think we can use them to bring them down one level at a time. Then the Sinaltans can put back the containers and take only the ones that belong to them."

"Better run it past Ava," I said, "but it sounds like the better option. I don't trust these people."

"Is that because they shot at us or because you saw something in their minds?"

"I've only gotten a glimpse at one of their minds," I confessed. "And she was focused on trying to control Jace. He'd disarmed her, but she used her voice to prevent him from capturing her. Their leader seems to have a really good shield. I need a little more time."

"You should take a swig of curequick."

I was tempted, but I still worried about the baby. "I can get through, but first I want to lay eyes on those children."

"Leave it to me. I'll tell them we want the ladders and communicate with the other ship—and clear it with Ava, of course. But it'll take time."

"Right, thanks." It was nice to have him working on the problem. Since my Change, I hadn't needed my big brother the way I once had. I could now do most things better and faster, and the fact that I had nearly two thousand years in front of me while he only had a single human lifespan put a wedge between us even if neither of us talked about it.

I turned off my earbud and started wondering if maybe there was another way into the container. I felt Ritter's presence before I turned.

"Come on," he said.

"Where are we going?" I was relieved for the distraction, even if the job he sent me to do meant I'd have to spend time with the Sinaltans.

"You'll see."

"Okay."

He was up to something, but the satisfaction he registered blotted out the pain he'd been experiencing earlier, though the blood staining his lime-green safety jacket was concerning.

Seeing my glance and interpreting it correctly, he pulled it off. "Bullet graze," he said. "I gave myself some curequick. I almost can't feel it."

"And your hand?"

He didn't look around before he dropped the duffel bag he carried, pushed me up against a container, and began kissing me and caressing my body, showing me exactly how healed his hand was.

"Okay," I growled as he pulled away. "I get the point. But where are we going?"

"We are going to see the stolen children."

"But Chris said we couldn't get into the container."

He laughed. "It's high, but the doors aren't blocked, so we can open it. I've done it a time or two before. Remind me to tell you about it." His hand dropped down to cup my belly. "We'll tell our son."

"Or daughter."

"Right."

Strange how often I forgot that Ritter had lived for almost

three centuries. Of course he'd traveled by cargo boat before and maybe even fought the Emporium on the high seas.

I reached up to give him a final, slow kiss. "Show me," I said.

He laughed and bent to pick up his duffel. "Get ready to do a little swinging."

Chapter 15

RITTER STARTED ACROSS THE DECK OF THE SHIP AS IF HE'D BEEN BORN on it. My internal compass was good, but since I'd cut my connection with Jace, I couldn't really gauge where we were heading, except that no life forms were nearby—or no unblocking life forms. I had to remember that some Avowed were particularly good at shields.

"Do you really think we can trust them?" I asked Ritter. "I mean, it all seems a bit . . . well, too easy."

He grinned catlike in the dim light. "They obviously don't know how to run an op, but I doubt they've had to do much subterfuge where they come from. Sounds like their ruling class has everything pretty much wrapped up tightly. But they seem amiable enough now that they know who we are. I think Master Leyton and his crew just want to come topside." A hint of sympathy ran through his words, and I understood why. The idea of being trapped under miles of ocean water, dependent upon technology for my survival, was something all my instincts said was a terrible idea.

"Their surface emotions do seem to indicate that, but maybe . . ." I shrugged. "They traffic in people. I don't trust that."

"Good point. Ava was asking them about that, and they said they needed workers. Apparently birth rates aren't high in Sinalta."

I frowned at that. "Strange. Unbounded here have to worry about getting pregnant when they wash their underwear together." In fact, the Unbounded gene's determination to replicate had left us with too many Unbounded descendants to keep an eye on. Ripe for people like the Avowed to prey upon. But at the same time, with so few of us actually undergoing the Change, reproducing often seemed the only way to keep the gene alive. Which reminded me about my failure.

"About the baby," I said, my steps faltering. "I should have been more careful about channeling Stella and controlling my nanites. If we'd waited and used sperm manipulation, our baby would have had a better chance. If he or she doesn't Change, that could be on me."

"What?" He stopped and stared, his eyes blacker than the night around us. "Is that what you've been thinking all this time?"

I tightened my hands into fists. "It's kind of hard not to worry about it. A fifty percent chance is much better than thirty."

He was quiet for a moment, and though no expression showed on his face, emotion rolled off him. It was both longing and gratitude, born of many years, out of experience and, yes, suffering.

"Well, you don't have to worry—at least not about giving our child a worse chance." He took my hands, uncurling them in his. "Ever since we stole Stefan's sperm to copy the process and get you—or, well, Jace, as it turned out—Cort worked on improving the manipulation. He turned it into pill form. Actually, that's what Stella and Chris used. And he gave me pills the night we married in Morocco. He knew any child we might have was my responsibility every bit as much as it is yours. I wouldn't . . ." His fingers rubbed over the flesh of my hand, trailing fire. "I would never put our child's future at risk. I know you think I'm old-fashioned, but after waiting centuries to find you, I would not have made love to you unless I'd done everything I could for our family."

I stared, shocked and amazed—and a little bit angry. It was so like Ritter to take it all on himself, the man wearing the pants and whatnot. "Why didn't you tell me?"

He shrugged. "I thought with Chris and Stella . . . I thought you knew." He tilted his head. "Am I in the doghouse? Because I thought telling you would make you happy."

I started laughing as the weight of worry flowed from my body. "No. I'm not mad." My arms went around his neck, and I buried my face in the hollow of his shoulder. "Thank you." *For taking care of me. For loving our child enough to worry.* I couldn't say any of that aloud, but he'd get much of it from our mate link because I wasn't holding back.

His arms tightened around me, and for a long moment we stood there, the world shifting around us, becoming brighter and full of promise. Until now, I hadn't understood how much the responsibility weighed on me. I should have told him before, but our becoming a family had happened a lot faster than I'd expected.

"Good, because there may be more to this whole Change than we know," he said. "When I was talking to Leyton just now, he hinted at their having the ability to tell whether or not a child will change when he or she is born. When I questioned him, he became a little vague, which I understand since he's apparently not a healer or scientist. But if that's true, maybe they've pinpointed what causes the gene to activate, and if we can identify it, we might be able to increase the chances of Changes in the future."

"That sounds promising." It might be false hope, but I clung to it. Of course, if we did increase Changes, the entire world would alter—it was already changing with the manipulation we'd accomplished thus far. And without the Emporium and Renegades fighting and killing each other, we'd definitely have more Unbounded.

That brought another unsettling thought: *What about the mortals?* More long-lived humans would affect the food supply, housing, wealth, and power. The balance would tilt. I pushed the thoughts aside. That was for another day. For now, I needed to find Kimber.

We drew apart and continued our search. We passed only a few more containers before Ritter identified the one he'd been looking for. Dropping his duffel, he removed an odd set of finger-to-elbow gloves and heavy sock-like boots.

"Jace has some of those." I'd glimpsed them in his duffel.

"Cort made a bunch of prototypes . . . before. . ."

"Right."

"They're a little hard to work out because they're magnetic and don't like to release. Takes a bit of strength to deactivate."

Suddenly, I wanted to try them. Me, the woman with recently conquered acrophobia.

"Don't worry," Ritter said, misinterpreting my rush of emotion. "I'll send down a rope ladder." When I didn't respond, he grinned at me. "Let me guess."

"I want to do it."

His grin grew wider. "That's my girl." *My girl.* And he meant it. For forever. Or at least two thousand years.

He reached into the duffle for another set of gloves. "Okay, so our target container is at the very top, the fifth row, but we'll stop at the top of the fourth." The gloves he gave me were smaller than his but still large, though the adjustment strap made them fit well enough. He gave me a demonstration. "The magnetic attachment is automatic when you touch the container. You move by flexing your muscles to depress the release while pulling back at the same time. Until you're confident, you'll want to keep three points of contact, moving only one foot or hand at a time." He gestured at the container. "You first. Don't worry. I'll catch you if you fall."

I was fine with that.

The climb up the four containers that were above deck was more difficult than I'd expected, and a whole lot more fun. My inches upward quickly became long arm reaches until we were perched far above the deck. I looked out, steeling myself against possible nausea and blinding fear, but I was still good—and I knew that every time I did something like this, I was making sure the fear stayed gone.

"This is the tricky part," Ritter said, coming up on my right and moving across the front of our target container. "Getting inside the container. Without a surface to stand on, it'll be difficult to open, but I know a few tricks. But first, let's tie on, just in case." He fastened a rope onto several metal hooks, wrapping one loop around me and another around himself.

I tried to mentally pierce the metal to see what was inside the container, but it only registered as a big blank. "They've got an electrical grid or something."

"And probably a lot of insulation for sound," he agreed.

Removing his magnetic gloves and balancing only on the boots while still attached to the side of the container below, he went to work on the lock on the right side, easily unlatching it. "The problem is finding purchase to pull it open. And we'll have to make sure no one is inside guarding the kids."

"Right. Well, get it open an even an inch, and I should be able to tell if someone is waiting at the door."

He leaned back, pulling on the bars, which refused to budge. He tugged harder, pushing against the side of the lower container. The door surged open a good handspan, and he lost balance, but the rope prevented him from flipping backward.

Life forces flooded to my senses. "No one's within about six feet of the door, but there are a lot of mortals," I said quietly.

"At least forty-nine."

I probed at the minds. "They're all . . . asleep, I think."

"Good." Ritter was already moving toward me and up onto the left door, pushing the right one open far enough to climb inside. He disappeared but returned almost immediately. "Clear."

I climbed inside and removed the magnetic gloves and boots. Instead of darkness, a single bright light burned on the wall of the container, sitting above a backup generator and giving a surprising amount of light to the shallow front area of the container. The rest of the space appeared to be divided in two enclosed sections with a narrow hallway down the middle, reminiscent of a college dorm.

A woman's voice came to us from the back of the container speaking in what sounded like Sinaltan. Footsteps came toward us as she spoke. Ritter moved close to the division on the left, keeping out of her sight. I remained where I was as a woman with a long red ponytail, skinny jeans, and a gun at her waist came into view. Her mind was dark and blocking.

"I don't know what you said," I told her, "but there's been a change of plans."

"What change? Did we transfer already?" she asked with the same accent as Leyton's but less pronounced. "I didn't feel the movement. This group has been restless. It will be good to get them out of here and into regular quarters. And why are we speaking English?"

"We're still on the cargo boat. And I'm speaking English because I'm American."

Her hand went to her gun, but she didn't draw, which was good for her because Ritter had opened his shield to let me channel his ability. She'd never get the weapon from the holster before my tranq hit her. "If we're still on the cargo boat," she asked, "where is Graeme?"

Graeme. I filed that away for future consideration. Whoever Graeme was, he was apparently on the boat. Did that mean we'd overlooked someone, or had her ally been knocked out with the other mortal sailors?

And what if he wasn't mortal? His body would cycle through the drug faster than the others. I told myself it didn't matter now that the Sinaltans had surrendered—even if it had been forcibly. Then again, I didn't quite buy their explanation that they thought we were Renegades.

Shelving those thoughts for the time being, I held out my hand in a typical human gesture. "I'm Erin Radkey. I'm with the Emporium. Your allies." My gaze flickered to Ritter. "And so is he."

She startled a bit and glanced his way, which told me her gift wasn't combat or sensing because she would have already noted his presence.

"I see," she said, easing her hand away from her weapon

and touching mine very briefly, a mere brush. I didn't get more from her than a nervous surface emotion, even with the contact. Her shield was as strong as the other Avowed, and I guessed she was another hypnopath. "I'm Uriella Sargente. Does Leyton know you're here?"

"Yes, he's headed back to his boat now to have a chat with your leaders."

"But we are still going to transfer supplies?"

"Everything except this container." I smiled, daring her to protest. "There will be no future transfers of human cargo."

"Does that mean we're ready to surface?" A light came into her eyes that were almost as blue as Leyton's. They glittered oddly in the light of the container.

"We'll be working that out next."

Her gaze strayed again to Ritter as if guessing something was wrong but not knowing exactly what. That made two of us.

"You said the children have been restless. What do you mean by that?" I pressed.

"Just that I've had to talk to them more. The boys started a fight, and a couple of the little girls wouldn't stop crying even when I ordered them too."

I quirked a brow. "Losing your gift?"

"No," the reply came too fast. "They're small, that's all. They forget." Pity rolled off her surface thoughts.

So, you're not as immune to them as you would like to be, I thought. It was a plus in her favor.

"One of the embryos has some experience with children and was able to calm them," Uriella added. "Plus, I gave them something to help them sleep."

Worry flashed through me. "I'd like to see them."

Uriella shrugged. "You're welcome to."

Ritter moved forward then. "Will we need a key?"

"There's a key if you want to turn the lock from the inside, but you don't need one from out here."

I extended a hand. "I'll take it anyway. Just in case."

She reached into the pocket of her outfit, which I noticed for the first time was a form-fitting black, woven with shimmering silver threads. It didn't look like anything commonly worn in America, unless maybe on the high-end model runways. Was that the fashion in Sinalta, or was the material perhaps from there?

"Thanks."

I left her standing near the entrance, but Ritter didn't follow me.

Aren't you coming? I said to him through the opening he'd allowed.

I have to make sure she doesn't lock us in. Never know what she's thinking . . . unless you do know?

I was getting tired of people asking that. Break through a few shields, and suddenly, everyone thinks you should be able to break down all shields—and do so immediately. *Not yet,* I told him.

I didn't have to open the doors to the two narrow separations to see the children because each side had sections of transparent plastic that gave me a view. On one side, twenty boys were all lying on the ground, wrapped in thin, shiny blankets. They mostly lay apart from each other except for a cluster of four younger boys close to an older boy of maybe eighteen or nineteen. Another older boy was sitting up in a corner near what looked like a portable bathroom that was secured to the wall with a metal cable. He looked both sleepy and angry, and the ugly bruise marking his cheek hinted that he'd been one of those fighting. In the fogginess of his mind, he was thinking regretfully of his mother.

In the opposite section, the twenty-nine girls were all near each other, heads on laps or cuddled together like spoons, circling a black-haired girl with bronze skin who was lying in the middle of the container. I recognized the girl as Kimber. She wasn't the oldest in the group, but apparently, she was the one Uriella had been talking about. One older girl near the outer circle lay staring up at the ceiling, her eyes opened. Despair oozed from her, and as I watched, a tear fell from her eyes.

I forced myself to clamp down on my shield to push away the children's emotions. It would be worse when they were all awake. Sighing, I reached out to Ava, tapping gently on her shield.

We've found Kimber, I said. *Tell Dimitri. She's here. Drugged, but okay, I think. He should look them all over as soon as he can.*

You're in the container?

Yes. With Ritter. There's a woman here too—Uriella Sargente. I won't be leaving her with the kids again.

Of course not.

Also, there's another Sinaltan on board, or at least someone Uriella's been working with. Just so we know.

No one has shown up, she responded. *Leyton and his men are already back on their ship. We're waiting for news. They wanted Dimitri to go with them to help those who went into the water, but we decided they can wait. We need to make sure their leaders agree to a discussion before we trust them further. Something about them makes me uneasy.*

For me, it's the kids, I said. *How can they justify it?*

Ava didn't respond, but I saw in her mind how doing

something horrific might be possible. Once, in another lifetime, she'd given a man paralyzing drugs and burnt his house down, the house they'd shared, the house where he'd murdered her and their baby daughter.

It's not the same, I told her.

I'll send Jace and Dimitri to help. But we won't be able to get the kids down until the container is moved.

They should do that first, then. Before the negotiations. I hesitated before adding, *Please.*

I'm going to the control room now. I'll make it happen.

Thank you.

I joined Ritter and Uriella. "When will they wake?" I asked.

She shrugged. "The drug should already be wearing off. I gave it to them seven or eight hours ago in their food. But for most, it's still in the middle of the night, so maybe it will be a while. It's warm enough in there."

"You're moving them like cattle," I retorted. "No pillows or beds or common decency."

"It's only until they get to our transport. We have adequate quarters there."

Likely similar to the crew quarters on the submersible, which were adequate unless you were a kidnapped child who had no choice in the matter—and then not even the most luxurious suite would be enough.

I shifted my gaze to Ritter. "Uriella will need to be transported to the Sinaltan ship."

"No!" she said, a little too vehemently. Then, seeing our curiosity, she added more calmly, "I'll be staying aboard. I'll be needed for the next transport."

I took a step toward her. "You must have misunderstood me before. There will be no more shipments that will need your particular talents. Not a single one."

"Right. That's okay. I'll await orders here then." Was that a touch of panic in her voice?

"No. You won't." We couldn't trust her, not when she apparently had no compulsion about trafficking children. "Unless . . . trafficking children is a crime here. Would you like to go to prison? I hear prisoners aren't too happy with those who abuse kids. You might die there a thousand times before your time is up."

"But . . ." The fact that she hesitated said volumes about her desire to stay above the ocean.

"Believe me, going back to Sinalta is for your own safety." I nodded at Ritter pointedly.

"Let's go," he said, moving toward her. "Erin will stay with the kids. I'm assuming if you normally stay on board that you have a way of getting down to the deck?"

"Yes." She glanced upward at what appeared to be a trap door on the top of the container before walking over to an odd pulley and cable contraption on a hook by the light. "Usually, I go up and then down, but the door will work."

"Good." I peeked out of the door to see Dimitri and Jace below. "Looks like our friends are waiting down there."

Ritter gestured to the door. "After you."

Uriella hooked her device to the left door panel, fastened another part to one of her feet, then stepped off and slowly disappeared.

"I'll send Dimitri up," Ritter said as he pulled on his magnetic gloves.

"See if you can find who she's working with. Graeme something. If he's Avowed, he needs to be sent to the Sinaltan ship as well."

Dimitri went in to see to the hurt boy first and also the other boys in the section who'd awakened. I dug in a food locker at the back of the container affixed to the wall above a bed. A small television and a portable toilet made up the rest of the space. Apparently, Uriella didn't have to sleep on the floor during transport like her charges.

I passed out rations as the children, still groggy from their hours of drugged sleep, awoke. I invited Kimber and the other older girl to help.

"We're really going home?" Kimber asked me, her voice wavering. "My mom, she must be going crazy."

"She is, a little," I said, "but that will be over the minute she hears your voice. I'll see if we can radio shore and get them the news. Meanwhile, I'll need help getting information from these kids—names and where they're from. If you think you can help me?" I offered her a tablet that Dimitri had given me.

"Sure. I work with kids a lot at the Mission on Ninth." Her face fell as she spoke. "Brenna is the one who did this—you have to tell them! I thought she was my friend, but she asked me to go with her to talk to her mother, and the next thing I know, I'm in here with all these little kids." Her voice sounded panicked as if she was about to cry.

I touched her arm, sending calming thoughts to the sand stream of her mind. "We know all about her," I said. "She won't be doing it again." If Marco didn't manage to catch her, I'd hunt her down myself. "It's really over."

For Kimber anyway. For the rest of us, it was just beginning because we needed to find out what to do about the Sinaltans before they hurt anyone else.

Dimitri appeared behind her and placed a gentle hand on her shoulder. Immediately, I felt her emotions stabilizing, much faster and more thoroughly than I'd been able to accomplish with my thoughts.

"You're Kimber Wheeler, right?" he said. "I'm Sam, a friend of Pastor Mike's. He told me about you. It's nice to meet you."

"Hi, Sam. You too. Did he say anything about my parents?"

Even his smile was calm and healing. "Yes. Don't worry. We'll contact them."

"I'll go and arrange it." I nodded at them and walked away, tapping my earbud. "Chris?" I said. "We need to get Stella to connect us with Los Angeles. I want to tell Kimber's parents that she's safe."

"Will do, but it's time to get everyone inside that container secure. They're going to move it now."

Chris had no need to worry. Long horizontal bars had been welded to the sides of the container inside the separations. The children clung to them as the container lurched into the air, moved for a few heart-pounding moments, and then set down. Shortly afterward, Jace was outside the open door, urging the children down a ladder to a lower container, then another and another until they reached the deck.

The ponytailed first mate awaited at the bottom with Ava. "Come with me," he said. "I'll show you to quarters. It's a tight squeeze, but there's plenty of grub, and our cook ain't half bad."

"Better make sure someone checks on them," I said. "A couple of the boys were fighting."

"Close quarters will do that," the mate said. "Don't worry. We've got a few hands below that can see to it." He raised his voice and announced. "Anyone fighting will go to the brig—after they swab the latrines. You know what those are, right?"

Kimber started to go with the others, but Ava stopped her with a hand on her shoulder. "We sent a message to your parents. They're getting a flight to Mexico now. You'll see them soon."

"Thank you." Kimber's gaze went past her to me. She

nodded, words of gratitude caught in her throat, but I already knew. I nodded and waved her on.

Offloading the Emporium containers and the loading of the Sinaltan supplies went smoothly, and by the time it was finished, and the hold of the Sinaltan ship closed, only Leyton and the female combat soldier I'd fought were still on board the cargo ship. We took them to the control room, where more chairs had been located and the master and mate of the ship escorted elsewhere for the duration of our conversation.

"Again, I sincerely apologize for the confusion at the beginning of our acquaintance," Leyton began. "We understand now that we should have verified the information with the leader of the Triad."

Ava inclined her head. "We accept your apology." At her side, Jace nodded while I wondered how the Avowed would have talked to Stefan since he was in prison. Had they tried to message New York? The idea was worrisome.

"My leaders also extend their sincere apologies," Leyton continued. "In fact, they have extended a rare honor and have invited you all to come to Sinalta with us. They would like to show you our beautiful city and discuss our mutual future."

I did not like the sound of that at all, being stuck under miles of water in the city of people who trafficked children and who had attacked us. "Why can't we do this virtually? If you talked to them, so can we."

"It is within our capacity," Leyton agreed, "however, they would like to get a feel for the new leaders of the Emporium. And they would come here, but several of our leaders are very advanced in age. Even though we are capable of making the journey in under two days, traveling is both a burden and a risk for them. Please, I urge you to accept our hospitality. You will love our city, and of course, you can keep your weapons with you. And again, I sincerely apologize for how we began." He paused before adding, "Please understand that this is a great honor as you will only be the second group of topsiders we have ever had below."

"Unless you count all the children," I couldn't help saying.

"Well, yes, but they become Sinaltans, so that is different. We give them a purpose."

A vein flexed in Ritter's neck. "You give them no choice."

Leyton waved a hand dismissively. "You will understand once you see the city. Please, come with us."

It was at that moment I finally broke through the man's shield. The time with the children hadn't been restful, but I'd been absorbing, and this invitation had given me the final impetus. In his mind, I found . . . honesty instead of deceit. He believed it was a major honor to be allowed to visit Sinalta. That was difficult to imagine with Brenna and Uriella's desperation to stay topside and even his own bitterness at not being able to surface, but the invitation and his belief in our alliance were clear. Stefan Carrington had been impressed with the city, so maybe Leyton's admiration was warranted.

Ava, sensing the breach of his shield, joined me inside his mind and intently studied his thought stream. She repeated questions about why we couldn't meet virtually and about his reasons for attacking us earlier, but everything in his thoughts matched what he had told us.

Finally, Ava stood and addressed Leyton. "We are grateful for the invitation to visit your city. We will have an answer for you within the hour."

He stood and bowed. "That is acceptable. Now if you'll excuse me, I'll return to my ship and make ready for the journey while we await your word."

After he left, Ava paced the room, looking at each of us in turn. "We must go," she said. "It's the opportunity to create an alliance that doesn't involve the former Triad."

"They just tried to kill us!" I protested.

"You saw his mind."

I nodded. "I saw *his* mind. But I have no idea what the Sinaltan leaders are thinking."

"Which is why we will go with our weapons." Ritter patted his sides. "Dangerous or no, it's an opportunity we can't pass up."

"I have to agree." Dimitri moved to stand by Ava as if to show his support. "I need to see them and find out more about their condition. We also need to learn if it's true that they can determine at birth whether or not a child will Change and how that is accomplished. Even with the cease-fire between Renegades and Emporium, it will help families determine the best care for their children."

"Meaning what?" I demanded, angry at myself for not questioning Leyton about that while I'd had the chance. "That we'd place those who won't Change for adoption?"

Dimitri nodded. "Possibly. Or maybe it will simply prepare families. For some, the knowledge that they missed out on eternal life is a bitter cup. Knowing before will prevent that disappointment."

The foreknowledge that Jace and I would Change might have made a difference. Same with Kimber or any number of Unbounded offspring over the generations. But would the good outweigh the negative consequences? Would my child suddenly be satisfied to live a mortal life just because he learned about it as a baby?

No.

Yet I was torn because maybe the information could lead to

an alteration of the gene that would allow everyone to Change, even Chris and my niece and nephew.

I sighed. "Okay, let's go."

Ritter shook his head. "Not Chris or Charles. We've seen how they treat mortals, so they will stay with you and help get the kids back to Mexico and then to the United States."

"They can do that without me," I growled.

Ritter's jaw set. "This isn't up for debate. Ava and I have already discussed it. Those children look up to you, and you're the only one who can make this crew take them back."

I snorted, rage in my heart. "Chris and Charles are completely capable. This is about the baby, and you know it."

Ritter's face was immovable, but the emotional waves coming from him were mixed—regret, concern, love, but all covered with determination to keep me safe. Maybe I should be flattered, but mostly I wanted to strangle him.

"We all know that something isn't quite right," Ava said into the sudden quiet, her voice as steely as her eyes. "You are our backup, Erin. You and Mari, once she's healed. Yes, we want to protect you, but there is also a very real possibility that we will fail, and you'll need to rally our people to fight against the Sinaltans."

I couldn't believe what she was saying. "So you know something is wrong, but you still choose to sail into the lion's den?"

Ava nodded. "To slay a monster, that is sometimes exactly where you need to be."

My further protests fell on deaf ears, and an hour later, I watched the Sinaltan ship move away and sink out of sight. I was both furious and worried . . . and only the life force burning inside me gave me the strength to turn away from the railing.

As I headed to check on the kids, a shadow moved into a

narrow alley next to a row of containers. At first, I thought the figure was only a sailor, one who hadn't been sedated during our initial boarding, but then my senses registered a swirling dark silver of a mental shield. *Unbounded*, I thought.

I sprang after him, drawing my nine mil. "Stop!" I commanded.

The figure turned, revealing a thin, strong, thirty-something man in navy overalls. I aimed at his face where I could see he wasn't wearing body armor. "Who are you?" I demanded.

"I'm Graeme Padovan, an Avowed from Sinalta. I came to warn you, but it looks like I'm too late."

So he was the Graeme that Uriella had mentioned, the man we hadn't been able to locate before the Sinaltan ship departed. Either he'd been topside long enough to lose his accent, or he was good with languages.

"Warn me about what?"

His gaze went past me out to the sea, now marked only by swelling and movement and the water slapping against the cargo boat. "It doesn't matter now. They're gone, and you will never see them again."

Chapter 16

MY FINGER TIGHTENED ON THE TRIGGER. "YOU HAD BETTER EXPLAIN yourself. Now!"

He adjusted his position slightly and leaned against the container on his left. "I would have told you before, but I didn't . . ." He shook his blond head almost violently—blond hair with the blue eyes that seemed to be prevalent among the Sinaltans.

"Didn't what?" I pressed.

"Didn't want to get involved. I already helped you once."

"You were the one who prevented the Sinaltan soldier from shooting me."

He gave a quick nod. "I couldn't let him hurt the baby."

A chill rushed over me. "You know I'm expecting?"

"I'm an empath. It's part of my ability."

That meant he was a sensing Unbounded like me, or at least in the same family of abilities. And maybe that gift was the reason for his placement here. As one of the crew, he'd be in the perfect position to oversee the transporting of Sinaltan goods.

If he could sense emotions or even see thoughts, he could make sure the setup was safe and that no one had a mind to delve into the identity of his people.

"You are lucky that I was able to recover so quickly from the sedation your people injected into me," Graeme continued. "However, if he'd known you were Avowed and expecting, the sailor would not have shot. It is a death offense to harm an expectant Avowed."

"Except I'm not Avowed. I'm Unbounded."

He shrugged. "Just because you have not taken the oath doesn't change what you are."

Maybe he was right. I was also having a difficult time differentiating between the two terms. "Okay," I said, relaxing only slightly. Because he wasn't combat, and there was no way he'd be able to take my gun from me before I could fire. "Then explain your comment. Your people attacked us because they thought we were Renegades and not representatives of the Emporium."

"No," he said. "I mean, yes, Leyton and his crew might think that, but I talked to Sinalta directly, and my sources say Brenna Dabney reported that the Emporium had been infiltrated. So I think it was a ruse."

"A ruse for what purpose?" I waved the gun for emphasis, losing what little patience I still clung to. Worry inside me grew by the second.

"I'm saying I think they told Leyton to make a show of it."

"No, he believed that we were loyal Emporium. I saw it in his mind."

Graeme stiffened, lifting his shoulder from the container. Too late, I saw that I'd told him my true gift. "You broke through his shield?" he asked. "Then the rumors are true that the Unbounded here still have that ability." He gave his head a shake as if to refocus. "Maybe they told Leyton that, but did you see if they said to come to the boat in force? Or did they tell him to only bring that small number of sailors?"

I hadn't seen either thing. Now my lack of foresight seemed glaring. "There wasn't a lot of time."

He nodded. "Well, it's amazing that you could even break through Leyton's shield. But what I think is that he was played, just like your friends, to get them to go to Sinalta. Obviously, they told him to try to take you by force but didn't have him send enough men. It was all to get you to trust them."

"Funny way of going about it," I muttered.

"It worked, didn't it? Anyway, my sources say they want to help the leader of the Triad take back control."

"He is in control," I said. "And his son is on your ship. His direct descendant."

Graeme cocked his head. "This descendant you speak of; he is more to you than that."

I pushed out my mental barrier around even my surface thoughts, hardening it. All he'd see now was a whirling mass of black power. He probably wouldn't be able to sense the baby's life glow either.

"They have spies topside," he said. "Like me. Like the one who freed Brenna. He has an ability that makes the muscles go weak." He sighed. "Anyway, they are determined to get what they want." He waited a heartbeat before adding, "What they desperately need."

"To come to the surface. To get land," I prompted. Every Sinaltan I'd met so far wanted this. "I'm assuming you want that too, so what's your stake in talking to me?" I shifted my own position to ease the throb beginning in my arm from holding the gun up so long.

"It's true," he said. "Some of us don't exactly agree with the way Sinalta is run or approve of the methods they use, but we do all want to come topside." He lifted his head toward the eastern horizon, where the sky was beginning to lighten, signaling the coming of sunrise.

"So you're a Sinaltan Renegade." I couldn't help the mocking in my tone.

"I guess you might say that, but there are only a few of us. The ruling families have used the school system and the media to change the hearts of the people. Most of us now view mortals as lesser creatures to be used or discarded as needed, even those related to us."

This sounded eerily like the former Emporium, and irritation swept through me. "If you don't agree, then why didn't you come forward sooner?"

His eyes narrowed. "I didn't think you'd be stupid enough to get on their boat and go with them."

His point was so close to my own feelings that I couldn't protest. "My friends do intend to work things out with them," I said. "There's no reason why their goal of surfacing can't happen. Land will be found, eventually, but we won't steal it from others."

"That's just it. We *can't* wait. It has to be soon." He looked around even though he had to know we were the only life forms in this section of the deck. "What you don't know is that the city of Sinalta is failing, exactly like our other city failed. We lost six million people overnight. Those who managed to escape are now in our only remaining city. We have four million people crammed into Sinalta now. And if you can't imagine what that means, think of the population of your Los Angeles, only we're squeezed into a much smaller area. Our other city was newer and larger, built after we arrived in our current location. Its failure was catastrophic. The mortals died instantly, and millions of Avowed were also permanently killed or lost to us."

"Let me guess. This was fifty years ago." When they first made contact with the Emporium.

He nodded. "But even before then, it was growing crowded."

"I thought there were still two cities."

"The mine workers live in several smaller locations carved into the side of the continent," he said with a mirthless snort. "But those can hardly be called cities. There are no amenities. Comparatively, this cargo ship is a luxury liner. No Avowed would deign to live there." He shook his head. "That's part of why I joined the movement. For the people who work in the mines—which means most of the mortals now—it's a death sentence."

A few of his statements weren't making sense. "I've heard of your advanced technology. Why haven't you automated more of the mines? And why is the city failing? Is it because of over-crowding? Can't you fix the city, extend it, or build another one?" That they hadn't already done so had to mean something important.

His gaze dropped, and shame colored his cheeks. "We don't know how to fix it. It's something to do with the temperature and oxygen level, and even the stabilizers, but those who built it have already passed on, and we've lost their abilities. We've tried to make up for that with advanced engineering, but it hasn't worked. We've also tried to figure out how to bring the city to the surface, even in the harsh Antarctic environment where we likely wouldn't be able to sustain life. But no one can figure out how. Perhaps our ancestors never foresaw this day. In a very real sense, we grew too complacent over the millennia." He lifted his gaze, his tone hardening. "I say we, but I mean our leaders because I've only lived six decades. They were too busy lining their buildings and roads and pockets with gold and rhodium."

Things were now clicking into place. With a city failing and four million Sinaltans at risk, I understood their leaders' urgency.

"Maybe we can figure out the tech," I said. "We are also advanced compared to the world's standards, and we have people with amazing abilities. And if not, we have connections in governments, and there is land available. It may not be the choicest, but it's better than under the ocean. In fact, people can go wherever they choose, and it doesn't have to be to the same place."

"And Sinalta ceases to be a country?" He shook his head. "It's unthinkable."

"I understand that, but it's better than being fish food."

He frowned. "You misunderstand. I agree with you. If I could take my family and disappear into the Amazon jungle or even the jungle of New York City, believe me, I would count myself lucky—and many of us feel the same way even though we might not say it, and even if they are like me and love our homeland. Our leaders have lost their way, and I believe there is nothing we can do to return to what once was. Most Avowed are too accustomed to living by the sweat of hardworking mortals. They believe the lie that they are owed a living. They don't know how to exist without the subsidies given to them by the government. But my family is hostage. They are the only reason I am here on this boat."

I steeled myself against the want in his voice and in his yearning surface thoughts that were strong enough for me to pick up even through my shield. "You're trafficking in children."

His head dipped. "And I should be punished. But it is only to save my daughter from the mines. She was born a mortal, but we chose to let her live. My wife works as a city engineer, and our daughter has a future working under her as long as I do my job here."

My breath caught in my throat, and I stumbled back a little to sit on a huge spool of cable. "What do you mean, you *chose* to let her live?"

"In Sinalta, only Avowed are permitted to reproduce." Graeme stepped from the alleyway and moved slowly to the other side of the spool, his hands raised to show he was unarmed. Light from the coming sun painted his hair with gold. "Children who will not Change are educated at placement centers, and then at age ten are sent to work, mostly in the mines but also in households. They will never have families or homes, and it's a stain on an Avowed family line to have such offspring. As it is legal for a woman to have a say over her own body, she is allowed to make the decision to have the child placed or to terminate."

"So it's true that you can tell if a baby will Change when it is born?"

"Look, I've told you enough. Even what I've said could mean death—for my family and me."

I glared at him, leveling the gun once more at his face. "I'm telling you it will mean death for you now if you don't tell me. Not permanent death, but death all the same, and I will get through your shield. I got through Brenna's and Leyton's."

He clamped his mouth shut, his chest rising. He didn't speak, so I took out the mental version of my machete and pounded hard. "You feel that? It's only the beginning. I don't want to hurt you or your family, but *my* family is on board your ship heading for what you believe is certain death. You know what you have done to save those you love. Well, I'll do far more to save those I love." I pounded again.

He winced. "Okay, I'll tell you. But I do so only with the hope that my child will have a true life above the sea, without death in her future."

"So you can tell if a baby will Change," I prompted. I still didn't know how I felt about that.

"We can after the baby is born, not before. That is, unless the child is born to a mortal or someone who hasn't yet Changed. Then it can be foretold."

"Why? The test can't be done in utero? Does it cause miscarriage or something?"

"It's not exactly a test. It's a who. And he can't tell if the baby will Change inside the womb because the signals from the mother's genes interfere."

"So it's a person, not a test." Disappointment spread through me. If only I'd known this beforehand. Maybe I could have convinced the others not to go.

"His name is Mikyn Zenos, an Avowed with the empath ability—or sensing, as you call it. His mother was a powerful healer, and his father was an even more powerful empath." He gave me a side glance. "His father was the last of those who could break through shields. It is rumored that he could tell before the birth if the child was mortal or an embryo Avowed. Mikyn's father died five hundred years ago, though. His wife was also the last of the gifted healers. Mikyn may not be as powerful as his father, but he is revered among our people because he has the power of life and death in his word."

I pulled my foot onto the edge of the spool and rested my gun hand on my knee, not quite pointing at him but close. I'd only trust him once I got through his shield, and my strength was waning. Even with my ability to recover, the efforts of the past few days were taking their toll.

Numerous questions came to mind, and I went over our conversation to determine which was the most important. "If you can't tell before the child is born whether or not it will Change, then you're saying your women can decide after the birth to keep the baby or not?"

"Like your own country, women are in control of their own bodies." His words were monotone, unfeeling. "But since they can't tell whether or not a child will Change, women have up until a month after delivery to decide whether to terminate or keep the child and endure the ignominy of having a mortal relative."

I stared at him in horror. "You murder them?" Nothing could have prepared me for this information. "That makes no sense. You're stealing children from here to work for you. And even if they don't Change, your children might have an Unbounded offspring later on. Until six generations it's possible."

He nodded gravely. "But the crowding in Sinalta will not allow many more to live in the city, and the most prestigious families are not willing to have their children go to the mines."

"But they're willing to murder them instead? That's going to be half your children!"

"Half?" Again he cocked his head at me. "More like seventy percent, which is why they sterilize all the mortals. Between a mortal and Avowed, it's only a twenty percent chance of Change, and that is too low to risk. With two Avowed, the chance rises to thirty percent. Usually, they can get it right with three or four pregnancies."

Horror pinned me to the spool. I imagined life forces winking out as the Avowed deemed yet another baby unworthy of life. "This practice is acceptable in your society?"

"The mother created the child, so it's her choice." He was

still speaking with that odd monotone, as if repeating something memorized. "Babies are not considered citizens until after their first month."

I couldn't respond to that because it was so ludicrous. "It's fifty percent chance of Change up here between Unbounded," I said. "I don't know the science, but we've figured out how to manipulate the sperm."

His back straightened. "My leaders will be happy to hear that."

"I can't imagine they don't already know. You've been in contact with us for fifty years, and the Emporium developed this over thirty years ago. But instead, your people are still killing children because they're mortals and then stealing our children to work as slaves?"

He held up a hand as if to stem the tide of emotion, and I realized I was pushing it at him. Maybe my machete had weakened his barrier. "Many of our mortal children still go to the mines. As I've said before, there are those of us who do not support or believe in the policies. I had two sons in the mines myself. They died after only ten years—that's about par there—and that's why I'm here making sure my Anina doesn't have to go." With the last words, his demeanor changed from impassive to visibly fighting tears. "I visited the mines often when I was there on leave, and I would do anything not to see another child of mine suffer that fate. I don't care that she's mortal. Right now, all I'm doing is holding on until I get her above the water where I can protect her."

Was his emotion real or faked? I couldn't tell, and there was still too much unanswered to readily believe him. "Okay, that explains the children you steal for the mines, but if you're so crowded, why bring our potential Unbounded to Sinalta?" I asked. "And I thought only Avowed were permitted to have children, but then you said if a person hadn't Changed yet, your sensing Avowed could tell about a baby in utero."

"Right." He pursed his lips as if tasting something awful. "There's another issue we face. After continual inbreeding over thousands of years, we are seeing some . . . mental collapses. Our medical personnel say it's simply bad luck that the very genes causing us to live long lives are also the same genes combining in strange ways with other similar genes to cause mental defects, and sometimes physical as well, though that's rare." He glanced in the direction of the sunrise, the light glittering like gold over the water. "I personally believe it's because humans were never meant to live without the sun and wind and sky." He sighed. "Unfortunately, many of these abnormalities are happening in the prestigious families, who continue to insist on intermarrying because of the power the practice maintains within their families. With the demise of our second city and the loss of so many Avowed, the situation has only intensified. When we lost our last gifted healer, things declined quickly. It's one reason why they bring in embryos from topside. If they pass the test and will Change, they are assigned to one of the ruling families to widen their pool of DNA. It is not a permanent assignment, and they will eventually have a choice about staying with that family once they give birth to an Avowed, though they usually stay connected because it means power. In the meantime, this widens the gene pool better than anything we can do within Sinalta ourselves, which our leaders hope will help the next generation. It's hard on the female embryos because they must give birth themselves, since the eggs die if we remove them, but it is only a slice of their thousands of years. And there are perks. The expectant Avowed is nearly worshipped. Anything she wants is hers."

"Except her body!" I jumped off the spool and faced him.

"Which I thought was the whole reason for your policy on babies. But I'm also betting it's the family and not the embryo who decides whether or not her baby lives, right?"

He nodded, his eyes hollow. "The ruling families nearly always choose termination of mortal offspring to protect their lineage and save themselves heartache." His expression didn't change, but anger came from him in waves, telling me he knew exactly how much suffering losing a child to the mines entailed.

"And what if this Mikyn person decides the embryo won't Change? What then?" This would mean most of the descendants they'd taken, and I already knew the answer but needed to hear it anyway.

"They are sterilized and sent to the mines with the other topsiders. Or sometimes they're kept as house servants or, uh, companions." He shook his head. "This is why I say that your friends—your family—have no chance there. There is too much the Avowed are not willing to give up, not even once they are above land, which is why they chose to ally with the Emporium." He hesitated. "But please believe me when I say that we are not all monsters."

"Those you work with, you mean."

"Yes. There is not much we can do except watch for our chance. Though, if we know you've imprisoned the former Triad leader, my guess is our Avowed leaders do as well. They will see that as a danger to Sinalta. They know Renegades will fight their way of life."

"What will they do to my team?" How much time did I have to find and free them?

He shook his head slowly. "They will not survive long. Only your healer will be spared to help keep the Avowed sane." Then he added half under his breath, "Although one might argue that they have already passed the point of no return."

My mind tumbled with the threat. "My team has spent hundreds of years fighting against people like your leaders, but it's the leaders they'll take issue with, not your people. There has to be another way we can help them find a resolution that everyone can live with." Now it was my turn to have tears in my eyes, and I blinked them away impatiently. "We have to make them understand that."

Graeme's chuckle mocked my emotion. "They won't believe, and if they can't be assured of a continent promised to them by the Triad, there will be war. We have lost much technology, but we still have weapons that could destroy your entire country. And enough precious metals to buy any soldiers in the world."

My throat suddenly felt dry and too salty, as if I'd been drinking the water that surrounded the cargo ship. "How long before the city fails?" I asked, finally lowering my gun to my side, not because I trusted him but because there was enough space between us to be safe. "Do they know that much?"

"A year for sure, maybe eighteen months. No more than that. And it will take months to bring everyone up and transfer them to the new destination." He hesitated. "As I said, my wife is one of the city engineers, and she's the main reason we're a part of those who want change. Because we know what they haven't told the public at large—that the city is doomed. And before you ask, yes, she and her colleagues have tried everything. They're mostly self-educated because we never dreamed such a thing could happen. My wife can't understand how our ancestors took the entire city under the ocean in a single day. That's why she and I both believe it was done through abilities we've lost."

"But you do have other abilities besides combat, sensing, and hypnosuggestion?"

"Yes, though most are gifted in hypnosuggestion."

So I'd noticed. "We must find a way to help my team and to get your leaders to let us try to resolve this peaceably."

Graeme considered for a moment. "Perhaps your healer can soothe their minds as they attempt to negotiate, but I think they feel they have already waited too long, and it has weakened their position. With time running out, I would not bet my families' life on their goodwill."

"No," I said, "not with your two boys already having paid such a terrible price."

He nodded solemnly.

"Then we'll make them give us a chance," I said.

"How?" So much hope packed into that tiny word.

"Do you know how to get there? To Sinalta, I mean."

Graeme tilted his head in a way that had become familiar. "Yes, because of my wife, I am one of the few who know the coordinates. Unfortunately, there's no way to get there. I spend six months here and six months there, and my replacement isn't due to rendezvous for another four months. Without the ship he'll come on, there's no way you can get to Sinalta, even if we could make it to the general area in time—which we can't. You do not have ships fast enough. A plane would make it, but then we wouldn't get under the water in time."

"But one of your ships would get us there, right?"

He stared, understanding dawning. "You have the transport we gave to the Triad."

"That's right. It's currently attached to the hull of this boat." I smirked at him. "So I am going to Sinalta, and you are coming with me." I didn't raise my nine mil, but the threat was there. Helping me was a risk, but I had every bit as much to lose as he did, so I wasn't giving him a choice.

"I'll do it," he said, after a long silence, "as long as we take my family when we leave, including my daughter."

"You have my word."

He sighed. "Even if we can get there, I don't see how we can help. Do you have a plan?"

"It's simple," I said. "We're going to blow up their city."

Chapter 17

OF COURSE IT WASN'T REALLY GOING TO BE SIMPLE, AND IT WOULD mean doing exactly what Ava and Ritter didn't want me to do, but if the situation were reversed, I knew the choice they'd make. They'd go after me. Because this was about more than just our family, it was about the world. The Avowed were as much of a threat to the world as the Emporium had ever been.

"You do know how to drive the ship, right?" I asked Graeme. Because he didn't seem that techy, and I really didn't want Chris to go with us. Half my family was already at risk, and he was more vulnerable than the others. Besides, his children and Stella needed him.

"Any child in Sinalta can drive a transport," he said. "Around Sinalta, we use the smaller ones, of course. Only the long-distance submersibles have the nuclear option for faster travel and are shielded for long distances, but the concept is the same."

"Good," I said. "Do you have everything you need? Because it's time to go. After I confer with my companions."

"I have a few things to get if you don't mind."

"One of my friends will go with you." I didn't trust Graeme enough to risk him disappearing until it was too late for us to do anything or tattling to his friends in Sinalta. "Come on."

I'd left Chris and Charles in the control room with the newly freed master and first mate, and when we approached now, I heard raised voices. I pushed inside, and the voices stopped. Guns weren't out, but Charles was flushed with fury, and Chris was flexing his fists the way he did in our morning sparing sessions when he was about to attack. It was a tell Ritter was trying to eradicate.

Chris glanced at me and nodded. "The captain here says he wants to continue his journey instead of going back to Mexico. That it'll be cheaper to take the kids with him and dump them there."

I narrowed my eyes at the man. "You'll go back to Mexico exactly the way you came. We'll have people there ready to help our team fly the children back to America."

"It'll make us late to our next stop," the master said.

I pushed into his mind, releasing a thought of fear into his stream of thoughts. It wasn't fair to manipulate him like this, but neither was taking those kids to Chile, and I didn't have time to babysit him. "You've taken enough money from the child trafficking. You *will* go back to Mexico, and you *will* make sure these kids get to the authorities waiting there. Otherwise, Chris and Charles will tell them you're responsible for all of it, and that will be the end of your career."

It was the thing he was afraid of most—that he'd be stripped of his post and end up as a poorly paid deckhand or, worse, be confined to land forever.

Then, because I spotted the flash of thought in his mind, I added, "And in case you have the bright idea of running and working in some foreign country, be aware that if you don't make getting these kids to safety your priority, we will all hunt you down and make you pay. These kids have suffered enough."

He stared at me, pale beneath his sun-browned face. "You win. I'll take them back. You've got our guns anyway." His gaze flicked to Chris and Charles. "Not like I can say no, is it?"

But he'd briefly thought about continuing the journey without telling them, surprising them with his destination upon arrival. "Right," I said. "Glad to hear that you agree." I turned to Chris and Charles. "I need a private word." I glanced toward the door where Graeme waited.

They moved in his direction while I turned to the captain. "I'm leaving your ship and taking that deckhand with me. Chris and Charles will be remaining to make sure you keep your word. If you don't, they will take you into custody."

I left the control room without waiting for a response, but the long-haired first mate came running after me. "You people . . . you're those new Unboundaried, aren't you?" He looked over at Chris and Charles and then at me.

I nodded. "We are." At least some of us were. "But we're not new. We've been protecting you for hundreds of years."

He nodded. "Okay. I believe that . . . and, well, thank you. You and the others."

For the first time since the rest of the team left, the knot in my gut eased. "You're welcome."

"I'll make sure to get the kids back to Mexico, no matter what." He gave another short nod and opened the door to the control room again, disappearing inside.

Charles was studying Graeme with experienced eyes. "Who's this?"

"Yeah," Chris added, "And why do you sound like you aren't going to be around to make sure we get the kids back?"

"This is Graeme, the Avowed contact on board, and it turns out the Sinaltans haven't been honest with us." I gave them an abbreviated rundown of what I'd learned. "So Graeme is taking me to Sinalta on Stefan's submersible."

"You mean us," Chris said.

"No, you need to make sure the kids get to Mexico."

"You need backup," Charles said.

"I *am* the backup, and this isn't a discussion." Ava had left me in charge, but I had to assert myself now before they decided they needed to protect me.

Graeme spoke up. "You don't get it. Your lives on Sinalta are worth barely more than a dog's. You'd—"

"Shut up!" I gave him a hard look. His comments would only make Chris and Charles more determined to accompany me. "And you're right, we're going to need more backup, but that means alerting all the Renegade cells about the Avowed, and Patrick needs to tell his father about the threat to America. We can't keep the secret like we did with the existence of Unbounded. Doing that nearly put the former Triad in control of the government. We need everyone ready to mobilize, especially Keene and Mari—once she's conscious—because we may need them both to get everyone out of there safely." By everyone, I meant our team because not even with Keene and me helping could Mari shift so many people.

"Right. Makes sense," Chris said. There was no denial in his surface thoughts, so maybe what I said really did make sense, even if I wasn't quite sure.

Chris pointed a finger at Graeme. "You had better not get her killed. Not even once." His gaze dropped ever-so-briefly to my stomach. I got the message loud and clear. I would survive death; the baby wouldn't.

I was still going.

"I'm depending on her to get my daughter out," Graeme retorted. "I have been hoping for a chance like this for the last nine years."

"He needs some gear," I said. "Go with him. But hurry. Make sure he doesn't contact anyone and examine everything he takes." I didn't need a weapon turned on me midtrip.

"I'll go," Charles said. I was glad it was him because I wanted a few minutes alone with Chris. I also knew that with his black ops experience, Charles would likely catch things even I would miss.

If only Ritter were here. But I pushed the thought away. I had to make my own decisions.

"I don't like this," Chris said when Charles and Graeme were gone.

"I know." I turned and began walking toward the place we'd climbed up to the ship and where our rope ladder was still attached to the railing, opposite the side of the ship where I'd watched Ritter and the others sink beneath the water. "I don't like it either, but it's all we've got. And Charles doesn't have the pull you and Stella have to make the rest happen. You have to go back and sound the alarm."

"Okay," he said, "but let me give you a quick rundown of how to steer that ship. I don't want you dependent on that guy. Don't worry. They're so simple my kids could drive them— once you know the basics."

"So I heard," I mumbled. By the time Graeme returned with Charles in tow, I was grimacing with impatience but pretty sure I could at least steer the boat. Once I hacked into Graeme's mind and got the coordinates, I wouldn't even need him.

When Graeme and I had climbed down the rope ladder and were in the control room of the submersible—or the transport, as Graeme insisted on calling the ship, he punched in a bunch of commands on the console.

"Show me what you're doing," I demanded.

He turned on me, suddenly too close in the confined space. "Is this what it's going to be like the entire trip?" he said. "With you suspecting everything I do?"

"Do you blame me?" I met his gaze straight on, my chin lifting in challenge. "You aided in the kidnapping of one of my family's descendants, a potential embryo. For all I know, that tapping you just did was you reporting that you captured me."

His sigh was resigned. "What can I do to convince you?"

"I think you know." I didn't add that I would get through his shield. Already, it was near failing.

He lifted his hands in surrender. "Okay."

Instead of vanishing immediately, the swirling silver of his shield drained away like water in a bathtub. I was in his mind before it was halfway finished. Of course, he was instantly aware of me.

Show me what you did just now, I told him. *And tell me how you really feel about what we're doing and about your loyalty to your leaders.*

He didn't resist. I stood there, his memories racing at me so quickly and with such ferocity that I was left gasping. There was more to Graeme's story, a deep bitterness that began when his Avowed mother had been staked to a pole in the ocean for punishment, her flesh eaten away by fish. I'd thought cutting or complete rotting in a sealed container was the only way to separate the three focus points to kill an Unbounded. Apparently, the Sinaltans had found a third.

What's more, Graeme Padovan wasn't coming with me because I was convincing or because he wanted to save his daughter. Or at least those weren't the only reasons. No, Graeme Padovan was taking me to Sinalta because he had a burning desire for revenge against the ruling families who had essentially condemned his sons to death.

That desire could make him a huge liability. I'd have to watch him even more closely.

I WAS SICK.

So sick.

You'd think that when nature chose me for the Change, I would have been given a little break in the morning sickness department. But with Dimitri's soothing touch and presence gone and the constant motion of the transport, I wanted nothing more than to vomit my guts out. Of course, when all you're doing is absorbing ocean matter, there's nothing in your stomach to throw up. After only ten hours, I was lying in the crew quarters' bottom bunk in a liquid mass of nausea.

"Here, try this." Graeme hunkered down beside me, offering a steaming cup.

"What is it?" I pushed off the safety harness and swung my feet down to the floor, ducking my head so I wouldn't hit the bunk above me.

"Nothing that will hurt the baby, and it might help you. These long-distance transports are always stocked with a variety of supplies, and it doesn't look like anyone has touched them. This is a tea made of a certain seaweed that we use to ease nausea. You might also try these crackers. You haven't eaten anything."

"I've been absorbing."

"It's not the same thing. You may be Unbounded, but you're

also human, and the human body likes to have something waiting in reserve for the baby, just in case."

"Why didn't anybody tell me that?" I grumbled, accepting the steaming cup from him.

He laughed. "With your healer nearby and steady ground, it probably wasn't necessary. During my wife's last pregnancy, she didn't leave our home once, not even to go to work because she'd have to take the transport, either through the city or the water, and since she is automatically given leave anyway, she chose to take it."

"They have a whole nine months off?"

"One of your years." A melancholy note entered his voice. "It's a reimbursement for the coming loss. A bribe." This last was nothing more than a sneer.

I sipped the tea and chose not to respond. Any apology wouldn't touch his pain but would only add to his need for revenge. "Um, not bad." And it wasn't too hot, either, which told me he had experience. "You made this for your wife?"

"Five times a day."

"You sound like you miss her." More than sounded. Need rose from him like a scent.

"I do. We have communication relays in place, and she has access, so we talk almost every day, but it's not the same."

"No, it isn't." Ritter had been gone less than a day, and the knot of anxiety was already almost more than I could take. "Plus, you can't be sure it's private."

He nodded. "Exactly, although we have a code we use to slip in messages, and when we get closer, I do have a way of reaching her without risk of anyone else overhearing. I'll let her know we're coming. She'll have some ideas to help. She's more active in our group than I am, of course, since I'm away half the year."

"Okay. But just her. We really need to keep this quiet."

"I know." He grimaced slightly and turned on his heel. "I'll leave you to rest. There's more tea in the cupboard if you need it."

After the tea and a few crackers, I was able to return to the control room, where Graeme sat staring blankly at the monitor.

"How much longer?" I asked.

"Twenty-eight hours."

I did a little calculation. "So at about nine, Wednesday night, LA time." Knowing the very great distance, it was faster than I'd dared hope. "What will the local time be?"

"An hour earlier. We reset our clocks to use your time zones after we made contact." He glanced over at me. "Better strap in. I have object detection on, and the programming is fantastic, but sometimes there's a jolt when it has to avoid things that are moving. It's either that or slow down. With the nuclear power engaged, you have to think of this transport as plane-fast, not boat-fast, though it's certainly not as fast as any jet. But there are a lot more things to run into down here than in the air. Live things, I mean."

"Right." Which might explain some of my nausea. I sat down and strapped in. "Any sign of the other ship?"

"You'd better hope not. If they see us, they'll take us into their hull and ask questions. No, I'm going another way."

That didn't sound good. "It better not be a longer way."

"Actually, it's shorter. We're smaller and can get through passages they can't. But they can also go faster, so they'll still beat us by a few hours."

A few hours, in which anything could happen. At least by then we'd know what my team's real welcome would be. For a moment, I entertained the embarrassing thought of what I'd do if Graeme's desire for revenge made him wrong about

Sinaltan intentions. His anger was enormous, like a blanket that engulfed him, so it was possible. He might also be one of those extremists who caused entire groups to suicide. If people could worship those like me simply because we lived two thousand years and couldn't be killed in ordinary ways, then it was entirely possible that Graeme himself was quite mad.

"So," I said, "tell me about your leaders. How does the government work?"

"There are five ruling families, and they fill the seats in the governing branch of our legislature. They're called statesmen, and they make the rules. The other branch is called the executive branch, and they administer the day-to-day. In theory, the branches are supposed to have equal power, but in reality the magistrate, who is the leader of the executive branch, is little more than a figurehead."

"And the rest of the Avowed?"

His head shook slowly back and forth. "They are every bit as imprisoned in their gilt cages as the leading families. I think that is what made the offer from the Emporium Triad so compelling to everyone. We would be ruling over a large country, maybe even an entire continent with plenty of room, while mortals to do the work."

"Well, that's not going to happen."

"I'm glad. Unfortunately, it takes time to see freedom as something all people should have, and we in Sinalta have been gods for a very long time."

Gods. It was the way the former Emporium Triad had seen itself. "Were they this way from the beginning?"

"I don't know. But none of us do. We can't even say for sure where Sinalta was originally built, but my wife believes it was near the Strait of Gibraltar."

Wherever they began, I was beginning to believe that the

rumors and conjecture about the mythical Atlantis had been based on truth. But if the Sinaltans were Atlanteans, they hadn't seemed to learn anything in their long years of exile from the rest of the human race.

"But your city went below the water in a single day? Is that true or only a myth?"

"Again, no one is left alive from that time, but the way our history tells it is that Sinalta was so advanced and the inhabitants so beautiful that people came from all over to see the city for themselves, but word got out about our abilities, and other nations wanted to control us. So we built a dome, and when we were ready, we left. We purposefully disappeared at the same time as a volcanic eruption so no one would look for us. It took months—years even—before we settled in the first location, and we moved several times after that in the first few hundred years, but ever since, we've been in Antarctica."

"It's pretty amazing."

He smiled. "I think so." Then his smile faded. "I often wonder how much of it is true and what would have happened if we hadn't run away."

I had nothing to say to that, but I gave him a sympathetic smile. "I can take watch now if you want to sleep."

He nodded. "I would like to. The computer is programmed with our route, and it will alert you if there are any issues. But just like driving one of your cars, slowing down and stopping never hurts."

"I think I can manage that."

The hours ticked by. I reached out mentally, searching for Ritter or Ava or Jace, but I couldn't feel any of them. I was supposedly the strongest sensing Unbounded in several generations, but what did that title matter if I couldn't pass the distance barrier? Mari had learned to do so with her ability, albeit with Keene's synergism help. Maybe I could learn to do the same.

All of which meant that until I was close enough, my team would remain in the dark about their potential danger.

I drank another cup of tea and ate more crackers and felt almost back to normal. My tongue still tasted of salt, so I drank too much water and had to figure out how to activate the tiny restroom. I was also constantly absorbing. The presence inside me burned with life, and I probed it gently.

Hello there, I said, more a feeling than actual words. Inside the baby's mind, the stream of thoughts was beginning, vague but present, also more feeling than anything. For the first time I felt the baby move, not with my body but with my thoughts as I saw it reacting to my greeting.

I'm here, was the emotion. It was satisfaction and curiosity all wrapped into one. I sat there for a long time, the connection open, a moment so private I didn't know how I could share it even with Ritter.

If we lived through the next week, I was going to try.

Then Graeme returned, and it was my turn to sleep again. The next time I awoke, a proximity alarm was beeping, and I nearly fell out of the berth in my hurry to get to the control room. Graeme was manually steering the transport now, and he'd turned on the larger screen on the sub's wall, which revealed nothing but blackness.

"We're close now," he told me. "I'm circumventing the perimeter alarms by taking us to a cave my wife learned about while working on the city dome and the shields that protect it. If we pass through the regular perimeter, I'll have to give them my name, and they'll undoubtedly give us an escort and take you into custody the minute we get through one of Sinalta's gates. They wouldn't hurt you." He hesitated before adding,

"At least not until the baby is born, but getting caught would make this journey pointless, right?"

He gestured to a mass on the screen that stood out as slightly darker than the rest of the watery world around us. "It's the backside of a cavern that stands between Sinalta and us. My wife's team uses it for a base when they're working on the underside of the city. The middle is hollow, and they blew out the water for air."

"Won't there be security here?"

"No. They know of the cave's existence, but not that it has an opening on this side. There are many underwater land-masses that have caves where we mine or grow food. They are natural protection for the city, but not all of them have been explored as thoroughly as you might think. My wife and one of her colleagues discovered the opening back here about a decade ago, and they're both of the same mind about leaving Sinalta, so they've kept it quiet. She'll meet us here with our personal transport so we can keep this one hidden for our escape."

It was a good plan, and since I had the tablet that could lock anyone except me out, I'd go along with it. "What is this group called?" I asked.

He shrugged. "We don't have a name." He shut his eyes wearily. "I guess that would make it too real. Something someone might report and that might get us staked."

I didn't have to ask what that meant because I'd seen the images of them staking his mother in the water.

"Resistance and revolutionaries are usually the titles that come up," he said. "The government calls us mortal lovers or dissenters." Again, the shrug. "It's all true. Valerine—that's my wife—believes in the goodness of human nature. But I haven't sensed any goodness in our rulers or those who blindly follow them."

I could understand exactly what he meant. Sensing provided insight into a person's true self instead of the face they showed to the world, and the inconsistencies were often painful.

That made me think of my child, lying in his blissful innocence. My shield would protect us both from the emotions of others, but I also needed to protect him or her from mine. Carefully, I fabricated a mental barrier, layering it carefully with smooth silver. As it was my own construct, I could get through it easily, but not by accident.

Graeme was now steering the boat directly at the black, looming mass of the cavern. Lit by the headlamps of the transporter, the dark, rough rocks appeared to be coated with an even blacker algae. The rocks looked cold and sharp and dangerous, which I supposed it was, this far into Antarctica.

"Where is all the ice?"

He chuckled. "Go upward, and you'll find plenty. But we're deep enough that the water doesn't freeze here, though the water is still very cold. A person, mortal or Avowed, can't last out there more than a few minutes. We've had more than our fair share of accidental deaths. That's why children who haven't Changed yet are not allowed outside the city. We've actually tapped into the Earth's core for the city's heat, which is part of the problem we're having with stabilization, but it has worked for thousands of years."

An alarm pinged, and he gently turned the transport, moving parallel to the rock. "There it is, up ahead."

I couldn't see anything on the wall screen, but the monitor on the panel showed a drawing of an irregularity. Graeme slowed, turning into the surprisingly large opening of a cavern. Shining rocks and sea life reflected off the headlamps of the transport, and when he flipped another switch, the effect doubled.

"What is that?" I said, staring at the rock that appeared coated with sections of fluorescent jelly. "Minerals?"

He grinned. "I thought you'd like that. There is gold as well as other metals on the rock, but that glowing surface is a unique sea creature. It's a specialty here. People claim they have aphrodisiac properties. It's not true, but they're hard enough to find and taste so great that no one cares to correct the myths."

I laughed. "Hopefully, I'll get to taste them. Though they're so beautiful that maybe no one should ever eat them."

"My wife would agree with you."

The passage narrowed, and he concentrated as we sailed onward. I tried reaching out again, thinking we might be close enough to Sinalta to reach Ava.

Noting the change in my focus, Graeme glanced back at me. "You can't sense Sinalta inside this rock. At least I can't. It's too dense. Only once we leave the cavern. And even then, you won't be able to see anything except that it's there. We have a grid similar to the one we put in the shipping container that prevents mental contact."

"How far away are we from the city?"

"About twenty-five of your miles. After we leave the cavern, it's up a couple miles."

He said it casually, and I realized that for them up and down didn't mean the same thing as it did to me. No doubt many of them went above and below the city on a regular basis.

The first part of the trip through the cavern took nearly thirty minutes, with me biting my lip until it bled. *Ritter,* I thought. *Where are you?* I hoped Jace hadn't irritated the Avowed to the point where they'd feel a hurry to shut him up.

With a little jerk, the transport stopped. "Sorry," Graeme said. "Almost passed it. This is the best place to park a craft of this size. We get out here and go a little farther on foot to a place that's better to board the smaller transport. The walls are too high here to do it easily. Valerine should be there soon."

"She's here now. And someone else." Two life forces glowed at an angle from our location. One dim and blocked, and one brighter. More people I'd have to rely on.

His eyes glazed a little. "Right. Good."

"She wasn't supposed to tell anyone."

"The other one is my daughter." He backed the transport up slightly, turned down another tunnel, and aimed the ship upward. The top of the wall screen now showed a slice of a dim world without water. Leaning forward, he killed the lights and the screen reflected only darkness. "We'll need flashlights," he said. "There should be some on board."

"I've got some too. And we'll need explosives." I headed to the sleeping quarters, where my team had left much of our gear. Now I put on Stella's armor, tucking weapons in the special pockets. I paused, looking at my machete. I couldn't conceal it without my long coat. Did Sinaltans wear coats? And what about my metamaterial cloak? At least that was small and thin enough to put inside a pocket.

Graeme snorted a laugh at me when I reappeared.

"Not going to fit in, huh?" I ventured.

"That's okay. I had Valerine bring you some things. I think it's best that you hide by simply fitting in."

"Where is the city's control room?" Maybe we wouldn't need to go inside the city at all but under it.

He grimaced. "The place to access most of the city's controls is located in the middle of the city beneath the parliament buildings. Depending on what our final target is, we can use the sublevels there to reach each area and set your charges."

I still had no idea what our final target would be, but I was hoping his wife would have some suggestions—and Ava, once I could contact her.

"I'm also not sure how we'll get you inside," Graeme added.

"Do you have a technopath in your group?" I asked before remembering that I didn't want to risk channeling a technopath to change my appearance.

"Good idea," he said. "The woman who discovered this entry with my wife is a technopath, and she should be able to forge you an ID."

"Right." I gave him a smile as if that had been my intention all along. Passing him a heavy bag of explosives, I picked up another. It was all my team had brought, and it would have to be enough.

He went up the hatch first, and I took a moment to set the tablet to security mode. If someone tried to enter the ship, it would alert me, and I could make sure to override any commands.

One way or the other, if I had to break through every last mental shield in Sinalta or blow the city to smithereens, I'd free my team.

Chapter 18

I FOLLOWED Graeme out of the sub, shutting the hatch behind me. He scrambled onto the rock and extended a hand, which I took until I was on solid ground. We started down a narrow passageway, the sides all sharp angles, rounded conclaves, and odd formations that could have been some native art but wasn't. Maybe sea creatures and ancient underwater volcanoes had been responsible, but it looked both beautiful and dangerous. Our breath turned white as it left our mouths, and the air felt icy cold, like prickling knives in my lungs. Ice crystals layered one wall and made some of our steps precarious, yet it was apparent that warmth was seeping up from deep within the earth because the waterway wasn't frozen, nor was the passageway clogged with ice. I had the sensation we were the only people in the entire world to ever lay eyes on this place, though I knew Graeme and his wife and possibly others had been here.

The narrow passage widened, and quite suddenly we came upon another waterway and a smaller transport with a door that opened upward like a hatch. A woman was peering out of this, the bottom half of her legs still in the transport and out of sight. Her eyes reflected our light, glittering a bright blue, and long blond hair framed a face so pale she appeared translucent. An intricate silver-colored headpiece lay across her forehead and around her hair like a crown, and a silver cord wrapped several times around her silvery-white fur coat that could have adorned a Greek goddess. Her face was eager, and her chin lifted in a manner that implied she was excited. She climbed out of the transport and moved toward us, her efforts encumbered by her long fur coat—one I envied because of the cold air. Even then, she looked regal.

Graeme hurried forward, catching her in his arms as she launched herself at him, a joyous smile spreading over her face. They crashed together and began kissing passionately, which reminded me they hadn't seen each other for two months.

Valerine Padovan was as tall as her husband, which made her look down on me slightly when she finally tore herself away from Graeme. Her eyes were heavily lined with black, and dark blue eye shadow covered her entire lid. She wore no mascara on her thick blond lashes, though, which told me she had a practical side. Our quick metabolism replaced so many lashes daily that mascara had to be touched up several times to keep it even.

"Anina?" Graeme asked.

Valerine laughed. "You already know she's here with me. I told her to stay in the transport." Her lyrical accent was far more prominent than her husband's.

I followed their gazes as they turned. Sure enough, a little girl as pale and blond as her mother was peeking out of the transport. Graeme hurried toward her, his feet sure as he jumped inside and picked her up. Love radiated from them, and for the first time I began to trust him just a little.

Valerine inclined her head and body in a slight bow. "Sorry about that. She insisted on coming when I told her. She's crazy about her dad." She made another tiny bow. "I'm Valerine."

"Nice to meet you." I tentatively tapped at her shield. It didn't seem as strong as those of the Avowed I'd met so far, but that made sense, seeing as she wasn't working topside. Still, married to Graeme, she would have practice in keeping him out. For now, I'd hold back and see what happened. If we were to be allies, I didn't want to force her cooperation.

"Thank you for what you're doing," she said. "Graeme told me you've promised to take us with you when you leave."

"I will do everything I can to fulfill that promise. But I'm going to need help."

She nodded. "I've been preparing for this for over a hundred years. I'm ready. In fact, I have some ideas to share with you." She turned slightly, watching her husband and daughter. "But it's cold. Let's get you inside. I've brought clothes you'll need to put on before we get to Sinalta. Hope you don't mind changing in the transport."

"I'll manage."

We moved together toward the transport, where Valerine pushed past her husband and settled into one of the two front bucket seats. Graeme gestured me to the back seat.

"Hope you don't mind riding back here. I figure it will be easier to change."

"No problem." The interior of the transport was slightly smaller than the average American minivan with the middle row of seats removed. With Anina taking up less space than an adult, I wouldn't have any problem changing. Heat rushed around me as I nodded at the child and slipped into one of the three empty seats in the back row, setting my duffel by my feet within easy reach.

In the front, Valerine shrugged off her fur coat, revealing a blue toga that matched her eyes and left one pale shoulder bare, reminding me even more of a Greek Goddess.

Glancing at me shyly, Anina settled in the seat farthest away from me in the back while her father settled in the other front seat. Valerine touched the control panel, and the hatch closed. As she started the transport forward, she gestured to a large cloth bag decorated with swirled silver braids on the floor between the rows of seats.

"Go ahead and open the bag. I think everything I brought will fit. We're about the same size."

She was being generous. While I was normally slender, my current outfit gave me a bit of girth, and she was on the too-thin side of willowy. "I'll need to keep my body armor on," I said.

"She's with embryo," Graeme told her.

Valerine shot me a smile. "That's wonderful. And an added protection for you here. Graeme probably told you."

"Or an invitation for kidnapping."

Valerine glanced back at her daughter and gave an abrupt nod. "That's a problem to fix, to be sure. But what I brought is not fitted, not until the cords are tied. There will be room enough, and the material is thick and tightly woven. No one will be able to see through it."

As I rummaged through the bag of clothing, I pondered our next steps. Right now all I had were my weapons, plastic explosives, and a plan to hack past their leaders' mental barriers. A lot would depend upon how much time we had and how much their leaders believed I had nothing to lose.

What I didn't have was a plan to rescue my team in the

event that I had to set off an actual explosion. And what about the innocents that might be caught in the crossfire? With each passing second, coming here seemed an increasingly bad idea.

I still had no choice.

Feeling eyes on me, I looked over to see Anina staring in my direction. She smiled shyly, flushing a bright red. Blond as she was, she reminded me of my niece when she was that age, except Kathy wasn't shy. I wondered if that was Anina's natural temperament or if it stemmed from the fact that she was a second-class citizen.

"Hi," I said.

She responded in a language I didn't recognize, and her father said, "English, Anina. You need practice."

"Hello," she said obediently, the red in her face deepening.

"You're ten?" I asked.

"Nine."

"Oh." Tall for her age. "I have a nephew who just turned eleven and a niece who's two years older."

"They are embryos?" she asked as if she already knew the answer.

I shook my head. "No."

"Oh, I am sorry."

Grief welled up inside me, unreasoning grief that I had no right to feel because Kathy and Spencer weren't any different than they were before I'd learned about the Unbounded. I was the different one.

"Nothing to be sorry for," I said. "They are too many generations removed to Change, but even if they were potential Unbounded—Avowed, rather—we have no way of telling until they are adults. Either way, they are awesome kids, and we are lucky to have them. They are so smart and funny. I hope you'll get to meet them soon."

Anina blinked in surprise as if she couldn't imagine such a world. "I hope so too."

Inside the bag, I found a white, sheetlike dress woven with tiny bits of glittering silver. There seemed to be too much material on the voluminous sleeves, and the attached silver cording on both the sleeves and the dress went on forever. Possibly the dress could fit over even my heavy-duty body armor. I held it up against me to measure.

A little giggle from Anina had me looking at her and grinning. "It's to protect the baby." I gave my belly a sharp rap, but only a dull thud reached our ears.

The dress was confusing to put on, but Anina took pity on me and showed me how to wrap the cords above and under my breasts and then in circles to my waist. The sleeves required similar wrappings down to the elbows and the wrappings were quite useful to secure a few weapons, though I doubt that had been their creator's intention. My real armament was on my body armor or strapped to my thighs and calves, but the slits in the sides of the dress allowed easy access while the folds hid everything underneath. I finished my ensemble with silver sandals that looked ridiculously inadequate for anything.

"You look pretty," Anina said. "But you should put your hair down, and you'll need a hair chain." She touched her own circlet of silver-colored leaves before leaning over to retrieve the white bag, pulling out a chain with a swath of blonde hair attached. "My mother will have to help. I don't know how to use this kind."

Neither did I, so I nodded and looked ahead. Unlike the long-distance transport, this one had a huge glass window separating us from the ocean instead of an electronic screen. I wondered at the difference, but the sea images spotlighted in the half of the window that was submerged riveted my attention. Was that silver gleaming from the rock lining the passageway?

"Rhodium," Graeme said, noting my attention. "Far more valuable than gold, even topside. We mine it down here and use it in almost everything, from headpieces to plating on our buildings. They are always looking for more veins, but of course we haven't reported this one for obvious reasons. We'll have to dive in a minute to reach the portion of the cave that Valerine actually reported in her notes."

I nodded. "How much further to Sinalta?" I felt a little like a child, but I'd been extending my mental reach since we'd arrived, and not catching even a glimpse from Ava or the others was cranking up my worry.

"Let's see . . . we'll be diving in about two minutes, then upward for three or so minutes to reach the second cave," Valerine said. "Ten minutes after that, we'll reach the mouth of the cave and start upward toward the city. Once we pass the grid about a mile below Sinalta, you should be able to mentally reach your people. The grid is on the same system that powers the dome, and without it the water would rush in and crush the plastic."

Graeme cast me a pitying look. "It's likely they will still be . . ." He broke off, glancing at his daughter, but I heard the word he didn't say: alive. "The families will want to see how much they can get from them first, and we're only a few hours behind their ship."

That was long enough to stake someone to a rock in the ocean, let them drown, and watch the fishes begin to feast, but I kept those thoughts to myself.

"You want a boy or a girl?" Anina asked into the awkward silence.

"Either one." I was going to add that I simply wanted it to

be healthy, but that wasn't quite true. I wanted an offspring I wouldn't have to bury before I aged another year. "Maybe a girl," I said. "I think my husband wants a boy."

"Girls are way better," Graeme said with a wink at his daughter. "They're definitely easier."

I'd heard the opposite where I was from, but life in Sinalta was very different from anything I knew.

"Hold on," Valerine said. "We're going down."

The next few minutes were fascinating as Valerine dived and navigated to the next cave. More time ticked by as we finally exited the cavern and began our ascent toward the city. Anina said something to her father, but their conversation fell away as I felt him—Ritter. Not his thoughts because his shield was strong and tight, but *him,* through our mate connection, and he was furious at something I couldn't see. I drew in a swift breath as I searched for Ava. She could protect herself mentally from prying minds as we talked, but I was too far away to protect Ritter that way. I found her, tightly blocked and angry but alive.

Ava, I knocked against her shield, and she pushed me away, which told me someone else had already tried to force her. I tapped a pattern she'd recognize.

She let me in, and I was relieved to see they were all okay. *Erin?*

Yes.

But how . . . you didn't.

Yes, I did. In the blink of a second, I transmitted everything to her without the tedium of physical speech.

It was a trap, I said. *They want Stefan back—or at least us and our mortal-loving Renegades gone.*

So we've learned. The instant we got to the capital and were escorted to a holding cell, we figured that out. They were most unhappy at our intercepting their future slaves and embryos. To be fair, I don't think Master Leyton knew what they intended for us. Wait a minute. Ritter needs something.

I felt the urge to beg her not to tell Ritter that I was here, but I saw it was too late. He was asking her about me, so he must feel me at least vaguely through the mate connection and would understand what it meant—proximity. Not telling him would have been only temporary, of course, but it would have given me more time to come up with a solid plan.

"Tell her I'm going to kill her," he said to Ava in a tight voice.

She chuckled without mirth. "You just did. But keep it down. Don't want them trying to break into my thoughts again."

I thought they couldn't do that, I said.

Right. Apparently not, or at least not the fellow they had in here. But he tried after one of their strong hypnopaths here ordered me to let him in. It was all I could do to reject the command. But never mind that. We've been talking to two heads of the ruling families here. They told us in no uncertain terms that they will not deal with us unless the original contract is upheld—which means giving them land that isn't ours to give. They also know we can't agree to that. I have the feeling they plan to attack the prison compound in Mexico to free Stefan. Are you able to reach anyone there?

She didn't mean mentally as she already knew we were too far away. *The Sinaltans have relays, but using their equipment means transmissions can be tracked. Graeme and his wife might know a way to send a short burst to Stella. They should be on high alert after Chris and Charles warned them.* The fact that Ava didn't censure me for telling Chris to mobilize everyone meant the situation was every bit as serious as I'd thought.

Well, if you can get through to the compound to give them an additional warning, do it. In the meantime, Dimitri has a little leverage. They want him to attend to their seer, Mikyn Zenos.

The Avowed who can tell if a child will Change?

I didn't realize that was who he was until I saw your conversation with Graeme. They only called him "seer." Apparently, he is feeling poorly, not physically but mentally. . . I think it's true what Graeme says, that he's the only one who has this ability.

Have you told these leaders that we'll do everything we can to help with their relocation? I asked.

She flooded me with images that communicated more quickly. She'd talked, presenting several plans, but the Sinaltans had listened and ignored her. They had also rejected her request to address the entire senate. Similar requests to see the media or to talk to the people at large were equally ignored.

It seems our Renegade, mortal-loving reputations precede us, Ava added, *and they aren't interested in a world where they are not gods. And that's what they are here to the mortals and even to the less powerful Avowed. Especially one of the leaders, Harren Tsaoussis. He's a powerful hypnopath, and I think he's the one who ordered Brenna and the others to keep their shields up. I haven't located the sensing Avowed who helped him, though. The man they had here earlier had little experience.*

She hesitated a moment before adding, *I think they all might be a little insane, or at least indoctrinated. They want a continent and sovereignty and to keep their current social hierarchy, which would be in violation of civil rights laws in almost every country. Dimitri has threatened to refuse to treat their seer if we are not released and given an audience with the senate, but I don't think his refusal will deter them for long.*

Which was a tacit approval of my disobedience.

Maybe I can create additional leverage, I told her. *I brought as many explosives as we could carry. My first thought is to get into the city control room and set some charges. Targets are yet undecided, but I know they're deathly frightened about losing their dome shield, and understandably so. Threatening them might be what we need to get you out of that cell. If we can get topside, they won't have the advantage, especially once all our people arrive.*

Threatening to blow their city shield isn't exactly ideal footing for peaceful negotiations, but it might get down to that, especially in light of what your new friend says about their atomic weaponry. But damaging something as serious as their shields would be seen as an act of war.

And isn't what they're doing to you already an act of war?

Yes, yes. But destroying their food supply might be more effective, and it would leave more room for negotiation because it's something we can replace. I'll get back to you ASAP.

I had no doubt that after centuries of working together, she would be able to communicate everything I'd said to Ritter and Dimitri even if they were being overheard. Jace was less experienced, but he was good at following commands. I only wished Cort were here and not in his grave, so I could be sure of where to set my charges. Trusting Graeme and Valerine wasn't my first choice.

Ava pulled away, leaving only a tiny thread linking us—one so small, I doubted even I would be able to detect it from the outside.

Silence reigned in the transport, and I looked around to see Graeme staring at me. Anina was leaning back in the seat, her eyes closed, with something suspiciously resembling wireless earbuds in her ears.

"You talked to them?" Graeme said quietly.

I nodded. "They're in a holding cell. You were right. Whoever is in charge isn't interested in compromise."

"I'm guessing they'll be at the parliament building," Valerine said. "That's where they keep important criminals, though it's been decades since we've heard about any. That's where I work too, only in the levels underneath in what we call engineering."

That might make getting them out easier—I hoped. "They're only safe for the moment because they want our healer to look at Mikyn Zenos."

"I see." Graeme exchanged a glance with his wife. Emotion wafted from him like a bad odor.

"What?" I pressed.

He sighed. "I'm not surprised they want your healer to examine Mikyn. Everyone in Sinalta has a stake in his future."

"Because he can determine if a child is an embryo."

"Yes. All parents and medical personnel are required by law to take newborns to the seer within two hours of birth, and a ceremony is held. But there's a rumor floating around that he was wrong about an embryo."

"You mean someone didn't Change?"

His glance at Anina was so fast that I wondered if I imagined it. "No. They *did* Change. Last year. After somehow surviving the mines for twenty years."

I felt the words like a punch to my gut. "But everyone he said *would* Change actually has?" I asked.

"As far as we know." He shrugged. "But there are four million people here, and if it happened once, it could happen again either way. In fact, if they're worried, I think it *has* to have happened before. Though if the child of an Avowed leader didn't Change, he'd hardly announce it." This time I didn't imagine the quick glance at Anina.

So it wasn't a perfect system, at least not at the moment, though it had apparently served the Sinaltans for several thousand years. My entire being itched with the desire to know how the man did it—to channel his ability and feel it for myself. Was there a gene he traced to its basic structure? Was it something that called out to him, shining like a beacon?

Valerine's jaw clenched and unclenched. "Mikyn Zenos should be executed," she muttered.

I wondered if she was thinking more about her lost sons or Anina. It didn't really matter. She was right. That kind of power, the power that allowed people to choose who was worthy of life or not simply because of a gene, shouldn't belong to any one person—or even to a group of people. The right to life was inalienable.

Anina was humming and moving her sandaled foot, exactly like any other kid who wasn't at risk of servitude for the rest of her life. Her parents had sacrificed to save her, but what about the thousands of other Sinaltan children, and those taken from above?

I experienced a shift in perspective. Up until this moment, my primary goal was freeing my team, but that wasn't what this was all about. I had to free all of them, both mortals and Avowed alike. Valerine was right. Mikyn had to be stopped. One way or the other.

Which meant Ava was right about targeting their food supply. We needed actions that would not only scare the leaders into releasing my team but make them reliant upon us until we helped move them from the ocean.

"You grow food here?" I asked. "Places we can blow up?"

Graeme snapped his gaze to mine. "We have places here in the city and in several caves like the one where we left the long-distance transport. They are all powered by energy from the

Earth's core, with our plants grown under special lighting. We also have fish and seal farms closer to the surface. We access those by using gates that lead under the city like the one we came in through. But if you're thinking those would be good targets, they aren't. Because we have facilities below the city where we store enough food to last seven years, as we have from the beginning."

From the beginning? It was odd phrasing, but I remembered something from my childhood Sunday School about a pharaoh and a famine in ancient times, so maybe that's what he was referring to. Even if that famine hadn't been in the same country, it could have affected the entire known world.

"But I thought a lot of the shipment from the Emporium was food," I said.

He nodded. "New kinds. Different from what we have here. Luxury items. You have a good variety that is appealing to us. Most of it goes to the head families, and then it trickles down to the rest. The shipments also contain raw materials that we use to make our cloth before we weave it with precious metals. And we order furniture and electronics because we don't have space for manufacturing. But for basic grains and such, the Avowed learned the hard way—when the people tried to starve us out before we sank the city—that we needed to be prepared. A lack of food was one of the things our ancestors feared most about going underwater. We've adapted, of course, and most of our food sources now come from the sea itself, but after the other city imploded, taking with it most of our food manufacturing plants, many more would have starved without our preparation. Our reserves are not as good as what we can get from our remaining sources or from topside, but it is a very wide safety net."

"I see." Having so much food available might complicate everything.

But then Valerine said quietly, "The power to all the storage facilities goes through the same systems that power the city. I don't have access to them, but we can set charges on the safety controls and shut them down. Most of the food will spoil, freeze, become waterlogged, or otherwise become useless. It is a good call. It will make them listen, and fewer people will be lost than from actually shutting down part of the city. Though we should also put charges on the dome, just in case." Sadness filled both her voice and demeanor, but there was quiet determination too. Valerine was a woman who would do what she needed to do.

"Then we should also target the five gates," Graeme said. "Not being able to flee or access outside food sources will mean more leverage. It means everyone is at risk, even the ruling families."

Valerine nodded. "They can be operated manually, so that means shutting the power to them from the engineering controls wouldn't be enough. We'll have to target each individually." Her gaze went to her daughter. "We'd have to leave one intact, at least until our escape."

We were silent, considering the implications. Their suggestions seemed both reasonable and shocking. But what other choice did we have?

"There is one more thing you should know," Valerine said, pushing something on the control panel that slowed our speed. "It's about the seer."

"Valerine," Graeme said. "It doesn't matter."

"What?" I demanded. We were now entering a narrow passageway that seemed to be made of some kind of opaque white plastic. Lights glowed from it, looking bright after the darkness of the ocean depths.

Valerine sighed. "Mikyn Zenos is Graeme's great-grandfather."

I frowned at Graeme, and he shook his head, his eyes fixed on the passageway ahead. "We are not close, not since he condemned my sons. I cannot abide the man."

Even so, it was a connection of family, and it meant maybe Graeme's loyalty was stretched even further.

"Tell me everything," I said. "About the food and Mikyn Zenos." Mentally, I reached out to Ava. *Sorry to interrupt your discussion, but you're going to want to hear this. I think we have a plan.*

Chapter 19

WE GLIDED UP THROUGH THE LIT PASSAGEWAY AND PAST A GATE, breaking the surface of the water in one of Sinalta's harbors. The female guard awaiting us in a floating booth waved at Valerine through the glass window without asking for identification.

"I always use this gate," Valerine explained. "She knows me and my transport. I sent her my general return time on my way out and radioed an update when we passed the security ring after we left the cavern."

I was guessing our welcome would have been different if Graeme and I had tried to come in Stefan's ship.

Valerine pushed more controls, and a soft moaning filled the transport. Then, miraculously, our ship rolled out of the water and onto a cobblestone road that looked like something from an ancient painting. Tall buildings of marble columns were inlaid with silver—or more likely rhodium—and gold. Statues graced every corner, most important figures wearing little more than fig leaves. Both men and women teemed on the streets, wearing togas of every kind and color, sandals, and glittering headpieces.

My first impression was that they had been stuck in a time warp here under the sea, but slowly, I saw that while the architecture was foreign and ancient, it mingled with technology I'd never seen in even the big American cities. This transport for example, that was both road and seaworthy, the 3D billboards advertising products I'd never heard of, and the buildings stretching far taller than any New York high rise, often with intricate walkways spanning the air between them. And everywhere the inlaid metals and elaborate designs. I saw no traffic lights, yet traffic moved without a hitch, so something was registering on the controls.

"Isn't all this marble dangerous?" I asked. "What about earthquakes?" Ancient cities had never been resilient to that sort of thing.

"We do have quite a few tremors down here," Valerine said. "But all this marble is a manmade lookalike. Only a few of the shorter structures are original to the city before submersion and are truly marble, though they've been reinforced. Those are mostly Parliament, and some structures and gardens belonging to the ruling families."

"Are all the areas so populated then?" I said, remembering Graeme's claims.

"Sinalta is made up of a center circle and two rings, separated by harbors," Valerine explained. "Where we are now is the inner circle, and overall it's the least populated—especially Parliament Street, where the rulers and their immediate families live. We're not that far from there. If there were more time, I'd take you to the outskirts. You'd see three times the number of people in the streets there and older structures. The mortals who serve the Avowed live there in small rooms in enormous apartment buildings."

"What makes it so bright?" I'd expected it to be darker in Sinalta since not only was it evening, but we were miles under the ocean.

"You only feel that it's bright because we've been in the dark. It's half-light now. At ten the city will switch to night. As for how, the lights are inlaid in the dome at random. There was some discussion about making only one source to mimic the sun, but anything bright enough to light the whole city took too much power and was too dangerous." Valerine paused. "At least that's what our history books say."

"Books," I mulled over that for some time, but of course they had books, probably both physical and electronic. Yet much had been lost, apparently, if they couldn't move their city or repair it.

Valerine brought the transport to a smooth stop before a tall building with impressive columns bordering the double, stained glass doors. Gold flowers and silver leaves wound up the columns. "We're here," she said with false levity, looking around at her daughter.

Sensing the change in movement, Anina pulled off her earbuds. "Why are we home?" she asked. "I want to stay with Daddy. He's been gone so long."

"We'll be back soon to get you." Graeme popped up from his seat and moved around it to the back, kneeling down in front of her. "Look, my precious. I want you to get a few of your most favorite toys together. We're going on a little trip, okay?"

Her eyes widened, and she began to speak in Sinaltan, but she wasn't good at blocking, and I understood the gist:

"Oh, I'm so excited. Can we go to the zoo again? I want to see the animals. And is Mom coming? How long are we going for? Can I take my sea lion doll? Will I need my matching sea lion fur coat?"

Graeme hugged her. "We're going for a week at least, and you can choose what to take, but don't pack too much, okay? Just one bag." He held up a finger.

Anina kissed his cheek and jumped out of the transport, waving before turning and running into the building.

"You sure she won't tell anyone about me?" I asked. "Any sensing Unbounded could get past her shield."

"I can't be sure." Graeme narrowed his eyes. "But she's not allowed to leave, and no one will visit her."

"I talked with her before we came," Valerine added. "She doesn't know who you are, but she knows it's important. Besides, as Graeme said, she won't see anyone. Anina doesn't have friends. She is not allowed to attend school with the embryos, and we don't let her go to the nursery with the other mortal children." Her lip curled. "They teach them to be subservient and beat them at will, so we pay an older neighbor on our floor to answer Anina's calls if she needs something." The tightness around Valerine's mouth told me there was no love lost between her and the neighbor. "Her help hasn't been necessary for years."

"We're only three blocks from the parliament." Graeme's smile became mocking. "Our reward for our jobs. Of course, we do live on the bottom floor of our apartment building. That's socially as low as you can get in this area."

Valerine tossed me a two-inch, intricately engraved coin with text I couldn't read. "We live in the apartment furthest to the back. The building is the only one on this street with gold roses on the columns. The number is three dash four zero five.

Insert the coin horizontally as far as it will go, and the door will open. In case you need to return here."

I committed the number of the building to memory because it never hurt to have a safe house, though if the op was compromised at some point, Graeme and Valerine's apartment might be the last place I'd want to go.

Valerine now slid from her seat and came to sit by me while her husband drove the transport. With a few deft twists, she had the hairpiece on my head; the rhodium leaves cold against my forehead.

"Luckily, your hair is only a little darker than mine," she said, giving a final finger-combing to the strands. "Or we would have had to remove the hair part. You wouldn't have blended in nearly as well." She tapped on the top of the transport, and something folded down in front of us. I'd thought it was some kind of video player like the one my brother had in his minivan, but it was a mirror.

Valerine smiled. "We are nothing if not vain in Sinalta."

I looked like something from a Cleopatra movie set. At least I'd fit in.

A tiny buzzing had Valerine fumbling for an earpiece, which she put in and answered like a phone. After a few seconds of conversation in Sinaltan, she ended the call. "Cherish will meet us there," she said. "She works with me, and she'll have an ID ready to get you inside."

Graeme's gaze narrowed on his wife. "Once we do this, there's no going back. They'll see us going into the building."

"Cameras?" I asked.

"No, it's not like that," he said. "I mean, yes, we have installed cameras, but down here . . . it's the people you have to worry about. The ones you think might be your friends. If it comes to it, anyone who sees us will testify against us later."

"No one has ever gone against the families. No one." Valerine's brow furrowed deeply as she sighed. "And quite frankly, there are more people who complain than those who will do anything."

"Are you sure we can trust your friend?" I couldn't help but ask.

They nodded. "She's one of the few I would trust with Anina's life," Valerine said.

We were silent as we drove the last few blocks to the city center, where the towering, close-set buildings gave way to luxury gardens, statues, and architecture that even to my untrained eyes had a different, more ancient feel. Everything screamed money and power. Fewer people were on the streets, now cobbled with designs that seemed impossible to create, with each structure becoming more elaborate than the last. Decadent was the word that came to mind.

Graeme slowed in front of a structure that reminded me of a Greek or Roman temple, then turned into an opening on the side that angled far down into the structure of the city. Once inside, he drove down one more level before parking the transport.

As we waited for Valerine's friend, we repacked my explosives from the duffels Graeme and I carried into Valerine's white bag and two others, one for each of us. Graeme also traded his sailor uniform for a white robe topped by a red, one-shouldered toga. Here, in this strange city that was both technologically advanced and archaic, he looked strong and able. Trustworthy. I hoped that was an accurate assumption.

Somewhere above us in this sprawling ancient building, Ritter, Jace, and the others were imprisoned. I could feel Ritter both like an ache of longing and a weight of responsibility. I knew he was upset that I was here. For him, the baby came first, and I had betrayed him. I hoped he would come around—if we survived. I was close enough now to detect if someone tried to get into his mind as we communicated, and to push them out, but still not close enough to extend my own shield, which left him vulnerable, so it was to Ava again that I reached out. Or maybe I wanted to stave off the inevitable.

I'm here at the parliament building. Any updates? I didn't really need to ask. I could sense her worry—something had happened.

They finally promised to allow us to address their executive magistrate tomorrow—if Dimitri looked at their seer afterward. Then suddenly they came back, insisting that Dimitri see their seer tonight instead of tomorrow. We're not sure why. If he's as fragile as they indicate, it would be better after he's rested.

Maybe they're worried the magistrate will be on your side?

Could be, but I believe he is only a puppet, just like Graeme indicated to you, but it was at least something besides the death they keep threatening us with. We need to find a way to make them release us, or at least allow us to go with Dimitri so we can fight our way out. I'm worried that the next time they come in, they'll simply drag him away.

They could also bring the seer to you. But they can't make Dimitri fix the man.

No, and so far I think that's the only reason they've held off on force. But there's some reason why seeing him is more important now than when we arrived.

Valerine says there's a night crew in engineering, so I'll poke around to see what I can find, I said. *From what I understand, the employees down here are all related to the main families, so someone might have heard something.*

Good. Meanwhile, we've been further discussing the targets. We still agree with your new friends that the food storage and gates will give us leverage but won't go so far that we can't dial the hostilities back. Since the Sinaltan leader first breached the agreement by holding us prisoner, we should have some leeway in our reaction. And blowing the gates at the same time should make them think twice about nuking us. See if Valerine can electronically turn off the gate you leave intact. With the other gates being physically damaged, that will help hide the fact that one is actually still functional.

Which might give us time to escape.

And the dome?

Yes. Her response was calm. *Valerine will know the best place to put it. If the shield is already having difficulties, one charge should be enough to do serious damage, if not to implode the entire structure. Because if all this fails, we can't allow them to send a bomb. No matter how fast our team acts on the surface, they wouldn't be able to stop that.*

Valerine says we can send an encrypted burst to Stella from here. But they'll figure it out, and it'll blow her cover, so we need to set the charges first. That meant less warning for those topside.

Let me know when it's done, she said.

I was about to pull back when I sensed Ritter reaching for me. Instinctively, before I could stop myself, I was inside the crack he opened.

I'm here, I told him.

Be careful.

No, Your Deathliness, I put into his thought stream. *I thought I would purposely try to get myself killed.*

That didn't amuse him, as I knew it wouldn't, but I wasn't backing down. *I'll be wherever you are after they release you,* I told him. *I'll bring the guns, and you try to bring the bad guys, okay? We'll make short work of them all. Together.*

That did get a flicker of amusement from him. We'd be okay. We would. I had to believe that.

I love you, he said.

I knew how much it cost him to say that instead of yelling at me for being there.

I love you too, Your Deathliness. Gotta go. Someone's coming.

I pulled away as a tapping on the hatch made Valerine jump and glare briefly at her husband, who like me had sensed someone approaching and should have warned her. "It's Cherish," he said.

He punched the control to open the hatch, revealing a curvaceous, black-haired woman with a large, hooked nose. Without a word, the newcomer somehow managed to slip inside past Valerine without touching her before coming to sit on the seat next to me. She was the only Sinaltan I'd seen so far whose skin was bronze instead of pale white and whose eyes were a dark brown.

"Hand," she said in more of that lyrical English, bringing to life a tablet on her lap. "I just need a picture and a hand scan, and you'll be good to go, at least until the update. No depending on it for more than ten hours, or it'll be detected and the ID quarantined until investigation. It's the best I could do." There was no apology in her voice.

She pulled the tablet away from my hand, lifting it to take a picture of my face. "There, all finished. You are now Lucia Pantazis. Clock starts now."

"Thank you," I said.

"Don't thank me. Just do it." Her dark eyes held mine. "Please."

I nodded, wondering at the intensity in her voice. "I'll do my best."

The hint of a smile came to the corners of her mouth.

"I don't care if you do your worst. Just help us." To Valerine, she said, "Call if you need me again."

When she was gone, Graeme said quietly. "Cherish is Avowed, of course, but she has a son in the mines."

A little more weight landed on my shoulders. One more person to save . . . or to fail.

"I've talked to Ava," I said. "The plan is a go—the food storage, the gates, and the dome shield. But she wants you to electronically shut down the working gate as well."

"That's a good idea," Valerine said. "We'd better hurry."

I didn't move. "Now that we're going inside, I need to need to know what's being said and how to respond. I don't know the language, but I can understand through you."

"Right." Graeme released a portion of his mental shield.

"You too," I said to Valerine. "I'll protect you from anyone else."

She hesitated only a second. I was glad because I needed to know if she really was on my side. At the same time, I marveled at how desperate she must be to permit the contact. If I couldn't sense whether or not someone was in my head, I'd fight to the death to keep them out. I'd seen too well what kind of things could be done inside someone's mind.

"Let's go," I said, climbing from the transport.

The parking garage resembled an ancient, well-kept house with columns, statues, and elaborate swirling inlays, but there was electricity in the fake lanterns along the walls. We reached a door made of plaster that resembled marble, and it slid open like an elevator door.

The doorway led to a narrow room with a desk. The older woman sitting there looked up and smiled as we crossed a tiled floor depicting Sinalta and her rings.

"Hi Priya," Valerine said a little too brightly.

"Back so soon?" Priya asked. "I thought you'd be away all day, with your husband coming back."

Graeme's mind translated the meaning of the senseless Sinaltan words into feelings and images without him thinking about it. As with passing information with Ava, it worked instantly.

Valerine smiled. "Yes. We are leaving soon to take Anina to the middle ring to see the animals at the zoo, and we'll stay a few days to enjoy the amusement park rides, but I forgot to assign the schedule for when I'm gone, and since our new employee arrived, we thought we'd give her a little tour."

The woman came around the desk and, to my surprise, kissed both Valerine and Graeme on their mouths. Graeme, responding to my thought, told me it meant that they were considered equals.

"Good to see you back," she said to Graeme. "Jonathan and I will have you both over for dinner soon. We would love to hear about your adventures topside."

"It would be a pleasure," Graeme said, but he didn't mean it. He'd spent four miserable hours being grilled about topside life during his last visit and had no plans to repeat the torture.

"I didn't know we were getting another engineer." The woman's blue gaze shifted to me. I put her physically somewhere in her forties, which meant she'd lived five hundred years, at least.

"We are. Thankfully. We've had a lot of extra work these past few months, and I need to brief her before I leave. I won't have time in the morning. So Priya, this is Lucia Pantazis." To me, Valerine said, "Lucia, this is my friend and co-worker, Priya Scala."

Kiss her on the cheek, Graeme told me. Which meant I was slightly inferior in this strange world. If I were much lower, I would kiss her hand.

Smiling brightly, I leaned in and kissed her cheek. She smelled of vanilla and raspberry, an odd combination here under the sea. I used the contact to increase my force on her shield, smashing it open on the third blow with my virtual machete. She wasn't nearly as strong as the others I'd met so far, except for Anina, and I hoped that was typical down here. I needed to find out what was going on upstairs with Ava and the others.

"Aapase milakar achchha laga," I said, copying the sounds from Graeme's mind.

I knew the accent wasn't perfect, but repeating it like this seemed to work because no alarm crossed her mind as she returned the greeting. "Nice to meet you also. Welcome."

After a hesitation, Valerine said, "Lucia is with embryo." I knew this was for my added protection, but it irritated me nonetheless.

"Wonderful news. Praise the ancestors." Priya reached for my stomach, and for a heart-stopping moment, I thought she'd feel the body armor, but her fingers barely brushed my robe.

Valerine sucked in a loud breath, and Priya glanced at her. "Is everything okay?" she asked.

"Yes, I just . . . I'm anxious to get back to Anina."

"Of course you are." A slight distaste had entered Priya's voice, and her thoughts were far more unkind. She didn't approve of Valerine's devotion to her mortal daughter. "That reminds me," Priya said. "The Scala family is soon to have a new member."

"Oh?" Valerine exchanged a look with Graeme, and her thoughts told me that she thought maybe one of the embryos from topside had been destined to be given to the Scalas.

"Yes." Priya grinned. "Bahar, my second cousin, has gone into labor." To me, she added. "She's married to Statesman Tsaoussis—yes, it's that Bahar. We should have a baby before morning." Her thoughts filled in the rest. The Scala family also had a stateswoman high in the ruling class, but Tsaousiss was the most prominent leader in all the ruling families, so Bahar's marriage had elevated them all.

I recognized the name Tsaoussis. He was one of the leaders Ava had been talking with—or contending with to be more accurate.

Valerine's shoulders relaxed. "But I thought she wasn't ready to deliver for another two weeks."

"She isn't." Priya walked back around the desk and resettled in her chair. "But apparently, this baby is a little impatient. We all have high hopes that he'll be an embryo. Third time's the charm, and poor Bahar has been through enough pregnancies in the past two years. I guess we'll know by morning if she'll have to try again."

I understood her meaning at once. This was Bahar's third child, and the other two hadn't been embryos but mortals, and from what Graeme had said about the ruling families, that meant Bahar—or her family—had opted for a post-birth abortion.

A rush of nausea had me fighting not to throw up all over the pristine floor. Regardless of what Graeme had said about it taking three or four pregnancies before the odds ended up in their favor, the stark reality was that every single birth had the same percentage chance—only thirty percent here in Sinalta—of a possible Change. Previous failures did not change those odds. But at least now I understood why those in charge were pressuring Dimitri to look at the seer immediately. The Tsaoussis and Scala families were having a baby, and a decision would be made about his future. They'd want the seer sane and ready to pass judgment.

So he didn't make another mistake.

Ava. I reached out through the space separating us. *I think I may have found out why they're so anxious. Statesman Tsaoussis's wife is having a baby, and they want to be sure the seer is in good health.*

I should have guessed. Depending on how the labor is going, we might have a few hours. Then they'll be back.

Right. I refocused on the conversation going on around me.

"We won't be long," Valerine was saying. "But it's nightfall. You'll be off soon, right?"

"Oh, yes, and with a little luck, I won't be in for days because I'll be off celebrating the new embryo." Priya laughed. "I might not be back before you are."

Valerine smiled tightly. "I hope it works out well, Ancestors willing."

"Well, if everyone will sign in, you can get your tour started." Priya slid a tablet across the table with the outline of a handprint on it. One by one, we placed our hands on the screen and were approved.

Valerine nodded at Priya and hurried past the desk to a door that she opened with a code. "Come along," she said, her voice sounding odd and unnatural.

On the other side of the door, I stared hard at Valerine. *You need to calm down,* I told her mentally, also transmitting the silent message to Graeme. *If you keep acting like you're doing something wrong, you'll get us all caught.*

"Right. I apologize," Valerine said aloud. Then, shaking herself, she added, "For the delay, I mean. Let's get right to the tour."

Which might mean we were being recorded. Sure enough, I glimpsed a camera by the door.

How many cameras? I asked Valerine.

Only at the entrances, she thought. *Here and near the doors below, which we use to manually work on the shield controls. It will be safe to talk in a minute.*

Good. I nodded at her to precede us down the hallway.

We passed a room where half a dozen people sat in front of huge screens, monitoring the city's enormous dome. So few people, it seemed to me, when the lives of four million were at stake.

I must have sent the thought to Valerine because she said in a quiet voice, "We have more here during the day, but really they're not needed. Everything was automated in the first millennium, and trading with the topsiders has facilitated that as our equipment became obsolete."

"Where is the old equipment?" Maybe those relics could give us some idea why their shield was failing.

"Stored below in one of the sublevels. I can show them to you once we're finished." She paused before rushing on. "If there's time. We may need to get out quickly, and it might be impossible to return."

The words were a not-so-subtle reminder of what she and Graeme were sacrificing, and I had to admit that without them, my job would be a lot harder.

On the third subfloor and down a long corridor, we set the first charges for the food storage. The second charge was down one more subfloor on the opposite side. Valerine made sure my detonator would work, attaching a booster to each explosive that would give me more reach. "The remote will activate the food storage and gate shields, once we get those in place."

As I pocketed the detonator under my dress, Ava's panicked thoughts surged down the connection between us. *Erin, our time has run out. They've shot Jace and taken Dimitri!*

Chapter 20

A SENSE OF INEVITABILITY FILLED ME. *GUESS THAT BABY WAS BORN,* I thought.

Peering out from Ava's eyes, I saw only Ritter's bulk blocking full view of my brother, but his life force was still glowing. *How is Jace? Is everyone else okay?*

He's okay, or he will be. The shot was in the arm, and Ritter is bandaging him now. Dimitri demanded his supplies and gave him an injection of curequick, so he'll be up in a bit. No one else is hurt. Dimitri went to placate them, but I don't think they plan to bring him back. At least they let him change into his bodysuit and armor instead of the prison scrubs they made us wear. They tried to put a toga on him, but he convinced them to let him wear his own clothes.

That's good thinking. It would give him protection once the fighting began. *But so far, we've only been able to set the charges for the food.*

How much longer for the others?

I don't know how far away the gates are, but I'm guessing a couple of hours for those unless we separate, and we still have the charge to set down here on the dome shield. That was the one that made me nervous because the last thing we wanted was for the city to collapse. But the charge was important as our backup protection against nuclear attack.

All right. Let me know as soon as it's done.

You think they'll hurt Dimitri?

No, I think once he does what they want, we'll become expendable, especially me. And as much as I know you'd like to run our Renegade cell in my place, I'm not ready to step down.

Very funny.

I've never been able to stop Dimitri from healing anyone when he sees a real need.

I wasn't so sure Dimitri would give in to them. I knew how much he cared about Ava, and I believed he'd put himself at risk to save her.

But you've also seen him do the opposite of healing, I said.

Yes. Sadness came through our link. *It eats him up when he has to do that. It's worse than killing someone with his sword.*

It may be necessary. This seer shouldn't have the power to condemn children.

He may be as much of a victim as we are. Just do your best, Erin. It's all any of us can do.

We'll hurry.

That would mean dividing and conquering, but I had been in Graeme and Valerine's minds long enough to understand that they had already passed the point of no return. That was enough for me to trust them.

Valerine was moving off, but I stopped her. "They've taken our healer to the seer."

Valerine frowned. "The baby must have been born."

"They shot one of my team. He'll be okay, but we need to hurry."

Graeme's brow creased as he scowled. "They'll never let your healer go. We need an Avowed healer too much, especially until a replacement for the seer is found."

"Will they hurt him if he refuses?"

"Oh, yes. Not permanently, mind you. But first they'll hurt your friends. Separating them will give them power over him. He'll have to jump through hoops for a promise to see them— and meanwhile they might already be dead."

"If the baby's here," Valerine added, "there's not much time, especially if your healer does what they want. Come on."

"No." Graeme held up a hand. "I can go now to the gates while you finish here."

Valerine drew in a swift breath of air. "It'll be too suspicious. I'm the only one with clearance to be where we'll need set the charges."

"You can give me the codes and show me where to do it—in your mind."

"But—" Valerine began.

"I'll call Cherish. She'll do half of the gates. She knows as much as you do, and she has clearance."

"But if her family found out . . ."

"They won't."

For a moment Valerine stared at her husband, and I could see in her mind that there was something she was trying not to think. But was she hiding it from him or me?

Finally, she nodded and held out her hand in invitation. At once, before he even touched her, he was inside her head, watching as she showed him where to place the charges. They exchanged no secret messages, and he didn't seem aware that her anxiety wasn't all related to the task at hand. The information dump lasted less than thirty seconds, and then he pulled away.

"I'll get a public transport to meet Cherish," he said, kissing her in farewell. "That way, you two will be able to take our transport back to get Anina. I'll meet you there."

"No," I said. "I'm going with you. At least as far as your seer's house. I need to see if I can free our healer and then get to the others. Valerine doesn't need me to set the last charge." I looked at her for verification.

"No, I don't. And it's probably better anyway. We have lockdown procedures. If the first charges go off before I get out, I'll be stuck."

I didn't like the resigned note in her voice. "We can't let that happen."

"There are other ways I can get out of the sublevels. Not easy ways, but possible for one person. So you two take the transport. Here, we can message you on this." She drew out an oversized earbud with a small, folded screen that I recognized as the phone she'd used before. "One of us will message you on this when it's all finished. I'll set the final charge and then take gate two offline—that's the gate we came through and will use to get out. But give me the second detonator, the one for the shield. I'd like to double-check the connection before you go."

We'd all agreed that the shield should be on a separate remote to avoid accidental detonation. The second device had a double safety and was small enough to tuck into an inner pocket near my breast.

It took only a minute, but she hesitated as she handed it back to me. "I don't plan on using it," I told her.

"I know. It's just . . ."

"Valerine." Graeme was already moving down the corridor. "We need to hurry."

"That woman at the desk isn't going to say anything when we leave here without you, is she?" I asked.

"Priya should be gone by now. And if her replacement asks any questions, well, you're in the database and will have the authority to escort Graeme." She glanced over her shoulder where Graeme had slowed his pace, turning to wait for me. Valerine put her body between us, taking my hand and speaking softly. "Look, I wanted . . . if something happens to us, will you please still take Anina topside?" She put her hand into the side pocket that angled over the front of her toga, pulling out a folded paper document and what appeared to be some kind of tiny data disk. "This gives you the right to take her. She'll be at our quarters."

I stared at the items in my hand. "But . . . how?"

"I told you before that I was ready. I've planned for everything."

"What does your husband say about this?"

She shook her head. "He didn't think it necessary, but so much could go wrong, so I made these this morning before you arrived. Anyway, I'm the mother and Anina is a mortal without citizen rights, which means she's my ward until she's ten, and then she belongs to the government. They can send her to the mines if Graeme and I don't do what we agreed—and it's pretty clear we're not. If we're caught . . . or if we're . . . you know . . . she must still get out."

"I promise not to leave her behind," I said, hoping I wouldn't regret the statement. But Valerine was risking everything she loved for her daughter, and if things went sideways, I wouldn't let it be for nothing. "But you must get the charge on that shield. And don't forget to send the warning to Stella."

She nodded. "You take the transport. I'll meet you at the apartment or even the cave. We have the location programmed in. Have Graeme show you how to access it."

I pocketed the documents and joined Graeme, who took one last, lingering look at his wife before plunging ahead. When we reached the entrance, the new receptionist at the desk was watching something on her tablet screen, and she barely nodded at us as we left.

"Mikyn lives just at the end of this street," Graeme said once we were out of the parking garage. "I'll drop you there and leave the transport one street over. Valerine's right. They'll lock down the area, and you don't want to get stuck. I'll meet you back at the apartment."

"All right."

He stared at the road ahead. "Mikyn's abode is more a mansion, and the front is a veritable fortress, but there's a side entrance I'll show you, and unless they've revoked it, I have a personal code for the family entrance."

"I thought you said you weren't close."

"We aren't, but when I'm here, I'm required to attend the baby ceremonies."

I stared at him. He had to watch parents receive their baby's sentence? The idea was unthinkable. Though we were only loosely linked at the moment, he could feel my distaste.

"All Mikyn's immediate descendants are required to observe and connect with him to see if we can figure out how he does it."

"And have you?"

A quick shake of his head. "I see it when he shows us, but I can't find it on my own after or before. Only if I'm linked to him."

"Were you there when your children were taken to him?"

"Yes. But not connected. That's not allowed."

So Graeme hadn't seen for himself that his children weren't embryos. I didn't know if that was kinder or more cruel.

"I'm sorry," I said.

He inclined his head, accepting the sympathy. "Valerine has wanted to act for years. Maybe if I'd listened to her, maybe if I'd bypassed the Emporium and contacted the Renegades . . ."

"Don't go there. Focus on the task at hand." Later we could discuss the past—if we got out of this alive.

"Right." He nodded vigorously as if to shake away the regrets.

"How many descendants does he have?" I asked.

"With our ability? Nine, the last I counted. Besides me, that is. There were over a hundred before the other city was destroyed. We've known about his mental issues for a while, and there was a concentrated effort to breed more empaths, but there just aren't that many with the ability who aren't already related. Most of the families have at least one empath, though."

"Who else will be there tonight?"

"The parents or their representatives, and someone from the senate, though in this case the father and grandmother are statesmen and will likely fill that role. Mikyn also has a personal assistant whose gift is combat and an assistant skilled in hypnosuggestion. They are relatives. There are mortal house servants, of course, but only one stays at the house and will be there this late."

"That's not much protection."

"It's not needed. No one here can go against the families." He gave a bitter snort. "It's not as if someone could assassinate him and escape to Mexico. No one goes in and out of Sinalta through the gates without being seen and recorded. Besides, no one can get into Mikyn's house."

"Except you and nine other sensing Avowed."

He nodded. "Only during ceremonies. Otherwise, the code won't work." He paused and then added, "We all hate it—attending the ceremonies. It's pointless, or it has been so far."

He pulled up at the edge of what would be considered a luxurious estate anywhere in the world. There was no sign of the overcrowding or ugly mortal areas of Sinalta that I'd been told about. It was all expensive Grecian architecture and lush shrubbery. Life forces radiated out at me from the house.

"I'm sensing a lot of people," I said.

He followed my gaze. "There must be more guards because of your healer's presence. Not sure how many from here."

"Seventeen." All of them blocking, but some obviously not well. They were in different rooms, though, not together. The one furthest removed might be the servant. "Could be more if they block well."

He laughed. "You mean as well as you? Unlikely. There's been no need. Look, I could take you as far as the door."

"I'll figure it out," I told him. "You need to get those charges set." I was already lucky that I wouldn't be climbing up walls and breaking windows, all of which I'd done in the past. Shaking out the metamaterial cloak, I drew it around me, including the hood.

"The coin Valerine gave you for the apartment will also let you inside the transport. It'll beep when you near it. To bring up the preprogrammed locations on the navigation screen, push this button. It'll alert you when you need to stop if there's any traffic to wait for. I've switched it to English."

It appeared very similar to the larger submersible, only simplified. "Thanks."

With another nod, I slipped from the transport and into the shadows of the shrubbery. Tiny, gleaming pinpoints of fake stars alleviated the overhead blackness, but I felt a distinct sense of loss when I looked for the moon and remembered there was none. As I moved down the cobbled walkway, I studied the path ahead that led to a back gate. Even as I edged toward it, a transport pulled up, and I stepped backward into the brush to hide. Seconds later, two men came past, speaking in Sinaltan. They carried no weapons and didn't look like guards, so they could be Graeme's relations, which in turn meant that two more of the seventeen inside the house were either guards or officials.

It also meant that these two men were sensing Avowed, and they might very well detect me, depending on how experienced they were. Delia Vesey from the former Triad had once hidden mentally from me, but even she wouldn't be able to now. But could I hide from these men? I tightened my shield, smoothing it over with glistening black from the inside. *Nothing to see here,* I thought wryly.

They passed me without glancing in my direction, intent on their conversation. Dissatisfaction rose from their surface emotions. Graeme hadn't been exaggerating when he said the seer's descendants were displeased with their forced attendance. Whether because they felt helpless, thought it a waste of their time, or were against the process entirely, I had no way of knowing unless I was inside their heads. And I couldn't risk that.

They were through the gate now, and I moved to intercept it before it clanged shut, waiting a few heartbeats before trailing after them.

A female guard stood at the side entrance, so I couldn't immediately follow them inside. Instead, I had to waste time breaking through the woman's shield so I could carefully release a picture suggestion into her thought stream: *Go check the gate and road, just in case.*

She obliged with an ease that sent a twinge to my conscience. At the door, a massive wood affair with no handle and only a keypad, I typed in Graeme's code, but nothing happened. Cursing, I eased around the house, finding more columns and a huge balcony. Graeme had said this was a veritable fortress, yet so far no animals leapt out at me, and I could detect no cameras or motion sensors.

Within moments I understood his comment. There were also no ground-level entrances to the back of the house, or even windows. Only the tall pillars and marble walls that were so high, I felt sick looking at them. Either the man didn't spend much time in his garden, or there was a door in the marble that opened, perhaps electronically. I felt along the marble, and sure enough, there were clear indentations of a massive door in the wall. No way to open it from the outside.

Sighing, I fumbled in my leg pocket for my grappling hook. It was smaller than the one Ritter used on the boat, but it would be enough to hold my weight if I could find a place to secure it. I was about to give up and pull a gun on the guard instead when I spied the head of a statue on what might be a balcony. I steadied myself and shot, nearly whooping as it wrapped and held. This grappling ensemble didn't have a motor to help me climb like some of our heavier ones, but the carvings on the columns would give my feet purchase. I longed for my boots instead of the ridiculous sandals, and for a moment I considered ditching them and the white toga, but I might still need the disguise to either fit in or at least mask my true intentions from casual observers. I looped the sandals around one of the cords on my dress and began to climb. Up, up, up, I climbed, my heart racing. It seemed to take forever. I didn't look down.

Finally, I was on a massive balcony and pulling out a glass

cutter. Hopefully with the guests present, alarms wouldn't be set, but I was ready to move fast in any case. I was grateful for the darkness and my cape that would obscure me from any cameras.

The inner fastening of the door was a simple lock, so a small, round cut in the glass sufficed to get me inside. I found myself near a large staircase and headed down it, following the direction of the life forces. At the base of the staircase, I was surprised by the large reception area that could have been a grand front entrance, though I was definitely near the back of the house. Columns, statues, and tapestries met my gaze while a gas fire burned in a majestic grate.

I walked across the cool marble floor, tranq gun in hand, my bare feet making no sound. Dimitri was here somewhere, and I needed to contact him, but that would mean chipping a hole in his considerably impressive shield and then helping him ward off anyone else who might notice and try to take advantage. I'd get closer first so I could be sure to protect him.

The life forces inside the house were divided into three different groups, ten in one room near the front of the house, one somewhere above, and six closer to me. Two more were at the front and back entrances. The ten was likely where the nine relatives had gathered, either with the servant or an official, so I moved toward the group of six life forces. That must be where Dimitri and whoever had brought him here were waiting. The wide hallway featured more marble statues, wall hangings, and scattered ornate furniture. I had the disorienting feeling that I was in a museum, not a place where people actually lived. How much of this had come from the original Sinalta before it sank into the ocean?

Voices came to me down the hall, and I paused to make sure they weren't moving in my direction. Then I continued, gliding along the wall until the voices were louder, and I could see they came from a partially open doorway. From the little I could see, it looked like a spacious library, with tall wooden bookshelves crammed with thick books bound in a variety of colors—white, brown, and black. Even my inexperienced eyes could see that none of them dated back to the age when the rest of the place had been created, and I wondered how many arctic sea lions had given their lives to preserve these words between their leather covers.

The voices became intelligible, and to my surprise they were speaking in English. "What is taking so long?" growled a man, his Sinaltan accent strong.

"He's been very unwell, Statesman Tsaoussis," replied a woman. "Getting him up after he's retired for the evening is never a good thing."

"The baby will be born within the hour, if he hasn't come already."

"Then, if you'll excuse me for saying so, shouldn't you be at your wife's bedside?" The tone was respectful, but I could sense a note of mockery in the woman's surface emotions.

"I'm not required there. She has her sisters and sedation, if that's what she wants. I need to make sure Mikyn is ready. I will not tolerate a mistake with this child."

"Then you should wait until morning."

"You know the law. It must be within two hours."

"Maybe the law should be changed." This came from a voice I knew only too well: Dimitri.

"Out of the question," snapped Tsaoussis.

"No?" Dimitri's mockery was far more apparent than the woman's. "I guess that would give the parents too much time to bond with a child they don't want to keep."

"You know nothing of our ways." The man's voice was angry,

almost vicious, but it didn't hide the desperation beneath the words. This child meant a lot to the statesman.

Distantly, I was aware of the solitary life glow on the upper floor moving lower—probably going down the same stairs I had recently taken. I ducked into a room opposite the library, pressing myself up against the interior wall. I could no longer see into the room, and I could only pick up half the words echoing across the hallway.

I waited, but I couldn't sense the person moving closer, so I concentrated on reaching out to Ava. *I'm here at the seer's house,* I told her.

That wasn't the plan.

I need to see how he's doing it, I told her. *And Dimitri needs backup. Graeme and Valerine will do what they can, and if they can't, then the food stores will have to be enough. Do you have a connection with Dimitri so you can tell him I'm here, or do I have to break through his shield?*

I sensed Ava's resignation before the thoughts formed. *I don't. I can't protect him the way you can. You'll have to break in.*

Doing so would weaken me, but I had to find out what was going on in that room. Maybe instead, I could slip into the seer's mind when he let the others in. But would he sense me among his kin? I should be able to block to some extent, but I suspected it wouldn't be enough. He would know. Would I have to battle him mentally?

The voices in the other room were louder now as Dimitri argued with the others. He was demanding that Ava be allowed to attend the ceremony. "If your seer is growing weaker, as you believe, you'll need a backup. Maybe she can learn."

Tsaoussis answered, but his voice was too low for me to hear, and I started to move into the hallway—only to be brought up short by a gun shoved in my face. I backed up fast, but the man came with me into the room. He grabbed my tranq from my hand, moving with lightning speed.

Combat, I guessed.

He wasn't alone. A shorter man with white hair and the slightest stoop was at his side. I couldn't see their life forces even though they were standing right in front of me. That meant the old man was sensing—and strong enough to block the other's glow.

The taller man spoke to me in a low, demanding voice, moving his gun toward me for emphasis.

"Sorry," I said, lifting my hands in surrender. "I don't speak Sinaltan." Mentally, I was already at his shield, pounding away with my machete even while enforcing my own barrier, pushing it outward to protect my physical body. And my baby. This close, he wouldn't miss if he fired unless I deviated his shot. His shield was strong but nothing like Graeme's or Brenna's. I slammed at it again. I could feel his strong surface desire to shoot.

"Stop," the old man said in English, raising a hand but not looking at his companion. "She is with embryo."

I could see their life forces now, glowing dimly.

The guard lowered his gun an inch, but he didn't step back. His return words in Sinaltan leaked disgust.

"Please close the door," the older man said to him mildly. "The others can wait a bit longer."

Scowling, the guard finally backed up, not lowering his gun further or taking his eyes from me. He pushed the door until it was mostly closed but not shut tightly.

"Forgive my friend here," the older man said. "He understands but doesn't speak much English. It's easier for empaths to learn languages. I'm Mikyn Zenos. Who are you? And what is that strange disappearing cape you wear over your toga? You're obviously a topsider."

I nodded, extending my hand to shake his. "I'm Erin Radkey, daughter of Stefan Carrington. I'm here because your great-grandson warned me that your people would capture my brother and his team after inviting them here for a peaceful discussion. And he was right."

Bam! I was through the guard's shield now and in his mind. He was furious at not being able to shoot me. He was also annoyed that someone had allowed me to sneak into the house. He blamed the older man's relatives because that had meant turning off the alarm and locking away the dogs.

Mikyn shook his head. "That is not what I've been told. We are concerned that after a recent change of power, the Triad does not plan to fulfill its accord with us. We will not wait any longer."

"You mean you cannot," I corrected. "Because the city is failing."

Mikyn's eyes narrowed. "You're an empath."

"Sensing, we call it, but yes, I am. And I don't care what you've been told. We aren't murderers, not of Unbounded, Avowed, or mortals, and we have every intention of helping your city. Unfortunately, you have betrayed us. You want the truth?" I paused, letting the moment sink in. "The truth is that if things continue, I will destroy your dome before you destroy our country. And I have the means." There, let him chew on that for a moment.

But it was the guard who reacted. He rushed toward me, gun rising. Baby or no, he was going to shoot me directly in the face.

I sent a flash of bright light into his brain. Instantly, he crumpled.

Mikyn jerked as if to help the man, then caught himself and stared at me. "You broke through his shield."

I nodded. "He was going to shoot me. Looks like breaking the law is a matter of politics here."

"Is it any different where you are from? How long before he recovers?"

I didn't know. Because the guard was Avowed, I hadn't been careful with my blast. But he would recover. "Tomorrow," I said. "Or maybe the next day. Sooner if our healer helps him."

The seer's gaze lingered on the gun still in the guard's hand. I could hit him with my ballistic knife before he moved a foot, and if I did, the baby born tonight and all the others in the future would have a chance at life.

He didn't go for the gun. "Now what?" he asked mildly.

"Now we go talk to the others and get them to release my team. We have no intention of allowing your people to die, but we will fight if we have to."

"And you think I have this power?"

I swept off my metamaterial cape, folding it up as small as possible and replacing it under my dress in my body armor. "I think you have leverage."

"That's assuming I believe you can carry out your threat."

I shrugged. "That's your choice, but those who betrayed my team should have given you and your senate the opportunity to hear us out."

"I admit that Tsaoussis and Scala have been known to spin things to their advantage. Very well." He dipped his head toward me in almost a bow. "I will listen, but a baby has been born, and I have a duty to do."

"You mean a child to sentence?"

He sighed. "You are not far from the truth." He gazed further into the room past my shoulder, and I wondered if his mind was wandering. Maybe in the next moment, he would go for the gun, and I could slay the monster.

Instead, he said, "You are connected with someone."

I'd forgotten my connection with Ava was still there, tiny and supposedly imperceptible. I couldn't even sense her thoughts at present. How strong was this man? "My leader." I fortified my shield along with the connection, ready to break it if it became a weakness.

The attack came almost immediately—a strong pounding with a mental object that was every bit as sharp as my machete. I pushed back hard.

Mikyn gasped, and the assault stopped as quickly as it had begun. "I cannot get past your barrier."

"No." I injected more confidence than I felt. "Graeme told me no one here could."

The seer waved the words aside. "They do not know I am able, or I would have yet another impossible job. But they don't need my skills to break through mental barriers."

"They use the hypnopaths."

"Yes."

Now it was my turn, and I knew I was fighting not only for myself, my baby, and my team but for all the world. I slammed my machete into his shield. Hard.

Maybe he wasn't expecting it, or maybe he let me in. I couldn't tell. But I was through and on the stage of his mind, watching his sand stream of thoughts. I didn't remain still. I spread a protective sphere around me in case of attack. Maybe this was what he wanted all along.

Mikyn's presence neared the outside my bubble. He probed. *You learned from someone very old and very powerful.*

I sent him an image of Delia.

Where is she now?

I killed her. I sent the story in a single brilliant burst. *Some of her memories live on inside me.*

You are not pleased with that.
She was evil.
Sometimes people are led to evil.
There is always a choice.
You want to change our way of life.
It must change.
Yes.

In that single word, I knew he had chosen a side. Or maybe the weight of all those babies' lives weighed too heavily for him to bear.

Mikyn watched me. "Come, I must see your healer."

"You don't look sick to me."

"I am. And so are Tsaoussis and Scala, and many others. They may not admit it, but we are a dying nation. If we don't surface soon, we will kill each other or ourselves."

He opened the door, stepping out into the hallway, and I followed, pausing to slip on my sandals and pick up my tranq from the unconscious guard.

Whatever was coming, I was ready for battle.

Chapter 21

*RIN? A*VA OPENED OUR CONNECTION, AS IF SENSING MY TURMOIL. *Have you found Dimitri?*

He's okay. I'm with the seer now. He has agreed to speak for us.

Approval came through, layered with concern that I was linked mentally with Mikyn. And she was right. Every minute I remained connected to the man was a danger. I pulled away, leaving his mind and coming back to myself but keeping my attachment to Ava strong.

When Mikyn and I entered the luxurious sitting room next door, the conversation fell utterly silent. Dimitri, three other men, and two women stared at me. Everyone except Dimitri wore layers of robes and glittering head decorations that reflected the overhead light from the crystal chandelier. One tall, bearded man was on his phone, and the other two Avowed males wore swords on their backs, Unbounded style, though the large assault rifle they each carried on a strap running from the left shoulder to right side of the waist was far more impressive. The taller woman, her hair pinned up elaborately and her face pursed, dripped with jewels and precious metals. By contrast, the round-faced, shorter woman was less decorative but far more pleasant looking.

The shorter woman rushed over to us, babbling words that could only involve me. How would the seer answer? My heart pounded as he hesitated.

Dimitri showed no reaction to my arrival, but his shield wavered, allowing me to connect. Instantly, I shared what I knew about Mikyn.

They are all unstable, he thought. *Mentally, but because of a repetitive gene. Something akin to bipolar disease. And I suspect that fewer and fewer Avowed are changing in the past two centuries because of it. Fortunately, the Unbounded gene always chooses the best options for reproduction, so it's not as bad as I expected, at least among the Avowed. I don't know about their mortal offspring. I think with proper treatment I could heal some, and with ongoing care, many others could live normal lives. But this explains their need for new blood. I've been working on all those I've met, but what I'm doing right now is only a temporary bandage.*

Not good, I said, to let him know I'd picked up the thoughts. *By the way, Ava is here too.*

How's Jace? he asked.

He's up and about, Ava said. *He's angry. He and Ritter are working on an alternate plan, just in case.*

I will get inside their shields, I said. *If worse comes to worst, we'll take these people down and come break you out.*

Easy, Dimitri responded. *Give it some time. Statesman Tsaoussis is unreasonable, and Scala takes her cues from him, but the other families who have not been informed of our intentions might be willing to work with us.*

Dimitri had more experience than I did in human nature,

but it seemed impossible. I wished Ritter and Jace were here so I could be certain we could take care of everyone in the mansion.

I may need to channel Ritter, I said.

He's standing by, Ava told me.

The exchange with Dimitri and Ava was over in two heartbeats, and then Mikyn was saying in English, "This is Erin, Triad Carrington's daughter. Erin, meet Statesman Tsaoussis and Stateswoman Scala." He gestured to the tall man and the bejeweled woman. "And of course my assistant, Magarete Santiagio." He laid a hand on the arm of the woman who had come over to us.

Magarete blinked in surprise. "But how did she get to you, Statesman Zenos?" she said in barely understandable English. "Where is your protector?"

Statesman? I thought.

That was surprising, but with the power of life and death in Mikyn's hands, it made sense that he'd also influence their lawmaking. This was the man everyone depended on to decide the future of their children, and people would be eager to please him.

Some, like Valerine, would also want him dead. They would blame him for every failed embryo and post-partum abortion, whether or not the rest of the senate were also to blame.

Statesman Tsaoussis's phone disappeared inside his robe. "How did you get here?" he demanded, his blue eyes flashing. His face flushed a dark red, contrasting with his puffy blond beard, which made him look like some kind of lion god.

Mikyn glared at him, pushing back his shoulders and standing tall. "A better question is why haven't you told me the truth about our visitors? I have seen for myself that they are willing to help us."

Tsaoussis stepped closer, looking down on Mikyn, and said with a sneer. "Lies. You heard how they were able to reject my demands to drop their shields. They obviously have something to hide."

"Or they simply don't want you to control them," Mikyn countered. "That strength may be exactly what we need. And for the record, this young woman broke through my mental shield."

There was a collective intake of breath, followed by utter silence.

"She is also with embryo." Mikyn jerked his chin at the guards. "They must not hurt her."

"You have a job to do," Tsaoussis said, ignoring the comment, "and so do we. The topsiders have gone against the accord. They have not arranged a continent for us as promised, and they have not sent the embryos and mine workers. And they refused to let us discuss this with Stefan Carrington himself. We believe he is their captive."

"It doesn't matter who we deal with inside the Unbounded organization," Mikyn said. "What matters is the future of our people."

"That is exactly why we must not trust them. Come, you have a job to do." The two men locked gazes, appearing ready to start punching each other. Then Dimitri was acting on their bodies, calming their fury and stabilizing hormone levels that threatened to escalate into a shouting match. I went along for the ride, watching in fascination as he soothed the beasts.

Stateswoman Scala stepped forward. "Come, Mikyn, my old friend. Bahar has given birth, and you know how much my granddaughter has suffered. The child is being brought here now. Please let the healer examine you before the baby arrives."

"For you, Turleen, I will allow it," Mikyn said.

Tsaoussis gestured to one of the other two men, who I assumed were his combat Avowed guards. "Take this topsider into custody and put her with the others."

"No," Mikyn said before I could pull out a weapon. "She will attend the ceremony."

Silence froze them in place for long seconds. "What?" Tsaoussis finally exclaimed, his tone one of controlled fury.

Mikyn inclined his head. "I want her here. She is the strongest empath I have ever met."

If he'd gotten all that from a brief visit, I wondered what else he had seen in my head. Or had his inability to get past my shield impressed him that much?

Tsaoussis's jaw worked, his beard moving up and down. He looked less like a thunderous Greek god now and more like a spoiled child. "Very well."

Mikyn allowed Margarete to lead him to a wide, heavy-looking, gilt armchair that could have doubled as a throne.

Tsaoussis gestured to Dimitri. "Please."

Dimitri walked over to Mikyn and began by placing his hands on Mikyn's bowed head.

I studied the others briefly as they watched. Tsaoussis and the woman were most surely hypnopaths and not likely as trained as their two guards. Down here, with no one to challenge their authority, the Statesmen wouldn't be bothered with daily combat sessions. That meant those two guards would be my focus once trouble broke out.

Refocusing on Dimitri, I went with him as he traced the synapses and pathways in Mikyn's body, searching for something that didn't fit. It was more a feeling than something he saw and completely physical instead of the mental mind stage that I used. Occasionally, he repaired a pathway or created a new one. If I channeled him, I would understand why, but for the time being, I would reserve my energy and simply watch.

There is nothing more to do, Dimitri thought. *He's actually better than the others, except . . .*

Except what?

I don't know. His anxiety is off the charts. If he were mortal, he would already be dead. I bet their doctor has him on all kinds of meds that aren't helping.

That's not surprising.

No. Sadness came through our connection, which surprised me. With Dimitri's love of family and deep value of life, I thought his anger at the seer would echo the fury boiling in my heart. I wanted Mikyn dead. Him and all the other statesmen. *I'll do what I can, but it will take more than one treatment to heal him further.*

Mikyn would probably need a psychiatrist, or maybe a priest to hear his confession, if they had that sort of thing here. I doubted it. A people who considered themselves gods would worship only themselves.

A soft vibration reminded me of Valerine's phone. Under the angry stare of Statesman Tsaoussis, I checked the message on the tiny screen.

It was from Graeme. *Halfway there.* Which meant he and Cherish must have separated and set the first two gate charges. They'd made good time. No word yet from Valerine, and with Mikyn here, alert despite his apparent submission, I didn't dare search for her mentally. We'd have to rely on tech. I had no idea how deep into the sublevels she had to go or what she would need to do to reach the place where she would set the charge for the dome shields.

Dimitri sat back in his chair. "He is as ready as I can make him in the time allotted," he said at last "I could do more if I had a few weeks. Would you consider—?"

"No," Tsaoussis said. His cheek twitched, and I wondered if it was a sign of regret. No way for me to tell as nothing radiated from his surface emotion. He looked at one of the guards. "Bring in the empaths and tell the guards outside to alert us when the baby is here."

The baby. Not my son. This wasn't a man who wanted attachment. Not yet anyway.

Nine men and women wearing togas and sandals filed into the room and made a circle around the seated seer. Dimitri, under the watchful eye of a guard, moved into a corner of the room behind them. Tsaoussis and Scala walked to the door, where an older woman appeared with a tiny baby wrapped in a plush blanket. As Tsaoussis addressed the woman, they formally extended their hands for her to kiss.

Dimitri loosely translated the conversation for me. *He is asking about his wife and the labor.*

You speak the language? I asked, surprised.

I understand some, is all. It's a derivative of ancient Greek.

That was something I didn't know about Dimitri.

The woman curtsied low, still clutching the newborn to her breasts. The woman, unlike the others here, dripped emotion, and her shield barely existed. *A mortal,* I thought, taking the opportunity to see her thoughts, which didn't need any translating.

"It was a difficult labor," she lied, "but your wife is fine. She will rest until the ceremony is over."

The labor hadn't been harder than usual, and sedation was used, but after the birth, the new mother hadn't been permitted to hold or nurse her child and was even now staring at the wall in her bedroom where the baby had been delivered. She had come here with the two babies before this, but three was more than she could bear, and she was now under suicide watch.

Instinctively, my thoughts went to the life burning in my belly, still protected from thoughts by the shield I'd woven there. Would I forgive myself if coming here hurt my baby?

Never.

Tsaoussis took the baby from the attendant—holding the bundle away from his body—and strode toward the seer. The baby, sensing the difference, began to cry. His tiny newborn wails tore at my heart.

"Oh, Harren," Stateswoman Scala said to Tsaoussis, taking the baby from his arms and rocking him. "You've done this before, even if it has been decades." Which told me Tsaoussis had cared for at least one offspring at some time in his life. He made no reply.

Mikyn accepted the baby from Scala, holding him with an expertise that spoke of many years. The baby remained calm.

Tsaoussis spoke in stilted Sinaltan, and again Dimitri translated: *Mikyn Zenos, I present this baby for seeing. Under the eyes of the Ancestors, give us your verdict.*

The slightest nod was the only answer. Mikyn's shield dropped in invitation, but not, I saw, to his whole mind. No, this was only a narrow slice, as he protected himself from his descendants. They weren't the only ones unhappy with their forced presence. As I had before, I walled off my own inner places, watching carefully for an attack. But no one appeared to give me particular notice, and I realized it wasn't the first time a family outsider had been invited to the ceremony. With my toga disguise, they might not even realize I was a topsider.

Come. Mikyn entered the baby's unprotected mind,

stopping not at the stage with the stream of thoughts but walking directly into them and diving upward. Then suddenly it wasn't diving upward but downward into a pool, following a path of energy similar to the way Dimitri followed the pathways of the physical body.

Time passed. Time stood still. Our hearts seemed to beat in unison with the baby's heart.

What are you looking for? I asked.

He motioned me past the barrier he'd created, and I stepped into a private conversation. *For the spark,* he told me. *This is the baby's self—or who he will be.*

I stared at a midnight blue sky with tiny dots of light, some shooting and some simply glowing.

There are a lot of sparks.

The one I'm looking for is more obvious than the northern star in your actual sky. It burns bright.

He was right. Nothing in the baby's pathways burned more noticeably than the rest.

And if you don't find this, you pass sentence on the baby?

Help me look.

I took hold of his gift and did what I'd never done with a sensing person before: channeled it. All at once I felt my senses double. I could see everything at once. I knew that the child would have blue eyes and dark blond hair and be tall like his father. He'd be soft-spoken like his mother, and he would love the color orange. He'd be partial to strawberries and dislike cilantro.

But I couldn't find the bright spark Mikyn was searching for.

Sorrow emanated from the old man.

You can't tell them! I didn't care that desperation leaked through my thoughts.

He sighed. *There is one more option.*

What? I was almost afraid to hear.

I can attempt to create the spark.

Shock spread through me. This man, this seer, seemed to be claiming that he didn't only foretell if the baby would Change but could make it happen? Amazement spread through me, trailing hope in its wake.

You can change the gene so it will activate? I asked.

Sometimes. But . . .

But what?

There is a side effect.

I could see what it was, sitting in his thoughts between us. This downside wasn't for the babies he saved like it was for the Unbounded that the Emporium had forced to Change early. No, the negative results were only for those it didn't work on, the mortals.

Horror replaced hope.

It's not the mines killing the mortals so early—it's you!

Yes, he agreed. *Or in part. But this one will die anyway if I don't try.*

The weight of the too many lives he carried was enormous. *You don't have to tell them! By the time they know the truth, you'll be topside, and he will be an adult with options that won't depend on his parents.*

Or you might have destroyed Sinalta by then if my people refuse to cooperate.

That is true too.

A heavy weariness came through our connection. *As you wish. I will not attempt to fix him. And it will not be the first time I have lied to them of late.*

Fix him. As if being mortal meant being broken.

Wait, how do you do it? I knew before the thoughts emerged that I shouldn't ask. Even if I knew and could copy the procedure, I wouldn't use it on anyone.

Would I?

Before I could retract my question, he gathered up all the stars in a single motion and spun them around us, whirling the mass into a blur of motion that was as beautiful as it was terrifying. Then I felt it, the exact moment he needed to act. And in his countless memories, I saw what would happen. He would send out a burst of light as bright as the light I used to knock out the guard, but here the light would be absorbed, causing some of the smaller stars to burst into flame and wink out. But when the flames all died down, one star might shine brighter than all the rest that remained. That was the spark, the gene that would one day cause the Change.

Or there would be no spark, and the lights winking out would mean years off the child's mortal life. Mikyn was manipulating the very structure of DNA to alter what might be, sometimes to miraculous results and at others to a devastating conclusion. This was what Graeme hadn't told me, or perhaps what he didn't even know. That Mikyn Zenos could manipulate DNA at its basic level.

My mouth opened in a silent scream.

Before he could release his flare, I jumped at the seer, or his representation, whipping out my machete. *You might kill him!*

I might save him.

I slammed my machete into his consciousness, sending my own light into him. Valerine was right: Mikyn couldn't be left alive.

Mikyn's mental scream of anguish shocked me out of my blind rage.

Dimitri, I said. *I-I've done something. Help him.*

I pulled away then, retreating to my own consciousness, opening my eyes to see the seer slumped back in his seat, the baby squalling on his lap. Dimitri was standing, his hands on the seer.

How is he? I asked.

He'll be okay, he thought. *I just need a few more moments. Stall them if you can.*

That's when I noticed the other empaths were unconscious on the floor, and everyone else in the room was glaring at me.

Tsaoussis grabbed the baby from the seer. "What is wrong with him?" he demanded of Dimitri. "This doesn't normally happen. What did you do to him?"

"It was just too much strain," Dimitri responded. "He'll be okay."

You should let him die. I couldn't stop the thought. *He's killing them—the mortal children.*

Erin, Ava's thought was calm and steady. *Channel Dimitri. Help him fix the seer, or none of us will leave here alive, and many more will die.*

Groaning mentally, I did as I was told, using my own and Dimitri's ability to find the wound and repair it. Just like Mikyn had done with the baby.

All at once, I understood why only Mikyn could do what he could do. He had two abilities instead of one, inherited from each of his parents. He wasn't channeling someone as I did, but he was both a healer and a sensing Unbounded.

Mikyn stirred. "I'm okay," he said weakly, "and the others will be too." He pushed Dimitri's hands away and looked around the room, his eyes settling on Tsaoussis and the baby. "He has the light," he said, his solemn tone a pronouncement. "The baby is a true embryo."

I couldn't stop my knees from shaking. Even though I'd severely hurt him, Mikyn wasn't going to tell them the truth! The baby was safe.

"He'll Change when he's thirty and two months old," Mikyn continued with a ring of truth that made my heart turn cold.

What? Valerine's phone vibrated in my pocket, but I ignored it, pushing out my thoughts and meeting Mikyn inside the still-crying baby's mind, though this time the seer was partially shrouded, protected. From me. But with my rage depleted, I was only interested in the baby.

Shhh, I told the child, sending calming thoughts of floating in warm water encompassed by a beating heart. The child calmed and started sucking on his fist, hunger beginning though not yet a pressing need.

I saw it, the light burning brightly, the spark of future Change. Also in the pathways of the baby's future, I saw the time that he would indeed become Unbounded. This wasn't a foretelling but a certainty now written in his DNA.

You did this, Mikyn told me.

No, I was channeling you.

Channeling? I didn't know anyone else could do such a thing. His disappointment hung in the air between us. *That is too bad,* he added. *I grow weary of this responsibility.*

You are also a healer, I said, almost accusing. He could heal himself instead of wasting Dimitri's time.

Of a sort. Not like your Dimitri here. But the ability has been helpful.

As he was the only one keeping his people sane and manipulating DNA, that was likely an understatement.

Your people don't know. Like with his ability to break through shields. What else was he hiding?

I can barely keep up with demand now. If I had extended healing beyond the leading families of Sinalta, I would be insane already. I'm not medically trained.

More excuses or the truth, it really didn't matter.

Tsaoussis unceremoniously handed his son over to the mortal slave, who hurried from the room, tears streaming down her face. He reached for his phone, and I reached for mine as well, aware that both the guards were watching me openly, their guns now drawn. With nine unconscious Avowed, I couldn't blame them. But I needed to set Ritter and the others free sooner rather than later, and I hoped the phone held the answer.

Green light, the text said, which must be Graeme's idea of code because I had seen no traffic lights in Sinalta. Determination blotted out the exhaustion brought on by the last hour's events. No, nearly two hours had passed since Graeme dropped me off for the ceremony. It was well after one in the morning.

I strengthened my connection with Ava, only to realize that she was already at hand, as she had been all along. *I guess you know the charges are set,* I told her. *We either start convincing them, or Dimitri and I make an escape.*

Tsaoussis was speaking Sinaltan into the phone, looking very upset.

Something seems to be wrong with a gate—gate two, Dimitri thought. *It's offline. He wants to know why they don't just fix it and stop bothering him, but apparently, they can't fix it.*

Right on time, I said. *The charges are all set.*

Tsaoussis began barking orders into his phone.

Whatever they've told him is concerning, Dimitri said, *because he's locking down the parliament building, including the engineering levels. He's ordered them to find whoever is responsible.*

Had Valerine already escaped? I had no way of knowing.

I hoped she and her daughter were already on their way to our escape vessel. I began backing away from the guards, but my movement caught Tsaoussis's attention.

He put away his phone and glared at me. "What have you done?"

"I've been right here," I said.

"And I suppose you know nothing about what is happening with gate two or the message that went topside about twenty minutes ago? I assure you that our technopaths will decode the message."

"No need," I said. "It contains a warning about the welcome we found down here and an order to protect our prison compound in Mexico, where we believe you will soon attack, if you haven't already. But since I already gave the command to rally our people before I came here on the transport you gave my father in good faith, which you have since broken, it is only a repeat of what my people already know. And now you have a choice—to deal with us honorably or to fight us. Because we will not allow you to destroy our people."

Tsaoussis snorted. "You underestimate us then, because we know exactly what we are doing. Seize her!" he said to the guards.

The confidence in his tone worried me. What did he know that I didn't? Had something happened topside?

Ava, I said. *Tell Ritter—*

His shield was already down, and instantly, I communicated the situation to him.

Retreat behind the seer, he ordered.

I was already moving, his channeled ability urging me that it was the best position. "Don't come any closer," I said, whipping out the larger detonator remote. "Or I will blow the charges I've set in all your gates and food storage lockers."

"Ridiculous!" Tsaoussis said. "You haven't had time to do anything like that."

"You're presuming I'm here alone."

The room was silent for a few moments after I made the pronouncement. Tsaoussis exchanged a glance with States-woman Scala.

"Stop this," Mikyn said, rising unsteadily. "This is not an idle threat. She can do what she claims. We need to listen. Call the senate."

Tsaoussis glared at him, but Scala once again stepped between them. "A full senate isn't necessary. The five families make the decisions here in Sinalta, and you have three of us right here." She walked toward me, her hands raised placatingly.

My mind screamed danger, though I couldn't tell from where it might come. "I want my team brought here too."

"Of course." Scala offered me an encouraging smile. She wasn't a beautiful woman, but she was compelling, and she radiated power. Something about her made my stomach tighten. *I need to get inside her shield,* I thought, unsheathing my imaginary machete.

Hack! Hack!

It was stronger than I'd hoped, or I had used up too much of my strength.

That was when I felt the remote ripped from my hand as if by an unseen force.

Scala smirked at me as the device landed in her outstretched hand. "There," she said. "Enough of that." I pounded her mental shield with my machete. If I hacked into her mind, I could incapacitate her. Same with Tsaoussis. But there was only one of me. I looked at Mikyn, and he raised his hand as if to indicate helplessness. I regretted hurting him now.

Turning, Scala strode back to Mikyn and Tsaoussis. Her arm swept over the unconscious empaths. "Time to clean up."

"I can take care of that right now." Tsaoussis drew out his phone and began speaking. "Gerold? This is Statesman Tsaoussis. Yes, I know I am speaking in English. I am doing so for the benefit of the topsiders here with me. You understand the language, correct? Very well. Then send reinforcements to Statesman Zenos's palace. Yes. A dozen should do. Oh, and the topsiders in the cell?" he added, almost casually. "We have all we need. Execute them immediately."

"No!" I said, taking a few steps toward them.

Tsaoussis smirked. "Yes. Sorry, my dear." To the guards, he added. "Shoot her but keep the healer alive."

Ritter's ability had me diving into a roll behind Mikyn's deserted throne while at the same time strengthening my shield. *Ping!* A ricocheting bullet hit the wall. The next one went into the crystal chandelier, sending shards raining down. Pushing out my shield to protect Dimitri, I shot my ballistic knife at a guard. He dodged barely in time, leaping over the throne to confront me. I was vaguely aware of Dimitri leaping past Mikyn's cowering assistant to slam his fist into the second guard.

Drop, swipe! Ritter shouted in his mind. I obeyed, carrying out the motion we'd practiced many times in our workout sessions. The guard went down, my gun pressed against his throat.

Abruptly, my channeling connection with Ritter cut off.

I pulled the trigger, and the guard went limp, blood spreading in a flood over the expensive carpet.

Ritter? Ava? I searched for them, but our connection was utterly gone. What did that mean?

I whirled, only to see that the guards who had been outside

the mansion were now inside, their assault rifles aimed in my direction.

"Stop this!" Mikyn shouted. "This is not the way. And she is with embryo!"

"She is slave-loving scum!" Tsaoussis shouted.

"You don't understand," Mikyn said, his voice louder and more urgent. "There is a far greater danger than to our gates and food supply. You must let them go. You must listen."

But Tsaoussis wasn't listening. "Shoot her!"

I dived behind the throne again as shots hurtled in my direction. Should I press the other charge? If I did, how much time would we have before the entire city imploded? Would it be time enough to get my team to gate two?

I didn't think so.

I stood and fired, taking down one guard. A bullet from the other rammed into my shield in the chest area, knocking me back. Pain spread through my lungs, punctuated by panic.

The baby!

"No, no, no!" Mikyn glared at the guard, whose eyes rolled up as he collapsed. I didn't have to guess who was responsible.

Mikyn snatched the detonator from Scala's hand.

"What are you—" she began.

Mikyn pushed the button.

The city beneath us shook. And shook. For long, torturous seconds we felt the vibrations. Then everything was still.

"What have you done?" Statesman Scala screeched. Her hand whipped out and slapped Mikyn across the face.

"The food stores are gone," Mikyn said, his voice monotone. "And the gates. Now will you listen? Or will they have to blow up our dome shield as well? We'll all die, and you have given them no reason to spare us."

Tsaoussis took out his phone and barked something into it, probably asking for updates.

Since no one was firing at me for the moment, I gingerly took a breath. My eyes locked on Dimitri's as he rushed to me, placing a hand on my chest. I knew he could see my pain.

My heart pounded, and tears sprang to my eyes. But it wasn't only the baby I was worried about. I couldn't feel Ava and hadn't been able to since about the same time I'd been forced to stop channeling Ritter. She was either blocking—or gone. I could, at least, feel Ritter faintly through our mate link.

Latching onto that link, I reached out to Ritter. For the briefest instant, I glimpsed something through his eyes—a group of men—and then . . . pain arched through me, so deep and all-encompassing that for a moment I could do nothing but hold my breath and grit my teeth.

Ritter! I screamed.

Chapter 22

"ERIN! BREATHE!" DIMITRI PULLED ME BACK FROM THE BRINK OF darkness. Pain still radiated throughout my body, but it now came primarily from my chest. "Good girl," he murmured.

I wanted to ask about the baby, but the words wouldn't come. "We need to go find them," I said. "Something happened to Ritter, and I can't feel Ava."

He nodded, pulling his medical bag over his head to a more secure position. "Let's go."

"Here." I handed him my backup gun.

No one stopped us as we ran from the room. My last glimpse was of Tsaoussis, his face bleached white with anger.

Outside, we ran along the cobblestones in the deserted street. But life forces ahead, glowing bright, made me stop and pull Dimitri into the bushes of a mansion. We held our breaths as the soldiers marched past. They were scarcely gone before we began running again, traversing half the block in minutes.

Finally, we reached the parliament building, but more life forces had surrounded it at intervals, inside and out, so we hunkered down again, this time in a cobbled courtyard with a grouping of short walls and statues.

"We have to get in there," I said. Not knowing what was happening to Ritter and the others was tearing me apart.

"We'll have to take out a guard and sneak in." Dimitri started to rise, but I pulled him down and held up two figures to indicate two people.

I waited, drawing out a small knife, but I relaxed when I recognized Graeme and his friend Cherish. They were dressed like Avowed soldiers but wore their rifles awkwardly, with the mark of those who were uneasy with weapons. I rose in front of them, keeping my weapons in hand, low and unobtrusive.

"Erin!" Graeme whispered. "Praise the Ancestors that you're okay. Have you seen Valerine?"

"No. Look, I need to get inside where they're keeping my friends. Tsaoussis gave the execution order."

He shook his head. "They've got it locked down tight. They have guards going through the sublevels now. Cherish made us guard IDs so we can look for Valerine. We're heading to the parking garage."

"I keep telling him Valerine knows those sublevels better than anyone," Cherish said.

"I'm sorry about your wife," I said, panic edging into my voice. "But I've got to get in there now."

Graeme nodded. "Of course, we'll help. But we'll need an excuse."

"You have the IDs, so we're your prisoners," I said. "You can say you caught us outside, and if they check with Tsaoussis, he'll verify that we ran."

"It might work," Cherish said. "But you'd better lose the dress so you'll look like a prisoner."

"Right." I tore off the headpiece and began unwinding the

silver ties from the dress. "You do know how to use those, right?" I motioned to the rifles slung over their shoulders.

Graeme shook his head, but Cherish nodded. "I've practiced a little."

"Right. Let's go then."

Dimitri and I hid our weapons inside our body armor as they marched us in plain sight up the majestic marble stairs leading into the parliament building, but a heavily armed guard stopped us as we passed the columns.

He spoke in Sinaltan, denying us entry, and too late, I banged on Graeme's shield to get him to let me in.

"We found these two topsiders in the street," Graeme said.

Tell him we must be the ones you heard escaped from the seer's house, I told him.

When he did, the guard shook his head and said, "I don't know anything about that. This is about the bombing. They've destroyed our entrance gates and food storage. We must capture whoever did this."

"Right. In the meantime, I have to put these in the cell with the other topsiders."

"Sorry. I can't let anyone in or out."

Oh, for crying out loud. I pulled out my tranq and shot him, the sound much quieter than a bullet but still loud enough to make me nervous. "Drop him behind that pillar," I said, "Hurry!"

Seconds later, we hurried into the building, sliding to a stop on the marble floor of a grand reception room when presented with six more guards. Wealth practically dripped from the walls, unlike the engineering reception somewhere underneath us.

"Orders from Statesman Tsaoussis," Cherish said. "We need to put these two with the other topsiders. Please don't waste our time calling the statesman like the man outside."

The guard motioned to the desk. "Long as you sign in. You're just in time," he added with a smirk. "I think they're having some excitement upstairs." The way he gloated, I was surprised they weren't all upstairs to watch, or holding a gladiator tournament to force our team to fight for their lives.

Cherish and Graeme put their hands on the pad at the desk, and apparently passed as no one stopped them from marching us up the wide marble staircase. "I'm not sure where to go," Cherish said at the top.

"Left," Dimitri said as Graeme and I were already turning, following the glow of life forces.

I could feel Ritter through our mate connection again, but his shield was tightly closed. No way to determine the extent of any wounds. I still couldn't feel Ava.

Was she already dead? I was searching mentally for Jace as we rounded a turn in the hallway and found four guards, two on each side of a mostly shut door that opened inward. Swords poked up from their back as they hugged the wall, peering inside. One of them turned and pointed his gun at us.

"Easy. We're with you," Graeme said, releasing his rifle and raising his hands. "Special topsider delivery here from Statesman Tsaoussis. Careful, this one is with embryo." He gestured to me.

The guard's eyes flicked over us. "The topsiders have taken two of my men hostage."

"How?" Cherish asked.

The guard flushed. "We came up here to carry out their executions, but there was already blood all over the floor—too much to be explained—so someone went in to investigate, and the one we thought was dead jumped us. The prisoners have guns now, and swords too."

As if to punctuate his statement, a volley of shots came from within, and two more guards rushed out the door. Before it shut, I caught sight of an empty desk, the elaborate tapestry behind it riddled with gunfire. Down a smaller corridor next to that, I glimpsed Ritter, moving like a red blur.

The guards were talking to each other and ignoring us. *Shoot now!* I told Dimitri and Graeme. We fired, taking out three of the guards. Then Ritter was at the door, wrenching it open. He slammed his fists into a guard, and Dimitri and I fired again as the man crumpled.

Everything was still. The stench of gunpowder filled my nostrils, making me want to vomit.

In the next second, I crossed the five steps separating me from Ritter. He caught me in his arms, not even wincing, though he was shot in his stomach and dripping blood. "I brought the bad guys as promised," he murmured, his face buried in my neck.

"I thought I'd lost you."

"We needed to protect ourselves from them. They tried to order us to stop fighting." He hesitated, and I knew that wasn't all. He hadn't wanted me or our child to feel his pain. I could sense his hurt now, and it made the ache in my chest feel like a mere slap.

Ava emerged from the open door, limping heavily and holding a man in front of her, sword at his neck. Jace followed with one arm in a sling but triumphantly waving a gun in his other.

"Sorry, I would have helped with that last bit, but I'm clean out of bullets. We all are, so you have good timing."

"We don't need him anymore," Ritter said, taking my gun and shooting the man in Ava's custody. The guard crumpled in a temporary death that was far kinder than what he and his buddies had in mind for my friends.

"We won't have long," I said. "There are more guards downstairs."

"Right. Let's go." Ritter handed me back my pistol.

"Wait," Cherish said. "If we can find our way to the back staircase, there's a corridor that leads outside. I've taken it a few times when I've had to present a report in chambers. It'll be guarded, of course, but it's our best chance to get out with minimal notice." She pulled out her phone. "I just need to access the schematics and see how to get there from here."

Ritter and Jace scooped up guns from the fallen soldiers and hurried partway down the hall to guard our position. Dimitri rummaged in the bag over his shoulder, taking out strips of cloth and shots of curequick. Ava and Ritter submitted to his ministration, but Jace waved him aside. "I'm okay. The other shot you gave me did its job, and the share of my blood that we spread on the floor will regenerate within the hour anyway."

When I stared at him, he laughed and said, "Never mind. Tell you later."

"Got it!" Cherish said.

We ran.

Cherish led us down a hallway, through a door, and down another hallway where we reached the back stairs. Shouts reverberated behind us, signaling that someone had figured out the prisoners were gone.

At the base of the stairs, Cherish turned, heading down a long marble ramp that was occasionally punctuated with alcoves, statues, and stone benches.

"They sure like their statues here," Jace muttered. "The more naked, the better."

"Hush." Ava's limp was easing, but her tight shield told me she was still in pain.

"Are you shot?" I whispered.

With the slightest of sighs, she released her shield. *Grazed. But I cut myself to add to the blood that we used to distract them. Ritter did too. It worked.*

Which meant it was a good idea, but I hated the need. I threw up a barrier against her pain, but I kept the connection between us open.

Ahead of us, Jace raised a hand with two fingers, and Ritter moved up behind Graeme and Cherish as they called out to the guards. The scuffle was so brief that we barely slowed our pace. A minute later, we came out on the street at the far end of the property, where we left two more guards unconscious.

"You know where the transport is," Graeme said. Blood was smeared across his toga, but none of it seemed to be his. "Go."

Ava turned to look at him. "You're not coming with us?"

He shook his head. "I have to find my wife. She hasn't checked in, and I wonder if the explosions down below blocked off her escape. Cherish knows the way, and with these IDs we should be able to get in." His eyes drifted to me. "We'll try to get to the house, but if you don't hear from me, go without us. Please take Anina with you."

"Of course," I said. Right now, we'd do what we had to in order to survive. But if I had to abandon the parents, it would be a failure I wasn't sure I could face.

Now it was my turn to lead. We found the transport a block over, and I hit the screen and chose Graeme's apartment. A short time later, we passed a group of large transports that seemed to be filled with soldiers and barricades.

"How far is the girl?" Ava asked.

I glanced at the screen. "Next block." My heart began pounding again.

Dimitri, in the back with Jace and Ritter, moved into the

empty space behind my seat and put a hand on my shoulder. "Breathe."

"Right." I did so, willing myself to calm. Normally, I thrived over the adrenaline rush, but it was different now because of the baby. "Someone else will have to drive when I get back from the apartment. I'll need to calm the child down."

"She may be asleep," Jace said. "Haven't you seen Chris haul his kids to bed when they fall asleep watching TV? They don't even stir."

I hoped he was right.

When I pulled up in front of the apartment, Ritter came inside with me. He'd removed his gray prison shirt and attempted to mop up some of the blood from his hastily bandaged chest, but he looked terrifying. I pulled out my metamaterial cape from my thigh pocket and tossed it to him. He held my eyes as he pulled it on.

He'd been expecting me to ask him to wait in the transport, but I knew it would do no good. He wouldn't wait or let me out of his sight. Besides, I *needed* him close. The terror of losing him had been too real.

The main building door was open, and I went to the back apartment on the main floor as instructed, swiping the coin vertically. The door chimed softly and slid open into the wall, shutting behind us after we stepped across the threshold. Inside was brightly lit as if waiting for its occupants to appear, though it was more likely the result of a scared child. The place wasn't as rich as Mikyn's, and far smaller, but it was still upscale. Graeme and Valerine had been rewarded well for their work. Except where their children were concerned, which in the end had made the difference in their choices today.

We found Anina in a bedroom with a beautifully carved canopy bed, the kind a real princess would use. She was asleep, her arms wrapped around a white toy seal, her hair spread out like a fan over her pillow.

A travel bag sat on the floor, full but not to bursting. I picked it up as Ritter gently folded the blanket around the little girl and scooped her up. We left without a word between us, the door shutting again on its own accord.

An affronted voice spoke as we approached the entryway, demanding something neither of us could understand. We turned to see an old woman in her doorway. Her eyes ran down my body armor, and she babbled more nonsense.

"Go inside," Ritter growled at her in a tone that didn't need a translation. "Now!"

With a gasp and wide eyes, the old woman backed inside, slapping at a control on the side of the door to shut it faster. She stared at us with wide eyes as the door closed between us.

We hurried out the lobby door. "Go, go, go!" Ritter said as we jumped inside. "We are about to be reported."

We'd gone only two blocks when sirens filled the air, but no one stopped us as we approached gate two. The gates themselves were underwater, but the manual controls were in the station above. Ritter and Dimitri took out the two lone guards who apparently hadn't been called to the capital and then activated the controls.

Minutes later, we were underwater and cruising downward. I breathed a sigh of relief. We weren't clear yet, but even if they followed us, we had enough of a start that we could make it to the hidden cave. There, we could decide whether to make a run for it and hope their faster ships wouldn't locate us in this huge ocean, or we could wait for Mari to bring backup. Because she would be recovered soon, maybe by morning.

A soft, hiccupping sob alerted me that Anina had awakened. She stared at Ritter with wide, desperate eyes that made my heart wrench. I reached for her, pulling her rigid body over to my lap.

"Hey, sweetie, it's okay," I said, easing through her mental shield.

"Where's my mommy?" she asked in Sinaltan. Even if I hadn't been able to understand her mind, I could have guessed the question.

"I don't know." I wouldn't lie to the child. "Your dad went to find her, but I promised your mom and dad to take you topside with me. We might have to wait for them there." I couldn't add that they might never make it out, that in fact, she might be the only Sinaltan to survive what might come next.

She buried her face in her hands and sobbed while I awkwardly rocked her, cursing the body armor that now felt like a straitjacket.

"Will we still be able to communicate with Sinalta after we pass through their grid?" Jace asked.

"Not with anyone mentally," I said, "and I wouldn't dare signal with the ship, not until we're close to land. They might find us. And I doubt there's been time to move a warship into the area."

"We can't leave here," Ritter said grimly. "They'll use their nuclear weapons against us."

Ava nodded from the front seat. "Agreed."

"We could sneak back into the city." Ritter looked at me. "Or some of us can."

I let the comment pass because my chest ached, and I was still worried about the baby. Would Dimitri have told me if the bullet impact had done lasting damage?

I drew out the smaller detonator. "There is always this."

I said it because we were all thinking it.

"No," Ava said unequivocally. "Not yet. I'm hoping it is enough that we have it."

"They'll find the charges eventually." Maybe they already had. But with such a large shield and so many sublevels, I was betting they hadn't—yet.

A niggling sensation beat at my mental shield, pressing but not threatening. Ava felt it too. "You think it's Graeme?" she said.

"No, he's not—" *that powerful,* I finished silently because Anina had stopped sobbing and was listening. "It's got to be Mikyn. He's more powerful than we guessed."

"Clearly," Ava said. "He has almost as much experience as Delia."

"But he was also the one who pushed the detonator and set off the charges."

"He was?" She was clearly surprised. "I thought you managed to do it."

"No." I exchanged a glance with Ritter. "What do you think?"

He frowned. "You have to see what he wants."

I didn't want to, but he was right. With Ava there, we should be strong enough together to combat any mental advance. I fortified my inner self, then cracked my shield.

What do you want, Mikyn?

I am in the process of gathering the statesmen at the parliament building, along with the executive members of our government. They now understand the risk to our city's dome and the reason for your actions. I believe I have enough support to remove Statesmen Tsaoussis and Scala from office. The emergency vote is about to happen within the hour.

And what about you? I asked. He was, after all, the one who had blown the explosives.

He showed me an image of him removing the memory from an unconscious Statesman Scala and also the guards. *Only Tsaoussis knows the truth, and he doesn't dare speak against me. I know too many of his other secrets. I did what I had to do to stop your people from becoming desperate enough to blow our city shields. It was also the only way I could set you free.*

I wouldn't say escaping was "setting free," but why argue semantics?

Even the acting statesmen for Tsaoussis and Scala will vote to have them removed, he continued, *though frankly, as far as leaders go, they are not much better. However, the other statesmen and I have a majority. Which means we are pleased to work with the Emporium and you as its representatives. But as you can imagine, no one is pleased about the imminent danger to our shields. We need a show of good faith.*

Ava, linked to me, was the one who responded. *I am the leader of this group,* she said, *in conjunction, of course, with Triad Carrington's son. I can speak for them.*

Please do, Mikyn said.

In the short term, if we can be sure you will disarm your nuclear warheads, we will remove the danger to your shield. We will need to be certain ourselves, and that means bringing in our own technopath and other officials. We will also need the return of all the children taken from above.

I will arrange it, Mikyn told her. *But as you know, many are no longer with us. Also, many of the embryos who are now Avowed have families.*

The latter will be given a choice, of course. For those who have died, reparations will be required.

How much recompense for the life of a child? The idea left a sour taste in my mouth. And for those without families, who would receive payment?

Agreed, Mikyn said. *But please, return from wherever you are and accept my hospitality for the remainder of the time you are here.*

Ava's laugh was almost mocking. *Thank you for the offer, but I assume you will take no offense if we do not oblige at present. We have had our fill of Sinaltan hospitality today. However, we will come to you soon.*

Mikyn's own mirth surfaced. *As you wish. But I hope you have an immediate idea to help us because everyone here is anxious. Not many outside the senate know of the shield failure, but rumors spread, and with the recent explosions, we are bound to see rioting and other trouble.*

Give us until morning, Ava said.

I severed the connection. "You think we can trust him?"

Ava nodded. "I don't see that we have a choice. But we'll send a coded burst to Stella after we've left their grid and see how Mari is doing. It doesn't matter now if the message is intercepted. They'll be expecting us to reach out to our people, and they still won't know exactly where we're heading, though I bet they've figured out that gate two is working manually."

"No doubt they'll have them all working soon," Dimitri said. "What I don't know is what we can do for them in the short term. We don't have the power to bring Sinalta to the surface, which would buy us more time, and we certainly aren't going to give them Australia."

"They once had the power to move the city," Ritter said. "Going up should be easier than going down, I'd think." He gave us a nostalgic half smile. "If Cort were here, he'd see the pattern needed and tell us what to do."

"Right," Ava said. "Then poke a little at us for not seeing it in the first place."

We laughed, and the old pain of missing Cort didn't seem as

bad. The laughter made my sore chest ache, and having Anina in my lap, clinging to me with such ferocity, wasn't helping, but I welcomed both. It meant we were both alive.

I was glad it was Dimitri in the front seat following the ups and downs and sideways of the navigation screen, but once we arrived at the place where Graeme and I had met Valerine, I had to lead them to the submersible.

"Wow. This is incredible," Jace said as our feet crunched across the cold ground, and our breaths came out white. "And to think that after Sinalta is moved, no one will ever see this place again." I nodded in agreement.

Somehow, I still had the tablet to the submersible in one of my pockets, and besides a cracked screen, it still worked. I opened the hatch with relief before handing it off to Jace. More miraculous was Anina allowing Ritter to carry her down the ladder to the control room.

We settled into the control room chairs, all but Dimitri, who remained standing as there were only five chairs. Little Anina sat between Jace and me, silent and afraid.

"We need ideas," Ava said. "Not just for getting out of here but for helping the Sinaltans. I'm afraid if we don't present a solid plan, relations are going to implode." Worse than they already had, she meant.

"We definitely need backup." I brought a hand to the area between my neck and breasts to test the sensitivity of my chest. I'd glimpsed some bruising in the smaller transport, though the pain in my chest seemed to be lessening—maybe because I wasn't running for my life at the moment. "But there's no guarantee that Mari will be able to find us here under all this rock. And it will take weeks to get a ship in the area."

"Mari may need Keene's help. To tell the truth, I'm not entirely sure if she'll be conscious yet without me there to help.

It may depend on whether Chris and Stella called for another healer."

"Let's give them until morning," Ava said. "We have to trust that they've been working on the problem as well. I told them not to attempt contact by radio, but I don't think we could get a signal in here anyway. We can always leave the cave again to talk with them."

"What if we use the Avowed transports to bring their people to the surface, where we can pick them up with our ships?" Jace said. "That seems to match their original plans." He set the submersible's tablet on Anina's lap with a game on the screen. "Play," he urged. "Try to make three in a row, and they'll disappear. Like this." He showed her.

She blinked without vocal response, but she set a finger on the tablet.

"Moving four million people will take a long time," I said. "And there's still the problem of where to put them." I shifted my position, wincing when my chest twinged.

Dimitri unfolded his arms and pushed off from the panel he'd been leaning against. "Let's take a short break. We need to check you out now."

I looked at Ava. "Go," she said. "You need to know."

About the baby.

Chapter 23

RITTER WAS INSTANTLY ALERT. "I'M COMING TOO."

Of course he was.

"Good. Because you'll heal faster once I stitch you up," Dimitri told him. "Give me a minute to gather supplies, and I'll meet you in the sleeping quarters."

I looked at Anina, who seemed to be enjoying her game. Jace was peering at the screen as well, and I couldn't tell which of them was more interested in the display. "Tell Jace if you need me, okay?" I said to her. "And he'll come and get me." She nodded, not smiling, but I understood that.

We went to the tiny sleeping quarters, where Ritter said, "What happened? I can tell something's off with you."

I told him about being shot after my link to him and Ava was severed. "I had my mental shield up, of course, but it hit me straight on."

His frown was thunderous. "I shouldn't have broken our contact. If you'd been channeling my ability—"

"In that much pain, you would have only distracted me

further." I motioned to his stomach, where blood was leaking through the bandage. It still had to be agonizing, even for someone accustomed to pain.

He stood there, not touching me, though only inches separated us. I waited for him to speak again, to say anything, but he didn't.

"So I don't know," I continued. "I don't think I broke any ribs, and I can still feel the baby's life force." I couldn't say the rest, that I didn't know if our child was okay or if I'd damaged something necessary to life. If I had, it was entirely my fault. I'd made the choice to put this baby at risk when I could have sent Chris and Charles, or even waited for backup.

"Say something." I took a deliberate step away from him. "I had to do it. For you and my family. You understand that, right?"

He closed the space between us once more. "I've waited over two centuries for a son—or daughter," he said. "So I won't lie and say this baby doesn't mean everything to me. I was furious when I learned you were here, but the instant I saw you in the parliament building, I realized that as long as you're all right, my world goes on." His arms went around me then, pulling me to him. "Because without you, there are no more babies, no . . . no love . . . only darkness and the revenge that kept me going all those years. I can't live like that anymore. I can't live without you."

He kissed me then, the emotion larger than both of us, and we were swept along, not controlling the passion but willing participants. It didn't matter that there were others close by or that Dimitri was on his way. There was only the two of us, desire burning so brightly that I almost couldn't breathe.

"This damn body armor." Ritter drew away, searching for the clasps. "It's like an iron girdle."

I was glad I was wearing an undershirt because Ritter had my armor halfway off when Dimitri came inside. "Good," Dimitri said, amused. "That will make my examination easier."

Ritter snorted. "I wasn't doing it for you." But his demeanor sobered instantly upon remembering.

I forced a laugh and pushed down the rest of the armor, feeling like a turtle shedding its shell. I was thin again, though distinctly aware of the fullness inside my belly.

"Lie down on this lowest berth, will you?" Dimitri waved his hand in the general direction.

"I can sense its life force," I told him as I stretched out on the berth, nearly hitting my head on the one above.

Dimitri knelt on the floor near me, pulling up my undershirt a few inches and placing warm hands on my belly. "I don't want to upset either of you, but back at the seer's place, after you were shot, I couldn't trace the pathways to the baby. I'm not sure what that means because everything happened so fast."

"Why didn't you tell me?" I asked. I felt Ritter holding his breath, and I didn't dare look at him.

"When would I have done that?" Dimitri said mildly. "When we were hiding in the bushes or shooting the guards? Or possibly when I was driving the transport here?"

He had a point.

"Well, check again now." Ritter knelt next to Dimitri and set his hand on my shoulder, rubbing slightly. A sensation of warmth spread through me. Whatever was in store for us, we would face it together.

Dimitri closed his eyes, and I reached out to his shield, but it was tight, and I didn't want to break in.

"This is odd," he said. "I can trace your veins and pathways, but it all stops when I reach your womb. I can't get past."

"Can I see?" I asked.

"Me too," Ritter said.

Dimitri's shield dropped in answer, and together we traced the pathways, with me sending the information to Ritter, finally coming up against a barrier—my barrier.

I let out a relieved gasp. "That was me," I said. "I put it there so the baby wouldn't have to . . . there was so much anger and emotion, and I didn't want the baby to get an overload from me. Or be at risk from anyone outside."

Dimitri chuckled. "That makes sense, and while it's probably a good idea for missions, I don't think it's a good thing to leave in permanently. Can you remove it?"

"Of course." I dropped it, erasing it with a mental wave of my hand.

Immediately, Dimitri began tracing the connection of the placenta to the baby and examining each tiny vein and neural pathway, with me going along for the ride.

"Everything looks normal," Dimitri said, his voice easier now. "If the baby was under stress, she isn't anymore. And I don't see anything that's a concern."

"She?" Ritter and I said together.

Dimitri laughed. "You wanted to know, right?"

"Yes," Ritter said.

We were about to leave when I saw in my daughter the place where Mikyn had taken me inside the Avowed newborn. Swirling stars. I felt the temptation to look, to see if one was brighter than the rest. In a rush, I shared the desire with both Dimitri and Ritter.

"That's assuming you have the gift without channeling Mikyn," Dimitri said aloud. "You do have sensing on one side of your family and healing on the other, but it doesn't mean you can do both."

I was almost certain he was right, and yet . . . Mikyn said I'd changed the baby, and while I'd been channeling him earlier, I wasn't all that sure I had still been channeling him. Besides, if I channeled Dimitri, wouldn't I then have both gifts, exactly like Mikyn? Yet what if I looked and my baby didn't have the spark? What then? Would I be tempted like Mikyn to change my child at the DNA level?

Could I simply look and not tamper? And what if I did see a spark? Would it only be my own I was seeing? Would seeing a spark set me up for later disappointment? And if I was able to do what Mikyn did, how many people would want me to foretell their children's lives? Or to "fix" their babies?

But of course I wouldn't tell anyone. It would only be for me.

Then what about Chris and Stella's baby? And any Jace might have? Would we be tempted to meddle?

What should I do? I asked the men.

"It doesn't matter if she'll Change." Ritter's voice was an anchor in the raging of my thoughts. "We can't risk hurting our child, mortal or Unbounded, and I don't want knowing the future to change what we feel for her."

He was right. I needed to step back from the precipice.

I sat up and let my feet fall to the floor, pulling away mentally from the baby and the others. "Right, then. Looks like we're having a daughter." To Dimitri, I added with a grin, "Thank you for setting my mind to rest."

He smiled and rose. "I didn't do anything." He looked at Ritter. "You next. And then maybe Erin can get a little sleep. Or, uh, I suppose you could get back to whatever it is I interrupted." He smirked at Ritter. "Just remember, we still have to come up with a solution for Sinalta by morning."

I switched places with Ritter, and Dimitri gave Ritter a shot of painkiller and began a rather long swath of stitches on his stomach, closing what was apparently an exit wound. On his back the entry wound was already mostly closed, but Dimitri gave it three stitches to close it completely.

Stepping up onto the edge of the berth, I brought down the duffle where I'd stuffed my extra clothes. I pulled on a comfortable bodysuit with built-in body armor that felt like weightless silk after wearing Stella's.

"I just keep thinking, what if the ability to bring Sinalta to the surface does still exist and they simply don't remember how to use it?" I said, thinking aloud. "Remember when we first learned what Keene could do and how confusing it was?" At first, I thought he had telekinesis because he'd lifted me when I'd been climbing, but he had simply increased my own efforts.

Dimitri glanced up from his work. "His is an odd gift, to be sure, and your theory is possible. But they might have bred out the gift completely. We've lost so many gifts ourselves over the years of fighting and trying to create combat Unbounded. It could be a lost gift that the Sinaltans need to bring the city up. Or several of them."

I gasped as something clicked in my mind. "We don't have levitators."

Both Ritter and Dimitri stared. "None that are known."

"I need to talk to Ava." I started for the door. "We have to send another message to Stella. I think I know how to bring the Sinalta to the surface."

It wasn't morning but only two hours later when Mari appeared in the control room of the submersible, which we had moved out of the cavern in order to communicate with the surface. She wasn't alone. As requested, Keene McIntyre was with her, as was Patrick Mann, son of the current US president and technopath. Jeane Baker, illusionist Oliver Parkin, and the New York Renegade's Brody Emerson, who was a powerful blaster, made up the rest of the Unbounded members. With the addition of Chris and our mortal guards, Charles and Marco, armed to the hilt, I had to admit that the ensemble was more than enough. If Jeane's presence didn't null their hypnosuggestion, Oliver's realistic illusions would confuse them, and as a last resort, Brody would be able to cause serious damage to their dome shield.

"Sorry we took so long." Mari leaned in to hug me. "Dying takes it out of you, you know?" She grinned as if she'd been waiting forever to say that.

I chuckled. "Only died twice myself so far, but I did wonder if we would have to wait another day for you to come. "

"I awoke yesterday morning after Keene came with another healer and worked on me." She grinned. "They sped things up a little, and I was trying to find you ever since, but I needed more rest—and Keene's help. All these tons of water make it somehow different from above."

"So tell us more about how we're going to sell them on this plan," Keene said. "And let's try not to get Mari killed this time."

"No one is getting killed." Ava rolled her eyes. "I hope you brought the computers I asked for. We're going to need them." To Chris, she added. "It's time to go up past the grid to contact Mikyn. We need to get his technopaths working on this as soon as possible."

As everyone went to work, I approached Marco. "I'm happy to see you," I said.

His smile was strained and his dark, constantly moving eyes were grave. "You heard we lost Brenna in the jungle."

I nodded. "We'll worry about that later. I know you did everything you could."

THE NEXT HOURS WERE BUSY FOR THE TECHNOPATHS AND SCIENTISTS, both in Sinalta and topside. The rest of us tried to rest, but we were too keyed up. As the time ticked to a reasonable hour, Mari, using coordinates from the smaller transport, shifted all of us to the parliament building, out of view of anyone. Only Chris and little Anina, now snoring softly in the middle crew bunk, stayed behind to make sure our retreat remained open.

We went to find Mikyn, and he led us into a huge half circle assembly room, where the entire senate awaited us in throne-like, padded chairs. Present were the five statesmen—each with a ten-person committee—and the forty members of the executive branch. Every person was Avowed, but the conciliatory tone Mikyn used to introduce us at a podium near the front was much different than it had been the previous day with Statesmen Tsaoussis and Scala.

It was almost a disappointment not to use some of the impressive arsenal we'd brought.

"We have a solution," Ava announced when she was given the floor. "It's temporary, but it will work until we gather the world governments and decide on plans for the future." She paused as everyone listened anxiously. "By working together, with your people and ours, we believe we can raise Sinalta to the surface once again."

Murmurs spread through the crowd, and snippets of conversation in both English and Sinaltan reached my ears:

"Impossible."

"Are they crazy?"

"Don't they think if we could do that, we already would have?"

"Please, hear me out," Ava said more loudly, banging on the podium with her hand. "The ability to move the city isn't new. It has obviously been done before, or you wouldn't be here. We now believe your levitators were responsible." More murmurs, but Ava ignored them. "Or at least they were partly responsible. You still have them among you, or at least one, former Stateswoman Scala, so that's a place to start. Admittedly, using only that ability, one levitator would not suffice, and maybe not even a thousand. But we have a man who can increase an ability at the atomic level. This is the ability we suspect you may have lost—or maybe lost track of. During the night, our technopaths and yours have worked together over city schematics provided by Statesman Zenos, and we believe we will not only be able to raise the city but also move it to a warmer place. Additional technopaths and scientists will want to view the calculations and do some of their own, and it may be that we'll need to harness some of the atomic power you have available to aid the move. But we are quite certain it will work. This will buy us the time we need to find you a permanent home. And you will remain a people."

A stunned silence fell over the senate, followed a hesitant clapping that soon grew into a roar of approval. But a man near the far side stood and raised a hand.

Mikyn Zenos waited until the din receded and then said, "You have permission to speak, Acting Statesman Scala."

The man inclined his head in acknowledgment. "Thank you. But you should know that former Stateswoman Scala is missing. We do not know where she is or if she would agree to use her ability in this way. We believe she may be with former Statesman Tsaoussis, who is also missing."

"There are others in your family who have this ability?" Mikyn asked, skipping over the fact that the two had apparently escaped custody.

The man conferred with his committee before answering. "At least seventeen. There may be more in the outer ring."

The poorer relatives, I thought.

"Gather them all," Mikyn said. "Have them here in seven days' time. We will reconvene then. Keep in mind that it will take several weeks before we can begin, and then more weeks to move the city. Effective immediately, we will also cease operations in the mine and will begin removing the workers in preparation for the move."

"Where will they go?" someone asked. "There's no room here."

"You mean we're closing the mines?" demanded another.

Amazement spread through the crowd, and I realized they'd planned all along to leave the mortals in the mines to work out their lives while the Sinaltans periodically returned with supplies and to collect the precious metals mined by sweat and tears and blood. And lives. Or maybe they might forget about them altogether. I gritted my teeth so I wouldn't scream out at them.

"That is part of the agreement," Mikyn said firmly. "But they will not make the journey with us. Ships are being sent to our location to collect and return them to their homes."

In reality, Mari had vowed to shift each and every one of them back to civilization, but we wouldn't tell them that.

"Those who are Sinaltans by birth," Mikyn continued, "will be returned to the nursery centers for now, or they may stay with their families. Embryos from topside will also be returned."

"What if they wish to stay?" This came from Acting Statesman Scala, his face flushed. "Some have families. And what if they want to take their children—our children?" His indignance hinted that this was a personal matter to him. Had he impregnated an embryo? Or had he forced one into staying with him because of a child?

Ava didn't allow Mikyn to respond but stepped back to speak into the microphone. "We have a list," she said, "and we will be contacting each and every embryo from topside personally, whether or not they have Changed. The choice about their future belongs to them and only them. As with removing the workers from the mines, it is non-negotiable." She paused and added, "We will not interfere with your society or laws, but to do business with other countries, you may have to revisit some of your ideas."

Mikyn stepped forward again. "I am sure we will come to a peaceful accord. I am grateful for the help of our Unbounded allies." A weak clapping came from the senate floor. "Are there more questions or concerns?" he asked.

Another man, who appeared to be a secretary of sorts, raised his hand. Though he wasn't armed, he sat with a group of people who were obviously security, judging by their swords and other weapons. "There is another issue."

"Speak," Mikyn said.

"We know that there are traitors within our midst, our own countrymen, and we still have not found the explosives placed on our dome shields. Please see the document we submitted this morning for the details. Regardless of the perpetrators' motives, they have committed crimes against Sinalta and must be apprehended and tried in a court of law for their crimes." His English was perfect but was as stiff as his back.

Must be their version of an attorney, I thought.

"What does that have to do with this meeting?" Mikyn was losing patience. "As of this morning, after we took our nuclear arsenal offline, the detonator for the remaining explosives was deactivated." He fumbled in a pocket and pulled it out. "It has been turned over to me. We will find the charges, and in the meantime, we are safe."

Without acknowledging the information, the man continued his line of thought. "We believe Anina Padovan, the minor child of the perpetrators, is in the company of the topsiders, as reported by a witness in her building. We move that with the charges against her parents, the child should now revert to the custody of the city. This will not only protect the child but will assure that the parents will not activate the charges themselves. Her presence will also aid in the search for her parents."

In other words, they wanted to use Anina as bait and to make sure Valerine or Graeme didn't blow the shields.

Mikyn looked at Ava, who looked at me. I started forward, joining them at the front. Ritter moved into place behind me, his hand close to his weapon. In the space of a few seconds, the mood in the room had become ugly.

Mikyn stepped away from the pulpit. "Is it true you have the child?" At my nod, he added, "You need to bring her back. I'll do everything I can to protect the parents. I think we'll get them off once they're found, though it may take a few years for the legalities to finish."

"In the meantime, what does Anina do?" I asked. "Serve in some ruling family's house? Live in the nursery and be treated like a slave?" I shook my head. "No way. She comes with me. I promised her parents, and for all I know, one or both of them might already be dead. Or they could be murdered in the search."

"It is a possibility," Mikyn said. "But the law is clear."

"Erin," Ava said. "We can't start a war over this. If Mikyn promises to protect the child—"

"*I* will protect Anina." I reached in the pocket of my body armor and pulled out Valerine's document and data disk. "All rights to Anina have been given to me, and I am her guardian until we find her parents, and they are able to take care of her themselves."

Mikyn scanned the document. "This works," he said, relaxing. "It's perfect, actually. They cannot dispute this."

He returned to the podium. "It's been brought to my attention that prior to the charges brought against the parents, the custody of Anina Padovan was transferred as is allowed by law, and thus, we no longer have rights in this matter. If you come forward, you can examine both the document and data disk." He paused as the attorney started forward. "As for assurance that they are serious about our agreement, the topsiders have been kind enough to give us the loan of their healer until Sinalta once again sees the sky." He motioned to Dimitri, who moved forward and stood by Ava. This time the murmurs were approving.

Shock filled me. Could I have heard correctly?

"Are there further questions?" Mikyn asked. "If not, our topside friends will be permitted to leave us now."

I turned my back on the assembly and stepped close to Dimitri. "No. You can't stay here! You see how volatile it is. They could change their minds tomorrow."

"That's exactly why I have to stay," Dimitri said. "I have to make sure they remain sane. I can help with that, and it gives them some measure of comfort to know they have leverage."

"They have a healer."

Dimitri glanced over my shoulder at Mikyn, who was

pointing out something in the document I'd given him. "He can't be trusted. You know that. He has too much power."

I did. And for all I know, this had been Mikyn's plan all along, to take control of the Sinaltan senate. Still, I didn't want to risk Dimitri.

I looked at Ava. "You can't allow this."

"I was the one who made the agreement," she said quietly. "Mikyn told me they wanted assurances. It was their ultimatum, like us wanting the mines closed. Or you wanting to take Anina."

I blinked hard, fighting tears. After we'd come so far, to leave Dimitri here alone among these people was a betrayal.

Ritter grasped my hand. "It won't be for long. We'll rescue him." The word rescue told me very clearly that he too considered Dimitri a prisoner, not a guest.

Ava nodded. "Our technopaths and engineers will be working with theirs, mostly electronically, but they'll need to examine things personally too. And Keene will need to be here for the move. We will not abandon Dimitri."

Mikyn turned from the pulpit and joined us. "I think it's best that you leave quickly," he said, his voice urgent. "Give everyone time to adjust and for the news to spread. They are still angry about the child."

"I agree." Ava motioned to Mari and the others, giving them the signal to gather.

Mari would shift us back to Chris and Anina, and then to Mexico from there, leaving the submersible in the cave for Graeme and Valerine with the hope that they'd be able to use it to escape. The submersible or smaller transport could also act as a base for us to shift back when we needed, even if negotiations broke down.

"Keep in mind that Valerine Padovan is one of your best

engineers," I told Mikyn. "She knows the city controls better than anyone." I hadn't really considered her ability before, but it was obviously related to science. Maybe she was even like Cort. If so, I wouldn't count her out just yet.

Mikyn nodded. "So I have been told, and I have informed the guards. I hope she can be found safe. The problem is that Tsaoussis and Scala still have a lot of friends here—and that advocate is one of them. It's going to be a rough few months until the city surfaces. We've already had a protest this morning in the outer ring that turned violent."

"It's going to be rocky even after that." Ava folded her arms and studied him intently. "Because you have a lot of changes that need to be made in your society. The sooner, the better."

Mikyn nodded. "Beginning with me. I know what I have to do."

I hoped he did because otherwise, Valerine was right about him. Without Mikyn foretelling their children's future, all children would have a chance. If he didn't stop, I'd have to return and eliminate him.

I would have no choice.

Ava and Dimitri moved off to join the others. Ritter took a few steps away, waiting for me to follow, but first there was something I had to ask Mikyn.

"If a pregnant woman had your ability," I said, "would she be able to tell if her baby was an embryo?"

The skin around his eyes wrinkled even more than usual as he studied me through narrowed eyes. "I don't know. I have never been able to tell in an expectant Avowed woman, but it might be different if it were your own body. If you channeled me, we could try together."

"No." The word came out a little too fast. "I just wondered." I had already made my choice.

Hadn't I?

"Very well. Safe journey." Mikyn bowed and withdrew to attend to a growing line of people waiting for his attention.

I joined the others. Ava stepped forward to hug Dimitri, her movements rigid and her mental shield tight. Tears shimmered in her eyes. Or maybe it was the light.

I hugged him too. As the Sinaltans had more to lose than we did, I had to trust that Dimitri would be all right. That I'd have many more years to learn what he was like as a father and that he'd be around to play with my daughter.

We left him behind then to find a private room where we could shift back to the submersible. Mari's ability was one we would keep secret from the Sinaltans for as long as possible.

Ritter stepped close to me, his breath hot against my temple. "We'll come back for him."

"I know." I took his hand as Mari folded the submersible around us.

We'd saved Kimber and the other children and begun freeing those in the mines. I could only hope that relations with the Sinaltans continued to be peaceful.

But if they weren't, we'd be ready.

TEYLA BRANTON GREW UP AVIDLY READING SCIENCE FICTION AND fantasy and watching Star Trek reruns with her large family. They lived on a little farm where she loved to visit the solitary cow and collect (and juggle) the eggs, usually making it back to the house with most of them intact. On that same farm she once owned thirty-three gerbils and eighteen cats, not a good mix, as it turns out. Teyla always had her nose in a book and daydreamed about someday creating her own worlds.

Teyla is now married and has seven kids, so life at her house can be very interesting (and loud), but writing keeps her sane. She's been known to wear pajamas all day when working on a deadline, and is often distracted enough to burn dinner. (Okay, pretty much 90% of the time.)

Teyla has worked in the publishing business for over twenty years. Teyla also writes romance and suspense under the name Rachel Branton. For a free ebook and more information, please visit http://www.TeylaBranton.com.